NIGHT OF THE
PARTY

NIGHT OF THE PARTY

TRACEY MATHIAS

■ SCHOLASTIC

Scholastic Children's Books
An imprint of Scholastic Ltd
Euston House, 24 Eversholt Street, London, NW1 1DB, UK
Registered office: Westfield Road, Southam, Warwickshire, CV47 0RA
SCHOLASTIC and associated logos are trademarks and/or
registered trademarks of Scholastic Inc.

First published in the UK by Scholastic Ltd, 2018

ISBN 978 1407 18800 3

A CIP catalogue record for this book
is available from the British Library.

Printed by CPI Group (UK) Ltd, Croydon, CR0 4YY
Papers used by Scholastic Children's Books are made
from wood grown in sustainable forests.

1 3 5 7 9 10 8 6 4 2

This is a work of fiction. Names, characters, places, incidents
and dialogues are products of the author's imagination or are used
fictitiously. Any resemblance to actual people, living or dead,
events or locales is entirely coincidental.

www.scholastic.co.uk

for Cate

The Immigration and Residency Act

From Wikipedia, the free encyclopedia

The 20— Immigration and Residency bill was brought before Parliament in late 20— and became law with the passing of the Act the following August. It brought into force the British Born policy which the Party had proposed in its manifesto during the general election of 20—. Broadly, the law prescribes that anyone not born in the UK who has been resident for fewer than twenty-five years has no automatic right to remain.

Everyone in this category was required to report to the new National Agency (NA) for assessment after the passing of the Act. Assessment was based on a points system which considered criteria such as employment record and income level, history of benefits claimed, fluency in English, criminal convictions, property ownership, professional qualifications and technical skills etc. About twenty percent of those assessed were permitted to stay, while the remaining eighty percent have mostly been repatriated. An unknown number absconded and remain in the UK illegally, running the risk of arrest, confiscation of cash and other property, and forced deportation. UK citizens have a legal obligation to report illegals to the NA.

CHAPTER ONE

Hey Soph,

It's 12 December. Almost the end of term. I should be in school but Miss D's off sick so Philosophy was cancelled and the others were arsing around Blu-tacking balloons and tinsel to the common-room ceiling. I couldn't be bothered. Checked out, went for a walk, ended up at the South Bank. Wrote an essay. Did some maths. Do you know it's possible to prove that infinity minus infinity equals pi?

Had my interview this week. Uni starts in 292 days. Just over 25 million seconds. If I get an offer. If I get the grades.

The Xmas market's up. Remember? All those overpriced stalls along the river? You used to love it.

I should go.

A.

He deletes the letter, empties the recycle bin, packs his laptop away, swallows the last mouthful of cold coffee. The cup's left intersecting rings of moisture on the table, a Venn diagram of empty sets. He wipes it clean with his hand, finds a philosophy lecture on his phone, jams his headphones in and heads outside.

It's nearly dark; the huge, projected images on the buildings across the river are already on: the right-angles of the English cross alternating with the curled flames of the Party torch. The images flicker, break up, go off, and come on again.

The voice in his ears asks if it's possible to prove that anything exists outside his mind.

It bloody better.

Everything that's happened in the last sixteen months (approximately 41,500,000 seconds)? He doesn't want to have invented all that; doesn't want to be stuck in the kind of mind that *could* invent it.

He's lost track of the talk. He clicks it off, hurries across the bridge and down into the station; when he reaches the platform, his train's pulling out. He studies the posters on the far side of the track (the usual government announcements; ads for yet another Second World War movie), glances at the headline in an abandoned newspaper on a bench (*Lucky for some? PM confirms 13 February General Election*), paces to the end of the platform.

When the tube comes, he gets into the last carriage, drops into the third seat on the right, restarts the philosophy talk and stares at the floor, trying to concentrate. The train judders and stops, judders and stops. The shiny shoes opposite him get off, are replaced by a pair of running shoes.

Proper running shoes, with cushioned and engineered soles, worn and scuffed like they've done hundreds of miles. He glances up. The girl wearing them has long dark hair that hides her face; she's reading, her book balanced on the backpack on her lap. She's wearing baggy grey tracksuit bottoms, cuffed at the ankle, and a navy-blue waterproof jacket. the sort that rolls up into its own pocket. Lightweight jacket, small backpack, trackie bottoms, trainers: she looks like she's ready to run.

The train slows into Camden Town. She stands, hesitates, and sits again; as she does she looks straight at him. Her face is pale, serious; she has dark eyes that lock on his. He blushes and ducks his head. The doors slide shut, the train jerks forward, picks up speed. Two minutes to the next stop. He counts down from 120 seconds. At 77 the lights flicker off, on, off again. The train slows, and stops.

They'll get going again in a minute.

He counts again, forward this time.

At 200 nothing's happened. The train's still stuck, the lights are still out; it'd be totally dark if people didn't have their phones out, making little blocks of white light along the carriage. Someone says *bloody London Transport. Couldn't organize a piss-up in a brewery.* A few people laugh. A kid starts to cry.

The train doesn't move.

It'll be another blackout.

Probably.

He looks across the aisle at the girl. The man next to her is looking at his phone, and its glimmer bleaches her face and makes dark hollows of her eyes. She's scared, he thinks. He switches on the torch on his phone, and leans towards her.

"You OK? It's only a blackout." (Probably)

"I know. It's just . . . I'm late."

He nods down at her trainers. "You'd have been quicker running."

"Yeah. Probably." She meets his eyes briefly, with a fleeting smile.

He wants to keep talking to her. "What's the book?" he asks and she tilts it towards him so he can read the title. *Four Quartets*. T S Eliot. Poetry. He gave Sophie a book of poems once. . . "Poems on the Underground," he says. "Don't see a lot of those nowadays."

It's a pathetic joke, but she smiles again. She lays one hand lightly on the book's cover. "Have you read it?"

"No," he says, and then, "Will you? Read some . . . I mean . . . if that's OK." Good thing it's dark; he can feel himself blushing. The girl stares at him for a moment, then she opens the book and leans forward to catch the light of his phone on the page. Down the carriage, the kid's still crying and the *piss-up in a brewery* guy has lost his sense of humour in the dark and is saying loudly, *What the hell is going on? And can't you shut that kid up, for God's sake?*

She starts to read.

He has no idea what any of it means. He catches odd words – *the light fails* – *a winter's afternoon* – but he can't put them together into any kind of sense; there's just her low, clear voice and a feeling in his chest like the beginning of tears.

No. *No no no no no.* Not *now.*

Only, he doesn't cry; at first it feels like he's going to, it feels like the same sense of building pressure, of something too strong to contain, but it's not. It's not the same, it's something different. *Lighter.* He hasn't felt like this for – definitely not for the last 41,500,000 seconds, maybe *ever,* and all he wants to do is go on sitting here, in the dark, listening to her voice, feeling whatever this is.

There's a sudden flare of torchlight. She stops reading. Two underground workers in big boots and high-vis jackets come stomping along the carriage. The kid's still crying; the man's still complaining loudly about *cyberterrorism* and *the need for heightened security* and *what the hell are the police doing about it, he'd like to know?*

"It's a blackout, sir," one of the underground workers says.

So.

Just a blackout.

Obviously.

He stands, shoulders his bag and stays close to the girl as they climb down onto the black gravel in the brick tunnel and walk along the dead rails to Chalk Farm station, and up the 54 emergency steps to the surface. The police are checking IDs at the barriers; he fumbles his card out of his pocket, is waved through, out onto the pavement. It's raining; it's utterly dark except for the lights of the police car and ambulance parked outside the station, reflecting blue off the wet road.

He stares. He knows this scene.

Déjà vu is a trick of the brain. Jas, who does A level Psychology, told him that: it's when one half of your brain registers something before the other, or something. Except. . . This isn't *déjà vu*. He really has seen this before. The blue lights. The wet road. The blue lights.

"Are you OK?" she asks.

He blinks hard and wipes his forehead with the back of his hand. "Yeah," he manages. "You? How're you going to get home?"

"I'll walk."

"Which way are you going?"

"Uh. . . Up the hill."

"Me too."

He lights the way with his phone. The power cut's knocked everything out: house lights and street lights, and it must go on for miles because there's none of the usual reflected city glow in the sky. The shops and cafés on the hill are closed, but in the pub halfway up there are candles in the windows, and the sound of muffled singing from the bar. *La-a-and of Ho-o-ope and Glo-o-ry:* the local Party, not exactly calm, but carrying on despite the blackout. Just past the pub, the Neighbourhood Watch are on patrol: Mr Smith from the flat downstairs, and Clyde from the block opposite.

"You need to get home," Smith tells them. "Stay in till the power's back on."

He nods; when the patrol's moved out of hearing, he asks her, "Where d'you need to get to?"

"East Finchley."

8

"That's miles."

"I'll go across the Heath."

The Heath's huge: he thinks of her running across it, in the dark, alone. *Anything* could happen to her.

"I can drive you, if you like."

"Can you?"

"Sure." He's not sure: he only passed his test last week, you're meant to stay off the road in a blackout, and Mum'll go mental if she finds out. But she's scared; he can't just leave her.

He doesn't want to leave her. They carry on uphill and round the corner; he pauses at the bottom of the steps and stares up at the flats. There's a faint flicker of candlelight in some of the windows, but the top floor is dark. Mum's probably still at work, or stuck on another tube. He turns to the girl.

"I need to get the car key. D'you want to come in?"

"What?"

She sounds startled, and he stammers, "I mean... It's freezing out here."

"Oh. Right. This is where you live?"

She follows him up the front steps and into the lobby. As the inner door clicks heavily shut behind them, he glances at her. The emergency lights glimmer weakly in the darkness, and her face is still shadowed, unreadable.

"You could stay for a bit, if you want? Wait till the blackout's over?"

"I can't. Sorry."

He doesn't want her to go; he says, "Sure. Won't be long,"

9

and runs upstairs. When he opens the door, Lulu leaps out at him like a miniature hellhound on speed.

"Get *down*, dog." He pushes her off, and lights his way into the kitchen with his phone; he still can't navigate this flat in the dark. He scoops up the car keys. Lulu whines at him. She's been shut inside all day.

"OK," he says. "OK... You better come," and she scampers down the stairs ahead of him; by the time he reaches the lobby, she's jumping up at the girl, licking her hands. "Get *down*, Lulu!" he says again, and, "Sorry. Sorry. She needs training."

"It's OK." The girl crouches to ruffle Lulu's ears. "Did you say her name was Lulu?"

"Yeah." He hasn't told her *his* name, he realizes; he doesn't know hers. "I'm Ash. You?"

"Zara. Ash what?"

"Hammond. You?"

"Jones. Sorry. I really need to get home."

Don't go, he thinks. He lets them out into the cold darkness, finds the car, slings the dog into the back, and clears his trainers off the front seat to make room for Zara. The headlights glare into the blackness as he pulls out and – he's not exactly wishing he hadn't offered to drive her home, but he can see why they tell you not to drive in the blackout: down the hill there's the white glow of the hospital, running on emergency generators, but everywhere else there's absolute, total darkness. He drives like someone's great-grandmother: sitting forward, hands tight on the wheel, peering ahead, going at 20 mph. This is safe;

braking distance at this speed is forty feet and the headlights reach four times that far.

It doesn't feel safe.

It feels like anything could fly out of the darkness at any time.

They inch up the High Street, past the closed tube station, up the narrow steep road to the Heath. Usually, from here, you look down on the lights of the city, but not tonight; the whole of London's blacked out. The road across the Heath is utterly dark except for the reflected glimmer of his own headlights in a fox's eyes that sends Lulu into a storm of furious barking; by the time she's shut up, they're at East Finchley. He drives under the railway bridge.

"You can drop me here," Zara says.

"It's OK— "

"I only live round the corner. It's fine. Drop me here."

He pulls over to the side of the road; she opens the door: in seconds she'll be gone.

"Wait," he says. "Can I have your phone number?"

She says nothing, staring straight ahead into the darkness.

"Zara?"

"I'll take yours." She unzips her backpack, pulls out *Four Quartets* and a pen, flips the book open to the back page. It's already covered in scribbled notes. She writes *Ash Hammond*. He tells her his number, slowly, carefully, watches her write it down and draw an irregular shape around it.

"Hey? You will call, won't you?" he says, but she's already out of the car; she shuts the door and the dark consumes her, instantly.

ZARA

The dark is absolute. It reminds her of starless and moonless nights when she was still a little girl, living on the farm, when she would walk along the track towards the woods and switch off her torch, and let the night wrap itself round her, so thick she could feel it on her skin, breathe it in. She could do with a torch now, but her phone's at home; it's safer not to take it out of the house. She walks blind, guiding herself with one hand on the garden walls, brushing damp stems that release scents of lavender and rosemary, snagging her skin on rose thorns. She crosses one road, turns the corner and climbs the shallow hill. There's a weak thread of candlelight in the living-room window where the curtains aren't quite closed. That'll be Mum, peering out into the darkness, wondering where she is. By the time she's let herself into the hall, Mum's waiting for her at the living-room door, a candle in her hand, her eyes wide in the dim light.

"Zara! Where have you *been?*"

"Săr'mâna, Mamă." Zara steps past her into the living room. Candles on the mantelpiece and the table make pools of warm light on the scuffed wooden floor and the red rug. She flops onto the sofa, leaning her head back. The light casts fugitive shadows on the ceiling.

"Where have you been?" Mum asks again. "It's *half past six.*"

"I know."

"So what happened? We said, straight there and straight home. Did you get it?"

Zara nods, unzips her pocket, fishes out the small rectangle of flat white plastic, and drops it onto the table. Mum picks it up and studies it: the lettering, the photo, the red-and-blue logo, the serial number, the fingerprint panel on the back...

"It's OK," Zara tells her. "It works. I had to use it to get out of the tube."

"What *tube?* You were supposed to take a *taxi!*"

"I know... He charged more for the card than you said. I had to use the taxi money to pay for it. It was fine." But her voice isn't steady, and she shivers, remembering the stark tower block in Camberwell, with its burned-out and boarded-up flats smelling of greasy damp and smoke, and the little man behind the steel door in the top-floor flat, surrounded with his computers and scanners and printers, the light flashing off the metal rims and thin lenses of his glasses. *I can't do it for a hundred and fifty. Sorry. Price has gone up. I take risks for this, you know.*

Mum sits next to her and takes her hands in hers.

"I'm *sorry.* I should have come with you."

"*Mum.* I'm safer without you. You don't sound English enough. You know that. Anyway, it was fine," and she pulls her hands out of Mum's and goes to the window, looking out through the crack in the curtains at the weak lights in the houses opposite, thinking of all the ways it wasn't fine: the glint in the little man's eyes as he stepped towards her and said, *if you can't pay. . . I mean, you need this, don't you?* and herself, stammering, *I can. I can pay*, and fumbling the taxi fare out of her bag, thrusting it at him, grabbing the flimsy slip of plastic still warm from the printer, and running. *Running*: following signs for the river along grey streets blowing with rubbish and dead leaves, past posters on the bus shelters shouting the same message she read later, on the scrolling screens on the tube, in the spaces above the windows, where once, sometimes, there used to be poetry.

DO YOU KNOW AN ILLEGAL?

IT IS YOUR DUTY TO REPORT THEM.

She ran as far as the river, and stopped for breath, leaning on the rail of the footbridge, looking at the city's reflected glitter in the water, the dark shapes of a dozen half-built towers and their stalled cranes along the waterfront – and, down on the terrace outside the concert hall, a tall fair-haired boy in a posh coat who she thought she recognized.

"You should have *called* me," Mum says.

Zara drags the curtains closed, and turns away from the window. She glances down at the phone lying on the table, imagining Mum, waiting next to it all afternoon.

"What could you have done?"

"I could have told you not to take the tube."

"And do what? Get another taxi? It'd already cost *hundreds*."

"Staying *safe*," Mum says. "That's the important thing. For another two months."

"February 13th. I *know*." She shoulders her backpack, takes one of the candles from the mantelpiece, and lights her way along the narrow hall, into the kitchen and down the cellar steps. The yellow candlelight wavers over her room – *home* – all the familiar things: the running machine, the crammed bookcase, the red-and-cream zigzags of the rug and the cushions. She kicks her trainers off, climbs into bed and remembers. . .

He crossed the terrace, hesitating as the huge illuminations across the river flickered off and on again, then he climbed the steps up to the footbridge and passed her: head down, earphones in, eyes on the ground. He was walking fast but somehow heavily, as if he were carrying more than just the bag over his shoulder, and she was sure then. She knew who he was.

He carried on over the bridge, above the dark river, into the falling evening, and without really knowing why, without stopping to think why, she followed him, dodging through the busy crowd, losing sight of him, finding him again on the stairs down to the tube station. She watched him pass through the barrier, onto the escalator, and down, out of sight.

She'd planned to run all the way home, but she could take the tube from here. It was the obvious thing to do. It was getting dark, she was late, Mum would be worried, and to run from here meant running uphill, away from the river.

She didn't want to lose sight of him yet.

She fished in her inside pocket for her emergency five-pound note, queued at the machine and bought her first tube ticket for months. Riding the escalator, she started to think that this was stupid; a stupid and pointless thing to do. The tube was risky. She'd be safer running. And she'd waited so long at the machine that he was probably gone.

And anyway. What was she following him *for?*

There was a train in when she reached the platform, and he was there, stepping through the doors at the far end. She sprinted and jumped aboard, dodging through the closing doors, and at the next two stations, she got off and changed carriages, moving along the train until she was in the same carriage as him, sitting in the seat opposite his. She took her book out, but from behind her hair she was watching him, not reading. He sat with his long legs stretched out into the aisle, earphones still in, a furrow of concentration between his brows. He looked unhappy. Of course. Of *course* he looked unhappy; what else had she *expected?* He glanced up and she dropped her gaze quickly, back to the poetry, taking none of it in.

The train slowed into Camden Town. She needed to change onto the other line here to get home. She stood, took a step towards the door, faltered, and stopped. The police were working the crowded platform, checking IDs, and she felt for the new card in her tracksuit pocket. *It'll pass any checks, that will,* the little man in the flat had told her, the light flashing from his glasses. *Fingerprinting. Barcoding. Anything.* Would it? She watched a policeman scanning the barcode on someone's ID, checking the screen on his scanner, handing the card back and stopping someone else who'd got out of her carriage.

She changed her mind, and sat down again. Fleetingly, she met his eyes; he looked quickly away, and she pretended to read, tracking the same words over and over again without understanding or even registering them. Then the train slowed, and the lights went out, and in the darkness he leaned forward and spoke to her.

Zara sits up, reaches for her backpack, takes out *Four Quartets* and flips to the back page, and his name.

Ash Hammond: the boy she recognized before he even knew she was there.

And his phone number, which she should scribble out or tear up *now,* because she can't get in touch; it would be crazy even to think of getting in touch with him. She should stop thinking about him.

She should just stop thinking about him.

CHAPTER TWO

Hey Soph,

*Zara hasn't got in touch. It's the 23rd December.
11 days. You can work out how many seconds that is
yourself, if you're interested. Basically, there's been
loads of time for her to call. If she wanted to. So,
logically, she doesn't want to.*

I wanted to talk to her again.

Forget it. I should just stop thinking about her.

A

He clicks print, deletes the document from the screen, empties the recycle bin, picks up the printed copy, opens the window, and crumples the paper in the flowerpot on the windowsill, on the old ashes. How many letters has he burned here? He's lost count. He takes his lighter out of the desk drawer, sets fire to the paper, watches it burn – $C_6H_{10}O_5 + 5O_2$ to $5CO + CO_2 + 5H_2O$ – carbon dioxide and water vapour passing unseen into the air; when the flames are out, he shuts the window, breathes on the glass, writes:

Zara Jones

Forget it. She's not going to call. He wipes her name away and goes along the corridor to the kitchen, past all the unopened removal boxes. Mum's sitting at the table with her laptop, a thick file of papers and an empty glass. She smiles up at him.

"So? Are you going out?"

"Don't know."

"You should, Ash. It'll be good for you."

"What will? A hangover?" He looks at the wineglass, then at her. "Is Aunt Kate still coming?"

Mum nods, shuts the file, and gets up to open the fridge. "Want something to eat before you go? There's a pizza. You could have that, before they ban it."

"Ban it?"

"Well, it's not BB, is it?"

It's not a great joke. But it's a joke. That's got to be a good thing, hasn't it? He smiles at her.

"Pizza's great. Thanks." He blasts it in the microwave and sits opposite her at the table to eat it with his fingers, scrolling through his phone, searching every social media site he can think of for Zara Jones, for the *nth* time. She's not anywhere. He flicks to the poetry site where he's saved *Four Quartets*; he's been looking for the lines she read, but he can't find those either.

The front door intercom buzzes, and he scrambles up to

answer it. She knows where he lives.

Stupid. It won't be her, can't be, and of course, it's not; it's Kate. He presses the front door release to let her into the lobby, goes out onto the landing and leans over the banister to watch her climb the stairs. She looks like Mum, but more *solid* somehow, stronger; he can't remember now if Mum used to be like that, before. . .

"Hi, you." Kate reaches the landing, dumps her bags down, hugs him. "How did the interview go?"

"OK, I think."

"Bet you get in. They'd be mad not to want you." She smiles, then frowns. "How's Julia?"

"Dunno. Same."

"Mmm." She goes into the kitchen; he lingers in the hall. Kate says, "Ju?" and there's a lot of talking he can't hear.

He should go out. He finds his coat, wallet, ID card; calls, "I'm going!" from the front door, and runs downstairs and downhill to the tube. There's a girl with long dark hair at the other end of his carriage. He changes seats to get a better look at her.

It's not Zara.

For God's sake.

Of *course* it's not her: the probability of meeting her again is *infinitesimal*; an average of four point-something million people use the underground every day. It was a one-off coincidence. It's not going to happen again. She's not going to call.

Forget it.

He switches his phone to a new chess problem, solves

it, gets off the tube. It's started to sleet. He hurries, past someone huddled in a doorway, past a new sign announcing that *this is now a zero-tolerance zone for drugs*, past a kid turning his pockets out for a patrol on the opposite pavement. As he rounds the corner towards the pub, he sees a familiar, tall, dark-haired figure ahead. He calls, "Lewis!" and Lewis stops, waits for him to catch up and greets him with a slap on the shoulder.

"Hey, Ash. Jas said you weren't coming."

He shrugs. "Changed my mind."

Lewis gives him a thumbs up. They carry on towards the pub.

"How've you been? What've you been up to?" Lewis asks.

"Not much. Revising." Waiting for her to call. *Forget it.* She's not going to.

"Already? Bloody *hell*, Ash. They're only mocks." Lewis grins and shoves open the pub door; a wave of noise and heat rolls out at them. Inside, a group of guys who look like they've been here all afternoon are bawling out Christmas carols; tinsel, paper chains and St George's flags hang from the ceiling. The others are here already, sitting at the corner table by the overloaded Christmas tree: Chris and Jas from school and Maya and Caitlin from Jas's band. For a fraction of a second Ash feels dislocated, already drunk. Everything blurs and sharpens again: Chris's lean face with its heavy-rimmed glasses under his untidy mousy hair. Jas's restless fingers tapping a beat on the arm of his chair, his dark hair flopping over his forehead; Caitlin leaning close to Maya; the

21

contrast of her paleness against Maya's dark skin.

He blinks his vision clear, and follows Lewis through the crowd, slings his coat over an empty chair, shifts his phone to his jeans pocket, and checks it's switched on. It is. Nothing from Zara.

Of course.

Just *forget it*.

"Evening, ladies." Lewis leans his hands on the back of Jas's chair, and greets Maya and Caitlin with a mock bow.

"Seen the latest polling figures, Lewis?" Chris asks.

"Yes." Lewis shrugs his coat off. The Party pin in his jacket lapel glints, as if the metal flames are really alight. He settles in a chair, leaning back with his hands in his pockets.

"Twenty points," Chris says. *"Twenty."*

"Anyone want a drink?" Jas jumps up from his chair, knocking the lower branches of the Christmas tree and dislodging a red-and-white bauble that rolls under the table. "Ash? What're you having?"

"Uh. . ." He wonders whether to stay sober or go for blind drunk, decides on blind drunk. "Vodka. I'll give you a hand."

They dodge through the swaying carol singers to the bar. Jas leans on the counter, flicks his ID card in his fingers to summon the barman, and grins at Ash.

"How long before Chris and Lewis finish with the politics, d'you reckon?"

"Closing time?"

"If we're lucky." Jas drums his fingers in a rapid rhythm against the sticky counter of the bar. The singers are roaring out something about shepherds and angels; even Ash can tell they're out of tune. Jas clutches his head and mimes a silent howl.

"Next time can we choose a pub where they've banned singing?" He drums his fingers again, and glances at Ash. "So? Did she call?"

"No."

Jas gives a lopsided, sympathetic grimace. "Want to make this a double?"

"Why not?" Ash watches the barman pouring drinks. "She was probably never going to," he says; he gathers up a couple of glasses and a bottle of lager and winds his way back to the table.

"Anyway," Chris is saying to Lewis, "you lot are finished. You're going to get smashed at the election. How many seconds to go, Ash?"

"Till the election? 13th February, yeah?" Ash slides a glass of wine across the table to Maya and hands a bottle of lager to Chris. "About 4,493,000. Where's Priya, by the way?"

Chris groans. "That long? She's in India for Christmas," and Maya says, "How do you *do* that, Ash?"

He shrugs and adjusts a beer mat so that it's properly parallel to the edge of the table. "Just do."

"We think he was abducted by aliens." Jas glances at Caitlin, who's counting on her fingers and doing sums on the calculator on her mobile phone. "Don't bother checking it, Cait. He'll be right. And can we drop the politics now, *please*? It's Christmas."

Chris scowls; Lewis grins and raises his pint of Yorkshire bitter. Ash picks up his vodka and tilts it in his hand, watching the light catch and reflect from the viscous liquid and the glass. *Light.* Something about light in the poem that she read... He listens absently to Jas talking about the band's next gig. "Day after Boxing Day. You'll be there, won't you, Ash?"

"Can't. Sorry." He downs a mouthful of vodka, feels the burn at the back of his throat. "I'm going away with Dad."

"Cool," Caitlin says.

"Actually not. It's a kind of revision boot camp for mocks."

"God," Jas says. "You said yes to that?"

"We'll send messages of support, Ash," Lewis says.

"You can try. There's probably no Wi-Fi. Or mobile signal." Which means she won't be able to call him. She's not *going* to call him. He swallows another mouthful of vodka; the carol singers launch into another drunken round of "Peace on Earth".

Four Quartets is open on her lap, but her eyes track the lines without reading them. She is only aware of his name and number, scribbled in the back of the book; as if they have burned through to the open page, obliterating everything else. *Ash Hammond.* He could tell her the things that she's half-wanted, half-feared, *needed* to know for the last year and a half. And, maybe, there are things he needs to know that she could tell him. Her phone's lying on the bookcase. She stretches out a hand. . .

No. *Stop it.* It's too complicated and too impossible. The only safe thing for her to do with Ash Hammond is not to know him.

She drops the book on the floor, wriggles her feet into her trainers and steps onto the running machine, starting slow and picking up speed until she's running fast, trying to reach the place where her mind will empty. It works, usually, this; it's an escape from herself, from all the tormented thoughts that wheel and circle in her head, restless and loud as disturbed birds at sunset. It's not working now. Her feet say *if, if, if,* and so does each throb of her blood in her ears, and the *shhh* of the motor is the *shhh* of his name.

Stop it. She slows and switches off the machine. In the chilliness of her cellar bedroom, sweat cools quickly on her skin. She shivers, bundles up clean clothes and a towel and runs upstairs. The kitchen smells of coffee and the sharp sourness of yeast. Mum, sitting on the stool by the worktop, glances up from her book.

"You look as if you've run a marathon."

It feels as if she's run around the world, and still not escaped. "Is there hot water?"

"Yes. Don't use it all. Max'll want a shower when she comes in."

In the bathroom, she strips off her sweaty running gear and climbs into the shower. The water whispers *Ash*. When she shuts it off, the last drops cling to the shower head, fat as question marks, before they fall and shatter on the stained enamel around the plughole.

She dries, dresses, and goes into the kitchen. Mum's working the risen dough: dividing it into three, pulling each piece into a rough square, filling it with cocoa, raisins, walnuts and Turkish delight: the taste of every Christmas Zara has ever known. She runs a glass of water, blows on the surface and watches the patterns change.

The front door opens and slams. Max comes into the kitchen, drops the post and the evening paper on the counter, wraps her arms around Mum and leans heavily against her.

"Hard day?" Mum says.

"Crazy." Max peels off her wet coat; she's still wearing her supermarket tabard. "We ran out of Brussels sprouts. People were so furious; I thought we were going to have a riot. And please don't tell me sprouts aren't BB; I've been hearing that one *all day*." Behind her glasses, her eyes are laughing now. "The Party's doomed, Ana. Blackouts, riots in Liverpool, *and* a sprout shortage on the day before Christmas Eve. And look at the paper."

Zara picks it up. Next to a photo of the Prime Minister climbing into an official car outside Downing Street the headline reads: GOING FOR GOOD? and underneath, in smaller letters: PARTY TRAILS BY 20 POINTS.

"Seven weeks." Max takes the cup of coffee Mum's poured for her; they head down the hall, and Zara leafs through the post: a couple of late Christmas cards for Max; a government reminder that under the terms of the Immigration and Residency Act it's an offence to employ, harbour, or conceal the identity of an illegal; and a Coalition leaflet promising immediate abolition of the British Born policy if they win the election – which Max says they will. *Seven* weeks.

She drops the leaflets in the bin, and takes the Christmas cards along the corridor. In the living room, Mum is unplaiting Max's cornrows and combing out her hair, making a cloud around her head; Max is sitting on a cushion on the floor, leaning against Mum's legs; the pool of warm light from the table lamp falls over them both. There's silence, except for the distant sound of music from the flat upstairs. Zara falters in the doorway. Max glances up at her, and smiles.

"How's the essay?"

Zara nods at her scrappy notes, scattered on the table. "I've started. . ." She *keeps* starting, but whenever she opens a book, the words slide off the page, leaving a blank screen where she plays over and over the film of Ash, climbing the steps to the footbridge over the dark river.

"What's the question?" Max leans away from Mum, pulls a sheet of paper off the table, and reads: *"Examine the ways in which Hardy presents the causes and consequences of Tess's feelings of guilt and hesitation.* That's easy enough, isn't it?"

It's too close: *guilt and hesitation:* it's like pressing a splinter under her skin. "I guess," she says, and Max scrambles up from the floor to put both her hands on Zara's shoulders.

"It's going to be OK, Zara. They're going to lose, and after the election you can register for A levels, and you'll ace them. You *will*. That last essay you did was great. And if you don't get a place at uni this September, you'll go next year."

"I know." She looks at her messy notes, and thinks, *what if they don't lose? What if they win again?* She imagines Max alone in this room with only the faint sound of music from the flat upstairs, and herself and Mum somewhere else: somewhere unimagined, unknown, a long way from here.

"I know," she says again, and she gathers up her notes and her book from the table, and goes downstairs to her room. It's freezing; cold seeps through the walls, the air is crystalline with it. She huddles in bed under the duvet and the blanket, leaning against her pillow.

In seven weeks, if the Party lose, she'll be legal. She can

call Ash. She catches her breath. She *will* call him. She must: she owes him.

But if the Party win?

Seven weeks might be all she's got, and it might take her that long to find the courage to say what she has to say.

She sits up, reaches down to the floor and picks up *Four Quartets.*

ASH

The singers finish a rowdy chorus of "Land of Hope and Glory". Ash studies the light, blurrily, from his third glass of vodka. Jas checks his phone and swears.

"What?" Maya asks. Jas passes her his phone, and she reads out loud, *"James. Don't forget about this evening.* That'll be your dad, right? *James."* She grins at him.

"Shut up, Maya." Jas swears again. "It's this drinks thing. At the House of Commons. He's been invited. He wants me to go."

"What *thing?*" Chris asks. "Is this the Party's Christmas party?"

"Something like that."

"With your dad as Santa?" Chris grins. "Handing over another sack-load of cash?"

"Yeah. Probably. Possibly not in costume." Jas groans, flops back in his chair with his hands behind his head, and knocks another bauble off the Christmas tree. "Don't suppose anyone wants to come with me? He said, if I wanted to bring someone. . . ?"

"Yeah, right." Maya turns to Caitlin. "I should get home. You coming?"

Lewis drains his pint and sets down his empty glass. "I'll come, Jas."

Chris laughs fiercely. "Of *course*."

"Ash?" Jas asks.

He can't face it. "Sorry. Can't. I should go home too." It's a lie. He's not going home: he can't face that either, not till Mum and Kate have finished however many bottles of wine and boxes of tissues they're going to get through and gone to bed. When the others have left, he wanders, head down against the sleet, turning at random into a street that's almost utterly dark except for a couple of illuminated windows reflecting in parallelograms on the wet pavement.

He knows this place, he realizes: there was a café here where Sophie talked herself into a job for about two weeks one summer. He keeps walking until he finds it. It's still open. It hasn't changed: same unmatched furniture, same old photos on the wall, same smell of coffee and fried food. The owner, Marek, is wiping down tables. Ash asks for a coffee, and when Marek brings it, he says, "Seen you before, haven't I? Weren't you here to see Sophie, once?"

"Yeah." He doesn't want to talk about Sophie. He nods towards the big sheet of plywood boarding the window to the left of the door. "What happened?"

"Stupid kids." Marek shakes his head and stares at the framed photo on the wall above the table: a group of World War Two airmen crouching in front of an old plane. He points to a man in the front row. "My grandfather. Battle of Britain. Let me know if you want more coffee." He smiles, and goes back to wiping tables.

Ash studies the photo. They had a talk on the Battle of

Britain in History Essentials in Year Eleven: sacrifice and heroism, a last-ditch defence of freedom, the turning point in the British struggle against tyranny. He thinks of planes falling screaming through the air, of violent, too early death.

He swallows the scalding coffee in one mouthful and goes to the counter to pay.

"Happy Christmas," Marek tells him. "Say hello to Sophie for me."

"Uh. . . Yeah. Sure. You too." He hurries out into the sleet, wanders again. The big Christmas tree's up in Trafalgar Square. They came here every year with Mum: Trafalgar Square for the tree, bus along Regent Street and Oxford Street for the lights.

He could do that now.

Stupid.

But it's still too early to go home.

He catches a bus, and sits in Sophie's favourite seat (upstairs, at the front, on the right). The Christmas lights sway above the wide arc of Regent Street: he's forgotten what they are this year, and he can't *see* because they're switched off, of course. It's an energy-saving measure, he remembers; there was something about it on TV last night.

Great.

He might as well get off.

He stays on the bus, staring at the dark street, and his phone rings.

He doesn't know the number.

It might be her.

It won't be her.

He presses answer.

She says, "Ash?" and it's still dark, but it feels as if someone's put all the Christmas lights on. It feels as if he's *plugged into* the Christmas lights: a huge jolt that leaves him fizzing and light-headed.

"Hi!" he says – and stalls. *God.* He's had about 950,000 seconds to plan this conversation and now he doesn't know what to say to her. "You OK?" (Brilliant.)

"Yeah. You? What are you doing?"

"I'm on a bus. On Regent Street. Thought I'd have a look at the Christmas lights."

"I thought they were switching them off early this year?"

"They are. They have."

"So. . . Basically, you're looking at some Christmas lights that are switched off?"

"Basically, yeah."

She laughs. "Hope the rest of the evening was better."

"No. This is the best bit. Because you phoned." (Too uncool? Who knows? Sophie would have. Talk about something else.) "So, what are you doing?"

"Writing an English essay."

"You doing A level?"

"Yeah. You?"

"Double Maths, Philosophy and Physics. You probably get more laughs from English."

"I'm doing *Tess of the* bloody *D'Urbervilles,*" she says. "Not a lot of laughs there."

"Oh." (He hasn't read it; he has nothing – zero – of

33

any interest to say about it.) "Where are you at school?"
(Pathetic.)

"I'm homeschooled."

"Oh. Right. Cool. Oh, by the way. That poem you read on
the tube? I've been trying to find it, in *Four Quartets*."

"It's in 'Little Gidding'. Near the end. Hey, Ash, I should
go. Running out of minutes."

"Oh. OK. But. . . Do you want to come for a run sometime?"

Dear Soph,

*She called. We're going running together. I think.
We didn't fix anything. But she wanted me to call back.
I think.*

*I looked up a bit of the poem she read. You
probably won't be interested. I gave you a book of
poems for Christmas once. Remember? Poems on the
Underground. Don't think you ever even opened it.
Anyway, listen to this:*

We shall not cease from exploration
And the end of all our exploring
Will be to arrive where we first started.

*I wish.
A xxxx*

CHAPTER THREE

Xmas Day. And no, you don't get a "Happy Christmas". Why the hell should you? It's not, and it's your fault.

We're doing the traditional thing this year. Last year was rubbish, going away to the sun. Getting away from it all. As if. So it's the full works today. Turkey. Tree. Crackers. Dad's come over for the day to play happy families, which hasn't stopped Mum drinking, by the way.

This is also rubbish.

For Christ's sake, Sophie. This whole thing, all our lives screwed up. Did you even stop to THINK?

Sod it. I'm going out.

He destroys the letter and changes into tracksuit and trainers. In the living room, Mum's on her laptop, Dad's flicking through the new biography of Churchill he gave him for Christmas (Mum's idea). They look up at him, and Lulu

35

leaps off the sofa, ears and tail up, every cell on high alert, all that *life*.

"I'm going for a run," he says.

"I'll come too if you'll make it a walk," Dad offers, but that's not what Ash needs, he needs to get out of here.

"Sorry. I need a run."

Dad shrugs and returns to his book. But Lulu hasn't given up hope: she's pelting round the room, yapping, skidding on the polished floorboards. She needs a run too; no one gives her enough time. Really, they should give her away, but. . .

"OK, Lulu. I'll take you." He ruffles her ears. "Come on, idiot dog. I'll take you to the Heath."

In the car he sits without switching on the engine, running one finger around the arc of the steering wheel. It's Christmas, a family day. She'll be busy. He rings her anyway.

"Hey, Zara. Happy Christmas."

"Ash! Hi! You too."

"Yeah, well, it's a bit crap, actually. What are you doing?"

"Writing an essay. Still. *Tess of the* laugh-a-minute *D'Urbervilles*."

"On *Christmas Day*?" He hesitates. "You don't want to come for a run now, do you? I'm taking Lulu to the Heath. I could pick you up?"

"I. . . OK," she says, and the grey day feels suddenly lighter; feels, suddenly, like *Christmas*. He drives to East Finchley buzzing with an electric fizz of excitement, and when he sees her. . .

God.

She's waiting on the pavement where he dropped her on the night of the blackout, in trainers, leggings and a sweatshirt. She's reading while she waits – *seriously* reading – a book in one hand and a pencil in the other. He parks a little way down the road, and for a couple of seconds she doesn't notice him and he's watching her unobserved, seeing her in daylight for the first time – this *beautiful* girl, who for some reason wants to come running with *him*. On *Christmas Day*. Then she sees him, and smiles, and that uncontainable feeling surges through him again.

She runs to the car, slides into the passenger seat, tucks her book into her bag, and turns to him. Her eyes are green, flecked with hazel.

"Hi," he says. "You sure this is OK? I mean... It's Christmas."

"It's fine." She shakes out her hair, gathers it in her hand, ties it into a ponytail; her sweatshirt's a bit too short in the sleeves, and when she lifts her arm he can see the underside of her wrists, the veins running beneath her soft skin.

He swallows.

"OK. Great. Let's go."

Lulu barks, and Zara twists in her seat to say, "Hello, Lulu," and scratches her where she likes it, on the short white fur between her caramel coloured ears.

Hampstead Heath is Christmas busy: crowded with families and dogs. In the car park, a kid and his dad are unloading what's obviously a new bike from their car. Dad brought *him* here, Ash remembers, the Christmas he got his first bike; he remembers pedalling with Dad hanging onto the back, running with him; the moment of realizing that he had been let go, was riding alone, keeping his balance. *He got it straight away,* Dad told everyone at home, over lunch.

"Ash?" she says.

He wrenches his gaze away from the kid and his father. "Nothing. Come on."

They jog down the path onto the Heath and break into a proper run, dodging puddles, walkers, dogs, other kids on shiny bikes. They head into the wood: it's quieter here, and Zara speeds up; he matches her. Faster, faster: he counts his footfalls, converting the number of paces to distance, but all the time he's aware of her, all the way through the woods and out onto the slope that runs down to the ponds. There's a prehistoric mound here (he thinks it's prehistoric; he doesn't really know) covered in dark trees, surrounded by iron railings. They stop, stretch, and sit on the bench that commemorates someone or other who loved this view.

"Thanks," he says.

"What for?"

"Meeting me."

"I wanted to see you—" and it's the best present of the day; an infinity of times better than Dad's blank cheque for a summer holiday after A levels, or Mum's IOU for a new laptop for uni.

"Yeah?" he says, and Lulu drops a soggy black tennis

ball that she's unearthed from God-knows-where at his feet; she barks at him with a series of little leaps backwards, front paws splayed. He leans forward to pick the ball up, and so does Zara and his fingers brush against hers with that electric Christmas feeling again. He hurls the ball down the hill; Lulu hurtles after it through the long grass in a shower of wet, brings it back, drops it and barks. He throws it again, and glances at Zara. She's smiling, watching Lulu flinging herself down the hill. He'd like to keep sitting here with her for the rest of the day, but it's Christmas.

"Zara? Do you need to get home?"

"I'm fine. Do *you* need to?"

He shakes his head, thinking of Mum and Dad, the silence in the flat.

"Ash?" she says. "Are you OK?"

"It's just. . . My bloody family." Lulu's back; he throws the ball for her again. "Mum and Dad split up. A few months ago. We've moved out, me and Mum, but they're doing this family Christmas thing . . . you know, all of us together, and it's so . . . I don't know. Forget it. What about you?"

"What about me?"

"Family."

"Uh. . . Just me and Mum, really. My dad left her before I was born."

"D'you ever see him?"

"No."

He picks the ball up and hurls it down the hill again. "So no brothers or sisters?"

"No."

"Same." He watches Lulu. She's lost the ball in the long grass – idiot dog – then she forgets that she's lost it, catches the scent of something else, tears off after that. Further down the hill, a couple of kids and their dad are trying out a mini-drone. It flies towards him and Zara, hovers over their heads, and lifts away. "My sister died," he says.

"Ash," she says; nothing else, only his name, and so softly that she might have said, "Shhh," but he tells her anyway, not looking at her, staring at the ground under his feet. "It was at a party. The summer before last. Quite near here, one of those huge houses. Someone's birthday; a friend of a friend of a friend; she wasn't even at school with her. Anyway. She took one of those illegal synthetic drugs. And it. . . She. . . There was this huge hall and a sort of gallery over it, and she was off her head, and she climbed onto the banister and. . ."

"Ash," she says again.

"I was there. I mean, not when she fell. Afterwards. Mum had asked me to pick her up." He falls silent, remembering the pelting rain, the ambulance parked on the drive, the blue lights reflecting off the wet tarmac.

He fumbles in his pocket for his phone, scrolls through the photos, and shows the screen to Zara. "That's her. Sophie," and Lulu, who is lying flat at his feet, finally worn out, cocks her head and thumps her tail. She may be an idiot dog in almost every possible way, but she was Sophie's and in all this time she has never forgotten Sophie's name.

ZARA

She lies on her bed and remembers. . .

There's a shop under the railway arches at Bethnal Green where she works at weekends. Gloria's Vintage Clothes: a cave of beauty under the vault of worn warm brick: satin, cotton, silk, lace; faintly scented air. When the door opens, the dresses and scarves stir on their hangers. She writes a poem called "I am still dancing".

On a rainy Saturday in January, she's hanging out clothes when the shop door clangs open, the scarves and dresses wake and shiver, and three girls sweep in on the wind. They move from rack to rack like restless birds: settling, moving on, settling again, chattering. *Oh my God, have you seen this?; Oh my God that's lovely; No, you HAVE to get it; Go on – get BOTH of them then;* and finally they buy so much that Gloria calls her to come and help pack their bags. She watches them as she folds clothes into tissue paper; long–limbed, glowing, posh girls, talking a language of shared, secret references and jokes. She hands the bag with the turquoise silk shirt to the fair–haired girl and hates her. She hates all of them. They are so confident, so *safe*. (The new Immigration and Residency

41

bill – the bill that'll make the British Born policy law, if it passes – has just been introduced by the government and is on its first reading in the House of Commons.)

It's a relief when, at last, the girls gather up all their bags and make for the door. The fair-haired girl is the last to go. She lingers on the threshold, looking back into the shop where the wind from the street is stirring the clothes on their hangers.

"Thanks," she says, and she smiles. She has blue eyes, and Zara catches, suddenly, a fragment of childhood memory: of summer above the farm and larks rising in hundreds into the sky. Then the girl lets the door fall shut, and is gone.

She comes back the next weekend. She's on her own this time, and she's brought a camera with her. Zara tidies clothes on the racks and listens as she chatters to Gloria.

"I've got this photography project I need to do for school. Is it OK to take pictures here? It's so *beautiful*," and Gloria, charmed and taken aback at the same time, says, "Yes, I suppose... OK."

"Oh, *thank you*. I'm Sophie, by the way."

A few impatient snaps, Zara thinks, and she'll be gone. But without her friends, Sophie is more thoughtful: quieter, slower. She takes her time over the photos: making studies of things seen from odd angles and in odd lights. She returns the next weekend and spends ages lying on her back in the middle of the floor to photograph the patterns of brick in the vaulted ceiling. At the end of that visit, she tells Gloria, "I've put some of the photos on my website. That is OK, isn't it?"

At home, Zara finds Sophie's website and scrolls slowly

through it. She's caught the kind of beauty that Zara herself sees at Gloria's: the brilliance of colour against the bare walls, the patterns and textures of printed cloth and brickwork. There are other pictures on the site too: close studies of trees and water, landscapes of London that transfigure it to a fairy-tale city of shining glass. When Sophie comes back the following Saturday, Zara tells her, "I looked at your photos. They're really lovely."

"Thanks." Sophie smiles again. She leans against a shelf and chats about photography and school and exams, while Zara sorts and tidies the hanging clothes; eventually she says, "I want to take some photos of the window. And you know? You should totally buy that dress with the green leaves."

She steps outside to take pictures that Zara looks at later, of monochrome reflections of the street in the shop's arched window, and Zara pulls out the dress. She noticed it when it came in: soft cream cotton printed with leaves of mottled green. At Easter, on the farm, she and Mum used to decorate eggs by binding leaves and flowers to their shells with old stockings and boiling them in vegetable dye; the dress reminds her of those patterns. She holds it against herself in front of the long mirror. Sophie's right. It would suit her. She'd have to work *for ever* to afford it.

She hangs it back on the rack and carries on working, pausing over a long shirt in soft needlecord that's the luminous blue of a summer twilight. When Sophie comes back in, Zara hands it to her.

"*You* should totally buy *this*."

43

It's half a joke, but Sophie buys the shirt, and when Zara's wrapped and handed it to her, she says, "Is there anywhere to get lunch round here? I'm *starving.*"

"Show her the Weavers' Café, Zara," Gloria says. "You're due a break anyway," and Zara takes Sophie to the basement café around the corner. They sit at a table by the window, under the display of black-and-white photos of old London; outside, weathered brick walls enfold a hidden garden of gnarled fruit trees and snowdrops. Sophie drinks black coffee and eats sugar out of the packet, pressing her finger into the golden crystals and sucking it clean.

"Why's it the Weavers' Café?" she asks.

"Built by Huguenot refugees. You know? From France? A lot of them were weavers. In . . . whenever."

"Oh." Sophie shrugs, swallows another mouthful of coffee, and glances down at the blue shirt, nestling like a scrap of fallen sky in the white paper bag at her side. "You're so lucky, working there. It's so lovely."

"You could ask Gloria if you could have my job. I'm going to have to leave at Easter. I've got sixteen-pluses. I'm going to be revising."

"Oh, yeah. So's my brother. Ash."

The memory gets stuck in a loop. Sophie licks sugar from her finger. *So's my brother, Ash. My brother, Ash, Ash, Ash. . .*

ASH

S

So Christmas was mostly rubbish as predicted but I did see Zara. I told her about you. She didn't say much.

What's to say? Except that you were a total idiot and you ruined everything.

Maybe. Maybe you were a total idiot. Maybe this was all your fault. And maybe, possibly, there's an x in y chance that it wasn't. Where the values of x and y are not known. Never going to know, am I?

A

He gets up from the desk; Lulu leaps off his bed, whines, thumps her tail. "In a minute," he tells her. "I need to send this to Sophie," and at Sophie's name she goes into overdrive, barking and scrabbling at his bedroom door.

"Shut up!" he shouts. "Sophie's gone. OK?"

They scattered Sophie's ashes on the beach in Cornwall that she loved when they were kids, where she used to run laughing into the freezing sea, throwing herself into the waves while he was still easing himself in, inch by inch. All that's left of Sophie is ash; all that's left is Ash; he wonders sometimes if Mum and Dad have thought of that too.

Must have.

It's too obvious to miss.

He prints and burns the letter, deletes the file. The computer screen flicks back to *Four Quartets;* he scrolls past the poetry and reads the notes at the end. Little Gidding is a real place; he hadn't realized that. He finds it on Google maps. It's only an hour-and-a-half's drive away.

He texts Zara.

CHAPTER FOUR

He texts: *Hi! Do you want to come out tomorrow?* and she sits back on her bed with her phone in her hand, staring up at the glitter of raindrops on the window, remembering. . .

A March Saturday in Bethnal Green; wind and rain blowing against the shop door, the Immigration and Residency Bill on its second reading in the House of Commons, the feeling in the shop as sombre as the weather. Zara's given in her notice. *Come back when your exams are over*, Gloria told her, but she knows where Zara was born; she knows – they both do – that she might never come back.

Gloria's busy with a customer, and Zara's folding T-shirts when Sophie arrives, hurrying in from the storm, her hair hanging wet and dripping round her face, her hands white with cold.

"Sophie, you're *soaking*. Here." Zara puts down the T-shirt she's holding, takes Sophie's arm, and steers her through the door marked *private* at the back of the shop, into the cramped office. She flicks the heater on. Sophie stands over it, hands held in the stream of warm air. She's staring at nothing, saying nothing. Rain drips from her sodden coat and pools on the floor.

"You look drowned," Zara says.

"I've been walking."

"In *this*? Here. I'll make some tea."

She switches the kettle on. Sophie gives her a bleak, bitter little smile.

"Tea in a crisis. How *English*."

"Sophie, are you *OK*?" Zara asks, and Sophie sits down suddenly in the desk chair and jams the heels of her hands against her eyes. A tear escapes, spills down her cheek and splashes onto her coat. She wipes her nose with the palm of her hand. Zara passes her a tissue from the box on the desk and sits on a box of printer paper at her feet.

"What's wrong?"

Sophie sniffs and draws in an unsteady breath. "You know the BB thing?"

Zara feels suddenly freezing and giddy; she holds onto the edge of the desk to steady herself. The crescendo of the kettle boiling is drowned out by the frightened roar of her blood in her ears. "Yes," she manages, but her voice sounds weird: odd and distant, not hers.

"We used to have this au pair," Sophie's saying. "Me and Ash. Jagna. She stayed in London after she worked for us. She met this guy... And... She came to see us yesterday. To say *goodbye*. She's going back to Poland. And... It's just... It's *so unfair*..."

"Yes," Zara says again, in the same strange voice; she sits tight on the box with her arms folded over her stomach.

"And my *stupid* parents," Sophie says. "Dad, anyway. . . You know what he said after Jagna had gone? He said it was just as well she was going home, because if she'd stayed after the law came in, we'd have had to decide whether to report her. And I said of course we wouldn't have and he said *but then we'd have been breaking the law.* He's such an *arse.*" She fishes a shiny turquoise hairband out of her pocket and twists at it. "He said it's probably best to avoid friends who aren't BB from now on. Even *Mum* said that. *You don't want to have to choose between reporting someone or breaking the law.*"

The hairband snaps.

"Right," Zara says, aiming for lightness, missing it by a million miles.

"*Zara?*" Sophie whispers.

She gives a weak, fleeting smile. "You'd better not know me, Sophie."

Sophie looks at her steadily, her eyes still brilliant from crying. "Fuck that," she says.

The thread of memory breaks and she's back in her own cold room, the rain glittering on the window overhead. She flicks the light off and clicks her phone on. A blue-white glow blooms in the darkness, and she rereads Ash's text.

Do you want to come out tomorrow?

She should say no, because what if he finds out that she's not BB? She thinks she could trust him not to report her: she feels as if she could, but she isn't *sure.* How can she be? And it's Mum and Max's safety she has to guard, not only her own. *His* too.

She thinks of his parents, telling him and Sophie to be careful about who their friends were, of the scrolling announcements on the tube. *Do you know an illegal? It is your DUTY to report them.*

But he *doesn't* know that she's not BB. Sophie made sure of that. *I won't tell anyone, Zara. I promise. Especially not my bloody family.*

And there's still so much she doesn't know. All her unanswered questions about what happened after Sophie died, the questions that have kept her awake at night and prompted her to frightened and fruitless searches online – all those questions are still unanswered. She couldn't find the courage to ask Ash yesterday. After he showed her Sophie's photo, they ran again, in silence; they didn't speak until he dropped her off, when he asked if she would come running another day.

She said *yes*, then.

She answers *yes*, now.

The rain dashes against the window all night. She lies awake, changing her mind a hundred times. In the morning, she locks herself in the bathroom, sits on the edge of the bath, and takes out her phone to call him.

"Don't tell me you're ringing to cancel?" he says.

She thinks *yes*. She says, "No. Just checking what time."

"When's good for you?"

"Whenever. I've got all day."

"Is 9.30 OK?"

"It's fine. See you then."

When he's rung off, she takes a long breath, stands and splashes handfuls of water over her face, tugs the plug from the basin and watches the pattern of the water as it empties. She scrubs her face with a towel and steps into the hall. Max has already left for work; Mum's in the kitchen, setting a tray with toast and a mug of black coffee.

"Oh, Zara. Can you take this up to Elsa?"

"Can't you? I'm going for a run. I'm going to be late." She hurries down to her room, changes out of pyjamas into running gear, and hurtles upstairs again. Mum's waiting at the top of the cellar steps, blocking her way.

"So who are you running with?"

"What?"

"I'm not *stupid*, Zara. You were out for ages yesterday, you were just on the phone to someone— "

"Are you listening to my *conversations* now?"

"No. Should I be?"

"Mum!"

"Who *is* it, Zara?"

She traces a crack in the floor tiles with the scuffed toe of her running shoe. "No one. . . I mean. . . I met him in the blackout."

"*Him?*"

"It's not like that," Zara protests. "He's just. . . He runs too. That's all."

Mum lets out a little breath and twists the ring on the fourth finger of her left hand, that matches the one Max wears. "Zara. . ." she begins.

"Mum. It's fine. We're just going for a run on the Heath, and the park police don't carry scanners, and anyway the new card's good."

"Just the Heath?" Mum says.

"Yes."

"And he doesn't know?"

"No! I'm not stupid either, Mum!"

She lets herself out into the cold white day; the rain has passed. Ash is already waiting, parked next to the railway bridge. She climbs into the car, slams the door – and blinks at him. He's not dressed for running; he's wearing the long woollen navy coat that he had on when she first saw him, jeans, and ordinary trainers.

"Ash? Aren't we going for a run?"

He shakes his head, and pulls out into the stream of traffic. They gather speed and sweep up the High Street. "Thought we'd have a day out." He gives her a quick, doubtful glance. "That's OK, isn't it? You said you had all day?"

Her thoughts are chaos and her breath feels locked in her chest. She can only manage a nonsense of all the wrong words. "Yeah. No. Fine. Where?"

"Secret." He grins briefly at her. She sits with her hands clenched as the familiar streets give way to the unfamiliar: to never-before-seen, half-boarded-up terraces of red-brick houses and shops, the swallowed villages of the city suburbs, the openness and emptiness of countryside. Through the fog of her fear, she wonders if they are going to Sophie's grave; she pictures a country churchyard under dark yew trees. The grey road unrolls through fields of brown earth, reaching to a wide horizon and a pale sky. Everything is monochrome, except the red crosses of flags hanging stilly in gardens and car parks, the scarlet jackets of National Service volunteers in the huge fields and a giant inflatable Santa in a pub garden, under a banner that says *Wishing you a Traditional English Christmas*. Another banner hangs from a bridge over the road: VOTE PARTY in stark black capitals on a white sheet.

"D'you get to vote?" he asks, and for a breathless heartbeat everything seems to freeze and shatter; then she understands that all he's asking is whether she's old enough.

"No. Not eighteen till May. You?"

"Eighteen last September."

"So –" Her voice sounds taut and brittle: can he hear that? – "Party or Coalition?"

"Coalition. Got to be, hasn't it? But I like some of what the Party's done about drugs. Enforcement. Sentencing. I would though, wouldn't I? With Sophie— " His fingers tighten on the wheel, his knuckles whitening, and he's silent for a moment, then he says, "She was anti-Party. She hated all the BB stuff," and she thinks, this is her chance. Now she can ask, naturally, casually, *what happened? Did they ever find out who gave it to her?* But there's that tension in his fingers, a rawness in his voice, a shuttered expression on his face. It's too hard to ask. All she can manage, her voice sounding strange and not her own, is:

"Yeah?"

"Yeah."

They slow down to fall in behind a National Agency van, its windows covered with such a thick mesh that it's impossible to see what or who's inside it.

ASH

He hopes she's OK with this; he's not sure. She's not saying much. Maybe she doesn't know what to say after he told her about Sophie yesterday. She wouldn't be the only one; none of the others – Jas, Lewis, Chris – knew what to say to him for a long time, and Mum and Dad still don't, but then he doesn't know what to say to them, either.

Not with Zara. This can't happen with her, this impossible bloody dead silence.

The National Agency van they've been tailing for a couple of miles turns off the road. "There's a deportation centre near here," he says. "It's OK. That's not where we're going." It's a pathetic joke; it doesn't make her laugh. He falls silent again.

Not far now: he leaves the main road for the meandering route round the edges of fields that he memorized at home, that feels like it's been deliberately designed as the longest distance between two points. Almost there: he wanted this to be a secret, but the signposts are giving him away.

Hamerton

Chapel End

The Giddings

She says, "Ash!" and the way she says it feels good; maybe

he hasn't messed this up, maybe it's going to be OK. He swings off the road onto a gravelled track that leads to a car park under trees, a white house and a small brick church in an overgrown graveyard. *"Ash,"* Zara says again, and he feels a sudden lift. It's OK; it's the right thing to have given her.

"Happy Christmas," he says. "Sorry it's late."

She laughs.

The church door is unlocked. They let themselves in. It's a simple rectangular space; the proportions feel right. Zara takes a book from her bag.

"Four Quartets?" he asks.

She nods.

"Will you read it?"

"'Little Gidding'? *All* of it? It's a bit long."

"I know." It's *bloody* long; he struggled through page after page trying to find the lines she read on the tube. But – listening to her, reading – he doesn't care how long this is going to take. He leans against a pew. The sense washes over him; his head is full of what it would be like to touch her, wind his hands in her hair, press his face into it, feel the softness of her skin against his. He swallows, tries to concentrate. She reads:

And all shall be well

And all manner of thing shall be well

She raises her gaze to his briefly; her green eyes are dark, dilated in the low light. That's almost the end. She finishes reading and closes the book. He's shivering: the floor is bare stone and the glass in the windows is thin and old; it must be below zero in here – but that's not why he's shivering, not only that.

She slides the book back into her bag and steps close to him. "Thanks, Ash," she says, and she hugs him, lightly and too quickly, and breaks away again, shoving her hands in her pockets and huddling inside her thin jacket.

"God. It's freezing."

He nods. "Let's walk." They step outside and walk through the long, wet grass of the graveyard, between the weathered stones, but her teeth are chattering and his fingers and feet are numb; it's too cold to stay out for long. They retreat to the car, and drive with the heating on maximum; he pulls to a halt in the next village outside the Fox and Hounds Free House. It's open for Boxing Day, the St George's cross hanging from the flagstaff in the car park, unmoving in the icy air. He turns to Zara.

"D'you fancy lunch?"

"Here? Uh. . . Sure."

It's a perfect country pub: dark wooden furniture, random pictures of horses on the walls, a muddy Labrador asleep on the hearth. There's a smell of wood smoke and food. They find a table near the blazing log fire. Zara huddles in her jacket and frowns at the blackboard menu on the wall. Meat and chips. Meat pies. "Tell me you're not a vegetarian?" he says.

"No. Um. . . I'll have the ham, egg and chips."

He grins and goes to order; leaning on the bar he lets his eyes range over the signs that decorate the back wall. *Dogs welcome, people tolerated, children must be on leads.* They should have brought Lulu.

"Hi? ID, please." The barmaid's smiling, holding out her hand.

"I am eighteen." He reaches into his pocket and passes her his card.

She nods. "Yeah. It's just I haven't seen you before. And we've had a lot of problems with illegals round here. Can I see hers too?"

He beckons to Zara; she gets up from the table and crosses the bar to join him. "She just needs your ID," he tells her, and she digs it out of her pocket and hands it over.

She still looks cold – pale and shivery; when the barmaid's handed her card back, he orders coffee for them both. They carry the cups to the table. He reaches his hands out to warm them at the fire; the logs crack, sparks fly up the chimney. Zara sits, silent, and he feels suddenly as if she's a million miles away from him. The brief hug she gave him in the chapel feels like a moment in another dimension. He doesn't know how to get back there. At last she says, "Ash? Can I borrow your phone? I left mine at home. I should call Mum. I didn't tell her I'd be so long."

He nods, hands her his phone, tells her the passcode – 1618 – and watches her go away from him, out of the bar, closing the door behind her.

ZARA

In the stone–flagged, whitewashed corridor behind the bar she releases a tense breath that condenses on the air. It's freezing here, colder than it was in the church and the graveyard. As cold as fear. Among the notices for darts competitions and quiz nights pinned to the board in the bar, there are pro-Party election posters. The Party emblem – the red-and-white torch that reminds her, always, of the knuckles of a clenched fist – is tattooed on the barmaid's wrist. There's a sign above the bar. *Not born here? Not welcome here.*

She makes her way shakily to the loos, locks herself into a cubicle, and sits down on the cold plastic seat. She unlocks Ash's phone, frowns at his screensaver, a muddle of numbers and symbols that she doesn't understand, and dials Mum's number, lets it ring three times, and dials again. This time it's snatched up on the first ring.

"Zara? Where are you? You've been *ages.*"

"I know."

"What's wrong? *S-a întâmplat ceva?*"

"Nothing. It's fine. I'm fine, Mum." She takes a long breath, the air stings with cold and the sharp tang of disinfectant.

"We. . . We're not at the Heath. He brought me for a day out. We came to Little Gidding."

"*Where?*"

"I don't know. . . About an hour and a half from London?"

There's a huge silence at the end of the phone.

"What was I supposed to do?" she asks. "I couldn't *tell* him, could I?"

"Just come home," Mum says. "*Treci acasa.*"

"Yes."

"Now."

"Yes."

She cuts the call, and opens the cubicle door. A woman is peering in the small spotted mirror above the sink to repair her make-up; she eyes Zara unsmilingly, and Zara wonders with another cold plunge of fear what she heard. Mum slipped into Romanian, but she kept to English all the way through, didn't she? Didn't she?

She hurries back to the bar. It's crowded now, with a group of men, red-cheeked with cold and Christmas hangovers. She squeezes past them to the table by the fire where Ash is waiting for her, with two plates piled with chips, slabs of fatty ham and oily fried eggs.

She's not hungry; she feels sick. She sits, slides his phone to him across the sticky dark wood of the tabletop, and summons *normal*. "Does it mean something? 1618?"

"It's phi. One-point-six-one-eight."

"What?"

"Phi. It's an irrational number."

"What?"

He grins. "Got a piece of paper and a pen?"

She fumbles in her bag for *Four Quartets*, and voices reach her from the group at the bar. *My mother-in-law's Christmas dinner. Now that is a reason for going on hunger strike.* A burst of laughter, and, *It's not a joke, though. I ask you. . . They're here illegally, and when they're locked up they have the nerve to protest. Outrageous.*

She finds a pen, hands it and *Four Quartets* to Ash, opening the book to the last page of scribbled notes. He leans over it, and draws two neat, straight lines.

And these deportation centres . . . there was an article in the paper.

"So. Have you heard of the Golden Ratio?" Ash asks.

"Uh. . ."

Like a bloody hotel.

"So, call this line A. Then you divide the other line. . ."

You know what? I reckon we should send them all to Scotland. They're always banging on about being an open society, aren't they? Let them deal with—

"Ash," she says, suddenly. He looks at her in surprise: she's interrupted him, she realizes, in the middle of something about lines B and C. "Can we go? I'm a bit . . . I don't feel. . ."

"What's wrong? Are you OK?"

"I'll be fine. I just need some air, or something. I should probably just go home."

He frowns, and she thinks it must be obvious that she's lying, but he only says, "OK." He closes the book and passes it back to her. They thread their way to the door, through the laughter of the raw-cheeked men buying another round from the tattooed barmaid, step out into the freezing air and drive away.

In the mirror, the pub and the village recede and vanish. She turns to look at Ash: his hands on the wheel, his profile, the curve of his hair round his ear. It's darker than Sophie's was: the dark gold of damp straw. He turns and meets her gaze.

"OK?"

"Yeah."

Damp-straw-coloured hair; eyes like wood smoke at dawn in Autumn. She folds her arms over a sudden feeling of hollowness in her stomach that's nothing to do with her uneaten pub lunch.

"Zara?" he's saying. "I'm not going to be around for a bit. I'm going away with Dad. It's been arranged for ages. And I've got mocks when I go back to school. But... We could run again maybe? After that?"

"Sure," she says.

"I mean... It's good, having someone to run with."

She nods. She keeps glancing at him as the rolling fields give way to suburbs, to London, to East Finchley. He pulls over to the usual place, under the railway bridge, kills the engine and turns to her.

"OK?" he asks again.

"Yes." She's not sure she is: her breathing is unsteady, her veins thrum, blood floods her cheeks. Further along the pavement, a Neighbourhood Watch volunteer is giving grief to a couple of kids; an Agency van prowls slowly down the other side of the street.

"I ought to get home." She fumbles the door open, scrambles out of the car, and leans back in. "Ash? Thanks for today. It was lovely." *Some* of it was lovely – the small church under the trees, the thin light through the flawed glass, the poetry in the place it was written for. And *him*: meeting her eyes when she glanced up at him, walking by her side through the wet grass, explaining maths in the noisy pub. But the rest was frightening and dangerous and she shouldn't see him again; she can't. She feels out of control: her body and blood running ahead of her to impossibilities; all her tightly held secrets threatening to escape her grasp.

It's OK. She's not *going* to see him till after his exams: weeks of peace, of safety. She ought to be relieved. But as the car pulls away all she can feel is how much she's going to miss him.

ASH

Hey Soph,

End of December. Stuck in Llan-somewhere with no other identifiable vowels, with Dad and a couple of hundred sheep. No TV, no Wi-Fi, no mobile signal. I'm getting a load of revision done.

I miss Zara.

I don't know what she feels. I know she hugged me at Little Gidding but that was just a thank you for going there, and afterwards it felt like she couldn't wait to get home. I know she said she was ill but it felt like that was just an excuse. She said to call her after mocks. But I don't know if she really wants to see me. I don't know I don't know I don't know.

I could do with you to explain this.

Whatever.

Happy New Year wherever whatever you are.

A xx

He deletes the letter, listens to the stairs creaking under Dad's feet. He flicks his bedroom light off; doesn't answer when Dad whispers, "Night, Ash," from the landing. In the dark, he goes to the window. A fierce winter rain lashes against the glass. There are no lights in the valley.

They stayed somewhere near here one half-term. There was a long zip-wire in a disused quarry; he went on it with Sophie (her idea). He remembers sitting in the truck as it climbed what felt like a hundred hairpin bends; from the top of the quarry they could see for miles. The wire ran high above a lake that was so far below them it looked like a disc of blue metal. *Jesus,* he said and Sophie laughed; she was laughing as they flew.

He wishes he could believe that somewhere she's still flying, still laughing.

CHAPTER FIVE

ASH

Dear Sophie,

18 January. Hey – I got an offer!!!!!!!

Got to get 4 10s. That's OK, though. I can do that. I think. God.

Mum and Dad are really pleased. Haven't seen them this pleased about anything, since

Got to go. I'm meeting Zara. I haven't seen her since Boxing Day, because of being away with Dad and mocks. I invited her to the end of exams drink last night. She couldn't make it, but she said yes to going running this morning.

A xxxx

He prints, deletes, stands to take the copy out of the printer, and Lulu hurls herself at him; she hasn't had much exercise while he's been revising and doing exams and Mum's been working hard too, on some case or other. They don't really have time for a dog.

They should give her away.

They won't ever give her away.

He sits on the bed and lets her leap onto his lap, scratches her head while she licks his face, then runs downstairs with her, into the sharp, below-zero cold; it's a good day for a run. At East Finchley, Zara's waiting, reading, her breath condensing on the air. She slides into the car, tucks her book into her bag and ties her hair back – *God*. He's missed her so much, he wants to tell her how much; instead he asks, "'Little Gidding'? Or *Tess?*"

"*Jude the Obscure.* Thought I'd do some extra reading."

"Right." He grins, pulls out into the traffic, takes the turning onto the long wide road up to the Heath. Jas does English (Ash tried asking him about those lines in 'Little Gidding' but he didn't have a clue), and he's only just got round to reading the set texts. *Extra reading* isn't even in the bounds of his known universe.

"So, are you going to do English at uni?"

"Not sure."

"Sounds like you should."

"Yeah. Maybe."

They jog down the path from the car park. He sets the stopwatch on his phone, and they start to run properly: off the main track, into the woods, and on, past the bench where he told her about Sophie, down the slope to the ponds, along the path to the tennis courts and the kids' playground and the café by the bandstand. At last, they stop, stretch, scoop up handfuls of icy water from the drinking fountain.

"What about you?" she asks. "Uni, I mean?"

"Maths and Philosophy. . . Hang on." He's forgotten about the stopwatch on his phone; he fumbles it out of his pocket, jams his finger down on it, but it's too late – the time's wrong. "Sod it. I'll just delete it."

"Why? Because otherwise it'll mess up your averages?"

"Yes."

She's laughing.

"What?"

"You're such a geek, Ash."

"*Hello?* Says the girl who writes essays on *Christmas Day?*"

"Says the boy whose passcode is . . . *thing.*"

"Phi."

"Phi. And what's your *screen saver?*" She reaches for his phone and he holds it out of her reach, above his head. *"Ash!"* she says and he grins and hands it to her; she frowns at the screen. "What is that?"

"Einstein. The equation for general relativity."

"Yeah. Right. Not geeky at all."

She's teasing him and he doesn't care. It feels good. They run again: along the path next to the running track, up the hill where Soph lost a kite once, letting go of the string, letting it go; through the wood, back along the gravel track. At the gate he bellows for Lulu. She slinks out of the trees. She's filthy. She stinks.

"Shit," he says.

"Literally." Zara grins.

He laughs, snaps Lulu's lead on, hauls her to the car,

shoves her onto the floor and looks at Zara across the roof. "We could run again? Next Saturday? Or . . . do you need to go straight home now? I mean, you could come to ours, if you like. Mum's at work. I could do us some lunch."

She hesitates, and says, "OK."

She says OK, and he feels warm with pleasure, all the way home in the stinking car. Inside, he hoists the dog in his arms and carries her upstairs so she won't get the stair carpet filthy, holding the door keys between his teeth. At the flat he says to Zara, "Ca'you ge'the door?" and as she takes the keys from his mouth one of her fingers brushes against his skin; her touch is as light as a breath but it sends that surge of electric feeling through him again. He steadies himself, carries the dog into the kitchen, scrubs at her with an old towel, but whatever she rolled in is as sticky as tar. He gives up.

Zara's studying the collage of photos on the kitchen wall: views of the Heath, the city, the river, close-ups of bark, brick, water.

"Sophie took those," he tells her. "Are you OK to wait for lunch? Dog needs a B-A-T-H."

"No. That's fine. D'you want a hand?"

In the bathroom, he holds Lulu down in the bath and Zara washes her, leaning so close to him he can feel the warmth of her skin. She's pushed her long T-shirt sleeves up past her elbows; he stares at the curve of her flesh, the fine hairs on her arms. . . She looks at him, as if she's felt him looking.

"Done," she says.

"Yeah."

He can feel himself blushing. He lets go of Lulu; she scrabbles out of the bath, shakes herself, and clambers, trembling, onto Zara's lap. He grabs her collar. "Lulu! Get off! Sorry, Zara. Sorry."

"It's OK." She stands up, drenched in scummy water, her T-shirt clinging to her skin. "Uh... I might need to borrow some clothes?"

"Clothes. Sure. Yeah." He leads her across the corridor into his bedroom, watches her looking round at his room, at his *life*: the neatly placed files on the desk labelled MATHS 1, MATHS 2, PHYS, PHIL, his laptop, the blackboard wall with its equations in his tidy writing, his *bed*. He still can't quite believe he's got here, into this universe where she turns to him with a laugh and says, "It's very tidy."

He grins back at her. "It's a geek thing," he says, and he hauls an armful of clean clothes from the wardrobe: tracksuit bottoms, sweatshirt, a fleecy hoodie: lots of layers because it's cold in here. The heating's gone off; she's shivering and so is he, like he was at Little Gidding: not only because of the cold. Every cell in his body feels alive, charged. He takes a step towards her, his arms full of clothes. Her eyes meet his: green, solemn; he's not sure what he's reading in them. "Zara," he begins—

—and Lulu noses the door open and bounds into the room, still damp from her bath, and leaps up at him. "Down!" he tells her. "Get off!" but she keeps leaping and barking. She probably needs food. Or thinks she does. Bloody dog. He pushes the clothes into Zara's arms. "Here. Have these. I'll stick yours through the machine when you're done," and he grabs Lulu by her collar and hauls her out into the corridor; she scampers ahead of him, sliding on the wooden floor, to the kitchen.

Bloody dog. But if it hadn't been for her, rolling in God-knows-what and needing a bath, there wouldn't be the prospect of the next – how long do clothes take to wash and dry? An hour? Two maybe – two hours of Zara here, with him. He grins.

Bloody dog. He clicks his fingers and she scampers back to him; he scratches her head. Thank God they never got rid of her.

ZARA

After he's gone, she stands for a moment, looking at the place where he was standing. She feels as if she's still running, her heart unsteady, her blood thudding in her veins. If Lulu hadn't come into the room—

Thank God she did. She can't get involved like that with Ash; it's too complicated. She takes a long breath and looks round the room again. It's *very* tidy: dark blue duvet smoothed on the bed, neatly written equations on the square of blackboard paint on the wall, laptop shut and precisely placed on the desk.

She wonders if, somewhere in the desk drawers, there's a dog-eared old copy of a local paper, folded open to a court report, a trial, a verdict in the case of Sophie Hammond's death. She tugs open the top drawer, but there's nothing here except a couple of charger cables, a calculator and a lighter, and her little act of invasion makes her suddenly ashamed. She pushes the drawer shut and glances edgily at the window. But the flat's too high up to be overlooked: outside there's nothing except the black branches of a tree against the grey sky, which feels fuller and heavier than it did this morning. A flake of snow drifts and settles on the rim of an empty flowerpot on the windowsill.

Snow.

She should go home. Instead, she strips off her damp clothes and dresses in his baggy grey sweatshirt and tracksuit bottoms, catching the faint faded scent of him beneath the clean smell of washing powder. She bundles up her clothes and finds her way along the corridor, past the stacked moving boxes, past the radiators clicking into life along the wall. She goes on into the kitchen, where Lulu is curled up in her basket while Ash contemplates the contents of a huge fridge.

"Hey," he says. "What d'you want for lunch? Here, give me those." He takes her clothes from her, shoves them into the washing machine and slams the door; water runs, the imprisoned clothes tumble over. She goes to the window, resting her hands on the warm top of the radiator beneath it. The snow is heavier now, beginning to settle in a white crust on pavements and roofs. Ash comes to stand next to her and they watch the ceaseless drift and flurry and fall, fall, fall, until along the corridor, the front door slams, and a woman calls, "Ash?"

"Mum," he says; he raises his voice to call, "In here!" and Zara turns away from the window as his mum comes into the kitchen. She's carrying a heavy briefcase in one hand and a bulging bag of shopping in the other. She halts in the doorway and gives Zara, then Ash, a questioning look. She has dark hair that needs a cut, threaded with silver. Her eyes are Sophie's colour: the same startling, summer blue.

"Uh... This is Zara, Mum," Ash is saying. "She... We

go running together. We were going to have lunch but the bloody dog needed a bath."

His mum smiles. "I'm Julia. It's lovely to meet you," she says, and her eyes and her voice are warm, pleased. *If she knew who I was. . .* But she doesn't, of course; any more than Ash does (*I won't tell anyone,* Sophie said, *I promise*). They sit down to a lunch of bread and hastily heated soup. Julia asks her about A levels and the conversation flows smoothly and safely to novels and poetry. They talk about *Tess,* and Julia reminisces about growing up near Howarth and reading *Wuthering Heights* for the first time in a moorland storm, and Zara thinks – inescapably – of Sophie, caught in a summer downpour on the Heath, tilting her face to the sky, drinking the weather.

"Well." Julia pushes her chair back from the table. "I've got some work to get on with." She picks up her briefcase, and leaves them alone in the kitchen.

"What work?" Zara asks Ash.

"She's a child-protection lawyer." He slams the soup pan into the dishwasher. "You're allowed to laugh."

"Laugh?"

"Sophie? Protection? Not such a great job there, Mum." He shakes his head. "Sorry," he says. "Sorry."

"No," she says, helplessly. What is she doing here? It's hopeless, impossible to ask him. His face closes down every time he says Sophie's name. She should go home. But she follows him into the living room, and they sit side by side on the sofa. Outside the big windows, the snow falls and falls.

They watch video clips and listen to music on his laptop; she finds his school magazine, with its glossy pages and colour photos, and flips through reports of music, drama, sport, chess, school trips.

"Are you in here anywhere?"

"Nope," he says.

"Not even for running?"

"I run by myself . . . usually." He smiles at her, but she doesn't smile back. She misses the running team. *Less than a month now, to the election.*

"You OK?" he asks.

"Yes. So, what happens next? After the posh private school? Posh university?"

"Ummm. . ." he says, in a way that makes it totally obvious, and she laughs.

"You are, aren't you? Which one? Oxford or Cambridge?"

"Oxford. If I get the grades." He looks at her, with a little puzzled frown between his brows. "You really haven't applied anywhere? Why not? Don't you want to go?" and she shrugs, thinking of the school trip to Birmingham, the bricky, leafy campus glowing russet and green in the sun, the talk about the English Literature syllabus; the sense of *worlds* opening before her.

"Don't know. So. *Oxford?*"

He nods. "Got the offer this week."

"Oh. So that's why you were so *buzzy* this morning."

"Partly," he says, and she doesn't ask what the other part was; she's afraid she knows, and she felt it too when he swung open the car door and smiled at her; his eyes like wood smoke— *Stop. Stop.*

"What about school?" he's saying. "Why don't you go?"

"I used to. But we moved house at the end of Year Eleven and I couldn't get into the college I wanted, so. . ."

She falls silent. She can feel blood throbbing in her cheeks. It's not exactly a lie, but there are volumes of truth missing from it too. She wants, suddenly, to kiss him. It would be easier and more truthful than talking. Instead, she stands and goes to the window. Behind the snow, the day is declining to evening. She should go home.

"It's going to be hell driving in this," Ash says. "Why don't you stay over?"

ASH

He falls asleep with his hand against the wall; thinking of Zara on the other side of it, curled up in the sofa bed in Mum's study, in a pair of borrowed pyjamas. When he wakes again, it's to the strange white-dark of the snowy night, and to Zara, leaning over him, saying his name.

"*Ash.*"

He struggles up. "Zara? S'wrong?"

"I got up to go to the loo. The living-room light was on."

"Mum," he guesses.

"Yes."

He flicks the bedside light on and hauls himself out of bed. His phone says 3:26:41; the heating's been off almost four-and-a-half hours. It's freezing. He reaches for his sweatshirt, pulls it on over his pyjamas, and makes his way along the hall. Mum's sitting on the sofa, leaning forward, fingers pressed against her temples as if she's trying to drive away a headache. She probably is: there are two empty wine bottles on the table and a toppled glass on the floor. He and Zara had some of the first bottle at supper but the second one is all Mum: all 75cl at 13.5% proof.

"Mum," he says.

She raises her face from her hands.

"Go back to bed, Ash."

He shakes his head. "What are you doing?" But he knows: it's on the table: *the Sophie file.* Autopsy report. Coroner's report. Letters to and from Mum and the police, letters from Charlie, the private detective Mum hired when the police found nothing. Charlie's last bill and sign-off letter that he's read so often he knows it by heart: *Honestly, Julia, I'd be taking you for a ride if I investigated this any further. I'm as sure as I can be that there's nothing left to find. I'm sorry. I know how hard it is to live with uncertainty, but I don't think we'll ever know exactly how it happened.*

He picks up a sheaf of fallen papers from the floor, tidies them, sticks them into the file, closes it, drops it on the table.

"I was going through Charlie's interview transcripts," she says. "I thought there might be something we missed."

"Mum. There's *nothing. . .*" It's impossible that something's been missed. It's all been read a hundred times; the pages are highlighted and tagged and covered in Post-it notes.

"Ash? Do *you* think Sophie would have. . . ? I mean. . . *Drugs. . .*" Her voice tails off. Any second now, she'll start crying.

"I don't *know,* Mum. I'll get you some water." He takes his time in the kitchen, letting the tap run, rinsing the glass before he fills it, making toast. By the time he's stuck everything on a tray and carried it into the living room, she's blowing her nose. He hands her the glass, sits opposite her on the coffee table; she tries to smile at him.

"It's pointless, isn't it?"

"Yes. You should go to bed, Mum."

She nods and gets to her feet, not quite steadily. He follows her along the corridor, and Lulu pads after him. His room's empty. He hesitates, goes to Zara's door, and says her name softly.

"I'm awake," she says.

"Can I come in?"

"Yes."

Lulu follows him, and leaps up onto the bed where Zara's sitting with the duvet tucked round her shoulders. She hasn't closed the curtains; the room reflects the strange luminescence of snow. He stands at the window, leaning his forehead against the icy glass. He feels her waiting for him.

"Mum can't stand it," he says at last, "not knowing."

"You never found out. . . ?"

"We never found out *anything*. We don't know who supplied her. She didn't buy it online. The police went through all her Internet records and card transactions, and there was nothing. They interviewed all her friends, they asked about her at Camden. Nothing. And there was nothing in her jacket or her bag. No packet or anything, so someone at the party might have given it to her. Probably did. But it was one of those mad parties, you know; hundreds of people, everyone bringing a plus one, the plus ones bringing plus ones, people crashing it. . . And it was happening all over the house and in the garden. They interviewed as many people as they could, but no one was exactly sure who was there. And – the thing is – she might not even have known – you can mix it in a drink. She might not even have known she was taking it. It might not—" He stammers to a halt.

"Ash?" she whispers. "Might not what?"

"Nothing," and suddenly – *shit. Shit, shit* – he's crying; one of those *stupid*, unstoppable. . . *Hell*. He fumbles out of the room. Flicks the corridor light switch. Nothing. Another power cut. He bangs into one of the removal boxes, gropes his way to the living room, sits on the edge of the sofa with his fists clenched between his knees, fighting for breath.

Lulu licks his hands.

Zara says, "Ash. *Ash*."

He says, into the darkness, "It was my fault."

"No," she says. "*No*."

"*Yes*. She tried before. Drugs, I mean. Mum and Dad were out and she was experimenting with something. I found her." He presses his fingertips against his eyelids: he can still remember it: the tree house in the garden at home and Sophie smoking God-knows-what that she'd bought God-knows-where, and him yelling at her, and her crying. "She asked me not to tell them. She promised she wouldn't do it again. And I didn't tell. And then . . . the party. . ."

"But you said," Zara says. "You said someone might have given it to her in a drink. If she promised you, Ash, that's the most likely thing, isn't it?"

"Maybe. Who knows? Maybe she kept her promise and maybe she didn't. I'm never going to *know*, am I?"

ZARA

So now she knows. She says, "Ash. . ." not knowing what more she might say, but he interrupts.

"Don't, Zara. Please. I don't want to. . ." A shudder runs through him. "It's freezing. I'm going back to bed."

He stands up from the sofa and she follows him into the corridor. It has no windows, and the strange snow light doesn't reach it. In the profound darkness, she stumbles, and he reaches for her and touches her hand to steady her. Only briefly, but it makes her skin wake and burn; she can still feel his touch, long after they have whispered goodnight at her door, and she has listened to him going into his room, closing his door, climbing into bed on the other side of the wall. She wonders if he sleeps. She can't. Sleep is impossible, now: knowing that what she was afraid of is true.

We never found out.

And worse:

It was my fault.

She lies in bed, feeling the memory of his touch on her skin. Outside the uncurtained window, the weather has turned to rain, melting the settled snow on windowsills and branches. The white reflected glow fades; the surrounding streets are still plunged in blackout. It's as dark a night as she's known: remorseless and bitter. *Certainty* is remorseless and bitter; she wishes she could go back to not knowing, to uncertainty and its comforting possibilities. Slowly, the black square of night lightens to an ordinary, slushy January day. The roads will be clear again, and the paths across the Heath: there's nothing to stop her going home.

She slips out of bed, steals along the corridor to the kitchen, and crouches by the washing machine. Lulu flings herself against her, wriggling, yapping and licking her hands. "Shhh. . ." Zara tells her. "Shhhh."

"Zara?"

She startles. Ash is leaning against the kitchen door. He looks as unslept as her: the thin skin beneath his eyes is bruised indigo. Lulu leaps at him, barking.

"OK," he says. *"OK.* I'd better take her out. Want to come?"

"Sure. Yes." She tugs open the washing machine and pulls out her clothes. They're still wet.

Ash swears. "Sorry. I forgot. Can you wear mine again?" and she nods, hurries back to the spare room and scrambles into the clothes he lent her yesterday. She needs to be out of here. She can't face Julia. *Mum can't stand it . . . not knowing.*

They creep out of the flat. On the stairs her hand brushes against his, and she shivers; she wants to knot her fingers through his, feel the pressure of skin against skin, flesh against flesh, bone against bone. She locks her hands into fists and buries them in her jacket pockets. They step outside into the raw air and the melting slush, and head downhill almost without speaking. From time to time Ash swears and tugs at the dog but otherwise he says nothing, as if he's retreated from last night's burst of truth into silence; and she. . .

She doesn't speak either, because she ought to tell him, and she can't.

They pass the bus stop, which someone has fly-posted with pro-Coalition election posters; so that all that can be seen of the usual government announcements now is DO YOU KNOW. . . YOUR DUTY. On the corner, Ash pauses.

"She needs a proper run. You OK to come to the park?"

She glances at him, meeting his grey-blue eyes. *No,* she thinks, *yes, no.* "Yes," she says, and they carry on to the park, climbing to the view point that overlooks London. The towers in the city are grey on grey in the misted air; it's the sort of view that Sophie would have photographed.

"What are you doing the rest of today?" he asks.

"I don't know. I ought to phone Mum, actually."

"D'you need. . . ?" He wriggles his phone out of his jeans pocket and passes it to her, and the lightest touch of his fingers against hers is enough to set her spinning again. She lowers her head so her hair hides her face, taps in his passcode, and takes a few steps away to make the call. She dials Mum's number but it's Max who answers. She's furious.

"Where have you *been?*"

"I texted Mum. I stayed over. Because of the snow."

"With strangers," Max says. "People you know *nothing* about," and she glances at Ash and thinks, not nothing – too much: way, way too much. She's carrying enough knowledge, now, to make her *snap*.

"Zara," Max says. "It's only twenty-five days till the election. Please. Come home. I've got a day off, anyway. We can do some work on *Tess*."

She watches Ash, flinging a stick for Lulu: long-limbed, fluid. "OK," she mutters.

"What?"

"I said OK, Max! I'll see you. Soon," and she cuts off the call, deletes Mum's number, and hands the phone back to Ash. "I should go home."

"Right."

"I've got work to do."

"Me too, I guess. I'll drive you."

He yells for Lulu, and snaps her lead on; they trudge back up the hill to the flats. She stuffs her wet clothes into a plastic bag, and climbs into the car still wearing his. On the drive, she stares straight ahead, at the wet road and the grey sky. They don't speak until he pulls up in the shadows under the railway bridge and says, "Do you. . . I mean. . . Are you still on for running next weekend?"

Run. She should run, because how can she be with him, knowing what she knows? She says, "I . . . I don't. . . Yes," because how can she not be with him, feeling what she feels?

Hey Soph,

So I told Zara about you. The tree house. Never
told anyone before: Mum, Dad, Charlie, Jas, Lewis,
Chris. No one. Not even bloody Lulu. Only Zara. She
was really nice about it. She kept telling me it wasn't my
fault. But how would she know?

I thought it was OK, telling her, only this morning
she was in a weird mood: really quiet, and she borrowed
my phone and she said it was to call her mum, but I
think I heard her talking to someone called Max. And
she deleted the number afterwards.

I know we're not together, but if she's got a boyfriend
why didn't she tell me? I've got no idea what's going on
with her now.

But I never knew what was going on with you either
and I knew you all your life, and I've known Zara
about 3,000,000 seconds. It's not enough.

Maybe she just can't deal with what a mess I am.

A

He prints, deletes and burns the paper copy; he's still leaning on the sill, watching the last of the smoke dissipate, when Mum says, from the doorway, "Ash!" and he slams the window shut and swings round. "Ash? Were you *smoking?*"

"No." He can tell she doesn't believe him. "I was burning some paper," he says, and he remembers, suddenly, why he does this; remembers Sophie, coming home from primary school in a state about a Maths test, and Mum writing *Maths test* on a piece of paper and burning it in the garden. *Burning the worry. There. Gone.* He wonders if she's thinking about Sophie; *there* and then *gone.* Maybe she is: she looks a bit sick, but maybe that's just an ordinary hangover.

"Where's Zara?"

"She had to get home." Maybe.

"She's nice, Ash."

"Yeah."

"And she's read such a lot."

"Has she?"

She laughs. "Yes. It was nice talking to her. Are you still going to the movies with Dad this afternoon? I'm sure Zara could go too, if you asked."

"She's busy."

With Max?

He doesn't want to go to the film. But he can't face arguing about it and if he's going to be out later he'd better get some work done now. He works through a Maths paper that's not as utterly absorbing as usual: other questions keep finding their way through it. He gives up, catches a bus into town and wanders for a bit before meeting Dad at the cinema in Leicester Square. The film's yet another Second World War movie, about the North Africa campaign, and he stares at the images of burning desert on the screen without registering them, wondering about Zara.

Who's Max?

The film ends, the national anthem plays. They make their way out into the drizzle. Dad lays a hand on his shoulder and steers him across the square. "I've booked us dinner. Celebration."

"What for?"

"Duh. *Oxford.*" Dad grins at him.

"Oh. Yeah. Right."

They cross the main road and wind through half-lit narrow backstreets to the restaurant; inside he blinks at the glitter of light off glass and silver and china. There's a huge framed photo of Churchill above their table. Dad orders real champagne and clinks his glass against Ash's.

"Congratulations, Ash. You know what? We should do a trip to Oxford one weekend. I'll try and make some time. Go and visit your college."

"I still have to get four tens, Dad."

Dad waves his hand, like that's *nothing*, fishes in his pocket and passes over a slip of folded paper. Ash unfolds it. It's a cheque for £250.

"*Dad. . .*"

"You deserve it. Enjoy it." Dad clinks glasses with him

again. "And I'm still paying for the summer holiday, yeah? Any ideas? What are the others doing?"

"Uh. . ." He swallows a mouthful of cold fizz. "Chris is going to India with Priya. I'll do something with Jas, I think. Europe, probably. There's a festival or something in Croatia he wants to go to."

"A festival?" Dad raises one eyebrow. "That's not exactly your sort of thing, is it?"

"Dunno." He did go to a festival once, with Jas: filtered light through the tent roof, an atmosphere of dope and wood smoke; just before Sophie— "I might not go to it, but we thought we could travel down there together. Stop along the way. Lewis might come too."

"Sounds good." Dad flips the menu open. "Don't leave it too late to buy visas, will you?"

"It's OK. I checked. Most of them only take a couple of days." He studies the menu; it's wholly carnivorous and it reminds him of the pub near Little Gidding. He thinks fleetingly of going away with Zara in the summer.

Stupid. He's not sure if she'll want to go *anywhere* with him by then. He's not sure she'll want to see him next *weekend*.

CHAPTER SIX

Ash.

She conjures fragments of him: damp-straw hair; wood-smoke eyes; long-fingered hands; a hesitant, puzzled frown; a defeated voice in the darkness. Every memory is a physical jolt, a missed breath. She is ragged with love. She opens his number on her phone, and, for what feels like the millionth time this week, she poises her thumb over *dial* – and stops. She wants to call, she longs to talk to him, she is hungry for his voice. But she's snared in a tangle of secrecy and danger and guilt.

How can she call him: knowing what she knows, hiding what she's hiding?

He hasn't called her either.

Maybe he's not going to.

Phone in hand, she prowls upstairs and into the living room. There's no one else at home: Max has left for work, and Mum's visiting Elsa in the upstairs flat. Zara leans against the living-room windowsill. The sky above the road is almost dark. The streetlight outside the door flickers on, reflecting from the shiny leaves of the big overgrown shrub that half hides the front gate and path. Evening already: she has consumed the whole day circling the same impossibility.

Can't be with him.

Can't not be with him.

She drops her phone on the table, goes into the kitchen, fills the kettle and sets it to boil. Over the soft roar of steam she hears her phone ringing. She runs, but before she reaches the living room, the call has cut off; the notification on the screen reads *Ash: missed call*. She's still staring at it when the phone stirs in her hand with an incoming text.

Tomorrow? Call me

She reads and rereads it: trying to find the meaning below the words. It's shorter than most of his texts: brusque – curt even. It sounds impatient, fed up.

It sounds – it feels – as if he might not bother getting in touch with her again if she doesn't call. And that isn't what she wanted; that isn't what she meant, ever, at all, by this week's long silence. She fumbles with the phone, stabbing the controls half blinded. By mistake, she video-calls him. His face unfolds on the screen; behind him she can see the dark square of the window in his bedroom.

"Hey," he says. He sounds guarded, but pleased too, she thinks, that she's called.

"Hey." She leans back against the windowsill to steady herself; her blood beats crazy in her veins.

"So?" he says. "D'you want to run tomorrow?"

It's just a run, that's all. No need to talk much – just the fall of her feet in time with his, her breathing in time with his breathing, the sense of him alongside her. "Yes."

He smiles, suddenly. "Cool. What time?"

"Whenever. I'm free all day."

"I'll pick you up. Nine-ish? Usual place?"

"Nine's fine."

Upstairs, a door closes, and footsteps sound on the stairs: Mum, hurrying back from Elsa's in time for the early evening news. "Ash? I've got to go. I'll see you." She cuts the call quickly, draws the curtains and switches on the TV. She and Mum sit side by side on the sofa to watch. They never miss the news these days. They watch like fortune tellers trying to predict the future: soothsayers peering into entrails, wise women studying the fall of cards, astrologers gazing at stars. It's all pointless. The news only tells you what has already happened. Only the future will tell what the future will be.

Even so, they watch.

The chimes of Big Ben fill the flat. There are twenty days till the election. Someone's thrown an egg at the Home Secretary, cutting short his speech about the success of the British Born policy: it spatters open against his coat in a mess of yellow and white; a young man is wrestled to the ground by armed police. The Prime Minister sits at his desk in Downing Street, outlining the Party's plans to extend the standard term of National Voluntary Service from eighteen months to three years. A polling organization gives the Coalition a nineteen-point lead over the Party. A police spokesman warns of terror threats in the run-up to the election, and pledges a hike in security: there will be increased monitoring of communications, extra spot checks on the tube, roadblocks, and checkpoints on routes in and out of major cities. A preview of the weekend's football, the promise of a double lottery jackpot, a forecast of cold foggy weather, and back to the Home Secretary's egg.

"I wonder what will happen to that kid they arrested." Mum picks up the remote control and flicks the TV off. "What are you doing tomorrow?"

"I was going to meet Ash for a run." Just a run, but she can feel her face blazing with all the other things it is.

"You need to be careful. Checkpoints. Searches." Mum gestures at the blank TV screen, and sighs. "Honestly... I grew up with all this sort of thing. I never thought you'd have to."

"I know," Zara says. "It's OK, Mum. I'll be OK. We're only going to the Heath. It's safe."

It's not.

The *Heath* might be, but secrets, guilt, love: those things aren't safe at all.

ASH

His phone wakes him on Saturday morning; he gropes for it and blinks groggily at the screen. It's 8:01:34. It's Dad.

He presses *answer.* "Yeah?"

"Sorry. I woke you up."

"Yeah. It's OK." He's meeting Zara in an hour; he rubs his eyes and sits up. "What is it?"

"I cancelled my meeting. Thought we could do that trip to Oxford today."

"Oh." He rubs his eyes again. He hasn't seen Dad since last weekend. But he hasn't seen Zara since last weekend, either. "Um. . . I'm supposed to be seeing someone."

"Someone?"

"Zara. She's. . ." What is she? He's still not sure. "We go running together."

"That's OK," Dad says. "Bring her too."

"Yeah?" She said she was free all day, he remembers. "OK. Thanks."

He rings off, calls Zara, doesn't get an answer. He decides it doesn't matter: she'll be waiting for him at nine anyway. He showers, dresses, grabs a quick breakfast while Mum frowns at yesterday's news footage of someone chucking an egg at the Home Secretary.

"I don't know why he's looking so annoyed," she says. "People threw eggs all the time during eighteenth-century elections. It's a solid English tradition. The Party should be in favour of it. What time's Dad picking you up?"

He checks his phone – "Now –" finds his coat, hugs her goodbye and runs downstairs. Dad's waiting for him in the midlife-crisis car: a reconditioned MG with sleek black paintwork, an oversized engine, and a tiny backseat that's designed for a sports bag or a box of wine bottles, not for anyone as long legged as him or Zara, but it's OK. She wants to see him, he'll sit in the back; he doesn't care. So long as she wants to see him.

The traffic's heavy; on the road across the Heath he tells Dad about the revision conference he went to during the week, about the physics lecture on dark matter: how it exists but can't be seen; can only be inferred from its effects. It makes him think of Zara, how there's something about her that he doesn't understand, can only guess at.

Dark matter = she already has a boyfriend called Max? Maybe.

But she's waiting for him, in the usual place, head down over her book; she doesn't move when they pull up alongside her, and he thinks, of course, she doesn't know this car, can't see him through the tinted windows. He swings the door open and slides out.

"Zara?"

"Oh. Hi?" She smiles, uncertainly, glancing at the midlife-crisis car.

"Hi. Listen. Dad's taking me to Oxford for the day. He says you can come too," and her face changes. Something's wrong. Something observed but unidentified. Dark matter.

"Ash, I..."

"What's wrong?"

"I can't..."

"But you said you had all day."

"I know... It's... I'm sorry."

And the day which he has been wanting so much collapses in on itself, implodes. "You said you wanted to see me," he says. His voice sounds uneven and too loud. He clenches his fists in his pockets to steady himself.

"I do, Ash. I... I just can't."

"Why not?"

"It's... It's complicated."

"Is this about Max, Zara?"

"Max?"

"I heard you talking to him on the phone on Sunday. Sorry. I didn't mean to spy or anything. It's just... The thing is, if you're already with someone, it's fine. I'd just like to *know*." From the way she's looking at him, he can't tell if she's about to laugh or cry, maybe both. "What?"

"Max isn't... Oh God, Ash." She bunches her hands against her face. "Max is my English teacher. And she's a woman. Maxine."

He has no idea what to say.

"I'm sorry, Ash," she says. "I just can't today," and she turns and runs, slipping through the crowds on the High Street.

"Ash?" Dad's opened his window. "What's the problem?"

Ash glances at him, and back at Zara. She's rounding the corner – almost gone.

But she said she wanted to see him.

"Ash?" Dad says.

"Hang on a minute." And he's running, dodging buggies, shopping trolleys, dogs, bumping into a newspaper billboard, shoving it out of his way, skidding round the corner. She's still running, a long way ahead of him; he calls after her but she doesn't look back. She keeps going and turns again, to the left and out of sight. He swears. By the time he reaches the turning, there's no sign of her.

He walks helplessly up the street of identical terraced houses in identical neat gardens. Halfway up, there's an overgrown bush just inside a gate, and a street lamp.

The leaves and the light: this is what he saw behind her when they were talking last night. He stops and peers at the house. Someone ducks out of sight in the bay window. He shoves open the gate, runs up to the front door. There are two bells, neither of them labelled *Jones*: he rings them both, simultaneously, pressing his face against the stained glass. Inside, he can make out a narrow lobby and two glazed doors. He keeps pressing the bell. A human shape appears behind one of the inner doors.

"Zara! *Zara!*" He hammers on the glass. The inner door flies open. It's her. She flings the front door open too, and snatches his hand away from the bell.

"Stop it! What are you doing?"

"I want to talk to you!"

"God, Ash." Her shoulders sag. "You'd better come in."

She glances quickly up and down the street, and hustles him inside. She doesn't want him here, he can tell, but he follows her anyway: into the ground floor flat, along a narrow corridor, through a tiny kitchen, down a flight of steps into the cellar. There's a big stack of moving boxes like the ones at home against the wall, leaving hardly any space for the running machine, the narrow bed, the rickety chest of drawers and the bookcase. The floor is strewn with scattered clothes and books; he recognizes some of them as hers: her tracksuit, her backpack, her jacket. The room is half dark – there's only a narrow window, high up in the rough whitewashed wall. It's cold. It feels damp. She *lives* here?

She tugs the geometrical red-and-white cover straight on the bed and sits down. He stands in the middle of the messy floor, hands shoved in his coat pockets.

"What about your dad?" she says.

"He can wait. I need to talk to you."

"What about?" She folds her arms tight across her body, and he drops his gaze to a pair of scuffed trainers and a dog-eared copy of *Othello* face down on the floor. He can't find the words for this.

"It's just. . ." he tries. "I just. . ." He shakes his head, and turns away from her, running his eye along the tightly packed top shelf of the bookcase, as if he'll find what he needs to say there. His gaze halts at a familiar paperback, tucked between two fat poetry anthologies.

Poems on the Underground.

He poises his finger on the top of the book, presses down, and wriggles it out of the shelf.

"Ash!" she says.

Sophie never read the copy he gave her – an unwanted present for her last ever Christmas – but Zara's read hers. The spine's cracked and there are sticky notes marking some of the pages. He flips backwards through the book. Back . . . back. . .

"*Ash.* Don't. Give it to me."

. . .and back till it falls open on the title page. . .

. . .and his own writing.

Happy Christmas, Soph, love from Ash

Zara's saying something, but it's meaningless; white noise. Right now all he can take in are these words:

Happy Christmas, Soph, love from Ash

OK. Think. *Think.* Sophie never read the book; he doesn't know what she did with it. Maybe she sold it online when she was saving up to buy a filter for her camera. Maybe, in a fit of philanthropy, she gave it to a charity shop, and Zara bought it.

What's the probability of that?

One in a million?

Even a one in a million chance is a chance; it's *possible.*

Only, why didn't Zara say anything? She must have seen the dedication. Why didn't she ever say, *I think I might have one of Sophie's books?* Why the hell wouldn't she have said that?

He looks at her, the book in his hand. His phone rings. He ignores it.

"This was Sophie's," he says.

She nods.

"Where did you get it?"

She doesn't answer, and he knows: suddenly, he knows and he feels like *he's* falling now, the world spinning around him.

"You knew her, didn't you? Sophie. You fucking *knew her!*"

She's standing, saying something, and he doesn't want to hear it; he only wants to get out of here. He blunders to the door, up the cellar steps, along the hall; she's running after him, but he reaches the front door ahead of her, wrenches it open, flings himself out onto the street and keeps running. Before he reaches the main road, he stops. She's not following. He leans against a wall and closes his eyes. The world keeps spinning.

She knew Sophie.

Dark matter = Sophie.

She knew her and never said.

His phone rings again. He checks the screen before he answers. It's only Dad. "Ash? Where on earth are you? I'm going to get a ticket if I'm here much longer."

"On my way."

He's still holding the book; he bends it to shove it into his coat pocket and walks back to the car.

"What—?" Dad begins.

"Don't ask. She's not coming." He slumps into the passenger seat. The heater's belting out hot air; he undoes his coat, feeling the weight of the book in his pocket. He stares out of the window as they pull away. This is the road that he and Zara took when they went to Little Gidding, and he remembers her long silences on that journey, all the space and time when she could have said something and didn't—

"... this week?" Dad asks.

"Sorry?"

"I said, didn't you get your mock results this week?"

"Oh. Yeah." They slam to a halt at the back of a queue of traffic waiting to get onto the North Circular Road. His phone rings; it's her. He cuts the call dead and switches his phone off.

"And?" Dad says.

"They were OK. Uhhh..." He's having trouble remembering; his brain's full of Zara and Sophie, Zara and Sophie. "Two nines and two eights."

"Oh." They've reached the front of the queue. There's a checkpoint at the junction. Dad winds the window down and hands over his ID card. Ash digs into his pocket, past the solid mass of *Poems on the Underground*, fishes out his card, passes it across. Ahead, a couple of cars have been pulled over and are being searched: he watches a bag being emptied, a bright blue dress spilling onto the verge. The soldier at the checkpoint nods, hands back their cards, waves them on. They join another traffic jam on the North Circular. Dad swears, and dials up the traffic news. Checkpoints at every major junction. A protest and roads closed in Wembley. Major hold-ups on the M40.

"Christ," Dad says.

"We could go another time." He absolutely doesn't want to do this now. He wants to go home: lie on his bed, stare at the wall; try and find a reason why in the 3,700,000 and more seconds that he's known her she has never told him about Sophie.

"No. We'll carry on." Dad shakes his head. They move forward a few yards, stop, move and stop again. "Two nines and two eights?"

"Yeah."

"And you need four tens for Oxford?"

"Yeah."

The outside lane's moving freely now. They pull out and pick up speed. The traffic slows. They stop again. Dad drums his fingers against the steering wheel.

"So what are you planning to do about that?"

"About what?"

"Your *grades,* Ash."

"It'll be fine."

"Two grades away from what you need in two papers?"

"They're *mocks,* Dad. The clue's in the title. Anyway, one of the eights was nearly a nine."

"Hmm." The traffic unclogs suddenly and surges forward. They pass a row of army trucks parked across the turn-off for Wembley, and swing onto the M40, past signposts for Oxford. "This girlfriend's not distracting you, is she, Ash? I know your Mum said she— "

"*No!* For God's sake! She's not my girlfriend anyway." He turns to stare out of the window. A thin grey fog lies over everything.

"Sorry," Dad says at last. "It's just... I don't want you to miss out on what you want to do. Don't waste your life." He doesn't mention Sophie, but it's her he's talking about: beautiful, brilliant, *stupid* Sophie who – how? – knew Zara well enough to give her that book of poems.

They never make it to Oxford. 32 miles into the M40, they hit a massive tailback. At the next junction, the motorway is closed, and all the traffic's being diverted onto local roads. Dad leans out of the window to talk to the soldier who's waving cars up the slip road. "Security precautions, sir," he says. For a couple of hours, they sit in traffic jams, then the radio announces that all routes into Oxford have been closed to prevent a threatened protest during the Home Secretary's visit that evening.

They turn back. The traffic coming into London is as bad as the traffic leaving it. They start and stop, start and stop; he switches his phone on to search for a different route and finds a string of texts from her – she's been sending them all day.

Ash. I need to talk to you.

Too late, he thinks, *3,700,000 seconds too late, Zara.*

Why the hell didn't she tell him?

Yeah.

Why didn't she tell him?

Why wouldn't you tell someone something like that unless—?

Unless—

He knows then. It's the same feeling as this morning; the same feeling of gravity suddenly failing, the long fall onto something solid, something that feels impossible but is inescapably, unbearably real.

Dad glances at him. "Are you OK, Ash? D'you need to stop for a coffee or something?"

"No. I'm fine. Can we just get home?"

"Sure. You're staying over at mine, yes?"

"Yeah. I need to go back to Mum's for some stuff, though."

It's another hour and more before they make it. He fetches the Sophie file from the living-room table in the flat and hides it in his backpack, and after supper at Dad's he locks his bedroom door, draws the curtains, sits on the bed with the file on his lap. He doesn't need to open it. He already knows; he feels heavy with certainty.

Prove it.

He flicks through the pages to the long list of party goers who were identified, checked out and interviewed by Charlie, Mum's private detective. At the bottom of the page, there's a much shorter list, of people who were there, but never tracked down.

– friends of Stephen Harris;

– friend of a friend (of a friend?) of Mark Sanders;

– and, highlighted in neon yellow – Anna. Long dark hair. Arrived with Sophie (?). Spent some of the evening with her. Left early (?). Not known to Sophie's other friends.

They've spent hours, days, wondering about Anna, who

maybe arrived at the party with Sophie, was seen with her during the evening, but not – at all – after Sophie had fallen. He helped Mum track through Sophie's photos, scanning all of them for a girl they didn't know with long dark hair. They found nothing. No one.

But he knows who she was now.

Night has fallen. The strip of sky in the window is dark and foggy; mist condenses in drops on the glass. She shivers, and calls Ash for what feels like the millionth time; for the millionth time, his phone goes straight to voicemail. He hasn't been answering her texts either. There's a string of them, going back to this morning, echoes of one another:

Ash. Please. I need to talk to you.

She *has* to talk to him.

She lies back and stares up at the ceiling. Anything – *everything* – that there might have been between him and her is over. She read that this morning, in his face, when he flipped that book open to his own writing and learned how she had lied to him. She was right, weeks ago, when she first met him: it was crazy even to talk to him; *insane* to think of loving him. How could they ever have ended up together, with that fatal secret lying between them, the secret that in the Party's England she couldn't dare tell him? She's read *Tess* a dozen times. She should have known.

They're finished, him and her, before they even started. But it's not only her love that's at risk. She thinks of Mum and

Max, curled up together on the sofa in the living room, in the warm light of the lamps, the curtains drawn tight against the world, the TV news flickering in the corner, counting down the days to the election. Less than three weeks to go. Almost there, but not there yet and she remembers Ash, staring into the darkness, talking about Sophie.

They interviewed all her friends.

He knows, now, that they didn't. She closes her eyes and pictures him, standing in this room, this morning, Sophie's book in his hand, saying *You knew her...* He's bound to tell: his mum, his dad, the *police*, and he knows where she lives; he'll tell them where to find her, but it won't only be her they find.

Mum. Max.

She shoves the blanket and the duvet aside, jumps off the bed, tugs on a hoodie, jams her feet into her trainers and checks her phone one more time. He still hasn't answered. She drops the phone on the bed, runs upstairs and into the living room. The Prime Minister's voice booms from the TV. Images of blocked motorways, of streets filled with smoke and riot police play on the screen. Max leans forward, picks up the remote control, and flicks the sound off.

"Zara? What are you doing?"

"I'm going to see Ash."

"*Now?*" Mum checks her watch. "It's very late. Almost nine. Can't you wait till tomorrow?"

"No! And it's fine. I... He's picking me up."

"Well. . . Call us when you get there."

She promises, and steps out into the darkness. The pavements glisten with frost, mist hangs in halos around the street lights. She runs to the Heath, and crosses it in night and fog; remembers. . .

CHAPTER SEVEN

Sophie — a couple of days back from holiday, her skin the colour of honey, her hair bleached by the sun to pale gold — sits on a bench on the Heath, flinging a ball for Lulu. She smiles a welcome.

"You OK?"

"Kind of." Zara sits next to her, picks up the soggy ball, and chucks it down the hill.

"Kind of? Oh. Sixteen-pluses?" The results came out this morning.

"No. They were fine."

"How fine?"

"Ten tens and a distinction in Add Eng," she says, and Sophie rolls her eyes. "Oh, not you too. Ash got nine tens and distinction in Add Maths and Add Phys. He did get a six in Spanish though. So it's not all bad."

She grins. Zara smiles palely back.

"What's wrong, Zara? You ought to be over the moon. No one gets ten tens."

"I am. It's just. . . You know the Act comes into effect next month? We should be registering for assessment. Not that there'd be any point. Mum'd fail. We wouldn't be allowed to stay."

"It's crazy," Sophie says. "I mean, you must be one of the only people in the country with ten tens. . ."

Zara just looks at her.

"Sorry," Sophie says. "So, did you decide? Are you leaving or staying?"

Zara fishes in her pocket and hands Sophie a slim rectangle of plastic: her new, fake ID card in the name of Zara Emily Jones. "We just moved in with Max. I'm not going to have a normal life for a year and a half. I. . . I don't know if I can *do* this," and Sophie starts to say something and she cuts across her. "Don't, Soph. Don't talk about it. I don't want to think about it today."

"Come to a party, then," Sophie says.

"A party?"

"Why not? I've been invited to this thing. . . Sort of invited. I know someone who's going."

"I don't know. I'm meant to be *hiding*, Sophie. And anyway—"

She gestures down at her tattered jeans, splashed with flecks of whitewash from the cellar walls, but Sophie's already pulling her to her feet, and she follows; across the dry grass of the Heath, under the bewildering sun, to Sophie's huge house. They climb the smooth wooden stairs to the top floor. Sun streams through the big skylight. Two doors stand ajar.

"That's Ash's," Sophie says, and Zara peers in at the dark blue carpet and curtains, the tidy bookshelves, the painted equation on the wall: $e\pi i-1=0$. "What's that mean?" she asks, and Sophie grins.

"It means my brother's a geek. Come on."

She leads Zara into her room. The noticeboard and the walls are covered in her photos: the studies of brick she took in Gloria's shop, views of London from the top of the Heath, holiday photos of blue sky and a silver sea, and a fair-haired boy with blue-grey eyes looking reluctantly into the camera. "Ash," Sophie says.

"Right. Not exactly your average geek."

Sophie laughs and comes to stand next to her. "You should meet him. It's *so* annoying he's not here now. He's at some stupid post-results picnic. Getting drunk on the Heath, and I really want you to meet him. You'd suit each other."

She stares at the photo for a bit longer. "Sophie, that's impossible."

"It might not be. He's – I mean, if he knew about you he wouldn't tell anyone. He's good at secrets. Anyway. Here. I've got something for you," and she turns away, reaches down a white paper bag from the top of the wardrobe and hands it to Zara. It's the green dress from Gloria's, with its mottled pattern of leaves.

"Present." Sophie's watching her, smiling.

"Sophie! You can't. "

"I have now. And it won't suit me, so you better have it. Please, Zara. I want you to."

She takes the dress out of the bag, and holds it up against herself, like she did in the shop. She feels changed.

"See?" Sophie picks up another bag from the bed, and empties it out onto her desk: glue, glitter, sequins, feathers and fake gems, and two blank white masks. "For the party. It says masks on the invitation."

"Masks?" Zara laughs. "What is this, eighteenth-century France?" – but she feels the attraction of it; of concealment, secrecy, disguise. They sit on Sophie's floor, decorating and sticking like little kids playing: a green mask for her, with flecks of red and gold, like the first coming of autumn in a wood; a blue-and-gold one for Sophie, like sun on water. Sophie places the masks side by side on her desk and photographs them.

They change into party clothes. They put streaks of colour in their hair (red and green in hers, gold glitter in Sophie's), and set out as evening falls. She waits outside the front door while Sophie has a shouted conversation with her mum – *Where are you going? Who's Ellie? Have you got her mum's phone number? How are you getting home? What time?*

Stop worrying. I'll be fine! Sophie slams the front door shut. They hurry through the shafts of late sunshine and shadow on the tree-lined street and catch a bus that takes them along the crest of Hampstead Heath. As they get off, at a wide road of trees and enormous houses, Sophie checks her phone and snarls. "Mum. She's told Ash to come and pick me up. Like I'm five. Oh, well. At least you'll meet him now," and they walk to the party house which sits behind high walls, the gates guarded by a couple of bodybuilders in dinner jackets, checking names on a list. Zara catches Sophie's hand in a last-minute panic. "I don't want to use my ID." It's new. She's not even sure it works.

"It's fine. They're not going to ask for it. You don't even have to give them your real name, if you don't want," and while Zara's thinking *real name* and wondering what that even means now, Sophie's smiling at the bouncer and saying, "I'm Sophie Hammond. Lily Paget's friend. Uh... Anna's with me."

They pass through the gates and along the drive, where strings of fairy lights wink like fallen stars in the trees. They climb the flight of stone steps to the open double doors and step inside, into a high hall with a geometric glass roof that catches the light like a faceted diamond. Bubbles pour from the top landing, drifting down into the hall, reflecting rainbows. Someone offers them champagne; Sophie takes two glasses, hands one to Zara, tucks her arm through hers and leads her into another huge room at the back of the house. A band plays. Coloured lights revolve. A girl wearing a black dress, a cat mask and a necklace like a jewelled collar catches Sophie's arm.

"Soph?"

"Lily!"

Other girls – Tabby in a shimmering purple dress, Mia in silver, Ruby in silk as red as her name – gather round, and Zara cradles her champagne and listens to them talk about holidays and parties and people she doesn't know. Someone asks, "Where d'you go to school?" and she almost answers with the name of her old school, remembers in time and says, "I don't. I mean, I'm sort of between schools at the moment." It sounds weird, and it's not safe to be weird now: she needs to be unnoticed. She mutters something about needing the loo, slips away and is slinking towards the front door when Sophie catches up with her.

"Don't go. Please, Zara. I get fed up with all that." She waves her hand towards the back room, all the girls in their expensive dresses. "And if you go, you won't meet Ash."

She stays. They sneak up to the top landing like kids at a grown-up party and spy on the hall through the banisters, watching the waitresses collecting empty glasses and bottles, and clearing up spilled champagne and broken glass, while the bubbles still fall, iridescent, around them. Fireworks start in the garden, and they lie side by side on the thick carpet to watch them through the glass roof. Rockets soar and burst in showers of gold, red, green, silver.

"You know," Sophie says. "It'll be OK. We can meet up. I'll come and see you. It'll be fine, Zara."

"Yeah. I suppose."

"It will. Come on." Sophie jumps to her feet. "I'm starving."

Downstairs, the room behind the hall is quieter than it was. The band are taking a break, and the party's mostly happening outside now, in the huge garden. "Grab that sofa," Sophie says. "I'll get some food," and Zara flops down into the deep sofa opposite the window. Outside, another brilliant shower of sparks falls and dies. At the table, Sophie's piling a plate with food, and chatting to a dark-haired boy in a black jacket and a plain black mask. He rocks on his feet, balances himself against Sophie, laughs, and staggers to the drinks table against the wall. There's the little explosion of a champagne bottle being opened, and when he turns back he's dangling a slender glass carelessly in each hand, between index finger and thumb. He passes one to Sophie with a bow, a flourish and a laugh. They touch glasses, and drink.

There's another explosion from the garden – not fireworks now, but lightning, white and dazzling, followed immediately by a massive clash of thunder and huge drops of rain that burst on the terrace. People dash inside, shaking rain from their hair and clothes, talking and laughing, clustering round the table to help themselves to food and drink.

The band starts to play: the music ramped up to maximum volume as if it's trying to compete with the thunderstorm. People dance; the lights spin red, green, purple. For one panicked heartbeat, Zara loses sight of Sophie, but then she's there again, in the chaos of colour and shadow, a bottle of champagne in one hand, the streaks of glitter in her hair sparkling under the lights.

She fights through the crowd to Zara's side, yells something that Zara can't hear over the din of the music, and pulls her into the dance, under the turning lights. Outside the storm is as wild as ever. Thunder crashes over the music, lightning floods the room with white light. They dance; dance. The other girls join them. Lily has lost her mask. There are dark streaks of rain on Ruby's dress. Sophie swigs champagne; her hair is drenched with sweat. She staggers against Zara; finds her balance and keeps dancing, wilder and wilder, as if the storm has got into her blood. Zara catches her arm and tugs her close. Sophie looks at her: wide eyed and startled.

"You need some water!" Zara shouts.

"What?"

"I'll get you some water! Wait here!"

She pushes through the crowd to the drinks table. For a moment she rests her hands on the soaked tablecloth. Her body is pulsing with the music. She's had enough now; she wants to get out of here. She wants to get Sophie – who's definitely had *more* than enough to drink – out of here. She grabs a bottle of water and weaves back through the dancers, the lights, the music, the chaos.

Sophie's gone.

The others are still dancing: Tabby, Lily, Ruby, Mia: purple and black, red and silver; the lights spin, the music pounds. Zara catches hold of Ruby's arm, and pulls at her. "Where's Sophie?" she yells, and again, and again, before Ruby shrugs, shakes her head and shouts something about ". . . the loo. . ."

Zara turns and pushes her way back into the hall. The bubbles are still pouring, and two of the waitresses are wheeling in a giant tiered silver cake, with candles that are already alight, burning like fireworks, sending up fountains of sparks. The dance music stops, abruptly, and in the ringing silence, from somewhere high up on the landing, a trumpet fanfare sounds: a slow *happy birthday to you!* The crowd

surges out of the back room, chanting, *Ell-ie, Ell-ie, Ell-ie!*
A girl in a silver dress and a silver mask walks up to the cake,
gathers her long hair in one hand and leans forward to blow
out the candles.

Zara scans the crowd. She can't see Sophie. She pushes her
way into the back room, where a few couples are still dancing
to silence, too twined round one another to break apart for
birthday cake. The storm is wild: rain hammers on the
lighted terrace, every drop a tiny explosion of silver, and she
runs outside, remembering Sophie, relishing a rainstorm on
Hampstead Heath. The dark-haired boy is sitting on the edge
of a big plant pot, his hair and clothes soaked, his mask pushed
up onto his head. His face is stark white, his eyes dark hollows.

"Hey!" she says. "Have you seen Sophie?"

"She was dancing," he says.

Someone screams in the hall.

Someone screams, and she knows – she can't know, how
can she? – but she's running anyway, back inside, through
the dance room. The door to the hall is blocked by a crowd
of people. There's a single shout – *get down!* – then everyone
is shouting, sobbing, screaming. *Get down, get down!* She
pushes through the crowd. One of the bouncers is pounding
up the stairs, taking them two at a time, and high above, high,
high above, Sophie is walking the balustrade of the galleried
landing, and laughing. Below her the bubbles are still pouring
through the air: they drift, shimmer, change, and Sophie
falters – slips – and falls.

Falls.

Falls.

The bouncer hurtles down the stairs, pushes through the crowd around Sophie, kneels next to her, presses thick fingers against her wrist, and then her neck. One of the waitresses has her phone out, and is stabbing numbers into it with shaking fingers. Ellie's crying. The silver mask dangles from her hand. The bouncer shakes his head and sits on his heels, his face grey and sick. Another man is moving the crowd away.

Zara steps past Lily and Ruby, crying in one another's arms, and out into the garden. The dark-haired boy has gone. She finds her way round the side of the house, out onto the street and walks home through the storm. She buries the ruined green dress at the bottom of the bin.

CHAPTER EIGHT

Fog smothers the Heath, gathering in droplets on the trees, falling on her like cold tears. She runs without stopping till she reaches the streets on the other side. The car lights blur silver and ruby. At the flats, she huddles in the doorway, and presses the buzzer for flat six. Julia's voice crackles over the intercom.

"Hello?"

"Hi."

"*Zara?* Are you OK? Come in."

She steps into the clear brightness of the lobby, and runs up to the top landing. Julia's waiting for her at the flat door, holding onto Lulu's collar. Zara looks fearfully into her face, but there's only concern, not fury, in her eyes. He hasn't told her.

"Ash isn't here, Zara. He's at his dad's for the night. Is something wrong?"

"We... I need to talk to him."

Julia frowns, but she says, "OK. Here. Hold the dog for a

moment. I need to take her out anyway. I'll give you a lift over there."

The trees are black silhouettes in the misty street lights; windows glimmer through the fog. They drive to a road that rises on a curve, and park outside a red-brick house that she knows: it's the old house, the one she came to with Sophie. She hadn't realized that Ash's dad still lived here.

"Number fifteen," Julia tells her. "Are you OK on your own? I should take the dog."

"Yes. Fine. Thanks."

She climbs the slippery wet black-and-white tiled steps. The stained glass in the front door gleams violet and amber. She rings the bell, a light comes on over her head, and a man with Ash's straw-coloured hair and blue-grey eyes opens the door.

"Hello?"

"Hi. . . I. . . I'm Zara. Is Ash here? Can I see him?"

He frowns at her, but he's only annoyed, not furious: Ash hasn't told him, either. "Is this about this morning?" he asks.

"Uh. . . Yes."

He considers for a moment. "OK. You'd better come in."

She steps over the threshold, into the hall and a rush of memory. There's polished marble on the floor, and the hall lights pick out little glints in the stone, and she remembers how the sunlight did that too, when she was here with Sophie. She climbs the stairs after Ash's dad, one hand on the polished oak banister, her skin remembering its warm smooth solidity. But on the top landing, both bedroom doors are firmly shut now, and there's dense night above the big skylight.

"Ash?" His father knocks at his bedroom door. There's a pause, a key rattles in the lock and the door opens. He says, "What?" and then he sees her.

He steps slowly aside, silently inviting her in.

She crosses the threshold.

ASH

He shuts the door and turns to her; she's soaked and shivering; he thinks she's been crying. He doesn't care.

"Ash," she says. "I need to talk—"

"Yeah." He's shaking too, but with anger. He has never been so angry with anyone in his life; has never *hated* anyone— "Fine. Let's talk. Let's talk about the party, Zara," and she looks suddenly afraid, her eyes wide and dark like on the night of the blackout, when he felt *sorry* for her, and he knows now: the tiny possibility that he's miscalculated, the 0.0001% chance that he's somehow got this wrong, all crashes to atoms. "You were there, weren't you? You were bloody there. You were *Anna*."

"I. . . Yes." She looks him in the face. She was there. She left secretly. She never got in touch with the police. And why all that unless—

"It was you, wasn't it? You gave it to her!"

She jolts as if he's hit her.

"*No!* Fuck you, Ash! She was my *friend!*" Her taut hands slacken and collapse into loose fists; her face folds. "God. Is that what you think of me?"

"What am I *supposed* to think? For fuck's sake, Zara! You

didn't tell me you knew her. You didn't tell me you were at the party. You didn't go to the police when they asked for witnesses. What am I meant to think?"

She stares at her feet. "I was going to tell you," she mutters.

"Yeah. Right. When?"

"Soon. I *was,* Ash . . . I promise."

"Fine." He picks his phone up from the desk, his hands shaking. "Fine. Let's call the police now. You need to tell them you were there. . ." and suddenly she's fighting him, grabbing for the phone, trying to wrench it out of his hand; it's like that morning on the Heath when they were messing about, and she was teasing him (like Sophie used to) about being a *geek.* He let her take it then. Not now; they're not *playing* now.

"Ash, no! Don't! I can't—" and she makes another grab for the phone. He holds it high, out of her reach, stabs at the screen. She tugs his arm. He mistypes, swears, shoves her away, enters 1618; the screen blinks open at the menu. He jabs at the phone icon, and she grabs at him again.

"Ash, listen to me. *Please.* I can't talk to the police. Not now. I *will,* but—"

"Why the hell not now?"

"Because. . . I. . . Please. Give me a bit of time. A few weeks."

"*A bit of time?* You've had—" For once he can't calculate the seconds. "You've already had a *year and a half,* Zara. How much time do you *want?*"

"I know," she says. "I just—"

121

"*Just* nothing!" He pushes her away again; she stumbles backwards, and he scrolls through his contacts, finds the number he wants, poises his finger over *dial*—

"I'm not BB!"

He stops, raises his head and stares at her. She's sitting where she fell, at the side of his desk. Her hair's damp; her trainers are wet and muddy; she must have run across the Heath, on her own, in the dark, to get here, to talk to him. To tell him—

"*What?*"

"I'm not BB, Ash," she says again and it's like – it's like discovering that the earth goes round the sun, the crazy improbable ellipses falling into one clear and elegant pattern. A *paradigm shift,* that's what it's called – *God.* Forget what it's called; the point is, she's not BB, and everything – *everything* – falls into place in his head with a *clunk* he can practically hear. She doesn't go to school. She doesn't go out much at all. She didn't dare come to Oxford on a day of roadblocks and security checks. Sometimes she panics about getting home. All the things he thought were about him are about something else, entirely.

He's still holding the phone, his thumb still poised over the dial icon. A moment later – less than a second later – and he would have called. It feels like if he's not careful the phone might make the call by itself. He swipes the screen shut, closes the menu, switches the phone off completely, and sets it very gently down on the desk.

"Not BB?" he echoes, stupidly.

"No."

"But you... You don't sound... I mean... You're *illegal?*"

She nods, and he walks to the window, leans his forehead against the cold glass. Outside, the darkness makes indistinct shapes of the garden: of the table on the terrace, the big tree and Sophie's tree house, the shed at the end of the lawn which Mum used as her office when they were younger. The same place and not the same place: a parallel universe where one single change has changed everything.

"Ash," she says at his shoulder; she's got up from the floor, has come to stand next to him. "There's stuff I need to tell you. About the party. You need to know. I was with her, practically all the time, and she never took anything. But then she went for food, and there was this guy, and he got her a glass of champagne. I saw him give her the glass, and he sort of jiggled it in his hand when he gave it to her. I... I think he was trying to get something to dissolve, or mix."

He stares out at the garden...

"It was a *spiked drink,* Ash. She didn't know. She didn't do it on purpose. It wasn't her fault. It wasn't *your* fault."

... The dark shape of the tree house.

"*Ash.*" She lays her hand on his arm. "Have you got that? It wasn't your fault."

He can't speak. He walks to the bed, sits, picks up the thick, tattered folder; all those useless statements, interviews that went nowhere, witnesses who'd seen nothing, while she—

He raises his head. "You *saw* what he was doing? And you didn't *stop* him?"

"I didn't *know*! I didn't realize... Not then. When he did that thing with the glass I just thought he was messing about. Like someone overacting in a stupid play, or something. He was really drunk. I thought Sophie was too. I thought that's why she fell."

"So when did you realize? When I told you about her?"

"I..." She drops her gaze to her muddy trainers. "No. It was on the news. That she'd taken an illegal high."

"When?"

"It... Not long after. There was something about the autopsy on TV, wasn't there?" and he remembers that report. He remembers Mum, trying not to cry, steadying herself to talk clearly to the camera: *Please... If you knew Sophie, if you think you might have any information, please get in touch with the police. We want to know how this happened. We want to make sure it doesn't happen to anyone else.*

"That was just... That was only a few *days* after..." Words choke him: he can't look at her. He stares down at the floor, at the shiny pink smear on the carpet where Sophie spilled some nail varnish once. Almost a year and a half. Almost eighteen months. About 45.5 million seconds, that's what it is: 45.5 million seconds of thinking it was his fault, of watching Mum and Dad fall apart, of Mum drinking.

"I didn't know what to *do*," she says. "How could I go to the police? And I thought, I kept thinking someone else must have seen him get the drink for her; I didn't think it could have been just me. Not at first. And Mum... I..." She falters into silence.

There's a piece of loose skin at the side of his thumbnail; he chews at it, biting it raw and painful, thinking about what she knew, all along, and he didn't. "So," he says. "That first day. When we met on the tube. Did you know who I was then?"

"Yes," she whispers.

He doesn't answer. After a long, long time, she says, "I should probably go."

He nods.

She doesn't move.

Another huge silence ticks past.

"Ash," she says at last. "I. . . It's late. They do a lot of ID checks on the buses at this time of night. Can you. . . Sorry. . . Can you give me a lift home?"

"Uh. . ." He rubs his hands over his face. "I can't drive Dad's car. Not insured. I'll call you a cab." He hauls himself up from the bed. The folder slides off his lap, the papers cascade out of it and fan out across the carpet. He lets them lie, goes to the desk and picks up his phone. All his actions feel slow and heavy, as if he's walked into a new stronger gravitational field that's dragging him down. He books a cab, and watches the car icon on the map, getting closer and closer. He says nothing until it turns into the top of the road, then he drops the phone on the desk.

"Your cab's almost here."

"Right." She clenches her hands. "Ash. One thing. If you're going to tell anyone about this, will you talk to me? Before you do? Please?"

He nods. They go silently downstairs together to the front

125

door, he opens it and stands waiting for her to go. She pauses on the doorstep, and he thinks she's going to say something, but she doesn't. What else is there to say? She goes down the steps and climbs into the cab. It disappears into the fog. He closes the door.

"Ash?" Dad calls. "Was that Zara leaving?"

"Yeah."

"Come here a mo."

He drags himself into the living room. There's a half-finished chess game that they started last week on the table; football on the TV.

"Everything OK?" Dad asks.

"Fine."

"Want to finish this game?" He nods at the chessboard. "Or watch—"

"No. I'm going up."

"Are you sure you're OK?"

"I'm fine. I'm just tired."

He nicks a bottle of whisky from the kitchen drinks cupboard and carries it upstairs. In his room, he sits at the computer, opens a new document and types.

Dear Soph,

Sorry. I mean, thinking you might have done it on purpose, because it seems like you meant it when you promised you wouldn't do drugs again. Not your fault.

Maybe not mine either. Except if I had told them, they'd have grounded you till Christmas. Only you'd

126

have talked your way out of it by the summer, knowing you. You'd still have been at the party.

With Zara.

She knew, and she didn't tell me. And I know about the BB thing. I get that. But all that stuff she did: following me on the tube and seeing me over and over again and never saying anything, not even HINTING, even after I told her about you and me and the tree house, and me thinking it was partly my fault.

You know what's funny? Yesterday I thought she might be getting interested in me. I'm such a fucking idiot.

A

He deletes the letter, and carries the whisky into Sophie's room, drinks sitting in the dark on the edge of her bed; crashes to sleep on her bare mattress.

ZARA

The lights are still on in the living room, a red glow behind the fog, shining off the wet leaves of the overgrown bush in the front garden. She tiptoes up the path, opens the door as quietly as possible, and creeps into the flat, but Mum must have been watching. She's waiting in the hall. She's furious.

"Where have you *been*?"

"I told you. I went to see Ash." She takes a step towards the kitchen, and the stairs down to her room, but Mum catches hold of her wrist.

"Wait, Zara. You were meant to phone when you got there."

"I forgot. Sorry." She tries to pull free. "Can I just go to bed now, please?"

"No. Stay here. You need to tell me what's going on."

"*Nothing.*" Nothing: he can't bear to see her, talk to her, be with her. *Nothing* is a huge heavy ache in her throat and chest. She scrubs her free hand across her face and closes her eyes hard against tears, but they won't stop. . .

"*Gata. Gata. Nu mai plânge. Totul are o soluţie.*" Mum has her arm round her now and Zara lets herself be led into the living room. She drops down onto the sofa and Mum sits next to her and holds her close, repeating, "Shh. Shh. It'll be all right."

When Zara stops crying, Max is there too. She's pulled the armchair up close to the sofa, and there's a tray of freshly made tea on the table. *Tea in a crisis. How English.* She picks up her usual mug and wraps her wet hands round it.

"Is this about Ash, Zara?" Mum says. "It is, isn't it?"

She nods, wordlessly, tightens her hands round her cup, and lifts it to her face to breathe in the warmth of the steam. The room is snug, cosy inside its red curtains, but she feels as if an icy wind is blowing through it. It used to be safe. She's not sure it is now.

"Zara?" Mum says.

"I. . . I didn't tell you. Ash. . . He's Sophie's brother."

Max says, "*Christ,*" and puts her mug down with a clatter; tea slops onto the scuffed table-top. "What have you told him?"

"Everything." Everything, except the most important thing: she never told him *I love you.* Max swears again, and Mum closes her eyes, so pale in the lamplight that Zara thinks she might faint.

"I didn't have a choice! He followed me here this morning. He found Sophie's book. He worked out I was at the party. And you know what?" She's crying again. "You were *wrong,* telling me someone else would have seen what happened. Because no one else did. It was only me. And it's been hell for them – Ash and his family – they've never found out. . ."

"Until now." Max takes her glasses off and pinches the

129

bridge of her nose with her thumb and forefinger. "What's he going to do about this, Zara?"

"I'm not sure. I told him I'm not BB." Mum gasps. "I had to stop him calling the police somehow, didn't I?"

"You should never have got involved with him in the first place! What were you *thinking*, Zara?"

"I wanted to *know!* And I'm not *involved* with him. . . It's not like that."

"OK, OK." Max leans forward and places one hand on Mum's and one on Zara's. "Do you think you can trust him, Zara? Not to say anything?"

She wants to say yes, but she thinks of Julia drinking and crying in the cold darkness, and his dad, lost on his own in the huge house that's haunted by memories of Sophie at every turn. "I'm not sure," she whispers.

Mum swears.

"You have to talk to him," Max says. "*Make* sure."

He never wants to see her or talk to her again, she thinks; he'll put the phone down.

She calls.

He doesn't answer.

CHAPTER NINE

Savage thirst, a desperate need to pee, a headache like a laser behind one eye, a feeling that he might be about to throw up: all wake him. It's middle-of-the-night dark; he's got no idea what time it is. He reaches for his phone, can't find it, remembers he's in Sophie's room.

Sophie.

Tonight, his mind doesn't flinch away from the thought of her. He feels his way to the loo in the dark, pees, swallows handfuls of cold water from the tap, and staggers back to his own room. Crossing the floor, he skids on a pile of loose papers. He flicks the light on and blinks at the scattered pages of the Sophie file – all those dog-eared sheets – and something else that catches the light and reflects it painfully, sharply, back to him.

It's the CD of photos that lives in an envelope taped to the back page of the file. Photos of the *party*. He should have *thought* of this.

He bends to pick it up, swallows a sudden lurch of nausea,

and stumbles to his desk. His hands are shaking as he slots the CD into the computer, and his blood feels fizzy, and that's not just the alcohol. She saw. She *knows*. He finds a memory stick in the desk drawer, downloads the photos onto it, checks the time at the bottom of the computer screen. 3:45:54. He can't call her now. But tomorrow. . .

He didn't want to see her again.

He needs to see her again.

Back in his own bed, he lies awake, thinking about Zara, thinking about Sophie. *Remembering* Sophie: barging into his room, interrupting his homework with questions about maths (*I don't get quadratic equations/angles in a circle/indices*) and once:

I've got these moral problems. For Philosophy. Listen. There's this baby on a train track—

Oh, yeah. We did that one.

So, what's the answer? Because as far as I can see whatever you do, it's wrong.

And he said – he can't remember, something smartarse probably. That might have been when she threw the nail varnish at him.

He lies awake for a long time, remembering, *As far as I can see whatever you do it's wrong.* It's almost dawn before he falls back to sleep, and bright sunlight when he wakes again. The fog has gone. Still hungover, he tugs on running gear, shoves the memory stick in his pocket, and gropes his way downstairs. The light in the kitchen is savage. Dad's at the table, with the newspaper, fresh croissants and strong coffee.

Ash sits opposite him and pours himself a mug of black coffee. Dad folds the paper and puts it aside.

"Whisky," he says. "You need to be careful, Ash."

"I know."

"I mean it. You can do yourself real damage."

"I know. I'm not *stupid*."

Dad frowns at him with *Sophie* in his eyes, and he wants to tell him: she wasn't stupid either, it wasn't her fault. He wants to tell him, only he promised Zara. He sips at his coffee, flipping through the paper. The Prime Minister's made another election speech, hailing the BB policy as a necessary defence of national resources, security and culture, promising to enforce it with greater energy if the government is re-elected on February 13th, denying the Coalition's accusation that the confiscation of illegals' property and their forced deportation amount to human rights abuses. *What rights do these people have? They are here illegally. They were given ample notice, opportunity and assistance to leave.*

He skips quickly through the rest of the news, stopping only to read a report on the trial of a woman convicted for giving shelter to an Australian friend, and sentenced to six months' community service. He folds the paper shut. There's one of the usual government announcements on the back page:

KNOW AN ILLEGAL?

IT IS A CRIMINAL OFFENCE TO FAIL TO REPORT THEM.

The words burn themselves into his brain; Sophie dances into his room, interrupting his homework.

So, what's the answer?

He needs to see Zara.

"Plans for the day?" Dad says.

"Think I'll go for a run." He shoves his chair back with a screech that sets all his hungover nerves jangling again, and steps out into the fierce light. He runs, blood and head pounding. He stops twice on the Heath – once to throw up in a bush, once to clean his mouth out with water from a dodgy-looking drinking fountain. He makes himself keep running: down the wide avenue of huge houses, under the shadow of the railway bridge, past all the tidy gardens, and up the path past the overgrown shrub.

The door's answered by a woman wearing gold-rimmed glasses, her hair in cornrow plaits, and he blinks at her, with a sudden, stupid plunge of fear that he's already too late; she's gone, he'll never find her again.

"Hi? Uh. . . Is Zara here?"

The woman frowns. "Sorry? Zara?"

"I'm Ash," he says, and her face changes.

"Oh. OK. You'd better come in."

He follows her through the narrow hall, into the front room. A dark-haired woman starts to her feet as they come in, so like Zara that she must be her mum. "Max?" she says, and he blinks again. Zara told him Max was her English teacher, so what's she doing here, opening the door as if she *lives* here?

"It's OK, Ana. It's Ash," and Max slips her arm round Ana's shoulders, and there's something in the way she holds her – another Zara secret falls into place with a huge clunk. *Max is my English teacher.* Yeah, right, Zara. What about

Max is my mother's lover? But it's OK. It's OK: he thinks he gets this now – how much she has been trying to protect.

"I need to talk to her," he says.

Max nods. "I'll tell her you're here."

But she's there already, standing inside the door, staring at him, her hands bunched in her pockets.

ZARA

His hair's damp with sweat, he's pale and heavy-eyed; he looks exhausted and a bit ill. She buries her hands deeper in her pockets.

"Ash? What are you *doing* here?"

"It's. . . I need to talk to you."

"We'll give you some peace," Max says, and Zara nods, without looking at her, still unable to shift her eyes from Ash. She feels Max and Mum slip past her, out of the room. The door closes softly behind them, leaving her alone with him. She's suddenly afraid, remembering what she made him promise. *Talk to me first if you're going to tell someone.* Why else would he be here?

"Ash. . ." she begins.

"Zara, listen. The thing is. . . I mean. . . I get it."

"What?"

"Everything. You not telling me. . . You couldn't. I. . . God, Zara. . ." and – how? She didn't notice this happen, but somehow the space between them has disappeared. She's holding him and he's holding her; his face in her hair, her skin against his skin; her mouth against his; he tastes of sweat and rusty water and stale alcohol and tears. She can feel his heart

136

thudding against hers. When at last they let one another go, they are both shaking. She takes his hand and leads him to the sofa; they sit with their hands locked together, fingers knotted through fingers.

"I wanted to tell you," she says.

"I know." He kisses her again. "I told you. I get it. It's like the baby on the train track."

"What *baby*?"

"It's OK. It's a hypothetical baby. No, listen. It's a moral dilemma. There's this baby, crawling on a train track. And there's a train coming, heading straight for him, and you can't reach him in time to pick him up, but you *can* change the points and divert the train onto the other track. Only then it'll run over an old man who's fallen asleep there. So, what do you do?"

"I don't know. That's *impossible*. Whatever you do, you kill someone."

"Yeah," he says. *"Exactly."*

She stares at him. Sunlight catches his dark gold hair. It floods the room, transfigures the street. She feels like summer, like a thousand larks rising, singing. The feeling coursing through her blood is laughter, but she's crying too. He frees one hand from hers and catches a tear on his fingertips. She leans her face against his.

"There's something I need to ask you," he says.

"Yeah?" She sits up. He digs into his pocket, takes out a memory stick, and flips it in his fingers. "Photos of the party. Charlie collected them. Mum's private detective. I . . . Would you recognize him, d'you think? The guy who gave her the champagne?"

She closes her eyes briefly, conjuring her memories of him: talking to Sophie, handing her the glass with a flourish and an easy laugh, sitting in the garden, rain pouring from his dark hair. "Yes. I'll fetch Max's laptop."

When she comes back into the room, Ash is leaning back in the sofa, loose limbed, eyes closed, face turned to the sun. She steadies herself against the door frame, dizzied that he is here, against all probability, all chance.

She watches him until he stirs, opens his eyes, and smiles. Then she sits down next to him again and sets the laptop down on the table. He plugs in the memory stick and opens the folder of photos. A list of named images unfurls down the screen. She clicks the first photo open, and catches her breath.

Ruby in her red silk dress and Lily in her black cat mask lean, laughing, into the camera – and suddenly, she's there again, in the high bright hall with the glittering roof overhead, the sour fizz of champagne in her mouth, the light kiss of a breaking bubble on her skin and Sophie laughing. . .

"You OK?" he asks.

She shifts one hand to hold his, clinging to him as if for balance. Blinking her vision clear, she studies the screen. There are figures behind Ruby and Lily, half seen, out of focus. She zooms in on them, taking her time. No. He's definitely not in this photo.

Nor in the next, or the next, or the next. She works through the file steadily, zooming in on figures dressed, as he was, as a lot of the boys were, in black with plain black masks. Once, she sees a bit of herself: her hand, and part of the skirt of the mottled green dress. She shivers, and carries on looking. She spends a long time on each photo. After the last, she turns to Ash.

"I'm sorry."

She wanted to find him: for Ash, for Sophie, for *herself*. To be able, at last, to *do* something.

But he's not there.

ASH

She seems as disappointed as him; more, even. She says, "I could try looking again?" but he knows – he reckons they both know – it won't be worth it. It's typical of the Sophie file: it's always raised more questions than answers. He ought to be used to that, but he's disappointed too. He was hopeful this time: the odds felt better than ever before. He runs a finger along the top of the screen.

"Maybe, if you wrote a statement. And I took it to the police..."

"It wouldn't work, Ash." She sounds certain, and he guesses she's thought this through a hundred times already. "If there's no photo, the only way to identify him would be to do a – what's it called? – an e-fit. And you couldn't do that. You don't know what he looks like. I'm the eye witness. I'd have to go to the police."

"You're not doing that," he says. He squints into the blinding sunlight. If not the police, then...

"There's Charlie, I suppose," he says.

"Charlie?"

"The detective Mum hired. He might have the tech for an e-fit. Only—" He breaks off, frowning. Charlie would want to know why Zara couldn't go to the police, and maybe they could trust him enough to tell him she's not BB; he thinks they could, but he's not *sure*, not 100% absolutely, definitely sure. This isn't something you can prove like a watertight calculation in maths. The whole idea feels too risky. He's starting to understand how it was for her, now, trying to calculate impossible unknowns.

"Forget it." He leans towards her and kisses her; she tastes of salt and the faint mint of toothpaste. Her hair is soft; it smells of something sweet. After a long time, they break apart. She closes the laptop gently.

"I just wanted to be able to do something *now*. Oh well. Eighteen days."

"Eighteen days?" He frowns at her.

"Till the election. Everyone says the Coalition's going to win, don't they? And they'll abolish the BB policy. I'll be legal. I'll be able to go to the police then."

"So that's what you meant, yesterday? About giving you a few weeks?"

She nods, and he feels suddenly as if something heavy has been lifted from him. He thinks of Mum sitting in the living room with the Sophie file in her hands, of lifting it from her, dropping it to the floor, telling her it's over.

"So we wait. Eighteen days. That's *nothing*." He jumps up and pulls her to her feet. "Come on. Let's go for a walk."

"Uh..." she says. "I'm not going out much right now. Unless I have to."

"Oh. No. Course." His mouth's suddenly dry, thinking of

141

all the times she's run and walked with him; all the times she might have been stopped, ID'd, arrested.

"What about going to Dad's? I'll call us a cab."

They sit close together in the taxi, fingers interlocked, leaning against one another; he turns his head to breathe in the scent of her hair. The house is empty; Dad's left a note to say he's gone to the gym. They raid the fridge for a late breakfast, and eat side by side at the table. He keeps looking at her; his heartbeat faltering every time he thinks of the slightness of chance; how improbable it is that he and she—

"Hey," he says. "I've just thought of something. I don't know your real name."

She laughs.

"Zara."

"Mmm." He lifts one hand and twists a strand of her dark soft hair in his fingers. "Zara *Jones?*"

"Uh... No. OK. If you want the whole thing: Catalina Maria Zara Ionescu. Catalina after Mum's aunt, Maria after her best friend at school. And Zara after Mum's Scottish penfriend. I've just been Zara Ionescu most of the time we've lived here."

"Ionescu?"

"Romanian," she says.

"Right." He pours himself another bowl of cereal and slops milk into it; he's suddenly starving. "So how did you end up here? I mean..." He halts. He feels as if he's saying this all wrong; the words slipping out of him carrying meanings that he doesn't *mean*.

"End up?" she echoes.

"I didn't. . . I don't. . ." he stammers.

"I know." She gets up from the table and goes to stand at the window, staring out at the garden with her hands bunched in her sleeves. "Mum did English at uni. She got pregnant with me when she was still a student. She had a big falling out with her family because she wasn't married to my dad. They're . . . old-fashioned. Traditional. Whatever."

He gets up too, and stands behind her, wrapping his arms round her and resting his head against hers: that sweet softness.

"Is that when you came here?"

"No. Later. We lived with Mum's aunt when I was little. In the country. I'll show you the photos sometime. Then she died when I was six, and Mum got offered a job here. We've been here ever since." Her voice falters. "I thought we'd always be here. Till the BB stuff started."

He tightens his arms round her. "Didn't you think of going back? When that happened? I mean, I'm glad you didn't. . ."

"We *thought* about it. Of course we did. And yeah, Mum and I could have gone. Not that I'd be able to write an essay in Romanian now." She shakes her head. "That would've come back, I guess. But I don't *know* anyone there, and things between Mum and her family are still rubbish. And what about Max? It's not so easy for Brits to get jobs and residency in Europe now, is it?"

"Uh. . ." he says; he doesn't know.

"The thing is. . . This is *home,* Ash. Don't get the idea that I hate it there, because I don't. I loved living on the farm. I love that it's part of me. But we've got a *life* here. Mum with Max, and Max's mum and dad and her brother are great. A proper family. And you were right. I do want to do English at uni. It's what I've wanted to do ever since I was in Year Nine."

She draws in a long breath.

"And everyone's said – haven't they? – all along, that the Party can't last. So when they brought in the BB policy, we had a choice. Uproot everything, lose all the things we cared about – or hang on here for eighteen months, and wait for the election and things to go back to normal. It felt like the obvious thing to do, and. . ." She shivers a bit and he kisses her hair. "We didn't realize what it would be like. All the forced deportations, and ID checks everywhere. . . We didn't think it would get so bad so quickly."

"Eighteen *months,*" he says: it feels an impossible time to live in secret; hidden; constantly afraid of discovery. "46.5 million seconds."

"Is it?" She twists in his arms and gives him an uneven smile. "I'm kind of glad I didn't know that."

"Only about a million and a half to go now," he says.

She shivers again. "So long as the Party lose. If they don't, then what's been the point? Mum and I'll have to leave anyway."

He lets her go, crosses to the table and flips through the abandoned newspaper to a report he skated over this morning.

"They're bound to lose," he says. "They're seventeen points behind in the polls."

Later that evening, after he's taken her home in a cab and walked back to Dad's, he goes into the garden and climbs the mildewy rope ladder up into the tree house and sits on the mouldy cushions. The memory is so clear that it's like being able to hear her, through some rift in time. *Ash, please. Don't tell Mum and Dad. I won't do it again. I promise.*

"I know," he says out loud. "Eighteen days, Soph."

CHAPTER TEN

In the morning, before he leaves for school, he breathes on his window and writes her name on the glass.

Zara Ionescu

He'd like to ring her, but he reckons she's probably asleep; he doesn't want to wake her. There are 1.5 million seconds to wait; let her sleep through as many of them as she can. He wipes her name carefully away, and heads out. It's like he's seeing the world through a new, more powerful lens this morning; things he's hardly noticed before leap into focus. There's a sign on the bus shelter halfway down the hill:

WHO IS YOUR NEXT DOOR NEIGHBOUR?

REMEMBER: **YOU** HAVE A LEGAL OBLIGATION TO

REPORT ILLEGALS

MAXIMUM PENALTY: £1000 FINE

OR 6 MONTHS' COMMUNITY SERVICE

He pauses to read it, thinking how she wasn't only protecting herself by not telling him she wasn't BB, because now he knows about her, he has *a legal obligation* that he has no intention of fulfilling. He carries on down the hill towards the tube feeling as if someone might be watching him. On the train, the same warnings scroll across the information screens. He picks up an abandoned paper, crumples up the election flyer that falls out of it (VOTE PARTY: VOTE PATRIOTISM) and sucks up the election news:

COALITION IN CHAOS?
2M ILLEGALS STILL AT LARGE SAYS HOME SECRETARY
ARCHBISHOP HINTS AT SUPPORT FOR COALITION
PM: THE WORK'S NOT FINISHED YET

And, buried somewhere on page seven, the latest poll gives the Coalition a sixteen-point lead over the Party. He drops the paper on his seat when he gets off the tube, hurries up to the ticket hall, through the barrier, and up the steps to the street. Forget the rest of the news. It's the numbers that matter. Sixteen points behind. One would be enough, and they are sixteen times that. Sixteen. *Sixteen.* It's going to be OK.

"Ash!" Jas is running up the steps behind him, taking them two at a time, his coat unbuttoned and flapping around him, his bag held loosely under one arm. They fall into step, and head for school.

"Good weekend?" Jas asks, and Ash thinks of kissing Zara goodnight yesterday in the narrow hall of the flat: her softness, salt taste, warmth. He's warm, now, with the memory; every cell in his body feels charged. *Good* weekend? Good squared, good cubed, good to the power of ten. . .

"Weren't you seeing Zara? How'd it go?"

"I. . . Uh. . ." He feels a sudden, urgent impulse to keep her hidden. "Actually. . . No. It didn't work out."

"What? So *was* she seeing someone else?"

"Uh. . . Yeah. I think." They stop for a random ID check; Ash takes his time putting his card away, putting a gap in the conversation.

"God. Sorry, Ash," Jas says. "You should've come over. Call next time, yeah?"

"Sure. I was with Dad anyway. Got stuck in that traffic on Saturday. Hours and hours of listening to him going on about my mock results."

"Tell me about it," Jas groans. "That's all I've been getting too."

They run up the steps into school, and sign in. In the sixth-form common room, Chris is sitting, leaning forward to read the heavyweight newspaper that's spread out on the low table in front of him, open at the page headed "ELECTION COVERAGE". Ash sits next to him so he can read over his shoulder; Jas drops into the chair opposite, takes his laptop and a copy of *Hamlet* out of his bag, and starts to type furiously at what's obviously some last-minute English homework. Lewis saunters across the common room, and sits on the edge of the table.

"Got a chess problem for you, Ash. Sending it now."

"OK." He fishes his phone out of his pocket; while he

waits for the link, he opens his contacts list and scrolls down to her name: a simple arrangement of four letters that sends another diffusion of warmth through him.

"Got it?" Lewis says.

"Hang on." He clicks away from Zara's name and opens the chess problem: it's the usual sort of thing. *Black to checkmate in three moves.* He frowns over it.

He wonders what Zara's doing now.

"Timing you, Ash." Lewis taps his wristwatch.

"Right." He switches his attention back to the screen. It's not difficult, this problem; he can tell it's not difficult; there's a rook and knight combination that ought to be obvious, but he can't get to it. He glances up. Lewis is grinning at him.

"Have you done this, Lewis?"

"Yep. Four-and-a-half minutes."

"Right." The squares on the chess board remind him of the geometrical patterns on the rug in Zara's room. He wonders if she's awake yet; what she's doing if she is. . .

"Time's up," Lewis says.

Chris looks up from the paper.

"That the first time he's ever got it faster than you, Ash?"

He nods.

"You feeling OK?"

"Fine." He catches Jas's eye. "Honestly. I'm fine." He swipes back to the contacts screen, and closes his hand round her name; holds her safe and secret.

ZARA

The day passes in seconds that feel years long; slow as the movement of glacial ice. At the end of the afternoon, she stands at the window watching the daylight fade and the street-lights flicker on. It's already dark when she sees Ash, hurrying up the street. She runs to let him in and in the safety of the hall, she holds him, pressing her face against him, feeling the rise and fall of his breathing. There are droplets of moisture on his coat and hair. He smells of outside: the city, air, rain. She holds him for a long time before she leans back to look at him.

"You OK?" he says. "How was your day?"

"Long."

He gives her a lopsided smile. "Yeah. I guess... How's *Tess?*"

"Still tragic. Neglected. I haven't been working. I can't concentrate on anything. All I've done is mess about with *have you evers.* Come into the living room. We're on our own: Mum's upstairs with Elsa and Max is doing a late shift."

Still with her arm round him, she leads him into the living room. She drags the heavy curtains across the window and lights the lamps, making the room safe and secret. Ash slings his bag and coat onto a chair, and stands, looking at her with the slight furrow between his brows that makes everything inside her melt and jolt, every time she catches it.

She kisses his forehead, tugs him to the sofa and pulls him down next to her. "What?" she says.

"Uh. . . Lots of things. Who's Elsa? And why's Max doing a late shift? I thought she was a teacher?"

"Elsa lives in the upstairs flat. Mum helps her out with meals and things."

"So she's the other doorbell? I rang them both on Saturday when I was looking for you."

"I know. She came downstairs to ask who you were." She catches a sudden expression of alarm in his eyes, and kisses him again. "It's OK. You don't have to worry about her. Her mum and dad came here from Germany in the 1930s. She's not telling anyone about us."

"Right." He slides his arm round her shoulders and draws her close to him; she rests her head against his shoulder; he kisses her hair. "And Max?" he asks.

"She was my English teacher when I was doing sixteen-pluses. And she's still teaching *me*. Only she doesn't work at school any more. She got arrested on an anti-government protest last spring. Got sacked. She stacks shelves at Tesco's now."

"God." He tightens his arm around her. "So is that how they met? Max and your mum? Because Max was your teacher?"

"Yes. At a Year Ten parents' evening. Romantic, huh?"

He laughs, and runs his finger down the curve of her cheek.

She turns her head to press her mouth against his hand. "And what's a *have you ever*?" he asks at last.

"Oh, you know. Those life experience lists. Have you ever been to France, sailed a boat, been in a helicopter – here." She leans forward to pick Max's laptop off the floor, flips it open and navigates to the site she was looking at this afternoon. "You do it." She cuddles against him and reads as he fills it in.

"How many bones have you broken?" she asks.

"One. Left arm." He flops back and stares up at the ceiling. "We were at Kew Gardens one summer holiday. I was nine. Mum went to the loo, and Sophie climbed this bloody enormous tree. I was trying to get her down before Mum got back."

She tucks her arm through his, through the arm he broke trying to rescue Sophie and holds him silently till Mum comes back from Elsa's, and beckons them to the table for tomato soup with rice. Over the meal, Mum talks Romania: she tells Ash about wooden churches, brown bears in the Carpathian Mountains, medieval towns, castles that never had anything to do with Dracula.

"She was a tour guide," Zara explains to Ash. "Can you tell?"

"Sounds great," he says, but then Mum's not saying anything about the brief visits to her mum and dad with their frozen silences which made Zara feel, even when she was little and didn't understand, as if she herself had done something wrong; all the bitter, unhappy things. But it's OK, really; it's good that Mum's talking so much; is soothing, smoothing. Zara watches Ash relax as he listens; at the end of the meal, she takes his hand and leads him downstairs into her room.

They sit cuddled together under the blanket on her bed and he works through a page of incomprehensible maths while she forces herself through a chapter of *Tess,* breaking off at the end of every page to look at him. Afterwards they lie silent and still, face to face: so close that she can see every pore in his skin, every fleck of colour in his eyes. The warm ebb and flow of his breath laps against her. She runs her hand over his cheek, his brow, his lips; learning the shapes of him. Time melts and runs away.

"Zara..." He breaks the silence. "Sorry. I've got to go. I told Mum I wouldn't be too late," and when she checks her phone it's somehow, already, after ten. She follows him upstairs. On the doorstep he takes something out of his bag, and hands it to her.

"For you." It's Sophie's copy of *Poems on the Underground.* She hesitates.

"She wanted you to have it, Zara."

She takes it then, and when he's gone, she sits in her bed and flips through the pages, turning back through the book to her writing on the title page, remembering how he did the same, just two days ago; how she thought that moment was the end of everything. She lies back, hugging the book to her chest.

ASH

The second Monday: ten days till the election: 864,000 seconds: a ten-point lead for the Coalition. He leans against the common-room noticeboard at break, staring at nothing, seeing her in her tiny damp, messy room. It's all he can think about: the numbers and Zara. He reckons he failed a Physics test this morning.

He wonders how she's coping. He spent the weekend – most of it – with her, not going out, not leaving the flat, and by Sunday he needed to *run*. She wouldn't go to the Heath. "I'm not going out," she said. "To get caught *now*..." and he told her that, statistically speaking, she was no likelier to get caught now than in any other of the roughly 46 million seconds that she's been living illegally. "It doesn't feel like it," she said, and later he decided she was probably right: when he took Lulu out to the park last night there were more police patrolling than usual. This morning, he texted Zara to tell her to stay in. He rereads her answer: *I am. But I think it's driving me a bit mad,* and a row of exclamation marks and screaming emoticons that he answered with a row of hearts—

"Shift, Ash." Chris moves him aside, pins a poster to

the noticeboard, says, "Coffee?" and goes to put the kettle on.

Ash straightens the poster and reads it:

POLITICS SOCIETY

MOCK ELECTION

FEBRUARY 13

DON'T FORGET TO VOTE

He went to PolSoc once when Chris dragged him along in the Lower Sixth; it was basically a version of what Jas calls the Lewis and Chris politics show: a series of arguments that felt unprovable and bad tempered. He didn't go again: he didn't see the point and he was getting enough arguing at home right then. It was before he and Mum moved out.

It doesn't seem pointless any more. And maybe there are some arguments you can't avoid.

"Hey, Ash." Jas is standing next to him. "You OK? You weren't at Chris's on Saturday."

"No." He stares hard at the noticeboard, suddenly so full of memories of *Saturday* that he feels unable to breathe or speak. Her hands on him. His hands on her.

"Ash?" Jas peers at him. "What's wrong? Is this still *Zara*?"

"Uh. . . No. Maybe. I guess."

"*Forget* her, Ash. She's not worth it. Look. Why don't you come to the gig next weekend? Loads of Maya's friends are coming. Or Dad's election night party?"

155

He's suddenly bursting with laughter; he smothers it, twisting his face into a smile that – he hopes – looks bitter and heartbroken. "Jas, I'm fine. I don't need setting up with one of Maya's hippy friends. *Or* a member of the Youth Party."

"God, no. Wouldn't do that." Jas grins at him. "How about lunch?"

"Today? Can't. Sorry. I'm going to PolSoc."

He won't be going to the gig or the party, either: he'll be spending those evenings with Zara. Memories of the weekend flood through him again. Jas is still studying him doubtfully.

"I'm fine," Ash says again. "Really."

He escapes from the common room; at lunchtime he dodges Jas and climbs the stairs to one of the History and Politics classrooms. Chris, Lewis and a handful of others, mostly from the Upper- and Lower-Sixth Politics sets, are sitting on the horseshoe of desks. He halts in the doorway, aware of uneasy glances from around the room.

"Hey," he says. "This is PolSoc, right?"

"Yeah," Lewis says. "Only . . . uh. . ."

"What?"

"Uh. . ." Lewis says again.

"Ash," Chris says. "It's. . . The thing is . . . we're talking about drugs policy today."

"Oh. Right." It feels like they're waiting for him to leave. He stays. He sits on a desk in the corner and listens as one of the Lower Sixth students gives a speech about the need to distinguish between big dealers and small dealers and to think about social conditions, and focus on education and rehabilitation rather than punishment: they're all arguments that he gets the point of, intellectually. But if he was face-to-face with *anyone* along the line that led to Sophie, he'd want to kill them.

"Have you lot actually checked the figures lately?" Lewis interrupts, with a quick glance at Ash before he goes on. "A straightforward hard-line crackdown does actually seem to have been producing some results."

"Yeah. That's right," someone else says.

"*If* you believe the figures."

"What d'you mean, *if?*"

"I mean this government'd be capable of *anything.*"

"Oh come *on!*"

– and the bell goes for the end of lunchtime, and Chris says, "Anyway. Ten days to go. Let's see what the figures say then, shall we?" and the room empties. Chris catches Ash as he's leaving.

"Ash. Listen. About all that." He gestures back into the classroom, takes his glasses off and polishes them on his shirt, saying, "About the election. I know the whole drugs thing matters. I'm not saying it doesn't. And for you. . . But there's other stuff. . ."

"Chris. For God's sake! You don't think I'd vote Party?"

"I. . . Well, no, but. . ."

"No way." He thinks of Zara, hidden and afraid and waiting. "No *way.*"

ZARA

She has slept late, run ten miles on the machine, showered, slept again, watched rubbish television, shouted at Mum, and read the same paragraph of *Tess* over and over. When Ash arrives, she presses her face against him to breathe in the smell of outside.

"I feel like the Lady of Shalott," she murmurs.

"What?"

"Imprisoned. Going *mad*."

"Ten days to go," he says. "Almost nine."

"I know. I know." She leads him into the living room. They flop down on the sofa; he lies with his head in her lap and she plays her fingers through his hair, chasing the droplets of mist that cling there, till he reaches up and catches her hand, prisons it in his and kisses her fingertips. Mum looks into the room. "I'm going to take Elsa her tea."

The front door closes and Mum's footsteps sound on the stairs up to Elsa's flat. In the silence that follows, Zara leans over and kisses Ash on the mouth, and he pulls her down on top of him and kisses her back. They lie in one another's arms for who-knows-how-many seconds, until the power fails, sinking everything in utter darkness. She rolls off Ash and the sofa and feels her way across the room, finds a candle on the mantelpiece and lights it. Strange shadows waver and dance on the wall.

"I better check they're OK upstairs. Come with me. She wants to meet you anyway."

"Who? Elsa?" He slides off the sofa and comes to stand next to her; his eyes grey-black in the faint candlelight.

"Yeah. She wants to know if you're good enough for me."

"If I'm. . .?"

She grins at him.

"So am I?"

"You'll do." She kisses him, lights another candle, and leads him out into the lobby and through the other door to Elsa's flat; up the stairs with their dark green walls and black-and-white photos that seem suddenly odd and unfamiliar, because of the candlelight, partly, but also because she's conscious of Ash seeing all this for the first time which makes her feel as if she's never seen it before, either.

In Elsa's living room, Mum has already lit the candles; the light reflects softly in the gleaming surfaces of dark-wood furniture. Zara and Ash sit in the shadows, in the smell of furniture polish and talc and mothballs, and Elsa talks to Ash about philosophy. When the lights come back on, she catches Zara's hand. "He'll do," she says, and Zara meets Ash's eye. They manage not to laugh until they're on the stairs. When they've recovered, they study the photos of cities hanging on the wall.

"She travelled a lot," Zara tells him.

"We could too," he says. "Europe. This summer. You could show me your village."

The village, and a hundred other places. She imagines long low dusty station platforms, and shafts of sun in narrow streets, waking with him in other cities, leaning on bridges over other rivers whose waters flow slowly, glitter silver. Paris. Prague. Florence. Rome.

"We could go to the Arctic Circle," he says, and she laughs again.

"That's an imaginary line, Ash."

"So? I do maths. I like imaginary lines. Go on. Let's cross it."

"Let's cross it," she says. They have crossed so many lines already, of secrets and danger; an imaginary line on a map is nothing compared with where they have already travelled.

ASH

The third Monday. Three days to go. The polls differ according to where you get them from, but averaging them all out, he reckons the Coalition are still nine point five points ahead. At break he and Jas sit on a table in the common room and listen to the latest episode of the Chris and Lewis politics show.

"It's not *fascism*, Chris," Lewis is saying. "It's *common sense*. Look. We're a small island. We've got limited resources and limited space—"

"Yeah, especially since the Party managed to lose Scotland," Chris interrupts. Lewis ignores him.

"We were getting overcrowded. Overrun. There were too many people coming in, taking benefits and jobs, putting too much demand on *everything*. The NHS. Housing. Schools—"

"Hello? Like we don't have NHS waiting lists and housing shortages now?"

"They're *getting* better—"

"Are they?"

"And anyway, the government can't just spend money it doesn't have. Anyway, that's the whole point. We've got limited resources. So people who were born here should come first. That's all the BB policy is."

"No, it's bloody not, Lewis! It's about *reversing* people's rights to stay. People came here legally and then the BB act changed the rules. That's an infringement of basic human rights—"

"Oh, great. I wondered when we'd get to the human rights bollocks. That stupid Coalition bitch was whining on about that too. Honestly, what's the big deal? People just move back to where they came from. And the ones who registered when they were *meant* to were helped with travel and everything—"

The bell goes for the end of break, and Chris, who looks as if he's about to hit Lewis, grabs his bag and storms out of the common room. Lewis gathers up his books. Jas flops his head back theatrically, closes his eyes and groans.

"God! How many more seconds of this do we have to put up with?"

"About a quarter of a million," Ash says. It's so close now. He feels a plunge of fear every time he thinks how close it is. But the numbers are still good.

He slides off the table. Jas follows him. Lewis is still sorting out his books; they walk out of the common room together and head for the stairs.

"You coming on Thursday, Ash?" Lewis asks.

"Thursday?"

"Jas's dad's party," Lewis says.

"Right." All his thoughts about Thursday start and end with Zara. "Uh... No. I... I said I'd stay in with Mum."

They reach the first floor and scatter to different classrooms; Ash watches the others go. He's been lying to them, and Chris, a lot. But he has to protect Zara; what else could he do?

And after Friday, he won't have to.

He runs up the stairs to get to Maths.

ZARA

He sits on the floor of her room with his laptop, wearing his coat under the duvet she's tucked round them both: the boiler's broken down and the flat is freezing. "It's too cold," she told him. "Go home," and he said, "No way. No *way*." She cuddles next to him. His fingers on the keyboard are white with cold. She leans over to breathe on them and he presses the back of his hand against her cheek.

"You know," he says. "It's half-term next week. We're going to stay with Mum's sister. I was thinking you could come too. It's in the country. Lots of places to run. We could go to Ely. Drive to the sea."

"Maybe." She doesn't want to think about it; it's impossible to think about next week without thinking about the election that lies in the way of it: a huge gulf between now and the future that makes her feel hollow and sick.

"Zara?"

"Yes. It sounds great." She shivers and he slides his arm round her shoulders and pulls her close. The page of equations on his laptop blinks shut. He's changed his screen saver from an illusion of constantly widening spirals to a photo of himself and Sophie on holiday: the sea and sky behind them, Sophie laughing into the camera, Ash with a look of slight reluctance.

She touches a finger to the screen.

"That was the summer holiday," he tells her. "Just before. . ."

"I know," she says. "Sophie had a copy pinned up in her room. It was how I recognized you."

"Oh, yeah." He grins. "When you stalked me on the tube."

"I wasn't stalking you. Not exactly."

"I wouldn't have minded." When he's stopped kissing her, he says, "Did you come to the house a lot? With Soph?"

"Twice."

"And I was never there. Shit timing." He falls silent and withdrawn, and she guesses he's wondering – like she has, a thousand times – what would have happened if she'd met him then; what would have happened if she'd met him on the night of the party – if he had come with them – if they hadn't gone at all—

It's not bearable to think about the past, any more than it's bearable to think about the future: all you can do is think about here and now, this moment, the rain hammering against the window, the sky falling dark, his breath against her skin.

This is all there is.

All.

All.

CHAPTER ELEVEN

Dear Sophie,

    Election Day, seven in the morning. The polls just opened, they close at ten tonight. We'll know the result by sometime early tomorrow morning. It's going to be OK, though. The Coalition are still 8 points ahead. They're going to win. Everything's going to be OK.

    A xxx

He picks up his polling card from the desk and studies it: his name and address, his voter number, directions to the local primary school which is the polling station for the day. When this arrived he was looking forward to voting as a vaguely interesting first-time experience; a mark of adulthood. It was unimaginable, then, how much it would actually *matter*.

He tucks the card into his pocket and walks with Mum to the polling station; they wait in the school hall where election notices are Blu-tacked to the walls among colourful collages of fairy tales. At the trestle table where the officials sit, he and Mum show IDs, are checked off the list, and given ballot papers. He says, "Thanks," his voice half stuck in his throat.

"You OK?" Mum asks.

"Fine." He carries his ballot paper to the voting booth. It's an open-sided box of raw wood on legs that looks as if someone's knocked it up out of an old packing case; it feels temporary, flimsy, easy to smash to pieces. He lays the paper flat, studies it, finds the Coalition candidate on the short list of names. A thick, stubby pencil is attached to the edge of the booth with a piece of hairy string. He marks a strong X in the right box, double and triple checks it, folds the paper, carries it to the ballot box, posts it into the slot.

And that's it. All he can do. For Zara. For Sophie. For Mum and Dad, for Ana and Max. He heads for school.

The school polling station is in the library, manned by students from PolSoc and the Politics A level classes. At break, he drags Jas to vote: they have their names crossed off lists, are given ballot papers to complete in one of the study carrels, and post them into the cardboard box labelled BALLOTS that someone – Chris probably – has prepared. It's all a near-perfect simulacrum of the real thing.

The result's announced at a special PolSoc meeting in the hall at the end of afternoon school: another mock-up of reality. Chris, Lewis and Mr Harrison (Politics teacher and acting returning officer) stand on the stage, Mr Harrison announces the total votes cast, comments on the low turnout, and finally announces the result – Lewis has 196 votes, Chris 227. There are cheers and boos in the hall, Chris gives a clenched-fist victory salute, steps to the microphone, and waits for the noise to die down.

"Thanks," he says. "And all I have to say is this: if you're old enough to have a vote in the real election, and you haven't used it yet, get to the polling station, and vote Coalition. Because this was just a game, but out there, it's real. And it matters. Thanks," and he steps aside to make space for Lewis.

"Congratulations." Lewis gives Chris a curt nod and Ash has a sudden memory of how he used to look when he was beaten at chess – also *just a game*. "Yeah," Lewis is saying, "get out there and vote. And let's hope the real thing delivers a more sensible result than this, because it's only the Party that's *realistic* and *tough* enough to make the hard decisions that this country needs to preserve *our* culture, and *our* values..." He pauses.

"Yes, well, thanks, Lewis," Mr Harrison says quickly. "And congratulations, Chris, and thanks to everyone who helped with the ballot and the counting, and I think I'm right that there's a special Politics Society meeting tomorrow to discuss the real result?"

The meeting breaks up, people pick up bags and coats, the hall empties. Ash and Jas wait for Chris and Lewis; they head out together into the dimming afternoon. The polls close in about five-and-a-half hours: another 20,000 seconds or so in which things can be changed. The numbers are good, but even so, his breath feels faster than usual.

He walks ahead of the others. Behind him, Lewis says,

"They are such *bloody* idiots," and Jas asks, "Is this the right time to tell you I didn't vote for you, Lewis?"

Chris laughs. After a pause, Lewis does too.

"What about you, Ash?" he asks.

Ash slows to let the others catch him up. "Coalition," he says.

"God's sake, Ash," Lewis says. "In the real thing too?"

"Yes. What did you think? That I'd vote Party because of Sophie?"

"I... No..." Lewis stammers.

A bus rumbles past; Jas rattles out a hasty "Going to get this! See you!" and pelts across the road with his coat flying, dodging a bike and a taxi, reaching the bus stop just in time.

"Anyway." Lewis gives Ash a friendly punch. "It's only politics, isn't it? Can't let it get in the way of friendship."

"Yeah. No," he says. They carry on to the tube station, where Priya's waiting for Chris, hunched against the February wind in a long padded coat, her dark hair blowing across her face.

"Hey." She kisses Chris's cheek. "Hi, guys. Who won?"

"Chris," Ash tells her. Lewis checks his watch, mutters something about his train, and runs for the barriers. Priya tucks her arm through Chris's and kisses him again.

"Well done."

"Yeah," Chris says but his voice is suddenly flat, dejected. "It's the real thing that counts, though, isn't it? And I couldn't even *vote* in that."

"You've done other stuff, though," Priya says. "All that

canvassing. And you're going to be on the phone till the last minute tonight, aren't you?"

"Anyway," Ash says. "Eight points ahead. It's going to be fine. Even without your vote."

"Yeah. I guess." Chris grins suddenly. "D'you want to come over and watch the results with us, by the way?"

"Uh. . . Said I'd watch with Mum."

"Sure. See you tomorrow." Chris gives another clenched-fist victory salute, and he and Priya walk away, hand in hand.

Next week – no, that's half-term; the week after – Zara will be able to come and meet *him* from school too. She'll be able to come to the pub, to Oxford for the day, to Chris's eighteenth – *everywhere* – because the Coalition are eight points ahead in the polls; it's going to be OK.

She waits for him huddled under blankets in the front room, hands cradled round a cup of coffee. The cold sucks up steam from the cup in curls that blossom and vanish. When he rings the bell and she opens the door to him, the air outside feels warmer than the trapped, freezing air in the flat.

He steps into the hall and shivers.

"I know," she says. "The boiler's still not fixed. We can't get anyone in to mend it unless Max is going to be here."

"Right." He frowns. "Even so, it might be safer if we stay here. They've upped security, and if they stopped us and ID'd you tonight it'd be. . ."

His voice tails off, but she knows what he means: it would be ironic and tragic and stupid, the sort of thing that would happen to *Tess*. But she wants to get out of the flat, out of the suffocating cold. She wants to hold his hand and tell Julia the truth at the exact moment that the numbers tip and the world changes.

"Mum and Max say it's fine for me to come over. They understand about telling your mum. And the journey'll be safe, Ash, I'm sure it will. If there's a checkpoint there'll be a queue. I'll have time to get out of the car. And it doesn't take that long, to drive to yours."

"Thirteen minutes. 780 seconds." He sighs. "OK," and they step out into the cold night. The air is clear and sharp. It tastes strong, as if there's something more than simply air in it. Shivering and dizzy, she holds onto the gatepost and stares up into the darkness. There's a sliver of moon, but the stars are invisible behind the haze of light pollution.

"Zara, come *on*," he says, and she lets go of the gatepost and climbs into the car. She winds the window down and breathes in the night, watching the familiar journey reel past: the shadow of the railway bridge, the wide avenue of enormous houses that remind her of the one where Sophie died, the road across the Heath with its dark woods on either side and infinite sky above. They clear the trees, and there's a glimpse of London in its huge valley. There are some localized power cuts: the city is a patchwork of constellations of light and hollows of darkness. Downhill again, past the old brick houses and the ghosts of Dickens and Keats, past the posh shops, past the white glow of the hospital that never goes out – and they're here.

Ash switches off the engine and the lights, and lets out a long breath of relief. "Let's get inside."

The flat feels beautiful: spacious and warm and clean in a way that makes her feel how grubby she is. She's been wearing these clothes for – she's not sure how long, but *too* long. She hasn't had a shower since the boiler broke down: only a couple of shivery, shallow baths in Elsa's chilly bathroom, trying not to use too much of her hot water, or stand-up scrubs in their own bathroom in water from the kettle.

"Ash? Can I have a shower?" she says.

"Course. I'll do supper. Pasta OK?"

"I thought pasta was the only thing you could cook?"

"It is."

"Pasta's fine, then."

In the bathroom, she stands under the shower for ages, breathing in the steam and the sweet, spicy smells of soap and shampoo, hearing his name in the shhhhh of the water. She dresses in his bedroom: it's the first time she's been here for weeks, and a couple of things have changed. On the wall above his bed, he's pinned up a collection of photos that she knows are Sophie's. There are panoramas of London taken from the top of the Heath on a bright summer day that catch the rush of clouds across the sky and the glitter of sunlight from all the glass in the city, and studies of dappled shadow and the play of light on the river. And on the blackboard wall, there are some pairs of numbers, labelled C and P: they're the latest opinion poll figures, she guesses. She studies the narrowing gap between them, and wonders what he'll be writing there tomorrow.

It's no good trying not to think about this any more. It's *here*.

ASH

She's left a bundle of her things on the kitchen counter: her jacket, her book, her ID card. He picks up the card and studies it, comparing it with his own. It looks identical – the NA logo, the hologram, the barcode – and he wonders how you get hold of a fake ID. He wouldn't know where to start looking; it reminds him of how Sophie knew, somehow, where to buy drugs when he didn't have a clue. He leaves the cards on the counter, unearths some pasta sauce and garlic bread from the bottom of the freezer, and sets a pan of water to boil, leaning over it to watch as it starts to stir and bubble.

"Hey," she says from the doorway; she comes into the room and sits at the table. She's wearing the grey sweatshirt and trackies that he lent and then gave her; her feet in thick socks, her hair wrapped in a towel. She's pale, her eyes dark-rimmed as if she didn't sleep last night. He didn't sleep much last night: he was – is – too full of tomorrow and what will happen. He only says, "Pasta takes ten minutes, doesn't it?"

"About that. 600 seconds."

He grins. The water comes to the boil, he dumps a pack of pasta into the pan and pours her a glass of wine; she takes a sip and he leans in and kisses her, tasting the sourness on her lips and behind it the sweetness of her. She catches his hand and pulls herself to her feet; they kiss all the way along the corridor to his room. . .

Some things, it turns out, take more than 600 seconds. Mum comes in from work to find him scraping burned pasta from the bottom of the pan into the kitchen bin.

"Honestly, Ash. How're you going to survive at uni?"

"On burned pasta, I guess," he says, and she laughs, but he only burned the pasta because of Zara, and she won't be at uni with him so the *pasta* will be fine, but what about him?

Without her, what about him? He drops the pan into the sink and runs the tap on it, watching the water glitter, thinking of her, of her, of her. . . Mum reaches past him to turn the tap off.

"I thought Zara was here this evening?"

"Oh. Yeah. She is. She's just getting changed. . . Uh. . . She had a shower. Their boiler's bust. We're going to watch the election results."

"All night? What about school tomorrow?"

"Mum, everyone'll be knackered. Teachers too. They'll all be watching."

"OK." She smiles suddenly. "So she'll be here for Valentine's Day."

Valentine's. . . ?

Of course. He's only been thinking about the 14th as the day after the 13th, but *of course*. Perfect. This is perfect; there's a kind of symmetry about it that lifts his hopes again.

"Can I buy champagne?" he asks.

"Well. . . Why not? Just for once." Mum digs a handful of

175

£20 notes out of her purse and presses them into his hand. He finds his coat and the dog's lead, and runs uphill with Lulu to the off-licence on the High Street. It's still open, an explosion of red and pink: balloons and hearts in the window, confetti scattered on the floor. There are a couple of bottles of real French champagne left among the sparkling wines. He picks one up carefully (it looks and feels as expensive as it is; the bottle made of thick weighty glass topped with a twist of gold foil) and carries it to the counter, feels in his pocket for his ID card...

"Shit." He was comparing it with Zara's. He must have left it on the kitchen worktop.

"Problem?" asks the man at the till.

"Left my ID at home. Hang on." He fumbles his phone out of his pocket. "I've got a photo of it. Will that do?" He swipes it open and passes it across the counter; the man squints at it.

"Date of birth... That's fine. You'd better get home, though."

"I know." He pays, picks up the heavy carrier bag, unties Lulu from the notice outside the shop and hurries for home: they'll have champagne for breakfast tomorrow, a celebration of *everything*—

A white van passes, slows, pulls to a halt ahead of him; the side door slides open, National Agents and police officers jump down. He turns to cross the road, and one of the officers calls, "One moment," and walks up the pavement towards him, hand held out. "ID check. Can I see your card, please?"

"Me?"

"Do I look like I'm talking to someone else?"

"No. Sorry." He checks all his pockets, in case he made a mistake at the off-licence, but he didn't; he knows he didn't. "Sorry. I've left it at home. It's just down the road. I could go and get it." He gestures down the hill, towards the flats.

"You know it's an offence to go out without a valid ID card, don't you?"

"Yeah. Mistake. Sorry."

"Can you get in the van, please?"

"What?"

"You heard. Get in." The man jerks his head towards the van.

He swallows, lifts Lulu in and clambers up after her; sits on a bench while she sniffs at God-only-knows-what on the floor; wonders if he could get away with showing them the photo on his phone.

His phone.

No.

The realization jolts him like a fall, knocking all the breath out of him. Zara's name and number are on his phone. What if they check his contacts? Track her down, find Ana, find Max, find *her*? He should delete her contact details, her name, everything – only there isn't time; the policeman's already climbing into the van. He lowers himself onto the seat opposite Ash, takes a tablet computer out of his pocket and balances it on his knees.

"Put your hand on the screen."

Ash does as he's told. White-blue light sweeps under his palm. "Am I under arrest?"

"Not yet." The policeman tilts the tablet towards himself, glances at the screen, and up at Ash.

"Name?"

"Ashley John Hammond."

"Don't suppose you can remember your ID number?"

"Yeah. LON-04-98302129."

The man raises an eyebrow, checks the screen again, and nods. "OK. But remember: it's an offence not to carry your card at all times. Go on. Straight home, mind. Get that card before you go anywhere else," and Ash practically falls out of the van, dragging Lulu behind him, scurries down the pavement—

"Hey!" the policeman calls. "You're forgetting something."

It's the champagne. He goes back for it, stammers, "Thanks," and with the bag in one hand and the dog lead in the other he pelts home, Lulu bounding next to him. In the lobby of the flats, he shuts the door and leans against the wall: out of breath, his heart beating at what feels like ten times its normal rate. It's OK. *Nothing happened.* But before he climbs the stairs, he deletes Zara's contact details and the list of her calls from his phone.

He's known her number off by heart since Christmas anyway.

ZARA

She has never felt so unbalanced: strung between hope and terror and suffused with the dizzy warmth of love. It's hard to talk to Julia; she's asking the same, easy questions as before, about novels and poetry, but love and hope and terror are a storm of feeling that Zara can hardly contain. She can feel it pushing to escape every time she opens her mouth to say a word. She keeps to quick monosyllables: *Yes. No. Yes.* When Julia hands her a cup of tea she clings onto it as if it's the only thing keeping her anchored.

"I need to make a few calls." Julia hefts her briefcase onto the table, and takes out a couple of sheets of paper.

Zara gestures to the door. "Should I. . . ?"

"No, no. Stay. It's fine. It's not confidential. It's election stuff. Ringing round to make sure people have voted."

"Oh. Right." At home, Max will be doing the same. Julia drains her tea and lays the printed lists, a pen and her phone on the table, and Zara goes to the window and leans her head against the cool glass. She looks down on streets and streets, the lights on in a thousand houses, the city poised between glitter and darkness. A line from "Little Gidding" plays on a loop in her thoughts. *History is now, and England.* Behind her, Julia is making one quick call after another. "Hi. I'm calling on behalf of the Coalition, you're registered as one of our supporters, I just wanted to check... You've voted? Great. Thanks... Yes, absolutely. A make-or-break election. I agree."

A make-or-break election.

She thinks how Julia has no idea how much that's true for her. Her thoughts run hours ahead, to tomorrow morning in this room, early daylight, the three of them sitting at this table and Ash saying, *Mum. There's something we need to tell you...*

Terror and hope.

She listens to the calls: another vote, another, another. It's going to happen. Another, and then Ash and Lulu are back. He stands behind her at the window, and wraps his arms round her. She feels his heart thudding against hers, and she thinks, he's holding it too, the same storm. Terror and hope.

He keeps holding her until Julia's finished phoning. After supper they carry cups of coffee into the living room. Julia scrolls through the TV channels, but there's nothing to see yet except reruns of vintage comedy. Ash picks up the empty cups and carries them out to the kitchen, and she takes *Four Quartets* out of her bag, opens it to "Little Gidding", and tries to read. The words blur and slide.

"Zara?" Julia says. "Is everything OK? With you and Ash?"

"Yes," she says. It's the one thing in the world she is sure of.

ASH

Back in the living room he cuddles next to Zara on the sofa. She's reading "Little Gidding", and his eye falls on the words he remembers her reading in the freezing little church.

All shall be well –

It will be, has to be, the numbers say it has to be.

Doesn't stop him feeling faintly sick.

Time bends, distorts, expands; it feels like a hundred hours pass before his phone flicks from 21:59:59 to 22:00:00. Voting's over now. There's a brief news bulletin: footage of polling stations around the country, reports of pro-Coalition protests in Manchester and Bristol being broken up by riot police, an interview with the Scottish Foreign Secretary (*"Do you anticipate changes to the border arrangements after the election?" "Let's wait for the result, shall we?"*), footage of the Prime Minister and the leader of the Coalition emerging from voting in their constituencies (the Prime Minister's overcoat, he notices irrelevantly, is exactly like the square-shouldered, long black coat that Lewis wears, like there's a Party uniform). At the end of the news, the TV switches to the election studio with its giant empty map of England, Wales and Northern Ireland on the wall. The final polling figures flash up on the screen: the gap between Party and Coalition has narrowed again, but not enough; he squeezes Zara's hand. "It's OK," he tells her. "Those numbers. . . They're OK."

Hours of nothing follow; just talk. At midnight, he goes to the kitchen to make coffee. Lulu pads after him. He scratches her head and gazes out of the window while he waits for the kettle to boil; there are more lights on than usual: all over the city, all over the country, people are watching and waiting. Then the lights go out, suddenly and simultaneously, in a huge blackout; only the hospital goes on gleaming into the darkness. The kettle clicks off, the indicator lights on the fridge and microwave go out. He fumbles for candles and matches in the drawer and makes his way back to the living room by candlelight. In the dark, Mum and Zara are leaning over Mum's laptop; there's a notice on screen, announcing that the election coverage will resume as soon as possible.

"How?" Zara asks. "If there's no electricity?"

"They'll have backup generators, I guess. Like the hospital. No coffee, sorry."

Mum fetches the wine from the fridge and pours three glasses. They crouch around the laptop. When the broadcast comes back on, the first results of the night are in: one Coalition win, one Party, both expected. Even so, he's disappointed; he wanted them wiped off the map.

They're eight points behind. They can't win. It's going to be OK.

There's a long wait. Mum's laptop dies, so he fetches his. It's low on battery; it lasts long enough for them to see the

Party hold a seat that they were expected to lose, then it too shuts down. They watch for another 47 minutes on his phone. When it runs out of power the results are finely balanced. No one's making predictions any longer.

"You two should get some sleep," Mum says. "You've got school tomorrow, Ash." She goes to bed; they stay on the sofa, cuddled under a blanket in the dark, holding one another. He feels too tense for sleep, but it comes: a broken sleep with weird snatches of dreaming.

He jolts out of it at 6:30. The power's back on; the lights glare; in the kitchen the kettle's boiling. The TV's announcing another hold for the Coalition, but—

He rubs his eyes and looks again. The scrolling headline at the bottom of the screen reads PARTY HEADING FOR CLEAR MAJORITY.

PARTY HEADING FOR CLEAR MAJORITY. . . The black on yellow headline sweeps across the bottom of the screen, disappears, and returns; she closes her eyes as if she can blank the words out, change the truth of them, but when she reads them again, they are still the same. PARTY HEADING FOR CLEAR MAJORITY.

"Ash? How?" she falters.

"I don't know. It doesn't make *sense.*"

On the big map on the screen, another area flickers from blank to the red-and-white stripes of the Party, then the scene switches abruptly to live coverage of the Prime Minister's victory speech, delivered at the Party Headquarters in central London. *This is a massive popular endorsement of the policies this government has followed ... a mandate for us to push further, faster...*

Ash jams his thumb down on the remote control; the TV falls dark and silent. He gets up from the sofa to open the curtains. It's early: a frail grey light is beginning to dawn and it's very cold. He comes back to her and takes her hands in his; his fingers are freezing.

"What's going to happen?" he says. "To you. . . ?"

She catches a shaky breath, sniffs, and blinks away

tears. "What d'you think, Ash? We'll have to get out. We can't survive another five years of the Party, how could we?"

A tear splashes on their linked hands; she's not sure if it's hers or his. She pulls her hands free of his and wipes her face. "I need to get home."

"Zara. . ."

"Ash. I have to get home."

He nods, and hauls himself up from the sofa. Lulu uncurls herself from the armchair where she's been sleeping and flings herself joyfully at him, scrabbling at his hands. He shoves her away.

"Bring her," Zara says, and he looks at her with that little furrow of puzzlement between his brows that breaks her heart, every time, never more than now. "It's early. If they think we're taking her for a walk, we're less likely to be stopped."

They let themselves out of the flat into the pale morning. In the car, she hugs Lulu on her lap as they drive through the quiet, almost deserted streets, past the posh shops, past the old brick houses, up the steep, narrow hill towards the Heath. The early sun is pale silver behind the trees; in the valley, London sleeps in a blanket of mist. *This city now doth like a garment wear the beauty of the morning* – Morning. Mourning.

There are traces of tears on Ash's face; a catch in his voice when he says, "Zara?"

She wants to touch him. She'll break if she touches him.

185

"Yes?"

"Where will you go? Home, or. . . ?"

"Home?" She thinks of the warm brick and shimmering colour of Gloria's shop, of walking with Sophie by the glittering river, of running with him among the silent trees on the Heath.

"I mean. . ." he begins.

"I know what you mean. I don't know."

They cross the Heath in silence, drive down the wide road of huge houses, pass under the railway and pull up outside the house. He switches off the engine. Lulu twists in her arms and licks her face. The street lights flicker and go off. She pushes Lulu onto the floor, and puts her hand on the door handle.

"Wait," he says. "When can I come and see you?"

"I don't know." But she does know. The street wavers and dissolves in the cold dawn light. She scrubs a hand across her eyes. "We'll be going as soon as possible, Ash. We have to. They'll be starting house-to-house ID checks any day now, won't they? They said they would, after the election. If they find us. . . It's not only us. Max'd be in trouble too. And you . . . if they found you here."

"So this is it?"

"It has to be."

She reaches for him, winding her hands into his hair, pulling his face towards hers. He tastes of tears. At last they let one another go.

"You'll let me know where you go, won't you?" he says.

"I'll come and see you, after A levels, or. . ."

She nods. But she wants him *now*, it's *now* she wants him, not months and months away. Only that's impossible. She kisses him again. She lets herself out of the car, and goes into the house without looking back.

CHAPTER TWELVE

—can't drive, not safe, blinded—

He gets as far as the Heath, parks the car, runs; Lulu leaps around him like Christmas has come again. *Christmas:* he ran with her here at Christmas, he told her about Sophie here at Christmas. He stumbles over the dog, shoves her away, shouts, "Get off, Lulu! Stop it!" then he crouches and pulls her close, pressing his face into her fur. "I'm sorry," he says. "I'm sorry." She licks his hands; they walk to the bench by the hillock of trees inside the iron fence and he sits and watches the daylight strengthen until he's so cold that all he can feel is cold. When Mum calls, his fingers are so numb he almost drops the phone.

"Where *are* you?"

"I had to take Zara home."

"You've got school."

"I know. I'm coming now."

She's made coffee for him. He pours himself a cup, takes it to his room; leaves it on the desk while he changes for school.

Steam condenses on the window; he writes her name on the glass. *Zara*. The letters run like tears.

Mum knocks at his door.

"Ash? Is everything OK?"

"Yes."

"Why did Zara need to go so early?"

"She just did, OK?" He turns away from her and wipes the opinion poll figures off the blackboard wall with his hand.

"Ash. . . ?" she begins.

"I've got to get to school." He shoulders his backpack, and pushes past her, out of the flat, downhill to the tube. The platform and the carriage are full of headlines:

VICTORY FOR COMMON SENSE

FIVE MORE YEARS

THE WORKS HAS ONLY JUST BEGUN, SAYS PM

He thinks about school. Chris'll be defeated and furious, Lewis gloating and triumphant, Jas cracking bitter jokes. He can't face it. At Camden Town he changes onto the other line; he gets out at Embankment and walks onto the footbridge over the river, stands where she must have been standing on the day she saw him, noticed him, knew him, followed him; while he listened to philosophy, trying to figure out if anything existed outside his head.

Zara.

He crosses the bridge, slumps down on a bench on the terrace, stares unseeing across the river: doesn't know what to do, where to go, what to think. Hours pass. People pass and then gather, in random knots of twos and threes.

Random?

He's not sure: there's a feeling of design in these small groups, standing at regular distances from one another; like they're not free-floating atoms, but joined by something. Some *intention*. He keeps watching. They start to move, one after the other, heading upriver along the terrace. He slips off the bench and walks with them, falls into step with a pale boy with dyed black hair and pierced eyebrows who's holding hands with a girl in a multicoloured patchwork coat. The boy glances at him.

"Yeah?"

"What's happening?"

"Who says anything's happening?"

They keep walking. He keeps walking with them: past the London Eye and the aquarium and memories of summer holiday outings with Sophie and Mum, and up the steps onto Westminster Bridge. Big Ben and the Houses of Parliament loom ahead of them.

They keep walking, a purposeful current, and not the only one: there's another crowd trying not to look like a crowd on the opposite pavement, and more on the Embankment. They cross the bridge, carry on down the shallow slope past the tube station, and into Parliament Square. People are converging from every direction on the broad expanse of grass in front of the Houses of Parliament, and suddenly they're not ambling but running, running hard towards the fence that encloses the grass, scrabbling up and over it, gathering in one huge, tightly packed, shoulder-to-shoulder crowd on the other side. Banners unfurl against the dull sky.

NOT MY GOVERNMENT!

RECOUNT NOW!

NO TO DEPORTATION! NO TO RACISM!

"Not in my name! Not in my name!" The chant starts somewhere in the crowd, catches like fire, multiplies. The girl in the bright coat and the black-haired boy join in, hands held, and in a sudden surge of fury he shouts too:

"Not in my name! Not in my name!"

The girl gives him a quick grin and grabs his left hand, someone else grabs his right; they stand, hands linked –

"Not in my name! Not in my name!"

– and, above the chanting, above the pulsing fury in his blood, he hears sirens, wailing closer and closer. Around the square, police cars and vans slew to a halt; ranks of police form up behind solid walls of riot shields. An amplified voice announces: *This is an illegal demonstration. You are to disperse NOW.*

Over to his right, a knot of demonstrators break away, clamber over the barricades, and are chased by police horses along the road past the Abbey; he doesn't see what happens to them.

He keeps hold of the hands; keeps chanting. A couple of rows ahead there's chaos, shouting, the clash of batons, a glimpse of blood running on someone's face.

The girl sits abruptly, pulling him down next to her; he keeps hold of her, but she's wrenched out of his grasp and dragged away. Hands under his armpits yank him to his feet; he struggles to break loose; there's a shove in his back and he's face down on the churned-up mud, tasting the filth of the city.

His wrists are twisted behind him and cuffed; as he's hauled up he feels his phone fall out of his pocket. He fights to get back to it, but they half-carry, half-drag him, still shouting, across the grass, past the broken remnants of the protest. They fling him into a police van and slam the doors shut.

At the police station, he hands over his backpack, his tie, the contents of his pockets: keys, bank card, travel card, the change from last night's champagne. He wonders if someone'll find his phone, wonders if it'll be the police...

Wonders with a sudden plunge of terror what happens if they do and Zara tries to call him.

The desk sergeant studies his ID and tells him to put his hand on the scanner. He watches the tremor in his wrist, the light swooping up and back under his palm.

"Ashley Hammond," the sergeant says.

"Yes."

She runs her gaze down the screen and frowns slightly; he thinks, probably, she's just read about Sophie. "Anyone you want to call?"

"That's still allowed, is it?"

"This is England, Ashley. We're not a police state."

"No?"

"Do you want to call anyone or not?"

He hesitates. Mum'll kill him. But he could probably do with a lawyer. "Can I call my mum? And... umm... I don't have my phone."

She pushes the desk phone towards him. "Do you need to look up the number?"

He shakes his head, dials, waits for Mum to pick up. "It's me."

"Why aren't you at school? They called me. I've been trying to ring you."

"Um. . . Yeah. No. I've been arrested."

"Arrested?"

"There was this protest. About the election. About everything." There's a long silence. He imagines her resting her elbows on her messy cluttered desk and pressing her fingers into her eyes, like she's got a hangover headache.

"Mum?"

"I'll be there. Give me an hour."

They lock him up while he's waiting, with a couple of strangers who don't talk to him and eye him suspiciously: he's wearing school clothes – smart shoes, suit, the long navy blue woollen overcoat that Zara calls his posh boy coat. . .

Zara. Don't call.

She won't. She'll think he's in school.

Probably.

He huddles on the bench and presses his face into his knees, breathing shallowly through his mouth; the cell stinks of sweat, of sick, of piss, of shit. He tries to count the tiles on the wall, can't concentrate, keeps losing count, thinking about Zara, the police, his phone. . .

Don't call me.

The cell door rattles open. It's the sergeant from the desk. "You're free to go, Ashley," she says, and he stumbles after her, out of the cell, along the corridor.

Mum's waiting at the desk, straight from work, in her lawyer outfit: smart suit, briefcase. She spends a lot of her life dealing with kids who are in trouble with the police, but it's never been him before. She says, "*God*, Ash."

"Sorry," he mumbles. "Mum . . . listen. . . Can I use your phone?"

"*Can I use your phone?* That's what you've got to say about this?"

"No. Sorry. I lost my phone. . . I. . ."

She jerks her head at the desk. "Collect your stuff. I'll see you outside." She pushes out through the door while he scoops up his backpack, shoves his balled-up tie, coins, keys, bank card and travel card into his pocket; he signs for them and escapes onto the street. He can still smell the cell on his skin; he takes a long breath of grimy air into his lungs, and looks round for Mum.

God.

Dad's with her.

They're standing a little way down the pavement, looking at him. It takes 35 paces to reach them. He stops, sticks his hands in his pockets because he doesn't know what to do with them, keeps them there when Mum pulls him into a hug.

"Are you all right?"

"Yes," he says.

"God, Ash. You need to be careful, you know. People

get hurt at these protests. Bella did a couple of cases, last year."

He wriggles free. "I'm fine. Can I borrow your phone?"

"No," Dad says. "You're talking to *us* now. We're having a proper conversation about this, Ash. For God's sake. Bunking off school. Getting arrested—"

"Rob." Mum puts her hand on Dad's arm. "I don't think this is the place—"

"Taking part in an illegal demonstration," Dad carries on. "What's that going to look like on your record? What the hell did you think you were doing?"

He tightens his fists in his coat pockets. "Protesting about the election result. What d'you think? Anyway, they didn't charge me."

"You think that means there won't be anything on your record?" Dad shakes his head. "And *protesting about the election result?* Maybe you didn't get the government you wanted, Ash, but they were democratically elected and—"

"Were they?" he says.

"Oh, for God's sake. Is this some stupid conspiracy theory about rigged elections? The result's the result. Get over it."

The result's the result; the result is – Zara. *Zara.* He turns to Mum. "Can I borrow your phone now, please?" and Dad says, "Just a minute," but Mum nods, takes her phone out of her bag and hands it to him.

He turns away from them, enters Zara's number and dials it three times. She's not picking up; in the end, he texts her. *Don't call/text me. I lost my phone at a protest. The police might find it. I'll let you know my new number when I've got one. I love you. Ash.*

He wipes his eyes, wipes the details of the calls and the text, and hands the phone back to Mum. They stand in an uneven triangle: three: a prime number: divisible only by itself or one: one three, three ones.

"Right," Dad says. "Let's get you home. Car's this way."

"I don't need a lift." But now he's contacted her he's feeling suddenly shaky. He doesn't argue when Dad says, "I'm not letting you get into any more trouble today, Ash," and he follows them along the street, down into an underground car park where Dad's left the midlife-crisis car. He clambers into the back and sits hunched up, not just because the space is cramped, but because the shakiness won't go and the stink of the cell on his clothes and skin is making him feel a bit sick.

They drive up out of the darkness into the grim day, join a queue of traffic inching its way along the street and sit, stationary, for ages; it's like the failed journey to Oxford again.

After ten minutes, Mum says, "I'll walk. It's going to be quicker. I'll see you at home later, Ash. Don't forget to pack."

"Pack?"

"We're going to Kate's tonight. Remember?"

He remembers wanting Zara to go with them.

He climbs out of the back seat to take Mum's place in the front; they edge forward another few yards and stop again. Dad swears and flicks the radio on. The traffic news announces gridlock all over central London. There have been other protests – at Oxford Street, King's Cross, in the City. Roads are closed; shops and businesses are shutting down early for the day. In an interview the newly re-elected Prime Minister says, *Yes: the government will certainly be looking at increasing surveillance to prevent further acts of disruption in future... Well, if we're talking about democracy, consider this: the government has a democratic mandate for its policies. What mandate do the protesters have?*

"Quite." Dad snaps the radio off, and overtakes a queue of stalled traffic to swing right into a side street, trying to find a way round the jams, but it's no better here. They come to a forced halt outside a mobile phone shop.

"Uh... Dad? I lost my phone."

Dad glances at him. The traffic shifts forward. "You mean the one I got you before Christmas?"

"Yeah. Sorry."

"This isn't like you, Ash. *None* of this is like you."

Not like him, but like Sophie, who left a trail of lost phones and bus passes behind her, who took risks, walked heights—

"Sorry," he says again. "I was thinking, I could get a pay-as-you-go? There was a shop there." He twists in his seat to look back over his shoulder.

"I'll order you one. I'm not stopping now," but they do nothing except stop: stop and start, stop and start; it's late afternoon by the time they pull up outside the flats.

"Listen," Dad tells him. "Stay out of trouble. Your Mum doesn't need this."

He flings the car door shut and runs upstairs. In his room,

he sits on the edge of his bed, staring at the columns of figures on the blackboard. Lulu whines and nudges him, and he shoves her away, changes his mind, and runs with her down the hill to the nearest mobile-phone shop.

It's closed by the time they get there.

He runs home, showers for ages to get rid of the stink of the police cell, stuffs some clothes in a bag for Kate's and switches on the TV. He watches the Prime Minister returning from Buckingham Palace to Downing Street, and the aftermath of the protest in Parliament Square: churned-up grass, toppled barricades, a scattering of dropped bags, scarves – his phone. What if she called his phone before he called her? What if, what if, what if. . . ? Feeling sick, he wanders into the kitchen and tugs open the fridge. The light reflects off heavy green glass.

It's the champagne.

He wrenches the bottle out of the fridge and hurls it across the kitchen. It explodes off the wall: glittering shards scatter everywhere, the floor's puddled with champagne, the air heavy with its sour sweet smell. Lulu cowers next to him and thuds her tail guiltily.

"It's OK," he tells her. "It's not your fault."

He fetches the dustpan and brush and starts to clear up: it feels like infinitely more glass and champagne than a single bottle should hold, as if it expanded as it exploded. He sweeps and mops. Lulu pads after him and gives a sudden whimper; when he turns to push her away, she's trailing blood from a deep cut in the pad of her front paw. He hauls her onto his lap and presses a tea towel against it. Blood seeps onto his hands; he's still sitting there – his hands covered in blood, surrounded by ruin – when Mum comes home.

CHAPTER THIRTEEN

She wakes, and for a half second she doesn't remember. Half a second, before everything returns to her like the sudden fall of darkness: the black on yellow words sweeping across the TV screen, the grey dawn over London, the taste of salt on his face, the defeat in Mum and Max's eyes when she let herself into the house. She couldn't face talking to them. She nicked one of Mum's sleeping tablets and fell into bed.

That must have been hours ago. She's woken to profound night; the slit window in the wall is as dark as the rest of the room. The power must be out. She gropes on the floor for her phone and switches it on. The screen gleams blue-white into the darkness. It's almost midnight, and she's missed three calls and a text, all from a withheld number. She opens the text. It's from Ash. *Don't text me. Don't call me,* something about a protest, and *I love you.*

She doesn't sleep again.

I love you

I love you

I love you, and at last grimy light dawns at the window, water runs in the bathroom, there are muffled voices in the kitchen. It's another day, and she can't avoid it because there will be things that have to be done; an ending to prepare for.

She drags herself upstairs into the living room, where Mum and Max are cradling cups of tea and watching the early morning news; she wonders if they've been here all night. On the screen there's a brief clip of a boy yelling and struggling as he's hauled to a police van – blood on his face, the towers of Westminster stark against the sky above him. Is that where *Ash* was?

She squints at the blurred crowd, but the picture switches back to the studio and to the news that the deputy leader of the Coalition has been detained by police investigating the outbreak of violence at yesterday's demonstrations against the re-elected government.

"Dear God." Max switches the TV off, and glances up at Zara. "Come and sit."

She curls up in the big armchair, bare feet tucked under her, arms wrapped round her body. The heating's still not working.

"We need to tell you what's going on." Max slides her hand into Mum's. "Ben's going to drive you two down to Wales on Tuesday night, then a friend of his'll take you to Ireland by boat. You'll need to pack, Zara. Only essentials, though. No more than you can carry."

"Tuesday," she echoes.

"It's the soonest we could manage. It takes time to sort these things, love."

"I know." Outside a car drives slowly past, and she watches it warily out of sight. Today, then Sunday, Monday, Tuesday. If he were here Ash would be adding up hours and converting them into however many seconds are left. Time when they might be found. Time when, maybe, she could see him again. . .

No. It's not safe. She turns back to Max. "What about you? Aren't you coming with us?"

"There are things I need to sort out here before I can leave. Work. This place."

"And is Ireland where we're going to stay? For good?"

"We don't know yet." Max takes her glasses off, and rubs her eye with the heel of her hand. "Maybe. It depends. . . We need to find somewhere we can all get permanent rights to stay. We're not sure where that'll be. But we will work it out. We're going to stay together. I'm not going to let those bastards. . ." She clasps her other hand round Mum's, and Zara remembers Ash, catching hold of her hand before she got out of the car yesterday morning, and herself pulling free of him, leaving him for ever.

She stumbles blindly up from the chair. "I'll go and pack."

She dumps the old rucksack that she had for school camping expeditions on her bed, and surveys her room. Clothes, shoes, books, folders of notes and essays, bits and pieces of jewellery, the glass animals she collected when she was nine. Laptop. Phone. Her *life:* to be reduced to what she can carry.

She starts with clothes, making a heap of underwear, sweatshirts, T-shirts, tracksuit bottoms, and a long shirt of green silk that Gloria gave her, and shoving them all to the bottom of the bag. Trainers. A level notes and texts. *Tess*. *Othello*. *The Romantic Poets*. *Paradise Lost*. She tucks them all into the bag with her battered copy of *Four Quartets* and picks up *Poems on the Underground*. Sitting on the bed, she turns slowly through the pages and stops to read.

O Western wind, when wilt thou blow

She closes the book and carries on, stuffing a rubbish bag with clothes she doesn't care about and books she can't carry, for the charity shop. It's almost full when her phone rings. It's a withheld number.

ASH

He walks along the lane from Kate's house, head down against the wind that sweeps across the flat land, pressing Mum's phone tight to his ear. It rings for a long time, then there's a silence; he thinks he can hear her breathing.

"Zara?"

"Yes." She says nothing else.

"Zara?" he says again.

"Ash, I'm sorry. I can't talk. I'm busy. Packing."

"*Packing?*"

"We're leaving."

"Already?"

"Tuesday night. We have to. It's not safe."

"I know, but. . ."

"I got your text. What's your new number?"

"I haven't got it yet. Ordered a new phone. I'll let you know, as soon as. . ."

"Yes," she says again.

"So. . ." He gropes for something to say, something to neutralize the silence, dissolve, deflect it; while he's still fumbling for words she says, "Ash. I can't. Not now," and she cuts the call dead.

He shoves the phone deep into his pocket and runs, flinging himself along the lane, out onto the road that angles through flat fields; on and on, through the village and beyond it, stopping only when breath and muscles won't carry him any more.

Around him the land reaches to the perfect straight line of the horizon and he catches a memory of Sophie when they first came here, wailing, *It's so flat*. Sophie: always, fatally, a lover of heights.

He'd like to keep running, but where to?

He walks slowly back to Kate's.

ZARA

By the end of Saturday, she's finished packing. There's only waiting now. She huddles on her bed in her room, under the old red-and-cream blanket from home that's too bulky to take with her to Ireland. The seconds of Sunday, Monday and Tuesday morning crawl past. She reads *Poems on the Underground*, watches TV on Max's laptop, and listens, always, for the ring at the doorbell which will mean that they've left it too late to leave.

She seeks out news and current affairs programmes. Not a fortune teller now, but a pathologist; not trying to work out what will happen, but what has happened; crouching over the dead body of hope, wondering how it died. She thinks of Ash and his numbers – *There's no way the Party can win* – the confident graph on his bedroom wall.

At lunchtime on Tuesday, she spots a programme in the listings: *How the Polls Got It Wrong: The General Election As It Happened.*

She switches to it.

It delivers less than it promised; there are no explanations. It's just a stitched-together patchwork of TV snippets from election day: interviews with politicians; interviews with ordinary voters; footage of polling stations all over the country, from the Scottish border to Cornwall; footage of ballot papers being counted in sports centres and town halls. And the pictures they missed while the power was out: a roar of triumph as the Party wins another seat; fists punching the air at Party headquarters; "Land of Hope and Glory" and St George's flags in Trafalgar Square; a boy downing a glass of champagne at another Party celebration somewhere in London; the Prime Minister. . .

No.

Wait.

Wait. She stabs at the laptop controls to rewind the programme, goes too far back, and watches the Trafalgar Square scenes again. She feels very, very cold and as dry-mouthed as if she's swallowed a handful of salt. Now. Again. The boy lifts the glass to his lips, drains it, drops his arm and turns away, the empty glass dangling loosely in his hand, then the camera pans away to another part of the scene. She drags the cursor back and watches again, though she doesn't need to. She recognized him at first sight.

She's seen him drink a glass of champagne before.

She presses her eye sockets into her knees and remembers. In the garden, fireworks soar and burst. Sophie goes to the table for food; a tall, dark-haired boy in a black jacket and black mask laughs with her, holds a glass loosely in his hand, presents it to Sophie with a flourish. He holds the glass with the same gesture; she'd recognize him just from that, she thinks, even if she hadn't seen his face later, in the garden.

It's him. The same boy: in her memory, on the screen.

The programme has run on. She drags the cursor back again, freezes the screen on the image of the boy, and stares at him. The boy who killed Sophie at the party, the boy whose Party has killed her future, her life with Ash, everything.

She stares at him, and a hard, cold purpose builds in her.

She will destroy him.

She saves half a dozen stills from the footage to the memory stick that Ash gave her, ejects it from the computer, and sits on the edge of the bed, flipping it over in her impatient fingers.

Come on, Ash. Call. I need to talk to you.

ASH

Tuesday afternoon. Mum sleeps; he walks the lane with Kate. Lulu limps alongside them with her injured paw in the air, and a ridiculous cone around her head to stop her biting her stitches.

"Any plans for the rest of half-term, Ash?" Kate asks.

He shakes his head. All his plans for half-term had Zara in them, but now. . .

The light is already starting to fail across the mathematical land of straight lines and flat horizons. It's getting late and tonight's the night she leaves; he thinks of her slipping away from him without a word, unable to bear another parting.

"Julia told me about the protest, by the way," Kate says.

"Oh." He kicks a stone off the path into the drainage ditch.

"Well done."

"Yeah? No one else thinks so."

"Your mum does, Ash. She's scared for you, that's all."

"Dad doesn't. Stay out of trouble, don't get a record, don't risk Oxford." He kicks another stone.

"You still want to go, don't you? To Oxford?"

"Yes." Doesn't he? Yes, only . . . *Zara*.

Zara.

Zara.

"Anyway," Kate says. "I think you were right to protest. People have to. This bloody government. Dan did a photo shoot in Calais last month. At the European reception centre."

"Where?"

"Oh... Well, if you're European and you get deported, you don't get sent home. You get dumped in Calais. They've set up this place; it's basically a processing centre. You know, helping people get resettled. Working out where they're going to be living, helping them with travel; all that sort of thing. Dan came back with all these portraits. Ordinary people who'd made decent, useful lives here, put down roots, and now—" She shakes her head furiously. A gust of wind and rain knocks against them. They turn and walk back to the house. At the door Kate feels in her coat pockets and swears.

"Left my key. No need to wake your mum yet. There's a spare."

He follows her round to the garden, where she lifts a flowerpot on the kitchen terrace, fishes out a damp key and lets them into the house. The sky is heavy with cloud and the electricity's out; the kitchen is almost dark. The cat slinks off the sofa and weaves around Kate's ankles.

"All right. I'll feed you. Can you find some candles, Ash? Middle drawer of the dresser."

He tugs open the drawer, lifts out a shoebox full of candles and matches, and pauses.

There's a rectangle of white plastic lying beneath it.

An ID card. He picks it up. It's Sophie's. She lost hers, he remembers, about the time they came here two years ago. She looks at him, solemn, from the photo and his vision slides and blurs.

He takes a couple of candles, puts the card back and the box on top of it; goes to the window, stares out through tears at the fading light.

ZARA

Come on, Ash.

She needs to tell him about this, but he doesn't call, and she doesn't know how else to get in touch with him. His last messages and calls were from a withheld number, he and Julia don't have a landline, and she doesn't know his email address. She sits on the side of the bed, fiddling with the memory stick, waiting, checking her phone every two minutes. Late in the afternoon, the battery plunges suddenly from twenty to five percent. She plugs the phone in, but nothing happens; the power's off. At the window, the day declines towards darkness; towards night, and leaving.

By half past five she can't bear to wait any longer. She slips on her trainers, zips the memory stick into the pocket of her tracksuit bottoms with her ID card, and tiptoes up the stairs. Mum and Max are still finishing Mum's packing in their room.

Zara creeps along the passage, opens the door to the lobby very slowly, steps through it and closes it gently behind her. The front door can't be opened silently. She bursts through it, and runs, taking the quickest route across the darkening Heath, along the yellow path, under the leafless dripping

212

trees, and doesn't stop until she's reached the flats. She presses the buzzer marked "Hammond".

There's no answer.

She tries again. Still nothing. Ms McDonnell (her form teacher in Year Nine) used to reminisce about the days before mobile phones, about sitting for hours on her boyfriend's doorstep, hoping he'd show up. She sits on the doorstep.

It gets darker. It starts to rain.

She wonders if he's taken Lulu for a walk, gets up, and jogs round his usual dog-walking circuit – down past the posh cafés on the High Street, through streets of big red-brick and stuccoed houses, uphill again, past the spot where he usually parks.

The car's not there.

She goes back to the flats and sits on the doorstep again. He talked about going to his aunt in the country. Was that this week? It *was* this week –

"Did you want something?" One of the local Neighbourhood Watch volunteers, in his bright scarlet armband, is eyeing her from the bottom of the steps.

She stands up. "No. I. . . I'm waiting for someone. Ash Hammond."

"Well, you can't wait here. This is private property."

"OK." She slinks down the steps, retreats to the corner, and glances back. He's still standing, still watching, waiting for her to go. She hunches her shoulders against the rain, shoves her cold hands in her pockets, and heads slowly up the High Street, flipping the memory stick over and over in her fingers. She passes the police station, stops, turns back, and stares at the lighted sign above the door.

She could post the memory stick in a letter to Ash – and maybe the police could find out who the boy is, could trace him buying the drug. But without her, there's no proof of what he did with it. She's the only person who knows at first-hand how he flourished that glass and handed it to Sophie. She's the only eyewitness to the truth that Sophie's mum and dad need; the truth that Sophie herself is owed.

She knows and she's always wanted to tell, and why shouldn't she now? There's no longer any point in silence. The worst thing that can happen is that she'll be arrested and deported, and she's leaving anyway – what does it matter whether she's deported by the National Agency or smuggled out with Mum?

Mum. She can't put Mum at risk.

But Mum'll be going, tonight, and there's no one else whom Zara's officially linked with, no record of the relationships between her and Max, her and Ash.

So do it.

Tell them.

Destroy him.

There's a phone box at the corner of the street. She runs to it, tugs the door open, steps inside, and lifts the phone, and as if this was *meant* to happen, it works. The dialling tone sounds a steady low *brrr*, her pound coin slips easily into the slot and the credit appears on the screen. She dials Max's number.

"Yes?" Max's voice is cautious, guarded.

"It's just me," she says.

"Zara? Where the hell are you?" She's never heard Max so angry, not even at school when she was Ms James.

"Max. Listen. I'm... There's something I've got to do, OK?"

"What?"

"Promise me you'll make Mum go tonight. *Promise* me."

"Zara, wait. Stop."

She puts the phone down, runs across the wet and glittering pavement and up the steps, and pauses for a moment on the threshold. Do it. Destroy him. She steps inside, walks to the desk, and says to the police officer on duty. "I need to talk to someone."

"ID?"

"It's... I've got some information. It's about Sophie Hammond."

"Who? I said, ID."

Don't hesitate, don't look scared. She hands it over as calmly as she can. His gaze flickers from the photo to her. He flips the card over and reads the back, taps something into the desktop computer and studies the screen. *Run*, she thinks. She says, "Like I said. I've got some information."

"Right. Wait there."

He comes out into the reception and ushers her through a door, along a corridor, and into a windowless room with a table, two chairs on either side of it. He points her into one of the chairs and sits opposite her.

"So."

"It's about Sophie. . ."

He chucks her card onto the table; it skates across the surface, spins and comes to rest.

"'*Zara Emily Jones*'." She can hear the italics and the quotation marks in his tone; his voice is heavy with disbelief. She swallows.

"Yes."

"Nice try." He nods at the card. "Where d'you get that?"

"I need to tell you about Sophie—"

"Where d'you get the card? Where's your family? Where've you been living? Who's been helping you?"

"I need—"

"Put your hand on the screen." He nods at a scanner set into the table, and she darts a glance from left to right: the locked door, the windowless walls, the policeman leaning forward over the table, waiting. She lays her palm on the screen. A wave of bright blue-white light sweeps to and fro beneath it; the silhouetted image of her hand burns onto her vision. She blinks at him as he takes a phone out of his pocket, studies it, and looks up at her.

"Catalina Maria Zara Ionescu."

"Yes," she says. "I need—"

"You're illegal, Miss Ionescu. You're under arrest."

She sits with her knees drawn up on the bench in the cell. Every time she's been out of the house in the last year and a half, the last – what did Ash say? – 46.5 million seconds, she

216

has half expected to end up somewhere like this. It feels fated, the inevitable end to the story. It doesn't matter; so long as she can make them listen to her, nothing else matters. She counts seconds, and loses the thread of the numbers; she struggles to remember lines from "Little Gidding". At last, the cell door opens and a different police officer comes in. He has bright blue eyes in a freckled face, under a thatch of straw-coloured hair: like Sophie, like Ash.

"Time to go," he says.

"Go where?"

"Deportation centre. It's a fair way away. Here. Have this." He's holding a bar of chocolate, offering it to her with a puzzled smile. "Tell me one thing. Why does a girl who's not BB walk into a cop shop? Didn't you know what'd happen?"

"Yes. I wanted to tell someone about Sophie. Sophie Hammond."

"Sophie Hammond? I worked that case for a bit."

"I know who did it." She wriggles the memory stick from her pocket and pushes it towards him. "There are image files on here. Pictures of a boy. He spiked her drink. I was there. I saw it."

"Jim!" someone calls along the corridor. "Get a move on!"

"*Please*," she says.

He takes the memory stick from her, nods, and slides it into his pocket.

CHAPTER FOURTEEN

The traffic's heavy and there are checkpoints on the approach to London. As soon as they get home he borrows Mum's phone and tries to call Zara, because he has to see her, tonight, before she goes. *Has* to, but her phone must be switched off or out of battery because his calls go straight to her voicemail, over and over again.

He gives up and drives to East Finchley. At the house all the windows are dark, and no one's answering the door.

They must already have gone.

He's missed her.

He drives slowly home, drags himself upstairs to the flat, halts at the kitchen door. Jas is sitting on the kitchen floor, leaning back against the wall under the collage of Sophie's photos. Lulu is on his lap; he's tickling her ears under the cone, talking nonsense to her. *Who's a dog? Who's a dog?* Sophie used to say that to her too.

"Jas? What're you doing here?" Ash asks.

"We're going to the pub, remember?" Jas lifts Lulu gently

off his lap, and jumps to his feet. "You weren't answering your phone."

"Lost it."

"Yeah. Your mum said." He gives her a quick glance and turns back to Ash. "So? You coming?"

"Suppose." He doesn't want to go anywhere. He might as well go to the pub.

They walk side by side down the hill without talking, and take the tube to central London, to the same pub where they met before Christmas. At the usual corner table, Chris is saying to Lewis, "Go on then. Explain *exactly* how the polls got it so wrong."

Lewis shrugs. "Well, they were just wrong, weren't they?"

"Or they rigged it." Jas drops into a chair, flips a beer mat off the table and taps it against his knee.

"Yeah," Chris says. "*Exactly.*"

"Oh, for God's sake," Lewis says. "This is *England.* Your lot lost, Chris. Get over it."

Ash leaves them to it, goes to the bar, buys drinks for himself and Jas. When he gets back to the table, Jas, Maya and Caitlin are shoulder to shoulder over Cait's phone watching a video of their band's latest gig, Chris is talking softly to Priya, and Lewis is flicking through the evening paper. Ash sits next to him and reads over his shoulder. *Post-election violence: government investigates suspected foreign interference. PM announces new appointments to House of Lords. House-to-house searches begin in*

London. . . Zara. He gulps a mouthful of vodka; his head spins. That's fear, he thinks, it's had time to take effect; the alcohol hasn't. Zara. Where is she now? How *safe* is she now?

"Ash?" Lewis says. He shakes himself.

"Sorry. What?"

"Chess problem?"

"Uh . . . no. . . I lost my phone."

"Get one of these." Lewis reaches into his jacket pocket, takes out a new phone, switches it on and tilts the screen towards Ash so he can see the quality of the HD, the speed of the internet connection, how accurate the speech-to-text function is. A fair-haired barmaid stops at their table.

"Can I take gla— the glasses, please?"

Lewis darts her a sharp look. He keeps watching as she moves on to the next table. "Bet she's illegal. Did you hear that? She was about to say 'glasses,' instead of 'the glasses.' Dead giveaway. She's Eastern European."

"You don't know that," Priya says.

"Bet she is." Lewis leans back in his chair, messing about with his phone. The evening stumbles past. Maya buys a round of drinks. Chris and Lewis have another argument. Ash thinks about Zara.

The pub door swings open, and two men walk in. They're wearing heavy boots and navy-blue uniforms with an intertwined, scarlet NA logo on the chest.

The room falls silent.

220

"Just a routine ID check," one of the men says.

Ash watches the fair-haired girl. She's serving at the bar now. Lewis was right, he thinks; she keeps taking orders but her frightened eyes flicker between the officers, the guy she's serving and the door at the back of the bar.

Run. Just run.

"IDs, please." One of the officers stops at their table. They hand over their cards in turn: Ash, Lewis, Caitlin, Maya (a long look at her card), Jas, Priya (a long look at hers too). Finally the officer turns to Chris, who's sitting with his hands jammed in his jeans pockets.

"And yours?"

Chris shakes his head.

"Chris. . ." Priya says.

The officer tuts. "Left it at home?"

"No. I've got an ideological objection to the ID card policy."

It's Chris's usual attempt to take a stand; it gets the usual reaction.

"I don't care what you've got, sunshine. Card. Now. Or I arrest you."

"Chris!" Priya says again.

The other officer's reached the bar. The girl's still there. Ash shoves himself to his feet.

"Show him your sodding card, Chris. You don't want to be arrested. Believe me."

He threads his way between the tables to the bar, leans on the counter. She's stuck, dealing with a punter who seems too drunk to remember what he's ordering. *Run,* he thinks again, but it's too late – the other officer's stabbing his fingers on the bar in front of her. "ID," he says, and for a second Ash meets her terrified eyes.

"It's in my coat." She gestures behind her.

"Right. Let's go and fetch it."

The officer ducks behind the bar and ushers her through the door at the back. When they reappear, she's in handcuffs and in tears. A table of men next to the TV give a drunken cheer as the officer steers her out to the white NA van parked at the kerb. The barman stares after her, mechanically wiping the same glass over and over; then he bundles the tea towel up, flings it onto the counter and turns to Ash.

"Did you want something, mate?"

"No. Sorry." He goes back to the table.

"Every bloody time," Maya's saying to Caitlin. Chris has both Priya's hands in his and is whispering something to her. Lewis's phone is lying next to his pint of Yorkshire Bitter. Ash sits down.

"What do *you* know about being arrested?" Jas asks.

He ignores him, leans across the table towards Lewis. "Was that you?"

"What?"

"That." Ash nods towards the door. "You were on your phone, after she collected the glasses. Were you reporting her?"

Lewis shrugs.

"You were, weren't you?" Ash picks up Lewis's expensive

new phone and clicks it on. The screen saver's the Party insignia: the torch that reminds Zara of a clenched fist. He holds the phone over Lewis's pint of beer –

"Ash! What the hell!" Lewis starts to his feet.

– and lets it go. It splashes into the beer and sinks to the bottom of the glass. In the semi-opaque liquid, the Party insignia blinks and goes out.

"You effing maniac, Ash! You effing bloody maniac! Do you know how much that cost?" Lewis sticks his hand into his glass, knocks it over, pulls his phone out of the flood and stabs his finger against the screen. Spilt beer flows across the table and drips to the floor. Ash stands up, puts his coat on, and walks out and away along the dark street.

"Hey! Ash!"

He halts. Chris and Priya are hurrying after him. He leans against a wall while he waits for them. He still feels dizzy, off balance; he has to blink them into focus when they stop in front of him.

"Nice one, Ash." Chris gives him an uneven grin, hunches his hands in his pockets and blows out an unsteady breath. "God."

"Yeah," Ash says. "I never. . . I know he said all that stuff at school but I never thought he'd actually *do* that."

"You know he's standing for election for the Young Party committee?" Chris says.

"No. I didn't." He flops his head back against the wall.

"You OK?" Priya asks.

"Don't know. Might've have too much to drink." The rain

223

falls on his face. The brickwork is rough and damp behind his head. Nothing feels quite stable.

"Coffee?" Chris suggests.

"Sure. There's a place near here. . . What about the others?"

Chris grins again. "Leave them. They were giving Lewis hell when we left."

They fall into step together. He heads for Marek's café, but it's not there any more; it's boarded up and it smells of smoke. He stares at it. He wishes he'd told Marek about Sophie.

Hey Soph,

Remember Lewis? We were in chess club together. He used to hang out at ours with Jas and Chris sometimes. There was one day when he'd been round and afterwards you said, "God, what a knob." Remember? Jagna was there, she was giving us dinner and she said, "What is knob?" You thought it was hilarious. You kept saying it for weeks afterwards. "What is knob?" You made me explain it though.

Anyway, Lewis. He's Party and when I didn't vote for him in the school election, he said it's only politics, you can't let it get in the way of friendship. But it doesn't feel like only politics. Not now. And how far can you hate what someone believes and does, and still like them? I don't know. I don't know.

Trust you to get it right. You liked the others, but you never liked him. You were dead right.

Ash xxx

ZARA

There is dense mesh over the windows of the van. All she can see outside is fractured darkness. Dark, dark, dark. It's as dark as it was the night she first met Ash.

She has no idea where they are going. There are two National Agency officers in the front of the van, and a few other women beside her in the back. No one's talking. One of the women is crying. Zara leans her head against the greasy fabric of the seat and closes her eyes. It doesn't matter where they're going; her journey will end where it was bound to end as soon as the Party won the election. Out of England, in a place where she doesn't belong.

She feels in her pocket for the chocolate, breaks off a piece and slips it into her mouth. It tastes as sweet as hope. The sandy-haired police officer nodded to her as she was loaded into the van, as if he was making a promise. Maybe she's done enough.

More dark. Dark, dark, dark, and a long curve in the road, the glint of a metal fence in the headlights, a glimpse of a long, low building, the sudden flare of a searchlight. The van stops, the engine dies, and the woman NA officer looks round from the front seat and says, "OK. We're here."

They pass through doors that slide and lock shut behind them, into a lobby of hard white surfaces. Zara sits where she's told to, in a plastic chair. A sign on the wall says *Reception* in English and in dozens of other languages and alphabets; she scans through them till she reaches *recepție*.

Say something in Romanian, Ash said, and she said – what else? – *te iubesc*. I love you.

"We'll check you in in a moment," the officer tells her. "Can you read English, by the way?"

She says, "Yes," and he crosses the lobby, and comes back with a printed leaflet. On the cover, there's a photo of a smiling woman in a sari and a man wearing the same navy sweatshirt as the officers who brought her here. The title is "Your stay at Oake Leigh." She opens the booklet and reads.

Welcome to Oake Leigh. We hope that your stay here will be comfortable and happy. Please report any concerns or problems that you may have to the staff, who are here to help and support you.

Underneath that, there's another photo of two smiling women sitting at a table over cups of tea, in blue plastic chairs like the one she's in. She turns to page two:

We understand that the first few days at Oake Leigh can be a confusing time, but our trained staff will do all they can to help you settle in and find your feet! On arrival, we will take your details and do a few minor checks and then you will be able to settle down in your new temporary home! You will be accommodated in one of our four houses: Larch, Elm, Beech

*and Ash. Staff will be on hand to help and support you if you
need anything during your first night.*

There's another photo of two women in a small bedroom
where the window is hung with curtains decorated with a
pattern of leaves. She doesn't read any further. She sits in the
chair with the leaflet in her hand, thinking Ash, Ash, Ash,
repeating his name to herself in time with the rapid thudding
of her pulse.

The other women sit silent in their chairs. The officers from
the van sit on the desk, sharing a packet of crisps and a bottle of
water. Time passes. It's cold. She's cold. She needs to pee.

More time passes.

She needs to pee.

It feels like hours before another officer hurries into the
lobby, and says sorry to the others, and something about
trouble in Elm. She has fair hair and blue eyes. Like Sophie.
Like the policeman (turning the memory stick in his fingers,
glancing from it to her, nodding. . .). She beckons Zara into a
windowless office with a light that flickers, and a sink in the
corner with a dripping tap.

"Can I go to the loo, please?" Zara asks.

The woman ignores her. She takes her photo and her
fingerprints, and studies the computer screen. Zara sits,
tight, on the chair, every muscle taut and clenched. Then the
woman tells her to stand up and searches her, running her
hands up and down her arms, over her back and chest, up and
down and between her legs while the officers from the van
watch.

"Please. . ." she says, but she can't hold herself any more. She wets herself, and the woman snatches her hands away with a tut of disgust. *It's not my fault!* she thinks furiously, *I told you I needed the loo!* but her voice feels turned to stone.

She stands silent, stinking and clammy, her tracksuit bottoms and her running shoes soaked in pee, while the fair-haired officer goes to the sink to scrub her hands under the hot tap.

"Right. Follow me," and she follows: through doors that fall locked behind her, along dimly lit blind corridors and staircases with peeling paint on the walls and missing ceiling tiles, to a small room with two narrow, empty beds. The green, leaf-patterned curtains at the window are frayed. There's a camera in the ceiling: a bulb of opaque black plastic.

"There's a shower in the corner," the woman tells her.

"I don't have any other clothes," she says.

"They should have taken you home to fetch them."

She says nothing.

"So you wouldn't tell them where you live?" The woman sighs, goes away and returns with a thin towel, a blanket, pillowcase and sheets, and a bundle of clothes. She pushes it all into her arms and leaves her.

Zara checks the door. It's locked. She cowers in the cubicle in the corner. It has a shower, handbasin and loo, and no door. She peels off her soaked clothes quickly, scrubs herself clean under a tepid, thin shower; dries and dresses in the stranger's clothes she's been given: boil-washed underwear, T-shirt and leggings. There are no socks. Barefoot, shivering, she makes the bed (everything is stained – mattress, pillows, blanket – with the phantom shapes of other women's blood or tears or sweat), and climbs into it. She pulls the covers over her head because there's a dim light above the door which won't go off.

Finally, she sleeps, but not for long. She jolts awake to find someone tall and bulky, in heavy boots, standing by her bed, watching her. She pretends to be asleep, looking at his boots through half-open eyes, her breathing taut and shallow. He stands for a while, watching; then he turns and goes away.

It's impossible to go back to sleep now.

She watches the window behind the thin curtains lighten from black to grey and listens to little noises in the pipes. At dawn, there's a sudden screaming and shouting somewhere along the corridor. A door slams. Then silence. Wide awake, she slides out of bed and pulls the fraying curtain aside. Outside there's a high fence topped with razor wire, and beyond it, some leafless woodland and dead, brown fields, and an empty horizon. Black birds wheel and toss in the sky. It reminds her of the countryside near Little Gidding. Perhaps it is; she remembers the conversation in the pub, the NA van ahead of them on the road.

It's too cold to stay out of bed. She climbs back in and pulls the covers round her, and lies shivering. She's freezing, and there's a familiar dull pain in the pit of her belly that's getting worse.

No. Not now. Please not now. The muscles in her thighs and the small of her back start to hurt.

She clambers out of bed again, and sits on the loo. She's

bleeding. She tears off a wodge of loo paper, stuffs it between her legs, pulls up her knickers and tracksuit bottoms, and crawls into bed, huddling under the cover, curled round the pain.

The light at the window strengthens. There's a knock at the door, a two-second pause before it swings open and the fair-haired woman from the night before looks in at her.

"You need to get up if you want breakfast."

"I. . . I've got my period. I don't have anything. . ."

"Oh. Right. You need to ask in the office. Downstairs."

"Can you let me out?" She sits up and swings her legs off the bed. She feels shaky and a bit sick.

The woman waves a hand at the door. "They're only locked at night. You can go anywhere during the day," and she leaves, letting the door fall shut behind her. Zara drags herself off the bed, into the corridor, and downstairs to the office. There are two male officers at the desk, leaning over a computer screen.

She waits, but no one notices her. After a couple of minutes, she edges into the room. One of the officers glances up at her. He's got cropped black hair. There are broken veins in his cheeks.

"Yeah?"

"I. . . Can I. . ." She can feel herself blushing. "I need some tampons and some painkillers."

He sighs, and gestures at the computer. "We're busy. You'll have to wait."

"Wait? How am I meant to—"

He straightens up. He's a lot taller than her. "You're new, aren't you? What's your name?"

"Yes. Zara."

"So, Zara, what you need to know is we don't like troublemakers here. Got that? Come back in an hour." He leans over the computer again. The other officer says something. They both laugh.

Another wave of pain surges through her. Sick and sweaty, she retreats into the corridor, and slumps down against the wall, pressing her face into her knees.

"Hey." There's a gentle hand on her shoulder. She raises her head and blinks away tears. A slim woman in a printed cotton dress and a long cardigan, her hair in cornrow plaits like Max's, is crouching in front of her. "What's the matter?"

"Period." She wipes her hands over her face.

"Ah. D'you need. . . ?" The woman fishes in her cardigan pocket and takes out a tampon. "Always keep a spare. What's your name?"

"I'm Zara."

"Grace." The woman takes her hand, and raises her to her feet, shows her to the nearest loo, waits for her, and takes her into the canteen. She fetches her a cup of tea and sits with her while she drinks it.

"Where are you from, Zara?"

"Romania."

"Ah. Europe. You'll be OK. You'll be on your way home soon."

"Will I?"

Grace nods. "Soon. In a few days. They send people back to Europe every two weeks."

A few days. She gazes out through the window to the high fence and the sky above it. The birds are still flying, and she remembers a fragment of poetry from Sophie's book:

. . . such delight

As prisoned birds must find in freedom. . .

Just a few days.

ASH

Lulu pushes her nose into his face and licks him. He groans, shoves her away, and forces his sticky eyes half open. There's a line of light along the bottom of the blind, sharp as the reflection off a shot glass.

He flinches; he definitely drank too much last night.

Last night. Zara left last night.

He closes his eyes again, rolls over and jams his face in his pillow, but Lulu's not giving up; she whines, scrabbles at him, and barks. She needs to go out. He hauls himself out of bed, drags on trackies and a sweatshirt and stumbles to the kitchen.

There's a small parcel addressed to him on the table and a note from Mum. *This came for you. Walk the dog!!!* It's his new phone. He tells Lulu, "Wait, dog," and she barks at him while he unwraps the phone and plugs it in.

He leaves it charging while they circuit the block. The sign on the bus shelter has changed again:

ARE YOU SHELTERING AN ILLEGAL?

HOUSE-TO-HOUSE SEARCHES WILL BE

STARTING IN THIS AREA SOON.

He stops to read and reread it, stomach churning, wishing he knew whether she got out safely and where she is now. Lulu tugs at him, and he runs home with her leaping next to him. There's just enough charge on the new phone to message Zara with the number.

When he's sent it, he sits with a cup of strong black coffee, wondering through his fuzzy headache whether her phone will work wherever she is now, how she'll get in touch if it doesn't, how long he'll have to wait—

His phone rings.

The screen lights up.

It's her number; it's *her*.

He snatches the phone up so hard he dislodges the charger; he fumbles to plug it in again. "Zara! Where are you? Are you OK?"

"Ash. *Ash*. It's Max."

"Oh. Right. Hi. Is Zara there? Max?"

"No. We thought she might be with you," Max says.

He's suddenly cold and sick and it's nothing to do with how much he drank last night.

"She went out yesterday evening," Max says. "She didn't come back."

"I'm coming over," he says. He cuts the call, grabs the new phone and the car keys and runs downstairs. Lulu barks furiously after him.

He drives the familiar route almost without noticing it; all he can think of is Zara, lost, lost, lost.

At the flat, Max opens the door to him. "You shouldn't be

here," she says. "If they do a search and find you here, with Ana. . ."

"I don't care."

She nods and he follows her into the living room where Ana's sitting on the sofa, as white and hollow-eyed as Mum, after Sophie. . . He hauls in a difficult breath and swallows hard.

"What happened?" he asks.

Max answers. "She went to the police. About Sophie."

"You think she did." Ana shakes her head angrily. "You don't know."

"Ana... What else?" Max looks at Ash. "She phoned after she went out yesterday. She said she was going to do something she should have done a long time ago. I think she must have meant telling the police about Sophie. And then she didn't come home."

"You think she's been arrested?" The idea is so terrifying he can hardly make himself say it.

Max nods. Ana closes her eyes, and Max sits down on the arm of the sofa next to her and lays her hand on her shoulder. He drops his gaze to the floor. Sun filters through the net curtains that stop people seeing in through the windows. It makes complex patterns of light on the floor and he thinks of the complex patterns of him, Sophie and Zara that have brought him here, now.

He raises his head and meets Max's eyes. "I'm sorry."

"Not your fault, Ash," she says. "I'm guessing you didn't vote for them."

He smiles weakly, and shakes his head. "So what now?"

"Good question." Max gives Ana the kind of look that makes him think they've been talking about this all night. "I think Ana should go anyway. Get to Calais. If Zara's been arrested, that's where they'll send her. And who knows when they'll start house-to-house searches here."

"If she's been arrested," Ana says.

Max sighs. "Ana. It's the most likely—"

"But we don't *know*." Ana clenches her hands on empty air in a gesture that reminds him of Zara. "I know, I know. The sensible thing is for me to go. But to leave . . . without knowing for sure what's happened to her. . ." She struggles up from the sofa and blunders out of the room; along the corridor a door slams shut. Max looks at Ash.

"She *must* have been arrested, mustn't she?" he says. "I mean, logically. . ."

"*Logically.*" Max smiles faintly. "Philosophy and Maths, yes?" and he frowns at her for a second before he understands what she means; right now, Oxford seems an immense distance away and not quite real.

"Oh. Yes."

"Well, you're right. Yes. It's the most likely thing. But Ana's right too. We can't be sure. And I can't think how to find out. Not safely. Not while Ana's still here. But she won't go without knowing."

He thinks about it. *It's an offence to conceal the identity of an illegal,* which makes it impossible for Max or him or *anyone* to go to the police and ask if Zara's been arrested because she's not BB. But— "What if I went to the police and told them she was missing? They'd tell me if they'd arrested her, wouldn't they? I could say I didn't know she wasn't BB."

"Too much of a risk." Max stands up and tidies some scattered papers on the table, folding a book shut, shutting the conversation down.

"I don't mind," he protests.

"Not only to you. Think. They'll know that's your car. And how many times have you driven here? Through how many cameras?" She gives him another faint smile. "Paranoid?"

"I don't know." He studies the play of light on the floor again. It was one of Sophie's favourite jokes for a while: *just because you're paranoid doesn't mean they're not out to get you.* It wasn't very funny then; now it's not funny at all. Now it simply sounds like a plain statement of fact: no way can he go to the police.

The patterns of light change, and he remembers suddenly, sitting here with Zara, wondering who they could tell about Sophie, and thinking of—

Charlie.

He looks up at Max. "There is someone else I could ask."

Get in touch, Ash, any time. It was what Charlie said at the end of his last visit, after he'd closed the investigation down because there was nothing to find. Ash never did get in touch because what was the point? There was never anything to talk about. But he needs Charlie now.

He parks at home, checks Charlie's website to make sure

the phone number hasn't changed, and calls him from the car. Through the windscreen, he watches Mr Smith from the Neighbourhood Watch patrolling slowly up the hill towards him.

"*Ash,*" Charlie says. "Hey, how're you doing? How's Julia?"

"Yeah, uh. . . Listen. Can I come and see you?"

"Sure. Anytime. Now if you want. I'm on the boat."

"Now'd be good. Thanks."

Smith's tapping on the car window; Ash rings off, swings the door open and gets out.

"Yeah?"

"You need to tell your girlfriend not to loiter on the steps when you're not in."

He blinks. "My—?"

"The one with dark hair? She was hanging round by the door. Yesterday evening. I told her it was private property. She. . ." and whatever else Smith is saying dissolves into random noise. *Yesterday evening,* she was here; while he and Mum were battling through traffic and checkpoints on the A1 and if *bloody* Smith hadn't moved her on, she might have waited till they got home. He might have been able to keep her safe from whatever's happened to her. He clenches his hands into fists; he wants to pound Smith, the traffic, chance, Smith. . .

"Get that?" Smith says. "You need to tell her."

"Oh, piss off!" He slams the car door, locks it and runs.

"I'm taking your name," Smith shouts after him.

Take it. *Take it.* Who bloody cares? He runs: down the

steep hill he climbed with Zara on the night of the blackout, past the ghost of Sophie swapping pocket money for drugs at Camden Market, onto the towpath alongside the oily canal, to the houseboat moorings near King's Cross station.

Charlie's waiting for him, sitting on the roof of his narrowboat with a mug of tea; vapour rises from it and dissipates into the cold air. Lost. Vanished.

"Hey! Ash!" Charlie greets him with a lazy wave, slides off the roof, gestures him aboard and through the low door into his messy office, and shoves a pile of papers off a sagging sofa. "'Have a seat. What's up? Or did you just want a chat?"

"No." He flops into the sofa and stares at his hands.

"Is this about Sophie?"

He glances up. Charlie's leaning forward in his chair, looking at him closely; he's got the sort of lopsided face that looks as if it's been in a lot of fights, but – *If there's anything, Ash, tell Charlie,* Mum said once. *You can trust him.* He didn't, then: he never told Charlie about the tree house. He says, "No. Yes. Sort of."

Charlie raises one scarred eyebrow.

"Someone – this girl I know – she's disappeared."

"Disappeared? Have you—"

"I can't go to the police. She—" He takes in a long breath, remembering suddenly, irrelevantly, Sophie challenging him to swim a length underwater in a pool on holiday somewhere; the refracted, broken sunlight on the tiles.

"Ash?" Charlie says, and he tells him, everything: Zara and Sophie, the party, the boy with the glass, Zara and him.

When he falls silent, Charlie says, "Christ." He picks up a paper clip from the floor, straightens it out, twists the metal till it snaps.

Ash waits.

"OK," Charlie says at last. "Let me do a bit of fishing. I'll call you."

"D'you think you'll be able to find out?"

"I'll do what I can, Ash."

He runs home, trying to empty his head, but his footfalls sound out *where is she where is she where is she* all the way up the hill.

In his room, he sits at his desk with his laptop. They've got tests next week. He opens a Philosophy past paper. The first question is: *Without freedom it is impossible to make moral choices. Discuss* and he thinks – of course, how can he not? – of Zara, wanting to tell the truth, and too constrained to be able to.

What if she has, now?

He slams the laptop shut, and goes to sit on the edge of his bed, hugging his pillow, trying to catch the scent of her hair, of her. It is already faded, out of reach.

CHAPTER FIFTEEN

He checks his phone every five minutes. More: every minute, with every breath, but Charlie doesn't call until late the next morning.

"Sorry it took so long," Charlie says. "Bloke I needed to speak to was away. Anyway. Yes. She's been arrested. As an illegal."

"Right." His voice feels stuck in his throat. "Do you know where she is? Did she go to the police? Did she tell them about Sophie?"

"Whoa, Ash. There's only so much it's safe to ask."

"Yeah. No. 'Course."

"Tell you what," Charlie says. "I'm still in touch with a couple of people who worked Sophie's case. I'll put out some feelers. See if they've heard anything."

"Yeah. Thanks."

He calls Max. Before he can say anything, she says, quickly, "Not now. Meet me. The Duke of Wellington pub. Near Archway. In an hour," and she rings off, leaving him staring at the screen. This feels crazy, like he's fallen into a spy film or something.

It feels even crazier when he arrives at the pub. It's a run-down, low building at the edge of a housing estate, one window boarded up. Inside, the carpet has the stickiness of years of spilled pints. Two tired-looking women are playing the fruit machines; an old man sits with a paper and a half of bitter at the table by the window. At the bar a girl's wiping glasses slowly, beneath a string of St George's flags.

"Hi," he says to her. "Can I have—"

"Are you Ash?"

"Uh . . . yeah."

"Max is waiting for you. In the park down the road."

"OK. Cool," though *cool* is not what he feels. He glances over his shoulder as he leaves the pub (the women carry on playing the fruit machines, the old man sips his half pint); at the entrance to the park he checks up and down the road before going in through the gate. *Just because you're paranoid. . .*

Max is sitting on a bench at the far end of the park, gazing down at London: the glass towers, the half-built skyscrapers, the stalled cranes. She doesn't speak or look at him when he sits down next to her.

"I heard from Charlie," he says. "She. . . She has been arrested. They found out she's illegal."

She nods slowly. "Did she go to the police? About Sophie?"

"He didn't know. He couldn't ask too much."

"No. Of course," and she looks at him then. The dull

midday light reflects off her glasses so it's hard to be sure, but he thinks there are tears in her eyes. "I think she did," she says.

"Yeah. Me too."

She takes her glasses off and wipes her face with her hand. "I should go. Things to arrange. Thanks, Ash. At least now Ana'll agree to leave."

She hugs him quickly and hurries away.

He watches her till she's out of sight.

He has no idea what to do now.

ZARA

You can go anywhere during the day, the fair-haired officer told her.

Anywhere has a six-metre, razor-wire-topped fence round it. The bottom two metres are a dense green mesh that stops you from seeing out, reduces the outside world to meaningless splinters of grey. She lays her hands flat against the mesh, and tilts her head back to look up at the expanse of the fence and the sharp wire and the sky. A faint rain falls into her face.

Western wind, when wilt thou blow
The small rain down can rain...

She shivers, and starts to run: looping the narrow yard, counting laps as obsessively as Ash would—

Don't think about Ash.

Run.

Thirty. The grey sky. The fence. The small rain.

Thirty-one...

"Hey!" The fair-haired officer beckons to her, impatiently, from the doorway. Zara approaches her warily; is there a rule against running in the yard that no one's told her yet? But the woman just says, "There's someone to see you," and Zara follows her inside and along the corridor, with its bare walls and missing ceiling tiles and cracked lino, wondering.

No one has visitors at Oake Leigh. It's a community of the illegal – the unknowable. So who – who can possibly have taken the stupid risk of asking to see her? I want to see her, therefore I know her, therefore I'm guilty: it reminds her of Ash, working his way through problems in logic.

Don't think about Ash.

The woman swings open the door to the office where they took her fingerprints on the first night, gestures her inside, and lets the door fall shut behind her.

Zara startles. There's a sandy-haired man sitting at the table. It's him: the policeman from Hampstead who knew about Sophie, who took the memory stick, who gave her chocolate and hope. Her heart quickens.

"Hi, Catalina." He smiles at her, and gestures to the empty chair opposite him at the table. "Come and sit down."

"Zara," she says. She perches on the edge of the chair. "Did you find something?"

He shakes his head.

"But that's why you're here, isn't it? Because of Sophie?"

He nods, reaches into his pocket and lays his phone on the table. "Is it OK to record this?"

"*Yes*," she says.

"Great. Thanks." He swipes the screen, and sets the voice recorder running. Time reels past in hundredths of seconds. "OK. Two things. First, which programme was it? I've been watching in my spare time. I've seen more reruns of that bloody election than I can cope with, and I still haven't found the one you got that picture from."

She gives him a pale smile. "Tuesday lunchtime. It was called... *How the Polls Got It Wrong*, or something."

"That's fine. I'll find it from that. Now..." He looks at her steadily; his eyes are an intense summer blue: Sophie's colour. "Next thing: can you tell me about the party? Everything you remember."

She rests her elbows on the desk, leans forward and talks; the trace of her voice spikes and falls on the screen of his phone. When she's finished, he says, "You remember it very clearly."

"I *made* myself remember. As soon as I realized what had happened to her. I've been waiting to be able to tell someone."

He sighs. "Guess you weren't planning to do it here," and she raises her head and gazes round the cramped, closed-in office, at the filing-cabinet drawers labelled Deportations (Europe), Deportations (Other), Pending Cases; at a year planner pinned crooked on the noticeboard and pock-marked with sticky dots and stars.

She gets up to study it.

"What's today?"

He comes to stand next to her, placing a finger on the calendar. "Friday. And look... The green dots are deportations to Europe. There's one next Thursday. Six days from now. Don't worry, Zara. You'll be on your way home soon."

Home? she thinks.

"Oh ... and here." He fishes in his pocket, passes her another bar of chocolate, and says with a lopsided smile, "Well, I'd better go and watch some more election coverage."

She smiles weakly back at him. She feels cold and hollow; she doesn't want him to go, but she only says, "Thanks for the chocolate," and trails along the drab corridor and upstairs to her room. Sitting on the bed, she lets a square of chocolate melt slowly in her mouth and gazes at the bare fields beyond the wire.

Six more days.

ASH

All he can think about is Zara: where she is, what's happening to her, but Friday, Saturday, Sunday pass and half-term ends and there's still no news. Back at school, he's only half conscious of anything: of Jas and Chris and even Lewis asking if he's OK; of Maths and Philosophy tests where none of his answers are what he's thinking because all he's thinking is – Zara.

Zara.

Zara.

He stumbles through the days, and nothing is clear or certain, not until Wednesday afternoon when Max texts him while he's walking up the hill from the tube at the end of the day.

DW6 –

– which, he guesses, in Max's not-so-paranoid universe, means the Duke of Wellington at six o'clock. It's worth a try, anyway. He takes the dog for a quick jog round the block, gets into the car, changes his mind and walks. He's going to be late, but it feels safer, more anonymous, than driving.

He has no idea if it's necessary to think like this.

Max is waiting in the pub this time, sitting in the corner

with a glass of orange juice, reading; he sits in the empty chair opposite hers and nods at the book that she's laid face down on the table. "*1984.*"

"I used to think it was fantasy." She gets to her feet. "What do you want to drink?"

"Uh... I don't mind. Orange juice is fine, thanks," and while she goes to the bar, he watches the muted news on the TV above their table: burning cars, police with riot shields, a tank parked on a street of terraced houses. Max returns, sits and leans across the table to talk to him, keeping her voice low. "Ana made it to Calais. She's staying at the reception centre there."

"What about Zara?" he asks. "Is *she* there too?"

"Not yet. But there's a group of deportees arriving tomorrow. Here." She takes a slip of paper from her pocket and hands it to him. "This is the phone number for the centre. Ring tomorrow evening. But don't use your phone." He frowns at her. "No one knows what's safe or not, Ash. It's just worth being careful."

He nods slowly, studies the long number on the paper, hands it back.

"You can keep that," she says.

"It's OK. Got it." He drains his glass and sets it down on the table. "What are you going to do?"

"Go and join them. As soon as I've got my visa sorted." She checks her watch. "I need to get to work, Ash. But I'll keep in touch, OK? Let you know what's happening."

"Yes. Thanks."

After she's left, he sits and stares at the TV. The news is on a loop, still showing the riots in whichever town it is, and he watches without making sense of what he's seeing: all he can think is, *tomorrow*.

She'll be in Calais tomorrow.

ZARA

Saturday, Sunday, Monday, Tuesday, Wednesday pass, in obsessive looping runs around the yard under the free circling of birds in the sky, in long restless nights watching the line of light above the door and the camera in the ceiling, listening to muffled shouts and crying along the corridors. On Wednesday night, she changes into her own clothes: her tracksuit bottoms and T-shirt, and the grey sweatshirt that she borrowed from Ash and never gave back. The faint smell of him that it used to carry has been boil-washed out of it, but if she presses her face to it and breathes in, she can almost recapture the memory. She stands by the window and parts the fraying green curtains. The searchlights glare along the fence; beyond there's only darkness: the rolling fields and broken woodland sunk in night, the birds sleeping and silent. She climbs into bed and huddles under the thin covers to wait for morning.

Sleep doesn't come.

. . .the rain

Is full of ghosts tonight, that tap and sigh

Upon the glass, and listen for reply . . .

I love you. Ash. I love you.

ASH

Thursday morning, and today he can call her. He wishes it could be more. He wants more; wants to hold her, his hands in her hair, his skin against her skin, his lips tasting hers. . .

So, go to France.

Mad.

Possible. Definitely possible: he googles it. Direct train tickets cost a fortune, but there's the old way: train to Dover, ferry to Calais, and he's got Dad's Oxford £250 which he was saving for Europe with Zara anyway; it'll easily cover the cost of the train and the ferry and a day visa for France. He can *get* there, but it means bunking off school, missing a Physics test, lying to Mum.

He finds his passport and leaves the flat earlier than usual. He's not sure he's going to do this. He walks undecided down the hill to the tube. On the train he stands next to the doors. The stations pass.

Mad.

Possible.

Mad, and then King's Cross and the moment to decide. People push past him to get off, other people get on, the door alarm shrills. He leaps out. The doors slide shut. The train pulls away.

He lets the crowd carry him up out of the underground and crosses the road to the mainline station at St Pancras. Light pours through the high glass roof. There's a train leaving for Dover in five minutes. He buys a ticket, runs, flops into a window seat; the train rolls out of the station and picks up speed.

As easy as that.

He grins to himself, texts Chris – *Not feeling great. Can u tell Miss D I'm going home. Cheers* – and leans his head against the window. England blurs past. His breath mists the glass; he writes her name with his finger, finds the recording of 'Little Gidding' that he's saved to his phone, and listens to it on a loop.

At Dover, he buys a ferry ticket and a day visa. On board he searches all the sitting areas and cafés for Zara, but of course she's not there; of *course*. There are other ferries and the trains through the tunnel; it's a slim chance that she's on this boat, and even if she is, she'll be hidden, shut away somewhere that he can't find.

Feeling a bit sick, he goes to stand on deck, facing south towards France and a pale line of light beneath the clouds, hands freezing on the rail, salty wind slapping his face. It takes an hour and a half to cross: 5,400 seconds that feel slower than usual. At Immigration, he stands in line, has his passport stamped and steps into France.

There's an information desk in the foyer of the ferry

terminal. He flounders, fumbling for the right words in French – he learned a bit, ages ago, can't remember a thing – but the woman at the desk says in English, "Can I help you?"

"I'm looking for ... um ... the place where they bring deportees from England. It's a reception centre, or something?"

She nods, quickly, in a way that makes him think he's probably not the first person to ask, spreads a printed map on the counter, and draws a circle on it. "It's here. You can take the bus. Number twelve."

He thanks her, changes some cash, catches the bus. The reception centre is a nothing sort of place on the edge of a big car park, a square building like a decaying motorway services hotel. The wooden fascias under the windows have rotted in the salt air. He edges past the group of men who are smoking on the steps. Inside, there's a reception desk, a water cooler, an artificial plant, a few sagging sofas and chairs and a wall-mounted TV. A couple of women with kids on their laps are watching a cartoon with the sound off.

He goes to the desk. A woman with dyed red hair looks up from her computer screen.

"Yes?"

"I. . . I've come to meet someone. I think she should be coming from England today."

"A deportee?"

"Yes. Catalina Ionescu. She's usually called Zara, though. I think her mum's already here? Ana?"

The woman checks her screen, and nods. "You're early

though. The group doesn't arrive till this evening. Around seven. Seven fifteen."

"Oh. OK. Is Ana here?"

"She went for a walk, I think."

"Right." He goes outside again, pauses on the steps to check his phone. Half past one. Six hours. By the time she gets here, he should be home.

Should be.

Won't be.

He needs to see her. He checks the map again, heads back to the bus stop. There's a long beach near the town; he'll take a walk while he waits.

ZARA

She looks out of the window for the last time: at the countryside she won't see again for – how long? For years and years, not until some now-unimaginable future when history has turned and changed.

History is now, and England.

The birds are flying, high and far, looking down – maybe – on the chapel at Little Gidding, where she read *all shall be well* and looked up and met his eyes. She leaves the window, and walks out of the room for the last time, along the shabby corridor, under the eyes of the cameras.

In the canteen, the leavers' group is gathered around a couple of tables, some with coats and bags, some with no more than the clothes they wear. The noisy air around them sparks with excitement, anger, relief, apprehension. She doesn't join them. She finds Grace, sitting quietly in a corner, and slides into the chair opposite her.

"You're going?" Grace asks.

"Yes." She swallows. "To some sort of centre in Calais. They help to resettle European deportees, or something."

Grace leans forward across the table, and whispers, "And your mum will be there. Waiting for you."

"I hope."

"I'm sure." Grace smiles at her. "And think. Tomorrow you're free. No more being afraid."

Free, and a long way from Ash. But maybe Mum'll have her phone, maybe he'll have texted her his new number, maybe she can call him. Maybe tonight she can speak to him.

"Zara," Grace says gently. "Time to go." At the other side of the canteen, a couple of officers are chivvying the women to their feet, into line. She gets up, hugs Grace, and hurries to join the queue as everyone files along the corridor and into the reception area.

A coach is parked outside. They wait.

An officer with a clipboard calls out names. In knots of fours and fives, the women are escorted out of the door, and onto the coach.

... the imprisoned larks escape and fly...

By fours and fives, the waiting group dwindles, the room empties, until there's only Zara and the officer left.

He drops the clipboard on the desk.

"What about me?" she says. Outside, the coach door folds shut. "I'm supposed to be going too."

"No, you're not."

"I am!"

"Change of orders. Here." He picks up the clipboard and shows her the list. Her name's there, but it's been crossed out and next to it someone has written: *Hold.*

"Hold? What's that mean?"

"Hold? Well, it's like. . ." He mimes, closing his fingers. "Like, hang onto—"

"I know what it means! I mean why?" She runs to the door and hammers on it, but the glass is dense and solid, as unyielding as thick ice. The coach jolts forward, gathers speed, lumbers around a bend in the road and is gone. Zara keeps banging on the glass. The officer grabs her arm, hauls her away from the door and pushes her against the wall.

"Stop that."

"But it's not fair! They said I was going—"

"I said, calm it! Or do you fancy a stretch in Willow?" He looks at her, steadily and hard-eyed.

Willow? She doesn't know what it means, only that it's a threat. Her stomach clenches, her mouth floods with a sudden taste of salt. She glances out at the empty road, bunches her fists and shoves her hands deep in her pockets. "OK," she says.

"That's better." He picks up the clipboard, and jerks his head towards the door to the corridor; she walks through it ahead of him. He shuts and locks it behind her.

She retreats to her room, stands at the window, and stares out through tears at the empty fields, the birds in the pale sky.

. . . *Winging wildly . . . on – on – and out of sight.*

ASH

The beach goes on for miles. He makes himself keep walking. When the light begins to fade, he turns and trudges back. He's starving. He sits at a café with a baguette and a strong coffee, then wanders the town.

There's a market in one of the streets that reminds him of the Christmas market on the South Bank. The stalls sell wind chimes, brightly coloured scarves and coats, jewellery, and he thinks suddenly of buying something for her; he's never bought her a present.

He chooses a silver necklace with a green stone that reminds him of her eyes. He doesn't have enough cash but his card works. He takes the slim tissue-paper packet and tucks it into his pocket.

It's 6:30 now: almost time. He texts Mum to fend her off – *Going to Dad's. I'll let you know if I'm staying over* – hurries back to the bus stop and catches the next bus. At the reception centre, the car park is dark and empty. He runs across it and up the steps into the foyer.

Ana jumps up from the sofa by the window.

"Ash? What are you doing here?"

"I. . . Max said Zara'd be coming today. I just wanted to

see her," and for a moment he's afraid he's done the wrong thing, but she's smiling.

"Have you bunked off school to do this?"

"Yeah. I don't care."

They sit together, waiting on the soggy sofa. He folds his fingers round the wrapped necklace in his pocket.

At 7:34 his phone rings. Dad. He kills the call but Dad rings again and again and finally he jams his thumb down on answer.

"Yeah?"

"Calais," Dad says.

"What?"

"What the hell are you doing in Calais?"

"What? I . . . Nothing. . . I . . ."

"*Christ,* Ash. Right. Listen to me. There's a ferry at nine. Be on it. I'll pick you up at Dover."

A wide beam of light sweeps across the front of the hotel.

"Ash? Have you got that?"

A coach draws up at the foot of the steps.

"I'll call you back."

He rings off. His phone starts up again straight away: a furious cheeping and buzzing. He turns it off, shoves it into his pocket, and follows Ana outside. The newly arrived deportees are climbing wearily down from the coach: a couple of women, a dark-haired boy about his own age, a woman with two tiny kids, a blonde girl who reminds him of the barmaid from the pub in Soho, a family with a baby.

She's not there.

"But. . ." He stares at Ana. "She *was* arrested. Definitely. Charlie said. So why isn't she here?"

"I don't know." Ana climbs up onto the bus and he listens from the bottom of the steps as she talks to the big man in NA uniform sprawled on the front seat. "Ionescu? Oh. Yeah. She was taken off the list at the last minute."

"Why?" Ana asks.

"No idea. Sorry." The man spreads his hands.

"But. . ."

"I said, I don't know. Not the sort of thing they tell us."

Ana stumbles down the steps and the coach door hisses shut behind her. She stands, staring at nothing, clutching one arm across her stomach, pressing the back of her other hand to her mouth.

"Ana? What d'you think happened?" he asks.

"I don't know." She takes a couple of steps back as the coach starts up, sweeps in a wide arc and rumbles out of the car park. When its lights have vanished, she says, "You should go home, Ash."

He nods. There's nothing for him here, and nothing he can do to help, and he wonders if Ana's thinking that if he and Zara hadn't met none of this would have happened.

He trudges back to the bus stop to catch the next bus to the ferry terminal. What else is there to do?

She sits shivering on Grace's bed; it's cold this evening, and the faded curtains drift and stir in the draught from the window.

Grace takes a cardigan from a bag of clothes under the table, and tucks it round her. It's bright blue. Sophie's colour: whenever anything came into the shop that was this colour she thought of Sophie.

She pulls it round her shoulders. "Thanks," she says.

Grace smiles, sits on the other bed and leans forward. "What happened, Zara?"

Zara sighs. "I was on the list to go. Then at the last minute they said I wasn't. That's all."

"And you don't know why?"

"No. I've been asking all day. All they say is orders are orders and don't make trouble, or I'll be doing a stretch in Willow. What's Willow?"

Grace's face tightens. She twists the beaded bracelet on her wrist. "It's the isolation unit."

"Oh. What's it like?"

Grace glances round her room. "Like this. Only with nothing you could hang yourself with. Be careful, Zara. You don't want to go there." Grace looks at her squarely, with a kind of bitter fear that makes her sorry she asked.

They sit in silence. A gust of wind blows against the window.

Western wind, when wilt thou blow?

Rain spatters on the glass, leaving stranded drops that catch the light from the room.

ASH

There's a storm in the Channel. He stands on the deck of the ferry, staring into the dark, breathing in air that tastes of salt and oil, feeling the judder of the engine and the lurch of the sea beneath him.

Halfway back to England, he throws up, hunched over the wet icy rail, the wind blowing rain and scraps of sick into his face. He stumbles off the boat at Dover feeling heady and queasy, waits in the passport queue marked UK NATIONALS ONLY. The immigration officer questions him about why he's been to Calais for the day.

For nothing.

For nothing.

He mumbles something about a break; she narrows her eyes and slides his passport slowly back to him. At customs, he shuffles in a queue through NOTHING TO DECLARE. Outside, in the foyer, he blinks into the harsh light, and halts.

Dad's there, sitting in a hard plastic chair, laptop balanced on his knees, face white in the screen light, wearing the dark woollen overcoat that Sophie always said was too big for him.

Ash swears silently and scans the signs for directions to the station, but it's too late. Dad's already seen him, has folded the laptop shut, is hauling himself out of the chair and pacing heavily towards him. Ash waits. What else is there to do? When Dad reaches him they stand, face-to-face, saying nothing. The silence stretches; he counts fifteen before Dad shakes his head, and gestures towards the exit.

"Car's this way."

Ash follows him out into the dark. The midlife-crisis car is standing on its own in the huge car park. He folds himself into the passenger seat. The headlights reflect off the falling rain and the wet streets, as the car roars away from the port, through the town, onto the motorway.

"*Calais*," Dad says. "Why the hell...?"

"I don't know." *For nothing.* "How did you even know I was there?"

Dad glances at him. "Location tracker on your phone."

"What? *You* can check that? For—"

"I wouldn't have if you hadn't lied to your mum about where you were! She was at the house when she got your text. Christ, Ash. I *told* you after the protest. She doesn't need this."

"*She* was at *yours?*" She never – hardly ever – goes to the old house.

"I've had an offer. Someone wants to buy. We were clearing stuff out of the attic." The attic's a black hole of memories – of *Sophie:* photos, books, toys, school workbooks, paintings.

He stares out of the side window; rain streams across the glass.

"I just wanted to get away for the day," he says at last.

"You bunked off school, Ash. You can't afford. . ."

"I know."

"Is this about Zara? Has something. . . ?"

"No."

"Or is it. . . I mean. . ."

"No."

Dad sighs. "Do you. . . Would it help to talk to . . . that counsellor?"

"Debbie. No."

Dad falls silent. The white lines and cats' eyes that mark the road gleam in the headlights. Beyond them everything is dark.

CHAPTER SIXTEEN

She wakes to the uncomfortable bed, the chill in the room, the frayed curtains, the camera in the ceiling: all the things she thought she would never see again. There'll be another group leaving for Europe soon, Grace told her, in a couple of weeks or so. She'll be on that. She's bound to be. Yesterday was a mistake. That's all.

She picks up Grace's blue cardigan. Outside it's still stormy, a strong wind flinging rain against the glass. She puts the cardigan on and heads downstairs. She didn't eat last night and she's hungry, but she's stopped before she reaches the canteen by the officer who wouldn't let her on the bus yesterday.

"You're wanted," he says.

She looks at him blankly. He jerks his head along the corridor.

"In the office. Police to see you."

"Police?"

"Yeah. What've you been doing?"

She looks at him blankly again.

"Joke," he says.

Ha-bloody-ha. She turns without smiling to accompany him to the office. Police. That explains yesterday. It must: she told the sandy-haired policeman everything she knew, but maybe there are things he wants to clarify, to hear again, to ask more about—

She stops short on the threshold. It's not him. A man and a woman are sitting at the table. They're not in uniform; the man's wearing an open-necked shirt, his jacket slung over the back of his chair. He has untidy, grey-blond hair and his eyes are grey-blue like Ash's, but they make her think of stone, not smoke. Everything about the woman is sharp edged: her haircut, her features, her grey suit. Neither of them looks like the sort of person who would tell you not to worry, or give you chocolate.

"Come and sit down," the woman says, with a brief, dismissive nod to the officer. He withdraws, closing the door, leaving her shut in with the man and the woman. She sits. The woman places a small voice recorder on the table and switches it on.

"So. Catalina Ionescu."

She nods.

"I can call you Zara?"

"I . . . Yes. I suppose."

"We want to talk to you about the Sophie Hammond case."

"Sophie? But. . ." Zara looks from the woman, to the stone-grey eyes of the man, and back again. "I've already told... I don't know his name ... the other policeman."

"PC McBride," the woman says.

"I've told him everything I know."

"I realize that." The woman's voice is as sharp-edged as everything else about her: her words clipped and precise. "But we've taken over the investigation, and we need to confirm exactly what information you gave him."

"OK. So... You're going to do something about it? Do you know who he is yet?"

"Like I said," the woman says. "We need to hear exactly what you told PC McBride. So. Let's start with the night of the party."

She tells them. They listen: the man leaning back in his chair with his eyes narrowed, the woman sitting forward, her interlaced hands resting on the table. When she's finished, the woman reaches into the briefcase by her chair. She places a laptop and a file on the table, opens the file, and slides a photograph towards Zara.

"And you say this was the boy?"

She glances at the photo. It's nothing new: just another still from the TV programme.

"It was him."

"You're sure?"

"Yes. Completely. Who is he?"

The woman gives a sideways glance at the man. "We wondered if *you* knew that, Zara. His name? Anything else about him?"

"*No.* I don't. I thought *you'd* be able to find out... You will, won't you?"

The woman doesn't answer. She slips the photograph back into the file. The man leans forward, resting his big fists on the table.

"Are you making this up, Zara?"

"What? No!"

"There was no one called Zara at the party. Not according to the bouncers' list."

"No... I know. I... Sophie told them my name was Anna."

"So you lied? Are you lying about this as well? Are you just trying to make trouble?"

"No! Sophie was my friend. He killed her."

"This boy." He opens the file at the photo and turns it towards her.

"Yes."

"I don't see how you can be so sure about that, Zara. It was a *masked* party, wasn't it?"

"Yes! But I saw him without his mask. In the garden. He'd pushed it up."

She mimes the action, pushing her hand over her forehead, up into her hair. The man closes the file slowly and slides it back towards the woman.

"You took a long time telling anyone this, Zara."

"Because—"

"What? Because it took you a long time to make it up?"

"No! I haven't made it up. This is the truth! Why would I lie? If I knew I was going to end up somewhere like this!"

He considers her, his eyes cold and hard, for a long time. Then he lounges back in his chair, feels in his jacket pocket, takes out a pack of chewing gum, pops a piece in his mouth and chews it. She smells mint. Her stomach flutters. Her mouth is as dry as summer dust.

"Could I have some water, please?"

"Tell us again. From the beginning."

"I've told you everything—"

"I want to hear it again."

This time, he keeps stopping her: teasing her answers apart, asking questions about every tiny detail, challenging her memories.

Finally, he says, "OK. Let's write this down." He opens the laptop, and starts to type with his thick fingers.

"Do you believe me, then?" Zara says.

He stops typing for a moment. He and the woman exchange another look; the woman nods slowly.

"Yes, Zara. We believe you."

ASH

His head's a mess. He's got Maths to catch up from yesterday; at morning break he sits in the common room, trying to work his way through a page of past questions, but all he can think is where is she, and why wasn't she in Calais yesterday, and is she OK or has something happened to her: something he can't imagine, doesn't dare to imagine.

The vectors of a, b and c are such that $c \times a = 2i$ and $b \times a = 3j$.

How can she be OK?

Simplify $(a + 2b - 6c) \times (a - b + 3c)$

What's she doing right now?

Simplify $(a + 2b...$

And where *is* she?

Zara.

Zara, Zara, Zara... He slams the laptop shut. What he needs is a run; that thinking of nothing that comes with running, but he's got lessons all day and he can't afford to miss them after missing everything yesterday (pointlessly, *pointlessly*). Dad told him last night he'd cancel his allowance if there was any more trouble, and he's saving to go and see Zara this summer, maybe to travel with her – which will be pointless too, if he can't find her. And how's he supposed to find her?

He gets up and paces to the pool table where Jas is practising shots. The four angles off the cushion and rolls precisely into a corner pocket. Jas glances up at him.

"Hey. What happened to you yesterday?"

"Nothing. Just wasn't feeling great."

"You OK now?"

Zara, Zara, Zara. "Yeah."

"You want to come over tomorrow evening? Movie. Pizza. The others are coming. And hey – if you get there early we could talk about the summer? We ought to plan."

"I guess." He rolls the fourteen against the six: green against green. He's still got her necklace; he forgot to give it to Ana. The balls click, spin apart, settle.

"Ash?" Jas is shifting his fingers on the cue, making the shapes of guitar chords. "You sure you're OK?"

He nods, walks to the counter, flicks the kettle on, makes himself a cup of coffee and takes it back to his laptop. The maths makes no more sense; he is muddled with memories of Zara, drinking strong black coffee in the flat, the taste of it on her breath when he kissed her afterwards. . .

The vectors of a, b and c

The vectors of a, b and c

"Ash? You done this one?"

Lewis drops into the chair alongside him, scrolls through a phone, and tilts the screen towards Ash; it shows the familiar chequered black and white: ranks, files, diagonals, a king penned in one corner by a rook and a bishop; but it's the *phone* he's looking at, remembering it sinking into Lewis's pint.

"Got a new one on the insurance." Lewis grins at him. "Apparently it covers accidents involving wasted friends. Go on. This one took me five minutes."

"I wasn't *that* wasted, Lewis." He rams his laptop and books clumsily into his bag and shoves himself up from the chair. "And what about her? What about that girl? Was she insured for a new *life?*"

He blunders across the common room and out of the door.

What about *Zara?*

Zara.

Zara.

He takes a long time to type up her statement. While he works, she waits, letting her gaze drift around the room. There's another green dot on the wall calendar: another departure date, on the Wednesday after next: twelve days from now. She tries to calculate twelve times twenty-four hours times sixty minutes times sixty seconds. She can't hold the sum in her head; Ash would have got it in a heartbeat.

Don't think about Ash.

"OK, Zara. Check this, please. Sign across the screen if you agree with it."

The man swings the laptop round to face her and she runs her eyes quickly down the text. The story is clear and accurate. Even so, she hesitates, poising her finger on the screen, before she shapes her name. Written with her finger, her signature is shaky and clumsy.

She pushes the laptop back across the desk, and the man checks what she's written, nods, switches the voice recorder off and puts it and the laptop into the briefcase.

It's OK. They just needed to double check what she told the other policeman. They needed a signed statement. That's all. She shifts her chair back.

"One moment." The woman leans forward, hands steepled, elbows on the table. "We've got a few more questions."

"But. . . I. . ." She swallows hard. "I told you everything. There's nothing else."

"No. This isn't about the party. That's all fine. Your statement's very . . . clear. Just a few other details we need to investigate." She flips to another section of the file. "Where's your mother, Zara?"

"My mother?"

"Yes. We know she was here. You both registered for IDs when the scheme first came in. So where is she now?"

"She left—"

"Left?" The man interrupts. "Without you? You're only seventeen, Zara. I think you're lying. I think she's still here. But where? Your old landlord told us you left your registered address shortly before the Act was passed. That's – what? – eighteen months ago. So where have you both been living since then?"

"Nowhere—"

"Oh, please." The woman takes over again. "We pick people up from the streets, you know. If you've stayed hidden for eighteen months, it's because someone's taken you in. So, who? Who, Zara?"

"No one."

The woman sighs heavily. "Let's start again. Where's your mum?"

They start again, and again, and again. The air in the room becomes thick and difficult to breathe. The light flickers and glitters. Something electric emits a low hum that gathers in her head like the pressure before a thunderstorm.

The man fetches himself a glass of water from the sink in the corner and doesn't turn the tap off properly. She counts the intervals between drips. Five – six – drip – one – two –

The woman sits back in her chair with her arms folded. The man unwraps another piece of chewing gum, and leans forward.

"Your mum," he says.

She smells stale breath and mint.

She says nothing, she counts: drip – one – two – three – four – five – six – drip – one –

The man slams his hand on the table. "You're going to tell us this, Zara. Sooner or later, you're going to tell us. So why not do us all a favour and make it now?"

Drip, drip, drip.

The woman takes a flask out of her sharp-edged bag, and pours out two cups of coffee. It smells rich and dark, not like the weak, bitter water in the canteen. It reminds her of drinking coffee at Ash's in the high kitchen with its view over treetops and roofs, of watching the lights go out on election night.

Don't think about Ash.

The woman takes a sip and flicks to the next page in the file.

"Well. We can come back to all that. Now. Friends. Have you been in touch with. . ." and she frowns down at the page, and reads out the names of everyone who was in her classes at school, all the members of the running team.

"No," she says. "I told them I was leaving. Going back to Romania."

"And you've had no contact with any of them? On social media? By email? Phone?"

"No." *You never know who's watching,* Max said.

The woman raises one, sculpted eyebrow, and makes a note in the file. "What about Sophie's family? Did you keep in touch with them?"

For an instant, it's as if someone's snatched the ground away from under her. She says, "No," and her voice sounds scared and breathless. She steadies herself. "I mean... I never knew them."

"You never knew them? You knew Sophie, but not her family?"

"No."

The light glitters. Something hums. The tap drips.

Ash: I never saw you, never knew you, never loved you.

"Never," she says. "No. Never."

ASH

In Maths at the end of the day, Mr Jamieson gives them the results of Tuesday's test. He keeps Ash back after the lesson for a quiet chat.

"Is everything OK, Ash?" he asks, resting one hand on Ash's scrappy test paper. "This isn't like you."

"Yeah. No. I'm fine."

He escapes into the corridor. Chris is leaning against the wall, waiting for him.

"63 percent? What's wrong with you?"

"Drop it, Chris."

"This isn't still about Zara, is it?"

He says nothing, and hurries downstairs to the sixth-form common room, shoves his Maths file into his locker and slams the door on it.

"Ash?" Chris has followed him. "I'm going to meet Priya. You want to come?"

"Dunno. Got to go to Dad's later." But that's not till 7:15, and the alternative now is going home to nothing. He nods. They head for the corner café that's about halfway between their school and Priya's. They don't speak. Chris walks with his hands jammed in his pockets, his eyes on the pavement.

At the café they grab a corner table. Chris picks up a packet of sugar and twists it till it tears and spills. He flicks the torn paper across the table and onto the floor. Ash frowns at him.

"Hey. Are *you* OK?"

"Me? I'm not the one who just got 30 percent less than usual in a Maths test." Chris mangles another packet of sugar.

"Chris—"

"She's here." Chris gets up and waves; Priya's threading her way between the tables, hands shoved in the pockets of her padded coat, shoulders hunched, long hair over her face. Chris stands up and touches her shoulder briefly.

"I'll get you a drink."

Priya hangs her coat over the back of the empty chair, sits down, and gazes across the café at Chris as he joins the queue at the counter.

"Priya?" Ash says. "Is everything OK?"

She turns to him. "He didn't tell you?"

"Tell me what?"

She sighs, rests her elbows on the table and props her forehead on her bunched fists. "My dad wants us to move to India."

"*India?* What? *Why?*"

She raises her face and gives him a crooked smile, gestures down at herself with a quick fluid movement of her hands.

"No... I don't mean why *India*. Why's he want you to move?"

"Why d'you think, Ash? The BB thing, of course."

"But you are BB. And your dad."

"It's still crap," she says. "I – all of us – we get carded everywhere. Whenever I'm out with Chris. Whenever I'm anywhere. And you get this look, every time, like: *is this a fake ID?* You saw. In the pub. Same for Maya, and God knows how long her family's been here."

"But . . . what about Bristol?"

She spreads her hands. "I can study engineering in India, Ash."

"What about Chris?" It's the real question, the point, the heart of the matter. He wishes he hadn't found it because her face crumples; she sniffs, wipes her nose with the back of her hand, and catches a tear on her forefinger. "Don't. . ."

"Sorry. . ." he says; he sits helpless and dumb while she fights to recover herself. When Chris comes back, they talk about trivial nothings; all the important things weighing unspoken around them like a gravitational field: like dark matter.

After Chris and Priya leave, Ash sits on till the café closes, then he makes his way to the river, crosses it, and walks to the South Bank to the terrace where he was standing when Zara first saw him. He stares into the dark water.

Dark.

Dark.

Shit.

It's already 7:23.

He doesn't reach Dad's till 8:09. Mum's there too; they're both waiting for him at the kitchen table, next to the big window that overlooks the garden. The tree house is a dark block in the oak.

"Where the hell—" Dad begins and Mum says, *"Rob."*

She gestures to the chair opposite Dad's. Ash drops into it and leans back with his arms folded, sitting silently while Dad uncorks a bottle of wine and Mum opens the oven. She's cooked. She hardly ever cooks these days. She sets a dish of overdone baked potatoes and a dried-out casserole on the table and sits down next to Ash. He looks at her.

"What's all this for?"

Dad starts to say something, but Mum says, quickly, "We just thought it would be good to have a proper chat."

"What about?"

"What do you think?" Dad says. "Your results at school are down, your teachers say it's as if you've mentally checked out. Then the protest – and Calais – and now you're an hour late. . ."

54 minutes. Not an hour.

"We're concerned, Ash. That's all," Mum says.

What about? Me? Or my A level results?

"We were wondering. . . You haven't seen Zara for a while. Is. . . ? Has something. . . ?"

Zara. Zara. Zara. He turns to the window, remembering her, standing there, and himself standing behind her with his arms wrapped round her, his face buried in the softness of her hair, promising her that everything was going to be fine.

"Ash?" Mum says.

He presses his finger on the handle of his knife, rocking

it to and fro, staring at the shifting reflection in the blade. "I don't know. I'm fed up. That's all. With everything. With living in a fascist state, for example."

He looks across the table at Dad.

"Oh, not this again." Dad pours himself a glass of wine and pushes the bottle towards Mum. "It's not a *fascist state*. It's a democratically elected government—"

"Yeah, with fascist policies."

"With some bloody sensible policies, actually, Ash." Dad swallows a mouthful of wine, and sticks his fork into a lump of dry casserole.

Mum stares at him.

"Christ, Rob. Don't tell me you *voted* for them?"

"I. . ." Dad runs his finger through a drop of spilt wine, then straightens up and looks Mum in the face. "Look. None of the others have any ideas about how to control drugs. . ." which might be right, but it's not enough; it doesn't make it right, doesn't counterbalance all the other stuff, doesn't counterbalance whatever's happened – happening – to Zara.

Ash shoves his chair back hard. It topples and crashes to the stone floor; he kicks it out of his way: kicks it again.

"What are you doing?" Dad's up from his chair.

"What's it look like? I'm going!"

"Ash—"

"I said, I'm going!" He storms across the kitchen, into the hall, snatches Mum's car key from the hall table, flings the front door open, and hurls it shut behind him. The glass vibrates in the frame. It doesn't break. He wanted it to break.

He stumbles down the steps, and halts. The midlife-crisis car is parked at the kerb. He tucks the key between his fingers, poises it against the car, and drags it along the side, digging deep, gouging a long angry scratch in the paintwork.

He's hurrying away from it when Mum calls after him. He stops and waits for her.

She lays her hand on his arm. "Let's go home. Want me to drive?"

He nods.

He's shaking.

He can't see straight; everything angles and stretches like refracted light.

CHAPTER SEVENTEEN

On Saturday morning, she hides in her room, curled up on her bed.

Western wind, when wilt thou blow,
The small rain down can rain?
Christ! if my love were in my arms
And I in my bed again.

"Hey!"

Someone prods her, stabbing a finger into her shoulder. She opens her eyes. There's a stranger in her room: a girl with tightly coiled fair hair and uneasy, restless eyes.

"How does the window open?"

"It doesn't."

The girl swears and sits on the other bed. She's pale and her hands are shaking. "I need some air."

"You have to go outside for that. To the yard. D'you want me to show you?"

The girl glances out at the torn sky. "Maybe. What's your name?"

"Zara. You?"

"Katya. Where are you from?"

"London."

Katya screws up her face. "I mean—"

"I know what you mean. Romania. You?"

"Poland." Katya chews at her ragged fingernails, stands, paces to the door, to the bed, to the door and back again. "How did they get you?" she asks.

"Complicated." Zara shrugs.

"They picked me up in a random ID check. Last night." Katya pauses to stare out of the window, swings away and paces again. "This is such shit. This BB policy. It's *shit*. You know, ever since we came here, my mum worked. She did everything legal. Paid her taxes. Everything. It's—"

"I know," Zara says.

"You know what? They interviewed me for hours last night. Where did I buy my ID? Where's my mum? Where've we been living; where's she been working? They can forget it. They're not finding out from me. No way."

Katya drops onto the edge of her bed and chews at her fingernails again. She has already bitten them raw and bleeding, and Zara shifts to reach across the space between them, to hold Katya's wrists and pull her hands away from her mouth. "'Let's go outside," she says, and she leads Katya downstairs and out into the yard where the bleak wind chases scraps of rubbish across the cracked tarmac. Katya prowls to the fence and presses her face to the dense mesh, and Zara stands next to her, seeing what she's seeing: the splintered fragments of earth and sky.

286

"I can't take this. I can't take it!" Katya slams her palms against the fence, spins away, and paces alongside it. Zara falls into step with her. As they walk, Katya knots her raw fingers through the slender gold chain around her neck, and fidgets with the little cross that hangs from it.

"It won't be for long," Zara says.

Katya stops walking and stares at her. Her fair hair blows into her face. An empty crisp packet flutters around their ankles, skitters away, and is trapped by the fence. "What d'you mean, it won't be for long?"

"You won't be here for long. They send people to Europe every couple of weeks. One group went on Thursday. Another one goes in about a fortnight. Less." She shoves her chilled hands into her pockets.

They walk again. A few drops of rain gust into their faces.

"Let's go in," Zara says. "You don't want damp clothes."

"You sound like my grandmother." Katya gives a fleeting half smile.

"Seriously. They don't dry properly. It's not warm enough."

Inside, they make their way to the canteen, and sit at a table by the window with tea in plastic cups.

"How long've you been here?" Katya asks.

"About a week." It feels like infinitely more. It's oddly difficult to remember what it felt like not being here. She fiddles with a pack of sugar. It bursts, granules spill, and she thinks of Sophie, licking golden crystals of sugar from her finger, the walled garden outside the window, snowdrops in the lawn. Katya takes a sip of tea, and picks at a crack in the tabletop.

"But you said a group went to Europe the other day? So why are you still here?"

Zara doesn't answer. She doesn't want to talk about the man and woman in the airless room and their endless frightening questions. She doesn't want to *think* about them. And anyway, it's over. They've got her statement. It's going to be OK. She wipes her dry lips with the back of her hand. "It was a last-minute hitch. I'll be going next time. With you."

Rain blows bleakly against the glass. At the other side of the canteen, someone's crying.

ASH

He doesn't wake till early afternoon on Saturday. He ought to work; he needs a run.

He heads out with Lulu. On his way downstairs, he finds specks of black paint in the grooves of the car key; remembers the *satisfaction* of carving that scar along the side of the midlife-crisis car. He'd do it again. He *would*: despite the odd lurch in his stomach that feels like vertigo.

He drives to the Heath, runs with Lulu to the top of the hill and pauses to recover his breath, gazing down at London. Zara loved this view. He blinks away sudden tears, thinking about her then, about her now: wherever she is, whatever's happening to her. He tries phoning Max, but her number produces nothing except a dead silence; when he gives up he sees he's missed a call from Dad.

He doesn't ring back.

He doesn't want to talk to Dad; he can't imagine ever wanting to talk to him again. He runs round the rest of the loop that he and Zara ran together at Christmas, and goes home. In the lobby he stops to check the post: a handful of junk mail, a postcard from Kate, and a hand-delivered envelope addressed to him, which he rips open. It's a letter from Max, dated yesterday, telling him that she's leaving to join Ana in Calais. Just that: nothing about Zara. Nothing. He drags the dog upstairs, drops the post on the hall table, and halts.

Mum's laughing in the kitchen.

He looks round the door. Charlie's there, sharing a pot of tea and a packet of chocolate biscuits. He nods up at Ash. "Hi. How're you doing? I was passing. Thought I'd drop in to say hello."

"Right. Hi." He helps himself to a glass of milk and a couple of biscuits.

"Dad called," Mum says. "Can you tell him what time you're going over there tonight?"

"I'm not going."

He goes to his room, opens his laptop, types *Hey Soph*, stalls, and stares out of the window. The tree blurs into the sky. He's roused by a knock at his door, slams the laptop shut and swings round in his chair. Charlie's leaning on the door frame.

"Did you find anything?" Ash asks.

Charlie frowns and touches his forefinger to his lips with a warning glance over his shoulder. He comes in and closes the door softly behind him.

"Yeah. Well, it found me, more like. Note through my door from one of the blokes who worked Sophie's case. Zara did go to the police. They were more interested in her fake ID than her story, but Jim talked to her about what she'd seen at the party. He gave me the details. Asked me to have a look. I got the feeling he wasn't going to be able to carry on with it himself."

"Why not? So, did you find out who he was? The guy at the party?"

Charlie hesitates. "I'm doing some digging, Ash. I'll let you know as soon as there's something definite, OK? I didn't tell Julia. Didn't want to stir things up. . . And on the subject of stirring things up, what's this about Calais?"

Ash ducks his gaze to his hands. He picks a fleck of black paint from his thumbnail and flicks it to the floor.

"Looking for Zara?" Charlie asks gently.

For a moment he can only nod. "She wasn't there. I don't know why." He looks up at Charlie. "Can *you* find out where she is?"

"She'll have been sent to one of the deportation centres."

"Yeah, but can you find out which one?"

"Ash. . . You're not going to be able to visit her."

"I know. I just want to know."

Charlie sighs. "OK. I'll see what I can do. I'll be in touch, yeah?" and he's gone.

Ash sits at his desk and listens to the front door closing.

A slammed door.

That's all there is: no answers about Sophie, no answers about Zara.

ZARA

Back in their room, Katya upends the transparent plastic bag of her possessions, tipping them noisily onto the table by the window, and rummaging through them: purse, travel card, useless fake ID, balled-up tissues, tubes of make-up, hand cream, a pack of chewing gum, an empty cigarette packet.

Finally she swears, sweeps everything back into the bag, and sits on the edge of her bed, chewing her fingernails. "Zara!" she whispers. She leans forward, across the narrow gap between the beds. "Have you got a phone?"

"What do you think? No one has. *God.* Did they take yours? Is your mum's number on it?"

Katya scowls. "No one's was. I'm not *stupid.*" She digs the pack of chewing gum out of the bag, tips a piece into her hand, tosses it into her mouth, and offers the packet to Zara. A scent of mint flavours the air with the memory of yesterday's remorseless questions, the closed-in room, the big policeman's stony eyes. She knots her arms over a sudden sick hollowness in her stomach, and swallows hard.

"No. Thanks. Why d'you want a phone anyway? Who would you call?"

"It doesn't have to be a phone." Katya's talking so quietly that Zara almost has to lip–read to follow her. "Any camera—"

She laughs.

"– or paper," Katya mouths. "Paper would do."

"No. Sorry. What for?"

Katya doesn't answer. She sits on her bed, staring at the camera in the ceiling, playing with the little gold cross on the slender chain around her neck.

"I know who might have some," Zara says. She pulls Katya to her feet, and leads her downstairs. Grace is sitting on her own in the canteen. She smiles and waves when she sees Zara, beckons them to her table, and asks who Katya is and where she's from. "Poland's OK," she tells her. "You'll be OK."

Katya winds her chain through her fingers and holds onto the cross.

"What about you?" she asks.

"Long story," says Grace, and Zara, who knows the long story, says quickly, "Katya needs some paper. Writing paper. Have you got any?"

Grace nods, and leads them upstairs to her room in Elm, which is fuller than Zara and Katya's bare room: a length of gold-and-green dyed cotton covers the bed, framed photographs stand on the windowsill, the drawers are stuffed with clothes. Grace hunts among the patterned cotton dresses in the bottom drawer and pulls out an exercise book with a red paper cover. She opens it, tears out the first couple of pages, folds them, pushes them into her pocket, and hands the book to Katya.

"Are you sure you don't need it?" Zara asks. Grace shakes her head.

"Started keeping a diary when I first came here, but. . ."

Nothing happens, Zara thinks. Or the only things that happen are things you don't want to remember.

Grace is rummaging again. She finds a biro, and passes it to Katya. "You'll need this too."

Katya hugs the book and pen to her chest.

"What's it for?" Grace asks.

Katya shrugs. "Just writing."

"Just writing?" Zara asks, as they make their way along the corridor and down the stairs. Elm is identical to Larch is identical to Beech is identical to Ash: same doors, same peeling walls and scuffed lino, same opaque plastic eyes in the ceiling that Katya glances at before she says, "Yes," and nothing more. She leads the way outside, into the drab afternoon. There's a break in the rain, but other showers are gathering. Side by side, they lean against the fence and stare up into the sky. Wind and rubbish swirl about their feet. "Tell me about Grace," Katya says.

Zara gives a long sigh and slides down to sit on the wet tarmac with her back against the fence; thinking about Grace turns her bones to water.

"Zara?" Katya says.

"OK. She came to England ages ago. Before the Party. Her family'd been killed. Somewhere in Africa. Some political thing. . . I don't really know. She got permission to stay, then when the Party got in they said everyone like her had to reapply and when she did they shut her up here. She's been in here for – God knows. A year? Waiting to hear if she's going to be allowed to stay or sent home."

A year of being here. It's too much; even to think about it is unbearable. Zara scrambles to her feet and runs: lapping the yard, pounding the cracked tarmac, trying to run herself into emptiness. To think nothing. To feel nothing.

It doesn't work. She needs open space. She keeps running; a hundred times round the narrow yard, maybe. She loses count, and then the rain starts again. She pulls Katya up from where she's crouching, scribbling in Grace's red notebook, and together they bolt for the doors.

In the TV room, the volume is at maximum. The canteen's crowded, stuffy, damp; the air shrill with competing conversations. Katya stands against a wall, chewing the fingernails of one hand, clutching her notebook in the other. Zara tugs her sleeve.

"Forget this. Come on," and she leads Katya along the ground floor corridor to a big, deserted room that overlooks the fenced yard. It's utterly empty apart from a couple of broken chairs that have been abandoned here.

"What's this?" Katya asks.

"Visitors' room. I mean, not any more, obviously." The room's a meaningless leftover from the time before the BB policy. No one at Oake Leigh has visitors any more.

"Visitors?" Katya prowls along the scuffed, stained carpet tiles to the door at the far end of the room. Zara follows her. They peer through the wired glass panel into a long passage.

Doors all the way along it divide it into a series of sealed spaces, like airlocks. Red lights at each door show that the electronic locks are switched on.

"Zara," Katya whispers. "If this was the visitors' room, that passage must lead outside."

"Katya? Are you—?" She tugs the notebook from Katya's hand and opens it to a rough sketch labelled *yard, office, canteen.* "Are you trying to find a way to *escape?*"

"Shhh!" Katya darts a fierce glance up at the black plastic bulb of the camera above the door.

"It's only a camera," Zara says. "They can't hear anything."

"Are you sure?" Katya snatches the notebook back, hugs it to her chest, and retreats to the far end of the room. She sits down on the dirty carpet with her back against the wall. Zara sits next to her; before she can say anything, Katya grips her wrist and points up to the ceiling. There's another camera just above them. *Only* a camera, surely; it's crazy to think anything else, but – *Much Madness is divinest Sense* – especially in this place. She drops her voice to a whisper.

"Katya. It's impossible to escape. Those doors are all locked, and there's no other way. And what's the point? I told you: there'll be another group going to Europe soon. Here. Give me some paper and the pen."

Katya hesitates, then she hands over the notebook and biro. Zara tears out a ragged sheet of paper, draws a grid of squares, and pauses.

"It's Saturday, isn't it? First of March?"

"Yes."

She nods and fills the squares with S S M T W T F S S M T W. The next group goes to Calais on the second Wednesday: the twelfth day from now. Eleven days to get through, including today. She flips the paper over, scribbles the sums that Ash would do in his head ($11 \times 24 \times 60 \times 60 = 950,400$ seconds) and thrusts the paper towards Katya.

"See? Less than a million seconds and we'll be out of here. On the way to Calais."

"You're sure about that?" Katya meets her eyes, steadily and unyielding and she's reminded, again, of the policeman's stony look and the sickly smell of mint. She swallows.

"Yes. Of course I'm sure. I saw them go——"

"Did you? Tell me exactly what you saw, Zara."

She describes it: the women gathering, queueing up, climbing onto the coach; the coach driving away without her, taking the bend in the road and disappearing from sight.

"That's all. Isn't it? You saw the bus go. You don't know where they took them."

"To Calais," she says. "They go to Calais."

"You don't know that."

She swallows again. "What are you saying, Katya?"

"Just. . . I'd rather get myself home."

"That's crazy," Zara says again. "You're going to be fine. We both are. It's Grace who might not be."

Katya touches the cross at her neck. "So I'll take her with me."

ASH

Hey Soph,

   So Charlie said he'd let me know when he knows
something definite. So he knows something already,
obviously, and I don't care if it's definite or not, I want
to know what it is. I've got a right, haven't I? You're
MY sister. Zara's MY girlfriend. And I'm not Mum,
I don't need protecting from this. All that stuff he said
about not stirring things up? They're stirred up already.

   A x

He deletes and burns the letter, grabs his backpack and runs
downhill. It's dark on the towpath; the only light comes
from the windows of flats on the opposite bank, reflecting in
smashed fragments on the black water. Someone shoulders
past him under a bridge; a bike zings past him at high speed.
He's never walked here at night before and by the time he
reaches the moorings he's edgy, fists clenched in his pockets;
he feels ready to fight Charlie for what he knows.

Only Charlie's not there.

The boat is silent and dark; when he steps on to the deck
and tries the door, it's padlocked shut. He wonders what to do.

Break in? How?

Wait? It's freezing.

He might as well go to Jas's. It's just round the corner from here – a millionaire's luxury apartment: the top three floors of one of the new blocks behind King's Cross. He jumps off the boat and jogs along the towpath to the road. He's almost at Jas's when his phone buzzes with an incoming text. His heart gives the brief thud that means *Zara?* but of course, it's not her. It's Jas.

Sorry. Can't make this evening.

It's no big deal. He has no idea what to do next. Go home. Go to Dad's. Go back to Charlie's. Nothing appeals. He wanders vaguely towards home and his phone buzzes again. It's Chris this time.

Did you get Jas's text? We're at mine instead if you want to come.

Yes.

No.

Don't know.

He leaves it to chance; walks to a bus stop, waits, and takes the first bus that comes: to Chris's, not home. Sitting at the back, he thinks about his conversation with Charlie, and takes his phone out to google *Deportation Centres*. A lot of the search results return *website not found* or *invalid address;* the couple of sites that are still live leave him shaky with sick fury.

There's a biro in his bag, and he wraps his hand round it; he'd like to cover every writable surface on this bus with *fuck the party.* But there are CCTV cameras, everywhere, five of them, covering every angle; he'd be identified, arrested.

He doesn't want to be arrested again.

Face it: he's too scared to be arrested again.

He stares at the cameras, wondering what force it would take to smash them, imagines doing it, using the broken pieces to carve *fuck the party* on the windows. He does nothing. He sidles off the bus, watches it go on, intact, undamaged, and slinks round the corner to Chris's house.

They're downstairs, in the basement den. Chris is lying with his head in Priya's lap; she's leaning over him so that her hair hides her face. Ash falters in the doorway. It's a mistake, being here. This reminds him too much of how he lay with Zara; he's too much in the way: he should go—

"Hi." Priya's smiling at him; Chris struggles upright and straightens his glasses.

"Hey, Ash."

"Hi. Why did Jas cancel?"

"Bust-up with his dad or something. I don't know, really. Ask Maya and Cait when they get here."

"Right." It's a relief that they're coming too. He comes into the room, drops his backpack and flops into a beanbag; carries on scrolling through Google while Chris and Priya fetch snacks and drinks. *Invalid address. Website not found.* When they come back, Maya and Caitlin are with them.

"So what did happen with Jas, exactly?" Priya asks.

"God knows." Maya slings her guitar off her back and leans it against the wall.

"This is Jas we're talking about." Chris grins at Ash. "It could be *anything*. Borrowing the car. Fireworks on the roof terrace. What else was there? Or maybe they're still arguing about his sixteen-plus results."

There's a beat of silence, before Caitlin says, "Anyway. It's bloody annoying. We were meant to be practising this afternoon."

"Oh, listen. . ." Chris scrambles up and slots a DVD into the TV. "I was going to show you this. . . I mean, I wanted Jas to see it too, but I'll send him a copy. It's your last gig."

He presses *play*; the screen flickers into life with Chris's film of Jas, Maya and Caitlin, performing in a dimly lit upstairs room in a pub in the backstreets of Camden. It's the gig Jas invited him to, Ash realizes; the one he didn't go to because he was with Zara. The camera tracks over Caitlin and Maya to Jas: his body curled over his guitar, his floppy hair hiding his face.

Ash goes back to the pointless search on his phone.

Deportation centre.

Website not found.

Website not found.

Website not found.

He swears.

"S'matter?" Chris asks.

"Trying to find out about deportation centres."

"Why?" Priya asks.

Chris sits up. "Jesus, Ash. You're not looking that up on your *phone?*"

He shrugs. "Yeah. Why not? You think they're watching?"

"God knows what they're watching. You don't want to get on some list," Chris says.

He thinks of the cameras on the bus with a sudden plunge of fear, and deletes the search with shaking fingers.

It's all taking him *nowhere* anyway.

CHAPTER EIGHTEEN

She wishes she could sleep more: you can lose time and place in the oblivion of sleep. But she keeps waking early. This morning she and Katya are almost alone in the canteen. Early birds. *Early birds in elm and larch, in beech and ash...* It sounds like a line from a bad poem. If she wrote it, there would be no birds, nor trees, nor air in it: no *delight,* no *winging on and on,* no *escaping,* no *flying:* only cold rooms, locked doors, the eyes in the ceiling, fear...

She digs in her pocket for the sheet of paper she tore from Katya's notebook, and unfolds it on the greasy tabletop. It's ragged-edged and grubby now; she has crossed off S S M T W T F. Only S S M T remain: then it will be Wednesday again, and she will be out of here, on her way to other fields, other birds, other skies; to a place where there's no fence across everything.

It's only morning. It's too early to cross off Saturday. She folds the paper, tucks it away again, and picks up her plastic cup of tea. There's a scum of dust on the surface. She blows at it, watching the patterns shiver and break. A long time ago, she leaned with Sophie on the parapet of Westminster Bridge, staring down at the Thames while a huge sun slid down the sky behind Parliament, and Sophie said, *Do you ever think about water? How it's all continuous. . . It all joins up—*

"Hey!" Big fingers stab impatiently on the table in front of her. She shakes herself out of the memory and looks up at the crop-haired officer with the broken veins in his cheeks.

"You're wanted," he tells her.

"Me?"

"Yes. You. Come on."

She throws a puzzled, frightened glance back at Katya, as she follows him out of the canteen and along the corridor to the office. She halts on the threshold, and takes an involuntary step back, but there's no escape.

They're here again: the sharp woman and the stony-eyed man, sitting side by side at the table, a file of papers in front of them. An empty chair is waiting for her. The woman gestures to it, and she sits, knotting her hands in her lap. Fear is a slow twist in her stomach. The light is still flickering and humming, the tap's dripping again. The man unwraps a piece of chewing gum; the air smells of mint.

"I told you everything," she says.

"We just want to check some of your answers." The woman flips the file open, and it all starts again: the same questions and others: questions about Mum, and where she is now, and where they were living and who with; questions about Sophie and how they met and how often and where; questions about Sophie's family. . .

"I told you," she says. "I only knew Sophie. I never met her family."

"Not even when Sophie took you to the house?"

"No."

"And you've had no contact with them since she died?"

"None."

"You've never tried to make contact? To tell them about this?"

"Never."

Finally, the woman glances at the man, gives an almost imperceptible shrug, closes the file, and slips it into her briefcase.

"You can go," she says, and Zara escapes into the corridor. Today is Saturday: there's Sunday, Monday, Tuesday to go before she's out of here. Hours and hours for them to come back again, for them to ask a question that trips her into giving Ash away.

One hand on the wall to steady herself, she makes her way back to the canteen. It's crowded now. The talking is louder than usual: sharper, more agitated. The air feels made of invisible threads pulled tight enough to snap.

She feels tight enough to snap.

She hurries out into the yard, stands with her hands against the fence, blinking into the broken daylight. Will they come again? Three days. All she has to do is to survive three days; to keep saying no: no one, nowhere, never. Never Ash, never—

"*Zara!*"

She spins round. Katya is running towards her across the yard.

"Zara! The list. . . For Calais. They've put it up. You. . ."

"What?"

"You're not on it."

Thick white clouds race across the pale blue sky. Birds wheel and dive.

"But. . . No. . ." She pushes past Katya, and runs inside, along the corridor, to the noticeboard. Behind the shatter-proof plastic, the printed list is pinned crooked. There's the date, next Wednesday, and a list of fifteen names. Katya's is on it. Hers isn't.

"Tell them. Tell them they've left you off." Katya's followed her in from the yard and is standing at her shoulder. "Go on. It's a mistake, Zara. It's bound to be."

Is it? She keeps staring at the paper. The letters seem to blur and slide and rearrange themselves. Nowhere. Never—

"Zara!" Katya nudges her. There's a frightened flicker in her eyes. "Go and tell them. I don't want to go without you."

Zara nods, knocks at the office door and pushes it open.

The fair-haired woman who searched Zara on her first night is sitting at the computer with a cup of coffee cradled in her hands. The crop-haired officer is leaning on the back of her chair, peering over her shoulder at the screen. They're laughing.

Zara thuds her fist against the open door again. The woman swivels the chair round to face her.

"What is it?"

"The list. For Calais."

"What about it?"

"I'm not on it."

"No." The woman turns back to the computer. She drains her coffee. The man picks up both empty cups and carries them to the sink in the corner. The woman taps her nails on the desk while she stares at something on the screen.

"But I should be!"

The woman sighs and looks up. "Are you still here? You're not on the list, Zara. End of. OK?"

"No! It's not OK!"

The woman swings her chair round again. The man turns from the sink, his hands dripping. He takes a couple of steps towards Zara. She doesn't move.

"I want to know why," she says.

"Orders." The woman shrugs.

"Orders?"

"From London. We've been told to keep you here."

"But . . . who by? Those police? The ones who came to visit? But—"

"Zara." The man steps closer to her. His broken-veined cheeks are raw. There's a claggy smell of coffee on his breath. "Stop asking questions, and go to your room."

"No."

"Are you asking for a stretch in Willow?"

"No, but. . . Please. I've told them everything I know. I've got nothing else to tell them." There's a phone on the desk.

She snatches it up and thrusts it towards him. "Call them. *Please*. Tell them—"

"That's centre property, Zara. Put it down."

"Tell them—"

"Put it down!" and he wrenches the phone out of her hand, and for half a breath she thinks it's OK, he's going to call them: she'll be going; but he drops the phone onto the desk, the woman leaps up from her chair and together they grab her arms and hold her tight.

"You were told," the woman says through gritted teeth. "You were told, Zara."

They drag her out of the room, along corridors she doesn't know, and stop at a locked door marked Willow. The woman punches a code into the keypad by the door and swings it open. They haul her into a short corridor with numbered doors to left and right and push her into room number five. It's a bit like the room she shares with Katya: plain and cold; a cubicle with a loo and shower in one corner, the eye of the camera in the ceiling. But there's only one bed, and no curtain at the narrow window, no sheets or pillowcases. The woman tells her to sit. She drops onto the bed. It's bolted to the floor.

"This is the isolation unit, Zara. We put people here when their behaviour is a threat to themselves or other people or centre property."

"I'm not—"

"Zara? It'd be a good plan not to argue."

She falls silent. The woman nods. She leaves the room, closing and locking the door behind her. Zara curls on the stained mattress, her back to the room, hiding from the camera in the ceiling. There are greasy marks on the wall, as if other people have pressed their heads and hands against it. It's cold. She reaches for poetry, but all she can hear is *we've had orders to keep you here*. For how long? She thinks about Grace, here for more than a year. No. No: she can't, not a year. Not a year of locked doors and the fenced yard with nowhere to run and the eyes in the ceiling and the silent watchers standing over you in the night and the visitors from London, the questions to which she can only answer nowhere, no one, never.

Nowhere, no one, never. It sounds like her future: going nowhere, seeing no one she loves, never getting out of here.

ASH

Dear Soph,

It's the 8 March. I haven't seen Zara since the 14 February. About 1,900,800 seconds. And when am I going to see her next? There's another deportation to Calais next Wednesday. I could go and try and find her then. Only what if she's not there again? She SHOULD have been on the last one; what if she's not on this one either? And there's no news from Charlie about where she's being held.

I just wish

I just want her to be OK, and she's probably not, is she?

A xx

Calais next Wednesday. It's all he can think of doing. He prints and deletes the letter, crumples the paper into the flowerpot on the windowsill and sets it alight. The thin smoke vanishes into the air. He slams the window shut, sits at his desk, and reads through the essay he's been trying to write all afternoon. He's managed two paragraphs so far. They're rubbish.

He shuts down his laptop and wanders along the corridor to the kitchen. Mum's hauled one of the moving boxes onto the table; she's sorting through battered and faded orange-spined paperbacks. *Tess of the D'Urbervilles* lies on top of an unsteady stack on one of the kitchen chairs. *Zara, Zara, Zara: everywhere and nowhere—*

"Thought it was time I got this done," Mum says.

"Yeah. Need a hand?"

"No. I'm doing this box, then I'm going out."

"Going out?"

"I am allowed, Ash." She hefts another handful of books out of the box, and studies them. "What about you? Isn't it Chris's eighteenth tonight?"

"Don't know if I can be bothered."

"OK." She flips through a couple of volumes, and places them on top of *Tess*. "If you aren't going to the party... You haven't been to Dad's this week."

"I'm not going to Dad's."

He doesn't want to go anywhere. He should stay here and work, except working's not working; he might as well go to Chris's party. He goes back to his room, rereads the paragraphs he's written, dumps them in a file called *philosophy bin,* and heads out to catch the tube at Camden Town.

On the train he remembers Zara on the day he met her, how she almost got off the tube at Camden before they spoke. If she'd stepped out of his life then before she'd even stepped into it, she'd be safe now with Ana and Max, somewhere a long way away...

He's so lost in thinking about her he almost misses his stop. He leaps out of the closing doors at Highgate, rides the lift to the surface, walks the couple of hundred yards to Chris's house. On the doorstep, he's stopped by another memory. He was going to bring Zara to this party, because when Chris invited him he was looking into a different future: the one where the opinion-poll numbers were reliable; the one where *democracy* was reliable.

He takes a long breath of chilly damp air, and steps inside, into a primal chaos of noise and heat. He dumps his coat upstairs and fights his way to the kitchen. Chris, leaning against the windowsill with one arm round Priya, raises a bottle of lager to him across the crowd, and bellows, "Hi, Ash!" He raises his hand in reply and turns away, thinking again of the parallel universe where Zara was here with him, her arm tucked through his; then there's a hand on his shoulder and Lewis's face in his—

"You look like you need a drink, Ash!"

He thinks of the girl in the pub, in tears; of locks and bars and razor-wire topped fences.

"Just piss off, Lewis! What the hell are you doing here, anyway?" He pushes past him into the living room. Coloured lights revolve; music pounds; the air's a compound of sweat, alcohol, perfume, tobacco, dope. He recognizes faces in the strange light. Jas, Caitlin and Maya are squashed on a sofa at the edge of the room. He heads for them, and then Lewis is there again, blocking his way, a solid mass against the changing lights.

"I was *invited*," he says. "Ages ago. And what was that all about? Telling me to piss off?"

"What d'you think, Lewis? That girl."

"What girl?"

"*Jesus.* In the pub? The one you reported?"

"*Her?* For God's sake, Ash. Are you still going on about that? Look, she was illegal. She *deserved* to be reported."

"Just piss off," Ash says again. He shoves past Lewis into the kitchen, grabs a bottle of lager from the table and goes out into the garden, up the slope, out of the spilt light from the windows, into the dark. He leans against a tree.

"Ash?"

Jas, silhouetted against the kitchen window, is climbing towards him. He calls, "Here," and Jas trudges up the garden to join him. He's smoking; his cigarette a faint spark in the darkness.

"You OK, Ash?"

"Yeah." *No.*

"Bloody cold out here."

"I know."

"Are you... I mean... Is this still about Zara?"

He tilts his head back against the damp roughness of the tree. "Yeah."

"God," Jas says. "Listen... Have you tried calling her, or...? I mean..."

"There's no point, Jas. There's nothing..." *Nothing.* He closes his eyes hard.

"Sorry," Jas says helplessly. Ash keeps his eyes closed,

listening to the muffled thud of the party, feeling the seconds slip past. When he opens his eyes again, Jas is still there.

"Coming back in?"

It's too cold to stay out. He follows Jas across the lawn. In the kitchen, a bottle lies on its side on the table; there's a pool of something viscous on the floor. The light gleams green and purple. A boy and a girl by the door are wrapped so tightly round one another that it's hard to see where one body ends and the other begins. He held Zara like that.

He shouts to Jas, "I'm going to go."

He heads upstairs to find his coat, past another entwined couple on the stairs, along the landing. Next to Chris's room, Lewis is standing with one hand on the doorframe, blocking the corridor; the light from the stairs throws his shadow weirdly on the wall, huge and distorted. From beyond him, someone says, "Can you get out of my way, Lewis?" Ash recognizes her voice: it's Caitlin.

Lewis laughs and takes a step towards her. "Oh, come on, Cait..."

"I said, get out of my way!" Caitlin says. "Just let me get past!" and from behind Ash, Jas says, "What the hell's going on?"

Lewis snatches his hand off the wall and spins round, his face shadowed in the angled light. Caitlin dodges past him; Jas slips his arm round her and holds onto her.

"Cait? Are you OK?"

"Fine." She shakes her head furiously.

"What the *hell*, Lewis," Jas says again. His eyes are hollow in the half dark, his voice uneven, and Caitlin puts a steady hand against his chest.

"Jas. Cool it. He's just drunk. And stupid."

"You should go," Ash tells Lewis. "Just get out," and Lewis looks from him to Caitlin to Jas, shrugs and shoves past them down the stairs.

"He's such a nightmare." Caitlin slips her arm through Jas's. "Come on. You look like you need a drink. Ash?"

He shakes his head and leans against the wall while Caitlin leads Jas downstairs.

Nightmare. He thinks of Zara, wherever she is now, whatever's happening to her; finds his coat, and walks home through the dark, still thinking about her.

ZARA

Thinking and fear must have exhausted her in the end because she wakes from sleep to the strangeness of the solitary room, intense dark at the window, and the glimmer of the strip light above the door. She needs to pee. Still half sleeping, she rolls off the bed, crosses to the cubicle and sits on the loo with her hands pressed over her eyes. *No one. Nowhere. Never. No one. . .*

The door opens and footsteps sound on the floor. She jerks her head up. There's an officer standing over her. "Just checking up on you," he says. He stands and watches her till she's finished.

When he's gone, she washes her hands for ages before she crawls back to bed. She lies awake. The dark at the window diminishes to grey, to the overcast skies of another rainy day. The grimy light strengthens and fails again.

As evening falls, they let her out of Willow, but they don't take her back to the room in Larch that she shares with Katya.

They take her to Ash.

It's just like Larch: same cracked lino on the corridor floor, same peeling paint, same eyes in the ceiling, same twin-bedded room with its frayed curtains. The other bed's empty. There's a crack across the bottom of the window, taped up: above the tape, the view is the same. Fence and fields and sky.

She doesn't want to stay in this room. *Ash*. It's a mocking reminder of everything she's lost: the warmth of his bed, of his breath and his hands on her skin.

She slides off the bed, goes to the door and hesitates.

They didn't tell her she had to stay here. Even so, she creeps uneasily along the corridor, aware of the eyes in the ceiling, watching her.

No one stops her. She goes downstairs to the canteen. It's crowded and noisy, and she lingers in the doorway, watching the knots of women talking loudly around the tables. Something's happened: the air is tight with agitation, with fear and anger. She walks to the nearest table.

"What's wrong?"

The answer comes in a rush, a muddle of different voices. "They are sending Grace home. She will be killed! Her brother was killed, and her father. They told her it's safe now – *safe!*"

"When?" she interrupts. "When's she going?"

"Soon. Today? Tomorrow?"

She thinks about being sent home to die. She thinks about being sent home to live with death. It's not bearable. She scans the room.

"Do you know where Katya is?" she asks.

"She went to see Grace."

She leaves the canteen and hurries towards Elm. In the

TV room, the volume's up high. Canned laughter rolls out into the corridor, and then is drowned by a sudden shrill electronic alarm that jolts her heart. It keeps screaming: on and on and on.

She runs, pushing through the door to Elm, hurtling up the stairs, slamming through door after door after door along the dim corridor.

Katya's there, her arms gripped by two white-faced officers: a man and a woman. "What have you done?" the woman's yelling at her. "What the hell have you done?" Katya's face is streaked with tears, and her hands and sleeves are soaked with blood.

"Katya! No!" Zara pushes blindly to Katya's side.

"It's not me," Katya sobs. "It's not me," and Zara grips hold of her stained hands and pushes her sleeves back and sees: it's not her. She's not bleeding. It's just her hands, her hands soaked in blood that's drying on her skin, and she looks wildly past her – into Grace's room – at the sharp-edged shards from the smashed camera lens on the floor, the packed bag, the familiar, worn cotton dress soaked in blood, and Grace's slight and motionless body.

"I helped her," Katya says. "It was what she wanted." Her eyes are horrified.

"It's OK," Zara says. "It's OK."

"Jesus." The woman officer shakes her head. "Let's get her away from here." They drag Katya along the corridor, and Zara darts after them, dodges around them to take Katya's stained hands in hers. She holds onto her, walking backwards, facing Katya, stumbling, saying over, and over again, meaninglessly, "It's OK. It's OK," and then abruptly, they stop, the man's eyes widen, and he mutters, "Shit." Zara glances over her shoulder. There's a group of women hurrying towards them, pushing through the door, halting, blocking the corridor. "What's happened?" someone shouts. "What's happened?"

"Grace is dead," Zara says.

Someone cries out.

"You need to clear the corridor," the male officer says.

No one moves, except a tall woman who steps towards him with her hands on her hips. "How?"

"We don't know. . ." the officer begins.

"She killed herself," Zara says.

"So why have they got Katya? What has she done?"

"She smashed a camera for starters," he says and the tall woman takes another step towards him.

"A camera? A camera? A woman has died because of you. . . Because of this place. And you talk about a broken camera?"

"No," the woman officer interrupts. "That's not. . . Look. Calm down, everyone. Just calm down."

But the women are closing in, shouting, "Let her go! Let her go!"

"All right!" The woman officer takes her hands off Katya and holds them up, palms out: defensive, surrendering. But the man's still holding her, both hands tightly round her arm, and two women are tugging at him, trying to pull him off. He swears and hits out. A woman spins away from him, dropping into a crouch, her hands to her forehead. The woman officer shouts, "Let her go! For God's sake, let her go and get on the bloody radio!" and at last, he lets Katya go. She slumps against Zara.

Someone's grabbed a radio from one of the officers and is smashing it to pieces against the wall. Other women are running, back along the corridor, crying, "Grace is dead! Grace is dead!" Zara tugs at Katya and they run too, through all the doors, down the stairs, past the TV room where canned laughter plays to nobody; the crowd has grown as it moves, gathering women from bedrooms and dayrooms.

The chant changes to "Grace! Grace! Grace! Grace!"

In the canteen someone overturns a trolley – plates crash to the floor. A woman climbs onto a table and smashes at a camera with her shoe – a couple of women crouch over a pile of torn magazines with a cigarette lighter – others wrench a fire extinguisher from the wall and hurl it against the window.

Above the chant – "Grace! Grace!" – the tannoy is repeating, "Roll call. Roll call," and the shrill electronic alarm is still shrieking.

Katya sways on her feet. Zara holds her hand tighter, and pulls her away from the canteen, along the corridor and into the visitors' room. She picks up one of the abandoned chairs and smashes it against the door that leads to the outside. Again. Again. The glass doesn't break. Again—

A shout. Other people have had this idea too: a group of women burst into the room from the corridor. They're dragging an officer; she's crying, and a cut on her head is weeping blood into her dark hair. They haul her across the room and halt alongside the door that Zara couldn't break.

"Open it," someone yells at the officer.

She shakes her head. "I can't. I can't..."

Someone grabs her hair and jerks her head back. Her throat looks very pale, very fragile.

"Open it."

"I can't!"

"Open it! *Open it!*"

Zara lets go of Katya's hand, and shoves past the women holding the officer till she's face-to-face with her, meeting her wide, terrified gaze. She grips her shoulders and leans in close. "For God's sake," she says quietly. "Tell them. They're going to kill you if you don't. It's not worth it."

The woman closes her eyes. "C–X–5–8–2–4," she whispers and one of the women holding her breaks away, and stabs the code into the keypad with shaking fingers.

Along the corridor, the lights blink from red to green. Another woman pushes at the door. It swings open.

Zara catches Katya's hand and runs – through all the doors, through a deserted reception area, out into rainy air. They keep running. Around them, the crowd breaks and scatters. The alarm is still sounding, splitting the night. Floodlights along the road reflect off the wet tarmac, catch the slanting fall of rain and the fugitive shadows of the running women, and—

Blackout. The lights die. The alarm stops. There's a

moment of silence and darkness, shattered in an instant by sirens and headlights and revolving blue lights. Police cars and vans slew to a halt ahead of them, blocking the road. A woman falters, dazed and frightened in a beam of light.

Zara drags Katya off the road, into the dark. They run. Underfoot, the ground changes and changes again: slippery tarmac, sodden grass, heavy clay. There's a sudden smell of cabbages. Light sweeps over them. It picks out the ploughed ruts in the earth. An amplified voice calls "STOP!"

Dodge the light. Run. Keep running. More claggy wet clay. More cabbages. Keep running. Can't go back. The wet clay gives way to long tangled grasses, brambles, twigs, thick stems: a dense hedge. It's the end of the field.

"Now where?" Katya whispers.

"Climb." Behind them the light is playing more slowly now, inching toward them. Closer. Closer. Can't go back. If she goes back they will never let her go. She lets go of Katya's hand and battles through the hedge, feeling for the solid lower branches with her feet, shoving herself through the tangled stems. Twigs crack as loud as gunshots.

She falls headlong into a drift of wet leaves on the far side of the hedge, and struggles onto hands and knees. "Katya?" she whispers.

No answer.

A beam of light plays over her head. She ducks, pressing herself down into the rotting leaves. The light moves on. It gleams off trunks and branches. Trees. A wood. She's in a wood.

She thinks of the view from the window, the fields and

trees. She can't picture this wood, or what's on the other side of it. Katya would know.

But she doesn't know where Katya is. Can't call her. Can't even whisper. The men are too close. They'll hear. She crawls forward, feeling for her, finding only cold wet leaves and brambles.

Stop a moment.

Stop.

She crouches, listening. Her own breathing, the beating of her blood. Rain pattering through the branches. A rustle of movement ahead, somewhere deeper in the trees – Katya? Out in the field, one of the men shouts something about "the wood".

Move.

She flounders out of the drift of leaves and scrambles to her feet, fights her way forward. Ivies snatch at her ankles. Brambles snag her clothes. Twigs break under her feet. And where – where – *where* is Katya? She stops and listens again.

All she can hear is the weather. Rain beats heavily through the branches, onto the fallen leaves on the woodland floor. A wind rushes through the trees, making them toss and crack.

She says, "Katya?" Doesn't dare shout. There's no answer: only the rush and beat of wind and rain. She wipes her face, and keeps going.

Keep going. Can't go back.

But it's easy to get lost in a wood. She might be going back without knowing it. She stops again. The cabbage field's behind her. Oake Leigh is behind and to her left. Isn't it?

A beam of light sweeps past her, glittering in the rain.

They're here.

They're in the wood.

In the wood.

She glances back. The light lances through the trees. She hurries on. Falls over a stem as taut as a tripwire. Up. On. On. The light keeps shifting and searching, the rain drums and hammers, the wind howls. Keep going. Keep going. Ahead the darkness seems less dense. The trees thin. The wood ends.

And now run.

Another field, sodden and rutted as the first. A footpath between hedges – faster here, faster – that tips her out onto a tarmacked road. Candlelight glimmers in the window of a nearby house. Everything else is darkness.

Which way? Impossible to know.

Run.

She passes the faint light of the house. Runs on into the dark. Rain slams into her face, her feet kick up water from the flooded road. She runs through an unlighted village, hesitates at a crossroads, plunges onto a narrow, twisting lane between high banks. Somewhere in the distance, the white beam of a car's headlights sweeps across the darkness. She keeps running, round one sharp bend and then another. The headlights gleam again, closer now, just ahead of her. White light glitters off wet grass at the roadside. She clambers onto the steep bank, slips, scrambles up again. A car slides to a halt on the road. The hedge here is thick and threaded with barbed wire. There's no way through; none. She clings to the sharp branches to stop herself sliding down the bank.

The car door flies open. The driver's a grey-haired woman, wearing a plain raincoat. An ordinary raincoat. Not a uniform—

"Oake Leigh?" she asks.

Zara stares at her.

"Quick," the woman says. "Get *in*. Before they find you."

CHAPTER NINETEEN

He wakes early on Wednesday: he hasn't made a conscious decision about Calais, but he feels jittery with possibility, too edgy to stay in bed. He thinks about it while he dresses. It's doable. It'll mean another argument with Dad. He doesn't care.

He shoves his passport into his backpack and goes along to the kitchen. Mum's sitting at the table in her pyjamas, talking on the phone and frowning over something on her laptop; she glances at him as he comes in and lowers the screen. Work, he guesses, only then she says "OK, Rob. Yes. I know."

He sits down opposite her, fists bunched in his pockets.

"Of course. I'll talk to him. Yes. OK. Bye."

"Is that about me going over there later?" he says. "Because I'm not."

"No." She lays her hands on the laptop cover, and looks up at him. "Ash... Have you seen the news this morning?"

"No," he says, puzzled, and then, suddenly terrified, "Why?"

"There's something. . . You'd better see this." She gets up from her chair, comes round to his side of the table, swings the laptop round to face him and opens it.

For an instant the screen is dark, then it flashes open to a news site. The headline reads MASS BREAKOUT FOLLOWS RIOT WOMEN'S DEPORTATION CENTRE, and beneath it there are eight photos in two rows of four, captioned ESCAPED, and he stares and stares at the third photo from the left in the bottom row, touches her face with fingers that won't stop shaking, wipes his other hand across his own face. . .

"It's Zara. Isn't it?" Mum says.

He nods.

"Jesus, Ash." She pulls the other chair up and sits close to him, her arm round his shoulder, holding him tight. He keeps staring at the screen, trying to make sense of the text under the headline and the pictures: riot, assault, arson; searches with dogs and heat-seeking drones; the army to be drafted in. Dogs and men with guns. *Zara.*

"Ash?" Mum says.

"What?" He refreshes the screen, in case there's a news update, but it flicks back to exactly the same headline, the same photos, the same text.

"It says she's Romanian. Did you know? That she wasn't BB?"

"Yeah. No. Not at first."

"It's why . . . everything, isn't it? The protest. Calais. Dad."

He shrugs.

She says, "God, love. I'm sorry." She stands up and gives

him a hug, and he rereads and rereads the screen while she makes toast and coffee. When she brings it to the table, he flicks on the TV news and stares at footage of dogs and armed police tracking across big open fields.

Mum reaches for the remote control and clicks the TV off, but it doesn't stop the images; he keeps seeing them. Dogs. Armed police. What's going to happen to her? And why did she run; Zara, why did you run? All she had to do was wait; she'd have been safely on a coach to Calais today.

He stumbles up from the table and out of the kitchen. In his room he flips his own laptop open; checks all the news sites, peers at satellite images of the deportation centre where she was being held. He scrolls out from images of the building to study the surrounding landscape of fields, woodland, scattered villages; he imagines her, running. . .

Why, Zara?

He gets up from the desk, paces the room, sits on the bed and hugs the pillow to his face, trying to recapture the smell of her, until Mum knocks on his door. He drops the pillow, calls, "Yeah?" and she comes into the room. Lulu follows her, eyes bright with hope.

Mum sits next to him on the bed, and takes both his hands in hers. She's dressed in work clothes: dark suit, smart shoes. "I have to go to work. It's a court hearing. Sorry, I really can't cancel."

"It's OK," he says.

"And you should be getting to school."

He shakes his head. "I can't. . . I just. . ."

"Ash. *Love*. There's no point sitting waiting for news all day."

He tugs his hands out of hers and wipes them across his face, scrubbing away tears. "I'm not going."

She lets out a long breath. "OK. But listen. *Promise* me you're not going to do anything stupid. This is dangerous stuff."

"I know that!" *Dogs and armed men.* "And no, I'm not going to do anything. How can I? I don't even know where she is."

She nods and gets up, puts her hands on his shoulders and kisses his head. Lulu leaps up from the floor and barks.

"Hell," Mum says. "No! Get down, Lulu. I didn't walk her this morning."

"I'll take her," he says; he grabs Lulu's collar and holds her as Mum lets herself out of the flat. When she's gone he realizes he could have told her about Sophie now.

Tonight.

He'll tell her tonight.

What will have happened to Zara by tonight?

He drives with Lulu to the Heath, walks where he ran with Zara and thinks of her, still running and running; unable to call him because she doesn't have his new number, unable to call Max because her phone isn't working any more. He tries it five times to check; every time there's just a hollow nothing at the end of the line. What would Zara do, hearing that same silence?

Maybe. . .

He yells for Lulu, clips her lead on, hauls her to the car.

This is stupid.

It's *possible*.

He drives to East Finchley, parks outside the house, and rings the doorbell for the upper flat. There's a long wait before the intercom crackles and Elsa asks, "Who's there?"

"Hi. It's Ash. Zara's friend."

"I know. Wait there. I'll come down."

She buzzes the door to let him into the lobby and while he's waiting for her, he picks up the post from the doormat and flicks quickly through it: a couple of letters, a government leaflet and nothing from Zara. Of course there's nothing. The breakout was on Sunday night; today is only Wednesday. There's hardly been time for her to write, and in any case where would she get a pen, paper, money for a stamp?

The inner door swings open. He turns to Elsa with the letters still in his hand.

"You heard the news?" she says.

"Yes."

"You thought she might write here?"

"Yes. . . If she thought Max was still here. But there's nothing." He hands her the post; she takes out the letters and drops the leaflet on a pile of other junk on the hall table.

"Maybe another day?" she says.

"Will you let me know?" He writes his phone number carefully, clearly, on one of the envelopes, helps her up the stairs and settles her in her chair.

Back down in the lobby, he closes her front door, opens

the outer door and pauses. He picks up the government leaflet and shakes it out.

A postcard falls from it and tumbles onto the doormat.

He snatches it up. It's addressed to Max.

There's no message.

On the picture side there are words, in black letters on a white background –

And all shall be well

And all manner of thing shall be well

– and he knows – he knows – he knows where she is. He knows where to find her.

ZARA

The attic room has a rag rug on the wooden floor, a narrow bed with a faded patchwork cotton cover and red cushions. She lies flat, gazing up at the skylight in the roof. It's open – she keeps it open all the time – letting in the garden air, the scents of grass, earth and trees. All she can see through it is the sky: a clean blue, washed fresh by last night's rain, blowsy with clouds that are fluffy white and edged with grey-blue. It might rain again later. Rooks call from the woods behind the chapel.

She'll be moving on soon, they've told her, will be passed from one kind stranger to another, hidden in attics and cellars and sheds, smuggled the length of the country and finally away to safety. It feels safe here; it frightens her even to think about the journey. Don't think. There is the blue square of sky, the brown scents of earth, the calls of the wheeling black birds, the red rug. Only this.

Outside, a car crunches on the gravel and a door slams. Visitors come to the chapel from time to time, in ones and twos. She goes there sometimes at dawn and dusk, when there's no one else around, letting herself remember December, and Ash.

A dog barks in the car park, high-pitched and excited.

"Stop it! Idiot dog."

She jolts off the bed, jams her feet into her trainers, and runs: down the stairs, through the hall, and out into the strong spring air where the wind buffets her face and the sunlight finds a thousand diamonds in the wet grass. She blinks through the dazzle and the glitter.

He's heading down the path towards the chapel.

"Ash!" she shouts.

Lulu barks. Startled rooks take flight, calling, out of the tangled wood. He wheels round.

She runs towards him across the sodden lawn.

ASH

— and he's holding her, shaking and almost in tears; for the last 6,000 and something seconds he's been telling himself that this is stupid, she won't be, can't possibly be here, and now . . . his skin against hers, the taste of her, his hands in her hair.

She pulls back to look at him. A tear spills onto her cheek; he wipes it away with his thumb.

"'Ash. . ." She's half laughing, half crying. She touches his face, running her finger down the curve of his cheek. "Did Max tell you I was here? Did she get the card? Does she know you've come?"

He shakes his head. "She's with your mum. In France. I just guessed you might have written. Went to the flat. Found the card."

"And you recognized it? You knew it was 'Little Gidding'?"

He grins at her. "Yeah." He slides his arms round her, tugs her close, kisses her again, but she shivers and pushes away from him.

"Ash, wait. We should go inside. I shouldn't be out here," and he thinks of her photo, her face, on all those news sites and TV channels. He nods quickly.

They take a couple of paces towards the house – and Lulu explodes into furious barking, strains against her lead, snaps the ring on her collar. She bolts through the grass and hurls herself snapping and growling at a black spaniel. He pelts after her, grabs for her, gets hold of the scruff of her neck and drags her out of the fight; gasps "Sorry, sorry," to the tall woman who's tugging the spaniel away.

"You need to keep your dog under control."

"Sorry. She doesn't usually. . . Come *on,* Lulu." He hauls her away, still growling, turns back toward Zara.

She's not there any more.

ZARA

She hides behind the chapel, leaning against the rough wall, her hands pressed to her mouth. The tangled grass and the leaning gravestones are a green-grey blur; the racing clouds seem to fall towards her.

"Zara!"

Ash is hurrying between the gravestones, with Lulu imprisoned and struggling in his arms. He puts her down at Zara's feet with one hand still locked through her collar, crouches down, and fumbles to reattach her lead.

"God, Zara. I didn't know where you'd gone." He fastens the clip, and looks up at her. "Hey? What's wrong?"

"That woman with the dog. She saw me. I mean . . . she recognized me." She closes her eyes. She can still see it all, in perfect, relentless detail: Lulu bounding wild and joyful into the fight, and the tall woman in the waxed jacket and walking boots hauling and shouting at her dog, and looking around angrily for Lulu's owner and seeing *her* – seeing her, meeting her eyes, *knowing* her.

"What?" Ash tugs at her arm. "Are you sure?"

"Yes! Yes. I know she did. . . God. Is she still there?"

He passes her the lead. "Hold her a moment," and she

wraps the loop tightly round her wrist while he edges along the wall to the corner of the chapel and peers round it. He hurries back to her, making tracks in the long wet grass.

"She's on the bench outside the house. She... She was on her phone."

She swears and leans against the hard cold stone of the wall. Rooks tumble in the blowing sky above the trees, and her mind reels with them, dizzied and scattered. Think. Think. What now?

"I've got to get away, Ash. Now. Before the police get here. And I can't go inside. If she sees me go into the house they'll all be in trouble. Christ. What have I done? What am I going to do?"

He slips his hand into hers. "Come on."

"Come where?"

"With me. In the car."

"But... You can't, Ash. If they find me with you..."

He keeps hold of her hand.

ASH

His fingers knotted between hers, the familiar feeling of her skin against his, the hardness of bone against bone. He's not letting her go, not now, no way.

"You can't," she says again.

"It's the only logical thing to do. You need to get away. You need to make it look like you've got nothing to do with the house."

"Yes, but—"

"I can't think of anything else, Zara. Can you? And she's already seen me with you, anyway."

She shakes her head; comes with him to the car, slides into the passenger seat. Lulu cringes at her feet, ears down, tail quivering guiltily. Bloody dog. She should feel guilty; what the hell has she done?

He starts the engine, rams the car into gear; the tyres crunch over the gravel in the car park and onto the bumpy track. He glances into the rear-view mirror. The woman's still sitting on the bench, staring after them. She's still on her phone. He accelerates, taking the rutted track as fast as possible, swinging out onto the road.

"Ash?"

"What?"

"Do you think she got your registration number?"

"I don't know." But he knows she might have; she had time. He drives as fast as he dares; the road's narrow, twisting, all blind corners. It takes them through the village where they stopped for lunch at Christmas, where the St George's cross still flies in the pub car park, and out again into open country. He carries on driving, taking turns at random: an illogical, he hopes unpredictable, route: over a bridge that crosses the A1, on, and on, eastwards into flat land, intersected with ruler-straight lines of trees.

Illogical won't help if the woman took his registration number. He counts all the ways this car can be spotted and followed: automatic number plate recognition cameras on the road, CCTV in towns. Drones. Police cars. Helicopters. This feels impossible. He slows, stops in the gateway to a field, kills the engine.

Lulu scrabbles at the door and whines. "No," he tells her. "Stop it."

"Ash?" Zara says.

"Hang on. Just need to think a bit." Think. If they know about this car – a sudden realization, a new plunge of fear. If they know about the car, they know about him: he's on the insurance. He thinks of all the ways he leaves a track of his presence: phone, ID card, bank card—

Phone.

He pulls it out of his pocket, unlocks it with shaking fingers, and switches it off, drops it in the well beneath the dashboard. He has no idea what to do next; he has no idea why they've even ended up here. He tilts his head to look at her.

"What?" she says.

"Nothing. Just. . . I don't get it. Why did you run? Why not wait till they took you to Calais?"

"Because they weren't going to take me to Calais. They weren't going to let me go."

"But that doesn't make sense. Why?"

"I'm not sure." She twists her fingers together. "I think it was because I told them about Sophie."

"*Sophie*—?" He checks himself. His mind's a vortex of bewildered questions but there's no time for them now. What matters now is that she ran, and he has to get her safe.

OK.

Think.

Think.

"Zara? The people who were looking after you. . . Who are they?"

"They're a sort of underground. They help people escape from England. People who've failed asylum reviews. People trying to avoid deportation centres." She shivers; he leans forward to switch the heater on.

"So, how does that work? Getting people out?"

"I'm not sure." She shivers again, and holds her hands out to the heat. "There's a network of safe houses. Then either boat to Europe, or over the border."

"Safe houses? D'you know where any of them are?"

"No. Except ... there's a vicar from a church in Lincoln. He visited us yesterday. Godfrey. I don't know the name of his church."

Lincoln. He reaches automatically for his phone, stops himself, leans across her to open the glove compartment and pulls out Mum's battered old UK atlas. A few papers – printouts of Google maps, scribbled directions – slide out of it onto the dog. He ignores them, flips the book open, finds roughly where they are and tries to trace a route from here to Lincoln on only minor roads, but the atlas is useless for this kind of planning. It's fine for working out long fast journeys, for drivers who are *safe* using A roads and motorways, but it doesn't show anything else in enough detail. And it's way out of date; it still shows Scotland as part of the UK.

He tries one route, comes up against the sort of big intersection with a major road that's bound to mean cameras, and tries again, heading further east this time, looping round towns and cities and out into the fens, where the pages are blank white, intersected with the dead straight lines of drainage ditches and roads.

It's so flat, Sophie complained—

He catches his breath.

"Hang on. Where's all that stuff that fell out of the book?" He reaches past her, tugs the papers from under the dog, shuffles through them; stops at the printed-out map of how to get to Kate's house from the A1.

He's got a sense of how this might be possible now.

ZARA

Around them, the weather is closing in, closing down the last scraps of blue, the last glimmers of spring sunlight. The sky darkens to the deeper grey that fringed this morning's clouds; the first raindrops shatter against the windscreen.

My love in my arms again.

But now she wishes him miles away, safe and alone in London. She watches the rain.

"Zara?" He slides the atlas onto her lap. "I've got an idea. Mum's sister lives near here. She'll help, I know she will. Look. . ." and he runs his finger across the page, tracing a route of small roads all the way to his aunt's house, with only one major road to cross. It looks possible, but—

"Ash, if we're stopped. . ."

"Yeah?"

"You'll be in real trouble. Because they'll know you know who I am. I mean, I was thinking you could just say I was hitch-hiking and you picked me up at Little Gidding, but that won't work, will it? Because of Sophie. They know she connects us. They'll know we must have known each other before."

"Yeah," he says.

"You can't do this. Drop me. Lend me some money. I'll catch a bus, and if you're stopped you can say that woman got it wrong. If I'm not with you, they won't be able to prove anything and—" She stops because he's taken her hands and threaded his fingers between hers, binding them, knotting them, tying them together.

"No," he says. "It's not what *you'd* do, is it? If it were the other way round? If it was me running . . . you wouldn't leave me at a bus stop with a couple of quid."

She tightens her hands in his.

"We should get going," he says at last. He kisses her fingers, and lets her go, pulls out onto the wet road and accelerates. Rain streams across the windscreen. The land here is flat and open, unrolling to the blurred grey horizon. It feels unsheltered, *unsheltering*: there's nowhere to hide. Then the rain thickens, blotting out the distance, narrowing everything to the running of water on the flooded road, the sweep and return of the windscreen wipers, the percussion of rain on the roof. She welcomes the storm; it feels like a hiding place.

On, on, almost there now; they slow and stop at the junction with the big road, waiting for a gap in the traffic. A police car flashes past, wheels kicking up spray, siren sounding above the drumming of the rain, blue lights reflecting off the wet tarmac. It sweeps into the distance. They watch it out of sight: Ash's hands white-knuckled on the steering wheel, her breath held. But it's gone; it doesn't return.

In teeming rain, they slip across the main road, skirt a village, and turn onto a lane that angles through flat open fields, crosses a river and brings them to a grassy track between high hedges.

At the end of the track there's a house, sheltered by trees.

Ash pulls to a halt on the gravel drive and, with Lulu leaping around them, they dash through the rain and huddle in the shelter of the porch. He tugs at the bell. It sounds hollowly inside the house. No one answers.

"Middle of the afternoon," he says. "She'll be at work. It's OK. There's a spare key at the back."

He runs to fetch it, and lets them into the hall. It feels deserted. It's cold, and half dark. There's a scattered pile of post on the doormat.

"Are you sure she's here, Ash?"

"I don't know."

He heads along the hall, and she follows him into a dimly lit kitchen where the air is stale and dusty. Along the counter, everything is switched off and unplugged; in the rest of the room, the half-light makes big shadows of a long table, a dresser against one wall, a computer at a corner desk, a floppy sofa facing heavy, bolted shutters. Ash flicks the light switch – it's almost a surprise when it works – and crosses the kitchen to the noticeboard on the wall by the fridge. He swears.

"They're away. Both of them. Her and Dan."

She comes to stand next to him. There's a calendar on the noticeboard; a line is drawn through the last fortnight.

"Looks like they get home tomorrow," Ash says.

"We can't stay here that long. Think about it, Ash. She's

your aunt. How long before they work out this is where we'll be?"

He looks at her doubtfully, the familiar puzzled furrow on his brow. Seconds tick away. At last, he says, slowly, "OK. Right. . . I think you should change."

She glances down at herself; she's wearing a red hoodie that they gave her at Little Gidding. It's very bright.

She nods, and he leads her upstairs, along the landing, and into a bedroom that's flooded with rainy light. The cover on the bed is a patchwork of faded cream and gold silk and above it there's a long photograph of a cathedral at sunrise, its towers wrapped in shadows and mist, lines of gold in the sky.

"Dan took that," he tells her. "He got Soph into taking photos."

He opens the wardrobe, releasing a waft of perfume.

"Help yourself. Kate won't mind. I'll just sort the cars."

He runs downstairs. The front door opens and slams. She stares into the wardrobe. A stranger's clothes; this feels impossible, but Ash is right. She can't go on wearing this top. She chooses the most anonymous outfit she can find – plain black leggings, a long black T-shirt, a grey hooded cardigan – changes, and contemplates herself in the wardrobe mirror. She still looks like herself. She runs her fingers through her hair. In all her ID photos – on the fake card, in the photos they took of her at Oake Leigh – she was wearing it loose. She gathers it in one hand and pulls it back from her face.

It changes her.

She scoops up her abandoned clothes and finds the

bathroom. There's a pair of nail scissors in the mirrored cabinet: short–bladed, sharp enough. She lays the red hoodie over the basin. For a moment, she hesitates, thinking of Ash's hands, playing through her hair, then she picks up the scissors.

They bite with a soft *scrrr*, her cut hair falls onto the spread hoodie. She works fast, hardly looking in the mirror until she's finished, then she studies her reflection. She looks sharper-faced, more dangerous: an angry kid who's hacked her hair off in an act of fury with herself or someone else. Better. She wraps her cut hair in the hoodie and goes downstairs to find Ash.

He's sitting at the cluttered desk by the kitchen window, his face white in the gleam of the computer screen, the printer clattering noisily at his side. He turns to her. His eyes widen. She rubs one hand over her unfamiliar shorn head.

"They're looking for someone with long hair."

"Yeah. Good idea." He gives her a fleeting smile. "It looks good. Come and see this."

She crosses to the computer desk, rests her hands on his shoulders and leans over him to study the screen. It's open to a map of Lincoln. Ash clicks on the mouse, the map disappears, and a thumbnail image opens: a photo of a grey-haired man in wire-rimmed glasses.

"That's him," she says, remembering the man who sat, yesterday, drinking tea in the kitchen at Little Gidding. "Godfrey."

"Thought it must be." Ash clicks all the tabs shut, and

swings the chair round to face her. "We can *do* this, Zara. Dan's car's here, so we leave Mum's and take his. It's about two-and-a-quarter hours. The route's easy. I've got the phone number for the church. We can ring when we get to Lincoln." He scoops up and pockets a set of car keys, tugs the papers out of the printer, tucks them into his mum's battered atlas, and pauses.

"Zara? What you said in the car? About you telling them about Sophie. About them not letting you go because of her. . . I don't understand. . ."

"Nor do I." She swallows against the sudden brackish taste of fear in her mouth, remembering Willow, and the cramped, airless office, the man and woman and their remorseless, circling questions. "I went to the police. I told them about the party. That guy. . ."

"So. . . Wait. Did you do an e-fit? Did they work out who it was?"

She shakes her head. "I didn't need to do an e-fit. I'd *seen* him. On TV. A programme about the election. I showed them. And then. . ." She swallows hard again. "They kept asking me if I'd told anyone else. They asked me if I'd told *you*. They just kept asking. . ."

She bunches her fists against her mouth. He stands up to make room for her at the computer.

"Is it online? Can you show me?"

She hesitates. "I don't know if it's safe, Ash."

"*Show* me."

"Yes. OK. Yes." She drops into the chair, and he stands

behind her as she places her hands on the keyboard, so close that his breath is warm on her bare neck. She moves the cursor to the search box, and types: *How the polls got it wrong*. "He was at a Party celebration. He was drinking champagne. Just like he did at the party."

She presses *enter*, and the results unfurl down the screen. The TV programme is near the top. She clicks it open, scrolls quickly through the footage and pauses it at the boy raising the glass to his lips.

"There," she says, and—

ASH

No.

No. Can't be, she has to have got this wrong; has to; it can't be—

Not—

He—

No—

No no no no no.

But—

His legs won't hold him; he drops to his knees on the floor, hammers his fists against the stone tiles.

No.

No.

No.

Lulu whines and scrabbles at him; Zara says, "Ash... Stop..." She grabs at his wrists. He slumps against the dresser. Lulu creeps onto his lap and he holds her hard, pressing his face against her: Sophie's dog; Sophie's little dog; all that *life*.

"Who is he?" Zara asks.

He raises his face from Lulu's fur and wipes his trembling hands across his mouth; tastes blood on his knuckles. He split his skin, smashing his hands into the floor.

"He. . . he— Fuck. Fuck."

He scrambles up, gropes his way to the sink, retches up bile. He's my friend; he used to come over to the house; Sophie *knew* him. She must have recognized him at the party, have felt safe with him, trusted him, taken the drink from him without suspicion, knowing that he was her brother's friend—

My friend. He closes his eyes against memories of him: laughing in the pub, running up the steps from the tube with his coat flopping around him, whispering nonsense to Lulu, crouched over his guitar on Chris's shaky film—

He wipes his mouth.

Not *Jas*.

He turns to her. "It can't be. He— "

Jas: endlessly asking if he was OK, coming to the flat to find him when his phone was lost to take him to the pub, standing with him in the freezing dark at Chris's party: unfailingly *kind*.

"I am sure," she whispers. "I saw him."

"But he. . . I don't. . . Why?"

"Ash. . ." Her voice tails into nothing; she doesn't say anything else, but she doesn't need to. He doesn't need her to tell him. There's only one reason, isn't there – to slip a hidden drug into a girl's drink? He can only think of one reason—

He throws up again.

Zara rests her hands on his shoulders. When he's finished being sick, she lets him go, opens the cupboard above the sink, finds a glass, fills it with water and hands it to him. It glitters. It's cold.

He drinks it fast. It sends a blinding sharp pain through his head. He folds into a chair, props his elbows on the tabletop and presses his fingertips against his temples. She sits opposite him and slides her hands into his; holding him. Her fingers are icy from the water.

He shudders; he's freezing too; it's very cold in here.

CHAPTER TWENTY

She leans forward and kisses his bruised fingers; he feels the condensed warmth of her breath on his skin. He rests his head against hers. The rain is still hammering against the big window. He doesn't want to move; he feels terribly tired. He'd like to crawl into the spare bed, huddle there with her, but they have to go; he needs to get her to Lincoln, to safety, to the people who'll know how to keep her safe. He raises his head.

"Ash. Who is he?"

It's hard to say his name; he has to force it out. "Jas."

"*Jas?* But. . . Oh, God, Ash. . . He's your *friend.*"

"Was."

She tightens her grip on his fingers. But it's time to go. He frees his hands from hers, and gets up from the table.

"Ash? Wait a moment. I don't understand. He's just a guy in your year at school, isn't he? So why were they so bothered about me not telling anyone about him?"

He gives her a crooked, bitter smile. "Because he's not just a guy in my year. His dad's given loads of cash to the Party."

He crosses to the computer where Jas's face is still frozen on the screen. *My friend.* He shuts the screen down, picks up the atlas and the print-outs, checks his pocket for Dan's car keys.

Map.

Directions.

Car keys.

"What else?" he asks. "For the journey?"

Lulu pushes her nose against his hand. She's going to be hungry before they get to Lincoln. He tugs open the cupboard next to the sink and hauls out a heavy bag of dry cat food. He's hungry too, suddenly; there's nothing in the fridge, and not much in the cupboards but he finds some biscuits and a bar of chocolate and shoves them into a plastic bag with the cat food and the maps.

What else?

They'll need to call the church, but not on his phone. Phone box. Cash. He rummages in the pot on the dresser where Kate keeps loose change; scoops up £5.20 in coins; turns away.

Wait.

He turns back and pulls open the middle drawer. Sophie's ID is still buried under the candle box; he pulls it out, glances from the photo to Zara. They're not at all alike (except he can imagine that in the future that didn't happen, Sophie might have cut her hair spiky and short and dyed it black: trying out a look). He slips the card into his pocket with the car keys.

ZARA

"Zara, come on."

He pulls her to her feet, out of the crazy tangle of her thoughts; pushes the plastic bag into her arms and hurries her along the corridor and out onto the drive where a car that must be Dan's is parked in the rain. "It's open," Ash says. "You two get in. I'll just put the house keys back." She climbs into the car with Lulu. The rain pours in silver streams on the windscreen.

Jas. My friend.

Oh, Ash.

She wraps her arms round herself, and watches for him. He's back quickly, running across the gravel, head down, shoulders hunched against the rain. He climbs into the driver's seat, ruffles Lulu's ears when she leaps up to greet him and pushes her gently back onto the floor. For a moment he sits, staring straight ahead; then he adjusts the mirror and his seat, checks the dashboard controls and starts the engine. His movements are controlled, deliberate. He double checks everything, then looks at her.

"Wait. I think you should sit in the back. Cameras. Facial-recognition software."

She slides out, clambers into the back seat, and remembers: they know his mum's car, they know *him*. "What about you?"

"Oh. Good thought." He twists round. There's a floppy hat among the mess of coats and stuff on the back seat; he points at it. "Pass that." She hands it over, and he jams it on and tugs the brim down. As they pull out into the lane, Lulu squeezes between the front seats, and lies down with her head on Zara's lap, thudding her tail.

The road angles left and right along the field edges, over the narrow river and through the scattered outskirts of a quiet village. *Quiet,* and the land beyond the houses is huge and empty. Maybe this will work. They only have to get to Lincoln. No one's looking for this car.

They leave the village behind. The straight flat road unrolls before them. The moving red dot on the dashboard satnav tracks north and east. She glances up from it to try and catch Ash's eyes in the rear-view mirror, but his face is hidden by the stupid hat. His hands on the wheel are clenched, white; he lifts them one at a time to wipe his palms on his jeans.

On, and further on. The rain sweeps across the land, and away. There's a sharp clarity in the light now, and in the distant line of the horizon, cleanly dividing earth from sky. It feels as if you can see for ever. *Be* seen for ever: in the bare landscape the car feels like a target in a computer game, a travelling dot like the one on the satnav. Sun dazzles like a searchlight off the wet road.

She shades her eyes, and leans forward to watch the

odometer and the dashboard clock: the slow change from mile to mile and minute to minute. As the day falls towards evening Ash pulls into a gravelled car park in front of a low, whitewashed, brick building. A sign saying Jim's Diner and a couple of tattered St George's flags hang above the door. The paint is peeling from the brickwork. It reminds her of the corridors at Oake Leigh.

"Should phone Godfrey," Ash says. "I'll go and see if they've got a payphone. D'you want to take Lulu for a pee?"

They climb out of the car into the raw air. Lulu barks after Ash as he crunches across the gravel and out of sight into the diner, and Zara drags her out of the car park and into the field beyond. A rough track runs alongside a deep flooded drainage ditch, and she walks along it until the diner is hidden from sight behind a dense stand of dark fir trees.

She stops and stares while Lulu snuffles in the long grass. The land is a thin line under the immense sky. The world feels pared back to its bones, to earth, water and air. She's seeing this place, she realizes, for the first and last time. All the things she's about to lose: this land, this sky. This love.

She tugs at Lulu and walks back to the car.

ASH

Pulling out onto the road, he checks the dashboard clock: already 4:46. Later than he thought, and Mum said she'd be home early – how early? He said he wasn't going to school; she'll be expecting him to be there. He wonders about going back into the diner to call her, but Godfrey's expecting them in half an hour. . .

No. Get going; get Zara safe. He can ring Mum afterwards; it'll only be about 35 minutes.

35 minutes.

2,100 seconds.

In 2,100 seconds (more or less) he'll have seen Zara for the last time until— Who knows when?

He's hardly registered this till now; his mind's been too focused on calculating how to get her safely to Lincoln to think about anything else. In 2,100 seconds she'll be going away from him, into a different future. She'll have another life and he won't be in it, she won't be in his.

"Ash? I don't have your new phone number," she says suddenly, as if she's been thinking the same thing: about how there's almost no time left.

"I'll write it down for you. When we get there."

"Better not. Best if I memorize it," and he thinks, of course: Lincoln isn't the end of danger for her; it's one stop in a journey that has an unknown and incalculable number of other dangers still to come.

"Ash? Phone number?"

"Yeah. Sorry." He rattles it out.

"Uh-uh," she says. "Slow down," and he thinks if he could, if he could, he would stretch out every second, every nanosecond, of every minute that they still have together. But time and distance reel past; by the time she's remembered his number securely they're already in the outskirts of the city.

ZARA

She watches the back of his head, his hands on the wheel, his eyes in the mirror. Damp-straw-coloured hair, long fingers, wood-smoke eyes – all the things she will never forget. Never. How long will it be before she sees him again, except in her head?

Already the city is closing around them. The fields have given way to suburban streets: houses, a primary school where the St George's cross hangs limp from the playground flagpole. On the wet pavement, a couple of Neighbourhood Watch volunteers are standing, watching the traffic go past. She ducks her head, hiding her face. When she looks again, the suburbs have given way to the city centre. They pass a terrace of derelict houses, an abandoned warehouse, a boarded-up office block, then they sweep up onto a flyover, and ahead she can see the cathedral, standing high above the city, honey gold in a sudden shaft of evening sun.

The road carries them closer and closer, through the ancient city – a timber-framed house, an old red-brick wall in which no two bricks are the same, low stone buildings – and quickly past the cathedral itself: a wall of tall arched windows, a miracle of glass framed in stone. She twists in her seat to look back, but it's gone now, for ever, hidden behind a screen of trees.

They drive on. Stone cottages. Big red-brick houses in dark leafy gardens. She glances past Ash to the moving dot on the satnav. Almost there now. They are rounding the last corner, passing a parade of shops, a terrace of cottages.

"What the hell?" Ash brakes sharply. There are temporary signs in the road: red and white; yellow and black:

ROAD AHEAD CLOSED

DIVERSION

Just past the signs, a few people are gathered on the pavement, peering over the blue-and-white police tape that barricades the road. On the other side of the tape, half a dozen police cars and army Land Rovers are parked. Blue lights turn.

"It's Godfrey, isn't it?" she says. "Something's happened."

ASH

"I don't know," he says.

"It must be, mustn't it?"

"It might not be. Wait here. Hang onto Lulu," and he slides out of the car, walks along the road and stops by the group of watchers at the police tape. He peers over it at the church in its square of grass and trees, the army and police vehicles parked on the road, the police officers and National Service volunteers. The soldiers look younger than him.

A uniformed policeman walks towards the onlookers.

"Move away, please."

"What's going on?" someone asks.

"Illegals. Come on. Out of here."

There's a sudden burst of movement as two young soldiers drag a white-haired man out of the church and down the path. Ash leans forward, trying to see the old man properly. He catches a brief glimpse of his face as he's hauled towards one of the police vans; only for an instant, but enough to recognize him from his picture on the church website. Godfrey.

The soldiers bundle him into the van.

Ash keeps staring.

"Oi. You were told to move on," the policeman says.

"Sorry. Sorry." He starts to back away.

"No, wait. Hang on. Let's see your ID."

"What?"

The policeman clicks his fingers. "I said, ID," and – blood pounding, heart in free fall – Ash hands over his card.

Run, Zara. Run, he thinks, but he stands frozen and dumb while the policeman studies his face and then his ID card.

"London, huh? What're you doing in Lincoln?"

"Visiting."

"Well, this bit's closed. Go on. Get out." He flicks the card back without scanning it; Ash grabs it from him and stumbles to the car.

Zara's cuddling Lulu, hiding her face against her. "It was him, wasn't it?" she says. "Godfrey."

Too dry-mouthed to speak, he nods, starts the car, does a clumsy three-point turn, and pulls away; zigzagging through a grid of streets, checking the mirror again and again, glancing at the red dot on the satnav; putting as much distance as possible as quickly as possible between them and the church, the police, the army. They head north, through suburbs, out into countryside.

"Ash, stop a minute," she says.

He keeps driving.

"Ash."

"OK. OK." He slows down, parks next to a five-bar gate, switches the engine off.

"Was that because of us?" she asks.

"I don't know."

"It might have been, mightn't it?" and maybe: maybe it was, if the police raided the house at Little Gidding and found something that led them to Lincoln. Or maybe it was a random accident. He shakes his head.

"What now?" she asks.

"I don't know," he says again.

He picks up the atlas from the passenger seat, flips it open and finds Lincoln: at the hub of roads that radiate out in all directions across the flat land. He feels her breath on his neck as she leans on the back of his seat and peers over his shoulder at the map.

"You should get home," she says. "You could drop me back at Little Gidding. It might be OK."

"It might not." He runs his finger from Lincoln to the A1 and south, down to the bottom of the page, towards Little Gidding.

It might be safe.

It might not be.

He flips to the front of the book, to the big map that shows the whole island of Britain, the major roads running like veins: east, west, south, north. . .

It's obvious, isn't it?

"Scotland," he says.

CHAPTER TWENTY-ONE

"Scotland?"

He looks back at her.

"Why not? It's the obvious thing to do. Look. It's easy," and he runs his finger all the way up the A1, through England and over the Scottish border, which, on this out-of-date map, is just a faint dotted line.

"We can't," she says.

"Why not?"

"Because. . . How long's it going to take to get there? What about petrol? How are we supposed to cross the border?"

He checks the mileage chart in the corner of the page. "About 210 miles. Four hours. Ish. We should be OK for petrol, it was a full tank when we set off."

"Four hours?" she says.

"Roughly." He checks the dashboard clock. 5:47. "We could be there by ten."

For a long time she says nothing, then she asks, "What are you going to tell your mum?"

Mum. He checks the clock again: 5:48. She's probably home by now, and he's not sure how long it'll be before she panics, or what she'll do when she does. Call the police? Maybe not, if she suspects he's with Zara, but it'd be good to make sure.

"Tell me if you see a phone box."

He pulls out of the gateway. There's not even a house in sight here, only more open fields. It's eleven minutes before they reach a small village at a crossroads: a few houses, a mini-market, the White Hart Inn. There's no sign of a phone box, but he reckons it's worth trying the pub.

He parks, scrabbles up a handful of loose change, runs inside.

The TV in the bar is showing local news; the scrolling headlines under the pictures announce a major triumph for the security services and with a shock he recognizes the church in Lincoln. He stares at the footage of police and army vans outside the square of grass and trees. The commentary announces four arrests: three illegals and a local man whose name hasn't yet been released. He turns away from the screen, and leans across the bar to call to the barman.

"Hi. Is there a phone I can use, please?"

"In the back."

He goes out of the bar into a corridor filled with cooking smells that make him think he should have brought more food from Kate's, but he wasn't planning beyond Lincoln then. The phone's mounted on a board by the loos, surrounded by tattered taxi cards fixed with rusty drawing pins. The whole thing looks ancient and he picks up the receiver half expecting the line to be dead, but it's not. He feeds coins into the slot, enters the first six digits of Mum's phone number, stops, cuts the call, and dials Charlie's number instead.

"Hi," he says. "It's me."

"Ash?" Charlie says. "You on a payphone? Hang on a mo. I'm going to call you back."

"It's OK. . ." he begins, but Charlie's already rung off. He waits, hand on the receiver, and snatches it up as soon as it rings.

"Right," Charlie says. "Where are you? Don't recognize that code."

"Uh. . . Not sure," and Charlie starts to say something but he carries on quickly, speaking over him, "Charlie. Can you do me a favour? Please? Can you tell Mum . . . uh . . . tell her I'm going to be away for a day. Maybe a bit more. But I'm OK. Tell her –" he glances left and right; the narrow corridor's empty, but he drops his voice anyway. "Tell her not to call the police. I'm OK, but I won't be if she calls them."

"Ash, what the *hell* are you up to?"

"Nothing. There's just something I've got to do, OK?"

"Ash, are you—?"

He puts the phone down. It starts ringing again as he hurries away along the corridor; he can still hear it from the bar.

In the car, Zara's hiding her face against Lulu again. *Bloody dog.* If it hadn't been for her none of this would be

366

happening – and he'd already have said goodbye to Zara *hours* ago, for the last time till God-knows-when.

He slides into the driver's seat with his thoughts spinning, and only one thing clear.

Get to the A1. Drive north.

ZARA

They're driving again, leaving the village behind, heading out into more flat, open country. She leans forward, resting on the back of the empty passenger seat.

"Ash? Was that OK?"

"Fine."

"What did she say? What did you tell her?"

"I left a message." He raises his eyes, meets her gaze in the mirror and smiles briefly. "We need to get moving. It would've taken ages to explain."

"Ash. . ."

"It's fine. Can you pass a biscuit?"

She rummages in the plastic bag, opens the pack of biscuits and passes it to him. Lulu whines and nudges her with her nose, and she feeds her a handful of dry cat food, wipes her palm clean of dog slobber on the seat, and stares out of the window.

The earlier brightness has gone. Thick clouds are gathering again; beneath them, in the west, there's a line of pale yellow light where the sun is setting. The long views of the afternoon fade and close in. It's deep twilight when Ash pulls to a halt.

"Almost at the A1. Better let the dog have a pee."

Zara clips Lulu's lead to her collar, and they walk her along the straggly hedge that borders the road. She's almost luminous in the darkness: Sophie's little ghost dog. Back at the car, Ash says, "Sit in the front. It must be dark enough to be safe now."

She climbs in next to him. Lulu curls up at her feet. They pass through a silent village, circle a roundabout, and swoop down a slip road to join the stream of traffic on the wide A1. It starts to rain. Drops on the windscreen catch the gleam of other cars' head- and tail lights and glitter silver, gold, ruby.

They're moving fast now. A road sign looms up out of the darkness, and the names of places she has never been to shimmer in the beam of the headlights as they sweep past. Leeds, Durham, Newcastle.

"A hundred and twenty miles to Newcastle," she reads.

"Two hours," he says.

"How far from there to Scotland?"

"Not sure. Another hour?"

Three more hours, and it's only half past seven. This seems suddenly possible, even easy. She'll be safely out of England before midnight. Today.

But the lights ahead are slowing. The needle on the speedometer drops from sixty to fifty to forty: slower and slower again. They come to a stop at the back of a long jam, behind a convoy of army trucks. Ash swears, and thuds his fist against the steering wheel.

The car's headlights catch the faces of the soldiers sitting under the sodden canvas roof of the truck immediately ahead of them. Right at the back there's a boy who looks no older than Ash, staring back down the motorway.

Zara pulls the hood of Kate's cardigan over her head, and drops her gaze to her knotted hands. The traffic moves, falters, and judders to another stop. Ash swears again. Lulu scrabbles hopefully at the door. Zara pulls her onto her lap, and scratches her ears. "It's OK," she tells her.

It doesn't feel OK, trapped in the stalled traffic behind a truckload of soldiers.

"Ash? What's going on?"

"No idea."

"Can we get off this road?"

"Not till the next exit."

He leans forward and shifts the image on the satnav screen. The next exit is just a few miles away, but the little red dot that marks their position is motionless, going nowhere. Zara reaches past Lulu to zoom the satnav screen right out, all the way to the Scottish border. It's marked with a red line that's thicker and more solid than the faint dotted line in the atlas.

It's a long way north.

"We won't make it today now, will we?" she says.

"Don't think so."

He shifts his hand from the wheel to wind his fingers through hers, holding onto her. It's as if he's afraid she's going to run, but she can't: where would she run to? After a couple of minutes the truck ahead shifts forward and he lets her go to shove the car into gear. They travel a few yards, and stall again.

Start. Stop. Start. Stop. Time reels past on the dashboard clock. Ten minutes. Twenty. Thirty. After another slow mile they reach a thick barrier of cones, blocking the main road, forcing all the traffic into the exit which she thought would be an escape. There are brilliant lights further along the main carriageway, beyond the cones.

"*God,*" Ash says.

Stark and brutal under the bright lights, the skeleton of a burned-out bus is lying on its side among wrecked cars and scattered lumps of debris. Fire engines and police cars surround the scene, their blue lights reflecting weakly from the wet road. A bus bombing. She's seen them on the news with Mum. She twists in her seat to stare back as they inch up the slip road and onto the bridge over the A1. Ten minutes pass, then twenty, and they're still stuck on the bridge.

"I don't get this," Ash mutters. "Why are we still going so slowly?"

"I don't know." It's impossible to keep sitting, not knowing. She releases her seatbelt, shoves the door open, grabs Lulu's lead, and swings herself out of the car.

"Zara!"

"I'm just going to see!"

She sets off along the narrow concrete pavement, Lulu trotting ahead of her. The harsh glare from the bomb site spills over the road. It illuminates everything, in sharp, remorseless detail: the stalled traffic, the falling rain ... and the checkpoint at the end of the bridge where a group of soldiers are stopping and searching cars.

ASH

Where's she *going*? For God's sake... He opens his door to follow her, but the truck ahead is revving up, starting to move. He slams the door and shoves the car into gear.

Zara. Just come *back*.

This is all sliding out of control, getting *impossible*. It's taken an hour to do twelve miles; a mile every five minutes; at this rate, it'll take ten hours to get to Newcastle. No. This traffic's got to clear soon. Hasn't it?

Come *on*, Zara.

The truck ahead jolts forward and stops again. Why? Why the hell aren't they moving? It doesn't make sense that they're still going so slowly, now they're past the bottleneck at the exit from the A1. And all this stop-start, stop-start will be burning through the petrol; he's not sure any more that there'll be enough in the tank to make it to Scotland.

Zara...

And then she's there, flinging the door open, bundling Lulu into the car. She turns to him. The white glare from the arc lights on the road below bleaches her face.

"What's wrong? Zara, what is it?"

"Soldiers. There's a checkpoint."

They stare at one another. Should she run? Impossible; they're trapped on the bridge, there's nowhere to run to. And it's too late; they're moving again. The army trucks lumber straight through the checkpoint. They're next. A soldier signals him to pull to a halt.

He does as he's told. What else can he do?

"Ash!" she says.

He doesn't answer; he's got no idea what to say, and the soldier's rapping on the window, gesturing him to open it. Lulu barks. He jams his thumb on the switch, the window slides open, Lulu scrambles across his lap and sticks her head out, yapping and growling. "Sorry," he says. "Sorry. Shut up, dog!"

"Jack Russell cross, yeah?" the soldier says, and Ash looks at him properly; he's about the same age as him, maybe even younger; a National Service volunteer. He's scratching Lulu between the ears. "My mum's got one a bit like this. Lovely dog. What's his name?"

"Um. . . Her. Lulu."

The soldier grins. "Sweet. . . All right, Lulu? Oh. . . Can you open the boot, by the way? Search."

"Sure." He doesn't know where the control for the boot is; he fumbles round the dashboard and under the steering wheel, apologizing again, "Sorry. It's my aunt's car. . . I don't know. . ." but the soldier's busy, ruffling Lulu's ears, blowing in her nose, letting her lick his face, telling her what a beautiful dog she is—

"Got it. Sorry." He swings the boot open.

"No worries." The soldier gives Lulu a last pat and goes round to the back of the car. Ash looks at Zara. The glare from the arc lights makes dark hollows of her eyes.

"It's OK," he whispers.

"No, it's not. What if—?" She shuts up, quickly, as the soldier comes back to the window. "Nice camping gear you got there," he says. "Bye-bye, Lulu." He scratches her head again, and waves them on, through the checkpoint, off the bridge.

"God." Zara tugs Lulu onto her lap and clutches her arms round her.

"It's OK," he says again.

He's not sure it is. In less than a minute, they've caught up with all the traffic that's been diverted off the A1 and they're stuck in another dense, slow-moving queue: red tail lights ahead, bright white headlights behind, solid blackout darkness on either side of the road.

He's got no idea where they are, no idea where they're going. This is all wrong. It's the A1 they want: the obvious route; the clean line north; the shortest distance between two points where the points are England and Scotland, danger and safety – but all the overhead signs are flashing: A1 CLOSED. He needs to stop and rethink this. Find another way.

If there is another way.

There *has* to be another way.

A turning looms up out of the dark. He swings into it, up a steep curve, takes a random left turn that brings them into a small town. The street lights and house lights are on, and at the far end of the main street there's a supermarket with a petrol station that's still open. He slows and pulls into the car park.

"What are we doing?" she asks. He stops in a parking space and flicks on the overhead light.

"Got to get petrol. Don't think we'll have enough to get us there. Not if we can't go on the A1."

"Have you got enough money?"

He shakes his head. "I've got my bank card."

"Ash! You can't! What if they've got a trace on it? And they check the CCTV at the petrol station? Then they'll know we're in this car, not your mum's."

He swears, and traces the arc of the steering wheel with his finger. "OK, then. . . I'll get cash from the supermarket here, and we'll stop for petrol somewhere else."

"But. . ."

"We can't *walk* to bloody Scotland, Zara!" He checks himself. "Sorry," he says, "Sorry," and he leans over to pull her into his arms. He rests his head against hers and closes his eyes. God, he's tired. He feels as if he's been driving for ever. The thought of the journey ahead exhausts him; he'd like to stop, lie down, sleep.

Can't stop. He kisses her, climbs out of the car and jogs across the car park to the supermarket.

There's a service till outside the entrance. It's out of order.

He goes into the shop, blinking at the flickering fluorescent light and staring, suddenly starving, at the rows of tins and packets; they finished Kate's biscuits a long time ago. He grabs rolls, cheese slices, chocolate, uses the last of Kate's change to buy a couple of polystyrene cups of coffee from a machine and carries everything to the till.

"Can I have cash back, please? Fifty pounds?"

He slots his card into the reader and enters his PIN, tensed for alarms, the shutters rattling shut over the windows and doors, police sirens on the road.

Nothing.

He takes his card.

The woman hands him two grubby twenties and a ten; he stuffs them in his pocket, slings the bag of shopping over his wrist, picks up the coffees. As soon as he's through the door, he bolts, pelting for the safety of the car, scalding coffee slopping over his hands.

ZARA

He's *running*. She leans over to open his door for him, and he flings himself into his seat, thrusts a plastic bag and a couple of soaking polystyrene cups at her, starts the car and drives.

"Ash? What happened?"

"Nothing."

But he's driving fast, his eyes flicking between the road ahead and the rear-view mirror. They turn off the main road, and keep turning, turning, turning. At last, he parks alongside the stone wall of a churchyard in an unlit village.

"Nothing?" she says. "So what was all that for?"

"Just in case. Can I have the coffee?"

She passes him one of the cups, and takes a sip from the other.

"Yuk."

"I'll have it, if you don't want it. I need the caffeine."

"Are you sure you're OK? To keep driving?"

He nods and gives her a pale smile, picks up the atlas and switches on the overhead light to study it, tracing a route with his finger. She pulls the hood over her head again; she feels very aware of the light on her face, of how the car is a point of light in the dark village.

"Ash? What're we going to do if there's another checkpoint?"

He shifts in his seat, digs into his pocket, and passes her a rectangle of slim plastic. An ID card. She flips it over, and Sophie's face stares up at her: unusually unsmiling, her blue eyes serious, her fair hair tied back in a ponytail.

"It was at Kate's," he says. "Soph lost it there, ages ago. I thought. . . You know. Better than nothing."

"Better than *nothing*? Sophie's card? Ash, I don't look anything like her!"

"It's dark."

"Won't stop them scanning it."

"Sometimes they don't."

"And sometimes they do. And if they do, they'll see her records, won't they? They'll know she's. . . They'll see she's dead, Ash. And then. . ." She drops the card into the well between the seats. "It's not going to help. It's a crazy idea."

"OK," he says.

"Really crazy."

"Yeah. OK. Fine. We'll turn round or . . . whatever."

He slams the atlas shut, flicks off the light and drops the empty coffee cup to the floor. She rests her head back against her seat as they drive through the silent village and out into the unseen country beyond.

On.

On.

Her eyes are prickly with tiredness now; they keep falling shut against the sweep and play of the headlights along the

379

road and the flick-flick-flick of the broken white lines. Her thoughts waver and slip away from her. She jerks her eyes open and rubs them.

"Sleep, if you like," Ash says, and she shakes her head, opens her window, breathes deep lungfuls of chill wet air, and breaks off some chocolate. She takes a piece for herself, and feeds him the other, feeling the soft warmth of his mouth on her fingers. She leans forward to look at the satnav. The red dot is moving steadily up the screen: she traces the road north, around York, and further north again.

They fall silent. The lights flicker and gleam into the darkness. It's cold with the window open but she'll fall asleep if she shuts it, and she thinks Ash might too; he looks drained with tiredness. She twists round, tugs the long coat off the back seat, tucks it round herself and pulls the hood of Kate's cardigan over her head. Her eyes fall shut. She forces them open and watches the road. They close again, and she lets them rest for a moment, for a moment, a moment...

"Shit!" Ash brakes hard and she wakes. The lights scintillate off a reflective red-and-white sign at the side of the road.

CHECKPOINT.

"Stay asleep," he says, "*Stay asleep!*"

CHAPTER TWENTY-TWO

"Ash. . ."

"Just do it, Zara!" His voice is a harsh, frightened whisper, and she flops her head to one side: pretending sleep, every nerve wide awake with fear.

Lulu barks as Ash slides his window down. There's a hiss of rain and a rush of cold air on the skin around her ears and neck as if the big floppy hood of Kate's cardigan has fallen back, leaving her exposed. *Visible.* But Ash is already saying, "Hi?" It's too late now, to tug the hood back, to hide herself again. She lies still, eyes half closed.

"Sorry?" Ash is saying. "Is there a problem?"

"Routine check. There's a night-time travel restriction in place across the county. Can I see your ID, please?"

There's a pause, and she imagines Ash, emptying his pocket, finding his card and handing it through the window to the policeman or soldier, whoever he is.

"That's fine. Thanks. And hers, please?"

This is it, then. Now she'll be asked to stir, to wake, to hand over the ID she hasn't got. She can pretend to search her pockets, pretend she's lost it: *Sorry... Sorry... Maybe it fell out at the supermarket.* It might work. It might.

"Your sister?" the man says, and she is suddenly dizzy with terror, because she knows what Ash has done, knows that he's picked up Sophie's card from the well between the seats and handed it out through the window to the policeman, soldier, whoever he is. There's nothing she can do. It's too late to stop this now. All she can do is lie still and listen above the frightened beating of blood in her ears.

"Yeah," Ash says. "She's been at an all-nighter. She's completely bloody trashed."

Through her half-closed eyes, she watches a beam of torchlight travelling across her lap, up her body. It's as if she can feel it burning on the side of her face. Her *face:* all over the news bulletins, and her *hair*, that never, never, never could be Sophie's.

The man laughs. "Where was it, this party?"

"Cambridge," Ash says. "She's got a mate at uni there."

"Cambridge? And where are you headed now?"

"Durham. She wants to look round the uni. Not that she's going to get any bloody A levels at this rate."

Through half-closed eyes she sees in the wing mirror the headlights of another car, slowing and coming to a stop behind them.

"Durham? Why this road, not the A1?"

"Because... Like I said, she got totally wasted last night.

We couldn't set off till late and she's been puking all the way and it's not so easy to stop on the A1."

"Makes sense. Nice of you, giving a lift to your kid sister."

"Yeah, right," Ash says. "I'm not going to be doing it again."

The man gives another laugh. There's a pause. Ash's window hums shut, muting the sound of the rain, cutting off the rush of cold air. The engine rumbles into life, the car stirs beneath her, and moves forward, with a little jolt at first, then smoother, faster, faster. She opens her eyes and turns her head. The hood's still in place. Ash's shadowed face is clenched tight.

"Jesus, Ash."

He doesn't answer. He keeps driving, his hands tensed on the wheel, and swerves into a road that looms up on the right: they pass through a sleeping village, through countryside wrapped in darkness, and then steeply uphill. The headlights search out high hedges and trees whose branches meet and interlace across the narrow road. They keep climbing until, at last, Ash pulls onto a grassy track. He kills the engine and the lights, folds his arms across the top of the steering wheel and rests his head on them. He's shaking. She's shaking.

"Jesus, Ash," she says again. "*Sophie's* card?"

He says, flatly, "Was too late to do anything else. And he hadn't scanned mine. I reckoned he wouldn't scan yours either. Sophie's. Whatever."

He sounds bleak, hollowed out. She lays her head against his shoulder. "Ash. You need a break."

"Yeah. I think we have to stop anyway. Did you hear what

he said? About night-time restrictions on driving?" He sits up, flops back in his seat and stares into the thick darkness along the track. "I don't know what to do now. Dark should be safer. . . I mean, there's less chance of you being recognized. But it's no good if there are going to be checkpoints everywhere. Because you're right. Sooner or later someone'll scan her card. . ."

"Ash. Stop. Think about it tomorrow. Let's just rest now, yeah?"

She leans past him to pull the lever for the boot, and switches the headlights on.

"Zara?"

"Wait there."

Think about it tomorrow, she told Ash, but she's thinking about it now. She ponders the impossible choices as she feels her way round to the boot. Torch, tent, sleeping bags. She pockets the torch and bundles the rest in her arms and walks through the beam of the headlights, along the track, and into the trees. Last autumn's leaves are thick underfoot. Soft rain falls through the branches. She stops at the first flat clear space in the wood and slides the tent out of its bag.

Use major or minor roads? Travel by day or night? Risk cameras or checkpoints? They don't have enough information to know what's safe.

She snaps the tent poles together, threads them through the clips, pegs the tent to the soft ground, and walks back to the car. Ash is resting his head on his arms again, cuddling Lulu on his lap. She slides into her seat.

"Ash? I know what to do. We need to find out what time the driving restrictions start. Because maybe they don't start as soon as it's dark. Maybe there'll be a couple of hours when it'll be OK to drive at night."

He sits up, reaches for his phone, swears and drops it back in the well between the seats.

"It's fine," she says. "We just have to find someone to ask. Tomorrow, though. Come on."

She douses the headlights. They walk hand in hand, in the swinging circle of torchlight, to the tent. Safely inside, they cuddle together on one sleeping bag and cover themselves with the other. Lulu curls up at their feet. Rain falls through the branches. She holds him.

They sleep.

Voices on the track wake her. The rain has stopped, and a bright, late morning light filters through the tent roof. Lulu barks at the tent flap, and Ash opens his eyes and jolts upright. She holds a finger to her lips and points towards the track.

"Hello?" someone calls.

Ash mouths, "Wait here," grabs Lulu's lead, and clambers out of the tent. Zara crawls across the floor, and peers through the flap as he climbs through the trees to the track. A man and woman with walking poles and rucksacks are standing, looking at the tent.

"You're not allowed to camp here," the man says.

"Sorry," Ash says. "Didn't know."

"Well, you do now. You better move."

"Sure. Sorry."

He drags Lulu back to the tent, ducks inside, whispers, "Stay here," bundles up the sleeping bags, and crawls out again. She hides and watches. The man and woman are still standing on the path, sharing a bottle of water and a bar of chocolate. Further up the track, a bigger group of walkers are heading down the hill. She wonders how many people have walked past while they were sleeping, and noticed the tent and the car that shouldn't be here.

Slow minutes pass before Ash returns. He crouches next to her and presses his mouth against her ear.

"There are people everywhere. Take Lulu down into the wood. I'll try and hide you."

He screens her from the walkers as she crawls out. She's on her feet straight away, running, Lulu bounding next to her: away from the track, further into the trees, leaping fallen branches, slithering on slick leaves. She runs a long way downhill before she stops.

She hunkers down behind a thick growth of holly, and peers through a chink in the leaves. Ash wrestles the tent down, grapples it into a messy bundle in his arms, and lugs it up to the track and out of sight. The ramblers are still keeping watch.

Did they see her, enough to know her?

Did they?

It's possible; the trees are sparse, not yet in leaf. There was a clear view from the tent to the track. *From the track to the tent.* She crouches lower behind the holly, one hand on Lulu's collar, the other on the damp ground to steady herself, and waits. At last, the ramblers walk on, slowly, with frequent backward glances. Zara stands up, shifts so that she can see the car, and drops down again, holding onto Lulu, willing her not to bark.

Ash is talking to a man in a navy waterproof jacket with scarlet lettering on the chest.

She curls behind the thickest part of the bush, on hands and knees on the damp ground. She's kneeling on a holly leaf. She doesn't move. She waits, shivering, clasping Lulu in her arms.

The car door slams.

She crawls across the spiky ground to the edge of the bush and takes a cautious look uphill. The man's gone. She takes in a long breath, and dashes up through the woods, dodges round the car, shoves Lulu onto the floor and flings herself in after her.

She risks a quick glance along the track. The man in the navy jacket has gone; the other man and woman have stopped higher up the track, and are looking back again. She shrinks down in her seat as Ash reverses out onto the road and pulls away, accelerating up the steep hill between the trees.

"What did he want? That man?"

"I was just asking him about the driving restrictions. And it's fine. They don't start till ten. So we've got a couple of hours of darkness when it's safe. We'll go then."

They turn onto a main road, and immediately off it again, meander across high moorland, and park in the gateway to a field on a narrow lane that feels like it's going nowhere. Clouds chase across the washed sky, making shadows that swoop across the grass. The brightness quickens, dies and quickens again. She opens the window; the air is cold and clean. It is a perfect, English spring day. The last English day. With luck, the last English day.

She leans back in her seat and tilts her head to look at Ash. "So we're just waiting now?"

"Yeah."

The sky reels above them. They walk Lulu, make a picnic of yesterday's stale rolls, and climb into the back of the car. They lie together on the seat, her face close enough to his to feel the brush of his breath against her skin, to see every shade of grey-blue in his eyes. He holds her. They don't speak. At evening they get out, and lean on the gate, watching the sun fall huge and red in the west.

"Time to go," he says.

They drive towards the sunset. The horizon is washed with colour, from deep blue to rose. The light fades as the road carries them down from the moors, through a small stone built town where they stop for petrol, and on to the A1. There's no checkpoint at the junction; they slip easily onto the big road, into the light stream of traffic that carries them smoothly and quickly towards the north.

ASH

The road ahead of them is flat, dead straight, almost empty; it's tempting to speed, to burn through the remaining miles, but to break the limit now would be beyond stupid. He makes himself stick at a steady 60 mph. A mile a minute: he measures the diminishing distance by the clock.

They sweep past places he's never been. Catterick. Darlington. Durham.

A blue sign gleams out of the darkness: Newcastle, Berwick, THE BORDER.

"Not far." He reaches for her hand.

"How're we going to cross, though?" she asks.

He's been thinking about this. Most of the border crossings are on major roads where there'll be passport and customs checks, but. . . "Have a look at the map. Near Coldstream and Kelso. There are some little roads there that cross the border. If anywhere's not going to have crossing controls, it's there."

She reaches up to switch the overhead light on. He blinks and focuses on the road. It's very quiet now, nothing in sight except a few tail lights a long way ahead of them, a couple of headlights a long way back in the mirror. He tenses at the siren and flashing lights of a police car, but it's on the other carriageway, heading into the distance, gone.

"Ash?" Zara's looking at the satnav; he flicks it a quick glance, takes in the thick red line across the screen. She's studying the border.

"Yeah?"

"Those little roads. . . They're not there any more."

"What?"

"They're not. Look." She poises her finger against the screen, but it's impossible to look properly while he's driving. He *needs* to look. He indicates, pulls onto the hard shoulder, flicks the hazard lights on, compares the map in the atlas with the one on the screen. She's right. In Mum's atlas there's a grid of small roads between Coldstream and Kelso that cross the national border. In Mum's useless, stupid, out-of-date atlas; on the satnav map they're just – gone. Closed, he guesses: to stop people doing exactly what they're trying to do.

"What about this?" She traces her finger up the line of another road that diverges from the A1 beyond Newcastle, heads north-west into open countryside and merges with the A68 before it crosses the border.

"There'll be a checkpoint."

"I don't mean drive over. Look. There are some little roads quite close to the border. We could drive as far as we can, and then walk."

He's not sure, at all; there are too many things he doesn't know to be sure if it's going to be possible. But he can't think of anything better. He flips off the overhead light and sets off again.

Zara's tapping at the satnav screen. "60 miles to the border. How many seconds?"

"About 3,600." He stares ahead at the wide, dark road and scattered tail lights, flicks a glance in the rear-view mirror at the glaring headlights of a big car coming up fast in the outside lane.

"60 miles," she says. 'There are running races longer than that.'

He gives her a quick smile. "Let's keep driving for now, yeah?" He checks the mirror again; the big car that was coming up fast behind them has slowed and tucked into the inside lane. They pass more signs to unknown places: Chester-le-Street. Washington. Gateshead, and a sign to The Angel of the North; a brief glimpse of huge rectangular wings. . .

"Ash? Did you see it?" She's twisting in her seat to look back. He peers in the mirror but the statue's already out of sight; all he can see is the road and the strong headlights of the big car behind. They swing onto the bypass around Newcastle. There are patches of darkness in the city glow: localized blackouts, probably. Three fire engines scream past on the opposite carriageway and he wonders what else is happening; remembers news footage of barricaded streets, soldiers, tanks, burning houses and cars.

"46 miles," Zara says.

46: not far, not far. He speeds up a bit. The white lines flicker past. He catches up with a slow lorry and pulls into the outside lane to overtake it; slips back into the empty inside lane. The car behind with the big headlights does the same. A sign ahead indicates the way to Hadrian's Wall. If that were still the border, they'd be almost there. But they *are* almost there; say, 44 miles now. Maybe this is going to be possible.

This has to be possible.

Another sign looms up in the darkness. This is the junction they need. He slows down, crosses the line of green cats' eyes that mark the slip road, takes the first turning off the roundabout towards Newcastle Airport and The Border. The road feels exactly the same as the A1; white lines and cats' eyes flicker and gleam in the darkness. It's almost empty too, just a couple of cars coming towards them on the opposite carriageway, a couple a long way ahead. He glances into the mirror: one car behind them. He looks again.

Again.

It's the same car.

It's the car that was following them on the A1.

He shakes his head. Stupid: it's not following them, it simply happens to be on the same road, heading for the airport, probably. It's the sort of big, expensive car that a businessman or politician would use; the sort of car Jas's dad drives. No one's following them because no one's looking for this car, unless. . .

Unless the ramblers in the wood this morning saw her, recognized her, reported her. They watched her crawl out of the tent and run through the woods. It's possible. He's known all day that it's possible.

Or – his stomach clenches – perhaps it was *him* they recognized. Perhaps *his* face is all over the news now too. Stupid. He should have thought of that this morning. He should never have talked to the ramblers on the track, or the man in the navy jacket.

He keeps flicking his eyes between the mirror and the road ahead.

"You OK?" Zara says.

"Fine." He takes his left hand off the wheel, winds his fingers through hers, holds onto her tightly for a mile or two, lets go of her to change gear and slow down for the roundabout at the turning to the airport. He carries straight on. The road narrows to a single carriageway, heading nowhere except a handful of villages and the border. He checks the mirror.

The other car's still following.

He's sure of it now. He feels a lurch of fear; the kick in the guts that sometimes wakes him from nightmares of Sophie, falling.

"Ash?" she says.

He swallows, he doesn't want to tell her this, doesn't want it to be happening, but when he checks the mirror the headlights are still there, keeping a steady distance. "That car. It's been following us since before Newcastle."

"Following?" She shifts forward a bit to peer into the wing mirror at the reflection of the strong lights. "It might be coincidence."

"Might be. Hang on."

He speeds up.

So does the other car.

He slows down.

So does the other car.

"The people in the woods," Zara says.

"I guess." He thumps the steering wheel; Lulu cowers and thuds her tail. "It's OK," he tells her, but it's not. They've been found and there's probably a roadblock somewhere ahead, waiting for them, armed police, soldiers with guns; people who are going to check Sophie's ID properly, who will arrest her and him. What'll happen to her? What'll happen to him?

He keeps driving. What else can he do? The car keeps following, and the odometer counts down the distance. They're only 29 miles away from Scotland now, but light years away from any chance of making it; it's going to be like one of those war movies where they shoot the guy on the border wire.

No. No way.

He sets his teeth, steers round a long bend. In the darkness ahead there are tail lights, set high and wide like they belong to something big; a truck, maybe, going more slowly than they are. He accelerates to catch it up. It's more than one truck; it's a whole army convoy, heading for the border, probably.

It doesn't matter where they're heading. It's a chance.

He flicks a quick look at the satnav. Ahead, there are minor roads on either side; if he's going to do this, it's got to be now.

"Hold on," he says.

ZARA

Suddenly, they're speeding, swinging out onto the wrong side of the road. The headlights tilt and skew. Roadside trees flicker like mad ghosts and fade into darkness.

They overtake two of the trucks, slew back into the left-hand lane, and swerve into a turning off the main road.

A horn blares and headlights flash angrily behind them, but they're away; they speed through the darkness along a narrow, stone-walled lane. The headlights sway and dance crazily ahead of them. Another road opens up on the left.

Ash wrenches the car into it, and kills the headlights. In the thin weak beam of the side lights, they hurtle half blind down a shallow hill. Big stone farmhouses loom out of the night and are gone again.

Lulu whines and clambers onto her lap. Zara holds onto her, staring into the wing mirror, tensed for the white glare of strong headlights on their tail, but there's only darkness. The lane dips and swerves and comes to a sudden stop where another road cuts across it, heading left and right.

Ash glances both ways, checks the mirror and swings left again; he flicks the headlights up and accelerates, skidding to a halt at a give-way sign.

They're back at the main road. It's dark, deserted, in both directions. Ash turns south, speeding back the way they've come, checks the mirror again, jams his foot on the brake, and makes another violent turn to the left.

They surge through half-seen country, climb, dip, climb again. At last they reach a narrow road through a dense plantation of fir trees, swing onto a forest track, bump along it for half a mile, and stop. He switches off the engine and the lights and slumps back in his seat, tilting his head to look at her.

"You OK?" he asks.

She takes in a long breath: it feels as if she hasn't breathed since they pulled out to overtake the trucks. "Yeah. You?"

"Think so."

She pushes her door open, and Lulu scrambles off her lap and out of the car. She follows. The ground is soft under her feet. There's intense darkness under the trees, scented with resin and damp earth; all she can hear is Lulu snuffling the ground, and the caress of wind in the treetops.

Ash comes to stand next to her. "Do you think we lost them?"

"Yes."

"Jesus," he says, and she reaches for him, pulling him close. He rests his face against her hair. His breathing is rapid and uneven. His heart thuds. She holds him till he has settled and steadied.

"What now?" she asks. "Do we walk from here?"

"Too far, I think. Let's have a look." He fetches the atlas

and torch from the car and lays the map on the bonnet. They lean over it together, studying it in the circle of yellow light.

Ash sets his finger on the page. "I think this is where we are. Too far to walk. But if we drive to here. . ." He traces a narrow road to a dead end, just south of a red dotted line which, for a few miles, follows the faint grey line of the border.

"That's the Pennine Way." He runs his finger up from the road to the dotted line, and over into Scotland. It looks easy.

"Do you know what the border's like?" she asks.

"No. Do you?"

"No." She stares at the map, overlaying the faint, almost invisible grey line with images from history and TV: barbed wire, watchtowers, minefields, thick steel fences. "Looks like the best chance, though."

They get into the car again, and drive cautiously to the end of the forest track. For a few minutes, they sit with the lights and engine off and the windows open. Still nothing: no beam of searching headlights, no thrum of an engine.

"OK," he says. "Let's go."

She watches the moving dot on the satnav. That's how they must look from the sky: a dot of light travelling through the huge, dark land, following the turns and undulations of the narrow road, skirting lightless villages, passing through an unmanned checkpoint. The road swings north into a river valley and diminishes to a track. The river flows fast in the looming shadow of the hills. The headlights gleam off the tumbling water, pick out the dark shapes of sheep on the moorland and play ahead along the road which ends, suddenly, in a gravelled car park. They drive to the far end. There's a low earthen bank here; the road continues beyond it, but the tarmac has been smashed up, and grass is already beginning to grow over the uneven surface.

They leave the car and cross the gravel to a noticeboard that stands alongside a rubbish bin, picnic tables, and toilets in a small wooden hut. Ash shines the torch on the board. It's a map. From the red triangle marked *you are here* a dotted line cuts diagonally across the hills, labelled New Pennine Way. To the north, the map is scattered with warning notices: MINISTRY OF DEFENCE LAND. KEEP OUT. She puts her finger on the board, on the word LAND. "That's the way, isn't it?"

"Yeah." He closes his hand over hers. "Come on, let's go."

They walk back to the car. She stuffs the last bottle of water and a sleeping bag into the empty food bag, while he removes the satnav from the dashboard, tears a page from the atlas, and shuts and locks the car. The metallic slam of the door and the electronic beep of the locks seem to echo for miles in the stillness, but nothing – no one – stirs. There's only the tumble of water and the dark shapes of the hillsides and the huge sky, scattered with stars and the faint light of a quarter moon.

They take each other's hands and begin to walk. Beyond the earthen bank, the destroyed road is pitted with unexpected ridges and drops, and they walk instead on the rough grass alongside the river.

They don't talk; they are both tense, listening for the sound of army patrols along the valley or on the hills above them. It's very dark, the moon and starlight faint, but they don't dare risk the torch. From time to time, she stumbles and he tightens his grip on her hand to steady her; he stumbles, and she steadies him.

Lulu, off the lead, runs easily ahead: a ghost dog, sniffing out the traces of sheep and soldiers. But after a while, even she tires, and settles to a steady trot at their side.

The road climbs the river valley, past abandoned, crumbling buildings. They look prehistoric, but it's probably only a few years since they were lived in; the atlas marked a named village here. They pass through it, cross the river on an old stone bridge, and follow the road in a big loop to the left, splashing through a stream that flows down from the hills. Ash comes to a halt.

"Wait." He tugs the torn-out page from the atlas and the satnav from his coat pocket. "I think this is where we need to leave the road. Have you got the torch?"

She peers at the screen, glowing in the darkness, the pulsing red dot showing where they are – in the middle of nowhere, on no official road – and shines the torch on the paper map. Beyond the abandoned village, the broken road runs west, on and on through miles of England. It never reaches the border, which lies to their north, somewhere over the bleak hills that rise away from the river.

"Which way?" She lifts the torchlight from the map and sweeps it over the rising slope. Alongside the stream, the ground is set here and there with slabs of stone that seem purposeful: the remains of a walkers' track, perhaps. They follow it up a narrower, steeper-sided valley where the stream leaps and falls in its rocky bed. It feels darker here: the hills on either side loom close. They keep walking, plodding steadily upwards. She loses track of time and distance: there is only sky, hills, the stony grass beneath her feet, Lulu, the fall of water, his hand in hers. Then at last they come to a fork in the track where one branch carries on along the stream while the other veers sharply left and up the steep hillside. Ash checks the satnav again and points uphill.

"That's north."

The upward path peters out, founders to nothing on a sodden slope where water stirs under the wiry grasses. It's hard going; she fights against the steep gradient, the boggy ground, the tough grasses snagging her ankles. It's as if England is holding onto her, tugging her back. They haul one another slowly up and up onto a bare moorland, and keep climbing until there is no further to go.

They have reached the highest point of the hill. The summit is crowned with a stumpy concrete post on a sprawling pile of stones. An old wooden signpost stands next to it, its arms snapped short.

"This is it," he says. He pulls the satnav out again. "Zara, this is it. Look," and she looks, sees how the red dot is almost lost in the thick red line that marks the border; how, just a couple of paces away, lies Scotland.

ASH

"We've done it," he says. "We've done it. . ." and they're running, downhill, over the border. He snags his foot on a clump of grass, falls headlong, pulls her down with him onto the soggy ground, holds her, shaking with laughter and relief. Till now he hasn't dared to believe that they would manage this; the probabilities were so heavily weighted against it.

Zara glances back over her shoulder. "We should go further in."

She's right. He hauls himself to his feet and they walk a few hundred yards downhill to a copse of fir trees. The ground is reasonably dry here; it's a good place to wait out the rest of the night. He drops the plastic bag, tugs out the sleeping bag, lays it down on the pine needles; they wriggle into it together. Lulu curls up at their feet.

He wakes to morning. Sunlight angles through the trees, there's a clear sky above them. He can hear Zara's breathing, birds, a dog barking in the distance—

He jolts upright.

"What is it?" Zara's awake too, struggling to sit up, blinking at the brightness.

"Bloody Lulu. She's run off."

They crawl out of the sleeping bag and duck under the branches, back to the southern edge of the copse. Beyond it, in the clear daylight, the moorland seems vast, endless. Lulu could be anywhere.

"There!" Zara tugs his hand and points. Lulu's trotting along the track at the top of the slope, sniffing the earth and the air.

He bellows her name. She keeps trotting, westward along the path, away from him.

"Lulu!" he yells again, and maybe she turns, maybe she doesn't; he is never sure. All he knows is that in the instant after he shouts there's a noise like a shot, and the dog stumbles, tumbles head over heels, doesn't get up. For a fraction of a second he registers them as two separate events: a shot and Lulu falling – and then they collide in his head and he knows what's happened and he's running, uphill, fighting the slope; his ears full of the echo of the shot, the thunder of his own blood, Zara calling, "Ash, wait!"

He stops and wheels round.

"No! Don't! Stay there... She's in England! I'll come back..." and he's running again, up onto the bare stone path and across the border. He falls onto his knees next to Lulu, laying his hand helplessly on her bloody fur, feeling the failing flutter of her heart. Lulu. *Sophie*. Lulu...

"Stand up! Keep your hands where I can see them!"

He lifts his head, blinking away tears. A tall soldier is walking towards him along the ridge, his rifle raised. There are others following him: just kids, his age, guns pointing at the ground. He catches the eye of a boy who's staring in sick horror at Lulu.

"I said, get up!"

He runs his hand along Lulu's trembling flank and gets shakily to his feet.

"You're under arrest," the soldier says. "This is restricted territory. Ministry of Defence. Didn't you see the signs? What the hell are you doing up here?"

"I..." He makes himself hold the man's eyes: don't look downhill, don't look into Scotland, don't look at the trees. "I was lost."

The soldier lowers his gun slowly. He nods down at Lulu and glances at the sick-looking boy.

"Your dog? Sorry about that. There are wild dogs up here. Savage." He shrugs. "Yeah. Well. Sorry. There's a vet in the village. I'll take you there on the way to the border police."

But it's going to be too late, he knows it is: she's lying still, her filmy eyes half closed; she seems smaller and flatter somehow; she hangs heavy in his arms when he picks her up.

CHAPTER TWENTY-THREE

There's a smear of blood on the screen of his phone. He switched it on at the vet's, to take their number, and at the same time he checked for a call from Zara even though he knew she couldn't have called, and of course she hadn't, but there were 102 messages from Mum, Dad and Charlie. He deleted them unopened, smearing blood on the screen. He couldn't face reading them, and he didn't want the army or the border police reading them either.

There's blood everywhere: his hands, his jeans, his coat. He held Lulu on his lap in the Land Rover and with every mile she felt less and less substantial; he's not sure she was even alive when he laid her on the table in the surgery. There was a look in the vet's eyes. . .

"Here we go." The soldier swings the Land Rover through the gates of an army barracks and pulls up outside a square, brick building. The sign over the door says BORDER POLICE. Inside, Ash hands over his ID card, places his hand on the fingerprint reader in the counter, and empties his pockets, handing over the blood-stained phone, the satnav, the torn page from the atlas, a screwed-up piece of chocolate wrapper.

They lock him up. He lies flat on the bench in the cell, eyes closed, thoughts in chaos. Lulu bleeds in his arms, Zara waits in the trees, Jas cracks a joke and clinks glasses with him in the pub, blue lights reflect from a wet drive, a geodesic roof glitters above a high hall, a tight circle of people gather round Sophie on the marble floor, someone holds onto him so he can't reach her. . . The images spin and return, return, return, till the door slams open.

"Ashley Hammond? This way."

He slides off the bench, is led along a tiled corridor into a square room; sits where he's told, opposite the soldier from the border and a policeman who's holding his ID, flipping it over and over on top of a file.

"You're a long way from home," the policeman says. "What are you doing here?"

Ash blinks. They *know* what he's doing here. He can still see, vividly, in his head, what he saw in the rear-view mirror as they drove away from Little Gidding: the woman who recognized Zara, staring after the car, talking on her phone, taking the number plate that would lead the police straight to him. They *know*.

Don't they?

He looks the policeman squarely in the face.

"Nothing, really."

"So, you've bunked off school and come all the way from London to do *nothing really?*"

He shrugs.

"Only it wasn't nothing, was it?"

His mouth dries. He doesn't answer.

"You were on restricted territory. The border's closed to civilians. So what were you doing there?"

"I don't know. I. . . I wanted to see what it was like."

"*What it was like?*" the policeman echoes. "So, who was doing this bit of sightseeing? Just you? Or was someone with you?"

He doesn't dare trust his voice. He shakes his head. The policeman studies him narrowly and flips open the file, and he holds his breath, because it's coming now, it must be, the accusation: *You're lying, aren't you? You were with . . . uh. . . Catalina Ionescu, you were helping her escape.* It must be coming now. There'll be witness statements in that file, from the woman at Little Gidding, from the ramblers on the Yorkshire moor; stuff he's not going to be able to talk his way out of.

"You. . ." The policeman pauses to check something in the file.

Yes. Here it comes.

"You were arrested at a protest in London last month."

His thoughts slide and tumble again.

"You want to watch out. You'll be getting a reputation as a troublemaker." The policeman slams the file shut and flicks his ID card across the table. Dazed, he closes his hand round it, stands, tucks it into his pocket. They take him back to the front desk, hand over his phone, the satnav, the crumpled map and chocolate paper. The soldier walks him outside; the daylight is brilliant, dizzying.

"Sorry about your dog," the soldier says. "You OK to find your own way to the vet's?"

He nods and stumbles down the shallow steps, along the drive towards the gates.

She didn't report them.

The woman at Little Gidding; she didn't – can't have – or the police would have known.

He closes his eyes for a moment, thinking about all the crazy things they did: avoiding roads, changing cars, overtaking those trucks: all the crazy, *unnecessary* things. He walks out through the gate, turns towards the vet's – and stops dead.

A big, bulky, black four-by-four is parked at the roadside.

ZARA

She hides in the copse, keeping to the shadows deep under the trees, watching between the cross-hatched branches. The light strengthens across the huge, open moorland. The soldiers have spread out along the line of the border: keeping guard. Two of them stand together at the high point where she and Ash crossed. She's close enough to see that they're young – just kids: National Service volunteers. From time to time a laugh reaches her. The risen sun glints from polished metal on their uniforms: a belt buckle, a cap badge. They look settled. They don't look as if they're going anywhere.

She can't keep hiding. She closes her eyes, and pictures, again, Ash: running up the hill, raising his hands in surrender, being walked away at gunpoint with Lulu hanging heavy in his arms.

Arrested: and they know he was helping her to escape. He'll be in real trouble.

Julia's a lawyer. She needs to call her.

She heads north, downhill, into Scotland. For a little way, the trees hide her, but the copse is only small, and soon she's out on bare open ground that offers no cover, no hiding place. She keeps walking, aware at every step of the soldiers watching her from the ridge.

ASH

He stares at the car. *Run,* he thinks, but there's nowhere to run to, and he's run enough; it's impossible to go any further. He stands and watches with a strange, detached interest as the passenger side door swings open, and someone climbs out and—

"*Mum?*"

She runs towards him, stumbling, half falling; he puts out a hand to catch her. She holds onto him, and her face drains, her eyes widen in shock. He's covered in Lulu's blood, he remembers, all over his hands and clothes.

"I. . ." he begins.

"Ash! What happened? Are you *hurt?*"

"It's not me. It. . ." He can't say it.

"Ash," she says again, slowly and carefully now, making every word clear. "Listen. Is Zara OK?"

"I don't know. . ." He stalls again; wipes his nose on his sleeve, and stares past Mum, past Dad who's standing by the car watching them over the roof, and along the road towards the hills where he left her on her own, with no food, no water: nothing except Kate's old coat.

"You were with her, weren't you? *Ash.* All this blood. . . Did Zara get hurt?"

"No. Not Zara." He shakes his head. "Lulu."

She catches her breath, and pulls him close and he presses his face into her shoulder. She keeps holding him, for a long time, resting her face against his hair. At last, she asks, "Is she. . . ?"

"I don't know. She's at the vet's. I don't think. . . Sorry." He pulls free and wipes his face with his hands. "I'm sorry. I had to help Zara get out. She. . . Sophie—"

"I know," Mum says quickly. "Charlie told us."

"Mum . . . it was *Jas*." He swallows hard against the sudden flood of sourness in his mouth.

"I know," she says again; she tucks her arm round his shoulder, leads him to the car and helps him into the back seat, like he's a little kid. She climbs in alongside him, and buckles his seatbelt for him. Dad heaves himself into the driver's seat and stares at him in the mirror, grim-eyed and white faced, and he remembers that this was how they sat – him and Mum in the back, Dad driving – when they came home after Sophie died.

"He's OK," Mum's saying to Dad, with a little crack in her voice. "It's Lulu."

He tips his head back and closes his eyes. He's so, so tired. All he wants to do is stop.

But he left Zara on her own.

"Dad? Can we go to Scotland?"

"*Scotland?* For Christ's sake, Ash—"

"I have to. I have to make sure Zara's OK," and he tugs at the handle but the car door's locked. Mum lays her hand on his arm; she's saying something about not having passports and not being able to cross the border without them. But he promised Zara he'd go back.

"I have to find her, Mum. I just left her on her *own*. Over the border. On a bloody *mountain*!"

"Ash, wait." Mum rummages in her bag for her phone. "We'll call someone. Scottish mountain rescue. They'll find her. She'll be OK."

"Your mum's right. Here." Dad passes a road atlas between the seats. "Show her where Zara is. Then I want you to direct me back to Dan's car. We're going to pick it up, and then we're going home. Got that?"

Of course. The car park in the valley by the river; he can reach her from there. He knows how to find her from there. He directs Dad back to the turning they sped round last night, along the winding country road, onto the single track alongside the river and into the car park. They halt next to the earthen bank. He climbs out of the car and stares along the broken road that leads to her. The light blurs and bends.

He takes a step onto the bank.

"Ash?" Mum says.

He halts and looks back at her.

"I've got to find her."

"Ash, no! You can't. People have been *shot* on that border!" She looks faint and sick, and he thinks of her sitting in the dark and drinking and crying. He closes his eyes and sees Lulu, tumbling over and over. That could have been

Zara, if they'd gone a few hours later. It could be him, if he goes now.

What choice is there?

He jumps from the bank onto the smashed-up tarmac. *"Ash!"* Mum shouts. He doesn't look back. He puts his head down and starts to trudge up the destroyed road, eyes only on the next pace, the next, the next –

"What the *hell* do you think you're doing?"

– and Dad grabs his wrist hard and yanks him round. Ash fights free, takes another couple of uneven steps up the road, and Dad gives him a hard shove that unbalances him, sends him staggering, reeling, sprawling on the hard ground. He starts to struggle up, but Dad's already got hold of his coat, is hauling him back onto his feet, shaking him, yelling into his face. "You've already got the bloody dog killed! Isn't that enough for you? Isn't it?"

Ash tries to break free again, but Dad's pushing him, backwards, back along the sharp uneven road. At the bank, he trips and falls again, and Dad heaves him up and drags him to the car.

"Rob! Stop it!" Mum shouts.

Dad bundles him into the front seat of the car, and slams the door behind him. Ash yanks furiously at the handle but the door's deadlocked. He kicks at it, swears, and flops back in the seat. Outside, Mum and Dad are shouting at each other.

He stares and stares along the impossible road, at the huge hills under the vast sky, the immense distance separating him from her.

Mum opens his door, and he struggles upright. She puts her hand on his arm to hold him where he is, and passes him her phone.

"It's Zara."

ZARA

The wind rushes around her, unbalancing her, flapping Kate's long coat and thrumming in the little space between the borrowed phone and her ear. She presses the phone close, blocks the wind out of her other ear with her finger, but it still gets between their voices; he sounds a very long way away.

"Zara," he says. "Are you OK? Where are you?"

"Walking down the mountain."

"How come you called Mum?"

"I thought you'd need a lawyer. I borrowed a phone. We found a number for her office. . . I spoke to someone. Bella. She gave me her mobile number. Why aren't you under arrest?"

"They didn't know. About you and me. That woman? At Little Gidding? I don't think she reported us. I don't think she can have."

"God, Ash." She thinks of everything: the dark and the terror, and Lulu tumbling over and over. "And that car, last night. Your mum said that was just her and your dad?"

"Yeah."

"And. . ." She hesitates. "Lulu?"

"I don't know," he says again. "I don't think. . ." He stumbles into silence.

"Ash?" she says.

"Still here. I'm in the car park. I could walk over and meet you? Can you wait for me?"

"Don't," she says. "Ash, no. You can't. There are soldiers all along that bit of the border. It's not safe."

"But. . ."

"No! Promise me you won't try. I'm OK. There's a place near here. They look after people who've come over the border. I'm going to be fine, but if you try and cross. . . Ash, don't. *Promise* me."

ASH

"*Ash*," she says.

He leans forward, resting his head on the dashboard, staring into the dark around his feet.

"Promise me," she says again.

"OK. But . . . you'll call me, won't you? Tell me where you are? Can you remember the number?"

"Yes. And of course I'll call. I'm not going to *disappear*, Ash."

He says nothing.

"Are you there?" she says.

"Yeah."

"I've got to go," she says. "I'll *call* you," and the line goes dead.

He thinks of her walking on down the hill; further and further away from him, into a place he doesn't know. He screws his eyes shut; keeps them shut when Mum opens the car door, takes her phone gently from his hand, says something about the vet's and Dan's car and seeing him at home. He keeps them shut when he feels Dad getting into the driver's seat and the big car starting, reversing, turning and last night's journey rewinding; opens them only when the tilt and sway of the road starts to make him feel sick. He stares at Dad's hands on the wheel, feeling the throb of a bruise on his back where he fell when Dad shoved him. Dad glances at him and says nothing. They cross the roundabout by the airport.

"How did you find us?"

"Is that it?" Dad says. "How did you find us? Not sorry or anything?"

"I'm not sorry." He gazes out of the side window at a plane lifting off from the airport. "You know what she did, don't you? Going to the police. About Sophie, and. . ." He swallows: it's still impossible to say his name without feeling that he's going to be sick. "Jas. . . She did it for us."

"Yes," Dad says. "I know." They sit in silence till they've reached the A1, then Dad says, "Charlie called your mum after you called him. Then Kate and Dan phoned when they got home to tell us you'd taken Dan's car. Charlie's got a mate in road cameras. He helped out. We were trying to stop you before you did something stupid. Not that that worked."

"It wasn't stupid."

"Speeding like that in the dark? I thought you were going to kill yourself."

"I thought you were the police. If you'd been in *your* car—"

"This is my car. Just got it. If you'd bothered coming over to see me when you were meant to last weekend, you'd have known that."

They fall silent again. Ash opens Google maps. London's 290 miles away: roughly 17,400 seconds, but it takes ages longer than that to get there. They don't reach Dad's till ten o'clock at night.

There are packing cases and bin bags in every room; Dad notices him noticing.

"Moving out in a couple of weeks."

"Oh." He doesn't ask where to; he goes straight up to his room and crashes into bed. He's shattered, but thoughts of Zara, Sophie and Jas, and a film track of flickering white lines and cats' eyes keep him awake till God-knows-when; it's hours before he falls asleep.

When he wakes again, it feels like the middle of the day. He drifts through the house in a daze of memory: Zara sits on his carpet in muddy trainers with rain in her hair and tears on her face. "Ash, I'm not BB." Sophie yells at Mum from the stairs; she perches on the back of the sofa in the living room where he's hanging out with Chris and Lewis and Jas. . .

He blinks himself back to now: a rainy March Saturday afternoon, Mum and Dad sitting at the kitchen table over a pot of strong coffee, Charlie leaning against the door frame, cradling a mug in his big hands.

"Hi, Ash," Charlie says. "We need a chat."

"About Jas?" Ash kicks a chair out from the table, drops into it and pours himself a cup of coffee. "Yeah. We do. You knew, didn't you? Why the hell didn't you tell me?"

Charlie sighs, comes to sit opposite him, tops his coffee up, and wraps his hands round the mug again. "Because," he says, "for one thing, if they learn that I'm trying to collect evidence against him then I reckon they'll shut everything down. And for another. . . I'm not sure how risky this is, Ash. I haven't been able to contact Jim McBride. And that might be coincidence, or it might not."

"Right." Ash pushes his chair back, and folds his arms. "So, you thought you couldn't trust me? You thought I'd say something to Jas? Or beat him up or something?"

"Would've been hard not to, wouldn't it?" Charlie says.

He shrugs. "Would've wanted to. Doesn't mean I'd've done it. I can keep a secret." He looks from Charlie, to Dad, to Mum, and back to Charlie.

"You'll need to be *careful*, love," Mum says.

"Yeah." His head still feels made of fog; he pours himself another mug of coffee, folds a slice of bread round a hunk of cheese and carries them upstairs, to Sophie's room. Dad hasn't started packing here yet; the walls are still full of her photos, of the arrested movement of light. He sits on the side of her bed: doing nothing, thinking nothing, for what feels like hours. He only moves when his phone stirs and cheeps with an incoming text.

His heart kicks. *Zara*. But it's not her. He stares at the message on screen.

Hey. Are you OK? Want to come over?

Jas. Of course. Unfailingly kind. He glances from the text to the photos on the wall. With shaky fingers, he texts back.

Fine. Why don't you come here? I'm at Dad's.

There's a just-too-long pause before Jas answers.

OK.

Down in the kitchen, Dad's blinking heavy eyed at his

laptop and Mum's standing by the window, where he stood holding Zara on a day when there was still hope. He leans in the doorway.

"Jas is coming over."

"Jas?" Dad echoes hoarsely, and Mum swings round from the window. He drops his gaze to his feet with a sudden plunge of doubt. "I'm meant to be pretending things are normal, aren't I?"

"But *here?* Jesus, Ash." Dad curls his hands into fists on the tabletop.

"I want him to come here. You don't have to see him. Go out, or something. But. . . Just. . . I have to. I'm going to have to see him at school, aren't I?"

Though that's not why he's doing this; not only that. He watches unobserved from the living-room window as Jas climbs the street, and pauses at the gate to stare up at the house, shoulders hunched, hands buried in his pockets. He used to come here a lot, Ash remembers, before Sophie died; running up the steps to the front door, taking them two at a time. But hardly ever, afterwards, and now he lingers, rolling a cigarette, smoking it, dropping it half-finished in the gutter, before he squares his shoulders and hauls himself up the steps.

Ash darts into the hall to open the door before Jas has time to ring the bell; Mum and Dad shouldn't have to see him, but he has to do this. He has to. He hustles Jas upstairs. As they reach the first turn, Mum calls up from the hall.

"Hi, Jas."

"Oh. Hey," Jas stammers. "Hi."

"Come on," Ash tells him; he runs further up and Jas follows; up, up, to the top landing, and past his own room, and into Sophie's. He feels Jas falter behind him, turns in time to catch a flicker in his eyes.

"Said I'd give Dad a hand sorting Sophie's stuff."

"Yeah. No. Sure." Jas comes into the room, and leans against the windowsill. Ash unpeels the Blu-tacked photos from the wall, slowly, deliberately, piling them up on the desk.

"So, what was wrong? Why weren't you in school?" Jas asks.

He thinks about *why*; he has to grip the desk to steady himself before he's able to say, casually, "Just feeling a bit . . . you know. Did I miss much?"

Jas laughs. "What d'you think? The usual. Another round of the Chris and Lewis politics show."

"Great." He unpeels another row of photos. Jas drums his fingers against the radiator.

"You know, Ash, we should start planning for the summer. I was thinking. . ." and whatever else he says is just a stream of noise in which Ash recognizes random words that remind him of dreaming with Zara. Berlin. Paris. Prague.

"Jas?" He interrupts, bluntly, laying one hand on the piled photos. "Do you want any of these? I mean. . . She. . . Sophie. . . She liked you, you know."

"Uh. . ." Jas twists his hands together. His fingers are stained, nicotine-yellow; his eyes are heavy-lidded, dark-rimmed. "No. You should keep them."

There's a long silence.

"Ash?" Jas says.

"Yeah?"

"I. . . I ought to go. Meant to be meeting Maya and Cait. Practice," and the air suddenly feels heavier. The light seems to dim.

"Sure. Yeah. Course."

He leaves the photos. They descend the stairs; he lets Jas out onto the street. When he turns away from the door, Mum's waiting for him. She holds him. He rests against her.

CHAPTER TWENTY-FOUR

"And you're definitely staying in Edinburgh?" he asks. "All three of you?"

"Yes. Ash, listen. What's happened about Jas?"

There's a pause before he answers.

"'Nothing. They've wiped everything, Charlie thinks. Phone records. Bank records. And Charlie's been talking to people from the party. No one else saw anything. Hardly anyone even remembers he was there. There's nothing..." His voice falls into the kind of silence that can only be broken by touch.

"I'm so sorry, Ash," she says softly.

"Yeah. Speak tomorrow?"

"Of course."

She listens to the absence on the line after he's rung off, then she picks up her coat and goes outside, through the garden gate, across the promenade, and down onto the shingle beach. The tide is coming in. She walks thoughtfully, slowly, to the edge of the sea, and throws stones into the green-grey waves.

Gulls shout in the sky.

ASH

Hey Soph,

 She's staying in Edinburgh.

 It's Sunday, nearly the end of March: another week of term, then Easter, then exams. They finish on the 16 June. 83 days = 1,992 hours = 119,520 minutes = 7,171,200 seconds, and then I can go and see her. But after that I'll be in Oxford, if I get the grades which I probably won't –

 I don't know. I don't know I don't know I don't know.

 A xx

He sends the letter to the printer, deletes the file, crumples the paper copy and stands up to open the window.

Lulu raises her head from his pillow and thuds her tail.

"Wait a minute," he says.

He burns the letter and carries her downstairs for a pee, brings her back up and takes her to her basket in the kitchen. Charlie's there, having tea with Mum.

"Hey, you two." Charlie gets up from the table, crouches down next to Lulu and fondles her ears.

"She's doing well."

"Yeah. She's going to be OK." He helps himself to a biscuit, snaps it in two, decides he doesn't want it and gives it to Lulu. He leans against the dishwasher, staring out at the sky.

She's staying in Edinburgh.

He checks his bank balance on his phone: he's got £7.60. He used up all his money getting to Calais and buying petrol in Yorkshire. He should have got his allowance yesterday, but Dad's obviously, unsurprisingly, cancelled it, probably till June. Probably for ever.

"Shift, Ash," Mum tells him, and he moves so she can put the mugs in the dishwasher. She looks . . . better. Not over it, she won't ever be that, but a bit better. She smiles at him. "You meeting the others at the pub tonight?"

"Maybe. Don't know. What are you doing?"

She glances at Charlie with a quick smile. "There's a movie we thought we'd try and catch."

He looks from her, to Charlie, and back again.

Oh. Of course.

Sophie would have got this weeks ago.

He catches the tube into town, and dawdles through the backstreets, past the building site where Marek's café used to be. In the pub, Chris, Priya, Maya and Caitlin are at the usual corner table, huddled over a phone, so riveted to whatever's on the screen that they don't even notice him.

"Hey." He drops into an empty chair. "I'd get a round, but I'm broke."

They startle, simultaneously, as if he's sent an electric shock through them, and jerk their heads up to stare at him. No one says anything.

"Guys? What's going on?"

"Uh... Ash..." Chris pulls his glasses off and fumbles them back on again. "Haven't you seen it?"

"Seen what?"

Maya bites her finger. Priya shares a wide-eyed look with Chris. Caitlin covers the screen with her hand.

"It's nothing," she says. "It's just some stupid... *Nothing*."

"*Tell* him," Priya says to Chris.

"Tell me *what*?"

"Look, Ash..." Chris tugs the phone from under Caitlin's hand. "It's probably fake news. It *has* to be."

"What?"

"OK. You know I get alerts? About anything to do with the Party? This came up earlier today," and Chris passes the phone to Ash and clicks *play* on a video link, and he stares and stares at her, gazing steady-eyed into the camera, telling her story in her low, clear voice. The party. Jas. Jas's dad. The Party.

At the end he lays the palm of his hand on her paused image on the screen; he feels lighter suddenly, lifted. There's no need to hide this any more; she's freed him to speak because now everyone knows; at least, not everyone, but—

He shifts his hand and checks the screen: 9,457 hits already and rising every second.

"Chris? Have you seen how many...?" But Chris is staring at something behind him. He swings round.

It's Jas.

Ash's blood pounds in his ears; his vision dizzies and glitters. When everything clears, hardly any time has passed; Jas is still folding his coat over a chair. His wallet slips to the floor; he stoops to pick it up, and tosses it in his hand.

"Drink, anyone? Ash?"

"*Drink?*" he echoes.

"Yeah. Uh. . ." Jas's gaze slides round the circle; he licks his lips. "Is something wrong?"

Ash scrambles up, and Caitlin grabs at him, closing her fingers round his wrist. "Ash. Wait. It *can't* be true. It just can't."

"What's going on?" Jas's eyes shift from Ash to Caitlin. "Cait?"

She stands and steers him into her chair, reaches past him for Chris's phone, and starts the video. The screen flickers; Zara speaks. Ash tightens his fists and stuffs them under his arms.

Maybe, just maybe, she got this wrong. Maybe there's a chance.

But Jas is staring at the screen, his gaze fixed and appalled. His throat convulses; there's a tremor in his hand as he drags it across his mouth. When the video ends, his eyes flick up at Ash, and flinch away again.

Caitlin tugs at his sleeve. "*Jas!* You've got to do something about this. You can't just let—"

He shakes her off. "Stop it, Cait. Just shut up," and he blunders to his feet, knocking the chair over. He snatches his coat up from the floor, bundles it in his arms, turns to bolt and comes face-to-face with Ash. His face crumples.

"Ash. . . I. . ."

"You did it, didn't you?"

"I never meant to *hurt* her. . ."

"You spiked her fucking drink! What else did you mean?"

"No! Ash, it wasn't like that! Nothing like that. I *liked* Sophie . . . I would never have. . . It was just. . . I don't know. I don't even *know*. Look, I used it and it was fine; it just made me feel chilled. I thought that was all it would do for her too. . . I never thought. . . I was drunk. I wasn't thinking. . ." He's crying. He drags his sleeve across his face; a silver string of wet snot stretches and snaps.

Ash says nothing.

"I wanted to tell you," Jas says. "After. I wanted to. I wanted you to know —"

— and Ash hurls a furious clumsy punch at him; another, another, another — sends him sprawling over the toppled chair, flings himself at him again. Then someone's bawling at him, hauling him off, grappling him in an arm lock. He twists round and meets the bloodshot glare of the pub bouncer.

"You're barred, mate."

"Whatever."

The man lets him go. He picks up his coat, walks past Cait crouching over Jas, and out onto the street. He leans against the dirty brickwork. His hands hurt. Weird lights dance behind his eyes. There's a hollow pounding in his head. A long way off, Chris says, "Ash?" and then, "What the hell are *you* doing here?"

He opens his eyes. Chris, Priya and Maya have followed him out of the pub, and Lewis, in his long black overcoat with the Party pin glinting in his lapel, is standing, staring at them.

"What's going on? What're you all doing out here?"

Chris hands over his phone, silently, and leans against the wall next to Ash. Lewis watches the video; before it's ended, he thrusts the phone back at Chris.

"That's rubbish. That's just ... *rubbish*."

"It's not, Lewis." Maya presses the back of her hand against her nose; a tear spills and splashes on her cheek. "You know it's not. You know what Jas used to be like. And he was out of his head that day, wasn't he? It was results day."

She breaks off as a car screeches round the corner and skids to a badly parked halt against the kerb. It's followed by three, four, five others; the street is suddenly full of cameras and microphones. There's a fight to be first through the pub door. The white glare of camera flashes ignites the windows.

"God!" Lewis digs in his pocket for his phone and stabs at the screen. "Someone needs to stop this! Did anyone phone his dad?"

"For God's sake! Don't—" Maya ducks out of the way as another cameraman rushes past them into the pub.

Ash exchanges a look with Chris. They hurl themselves at Lewis. Ash knocks his phone out of his hand; Chris kicks it.

It skitters across the pavement, topples off the kerb and drops into a drain. There's a distant splash.

He turns his back on everything and crosses the road. Chris calls after him, "Ash! Wait!" and he lingers at the corner while they catch him up.

Maya tucks her arm through his; Priya and Chris walk hand in hand. They follow the grey streets to Trafalgar Square and sit on the steps outside the National Gallery. Ash stares at the lions at the base of Nelson's Column. He smiles faintly. Sophie used to climb onto those lions, every time they came here. Beyond them, the lights are flickering along Whitehall; Big Ben and the Houses of Parliament stand brightly illuminated against the night sky.

He tells them about Zara.

"You could have told us," Chris says.

A bus lumbers round the bottom of the square, the familiar warning on its side. DO YOU KNOW AN ILLEGAL? IT IS YOUR PATRIOTIC DUTY TO REPORT THEM.

"I mean ... I get why you didn't." Chris drops an arm across his shoulder. "Listen. Do you need to borrow some cash?"

Hey Soph,

It's Monday morning. I haven't been to school. I'm not going.

The thing is –

Mum's OK.

Lulu's OK.

Maths, physics and philosophy are universals. They cross borders. That's kind of the point of them. It doesn't matter where I am. And I miss her so much.

And this is what you would have done. I think. I know this is what you would have done.

I love you
Ash

He prints, deletes and burns the letter; Lulu scrambles up from the bed. "No, stay," he tells her, but she follows him, of course, as he drags the big backpack down from the hall cupboard and packs it with clothes, his laptop, his notes.

He doesn't know when – if – he's going to be back. He's doing what Sophie would have done; stepping off an edge into something unknown.

He finds the tissue-paper packet with the green and silver necklace that he bought for Zara in Calais, sticks it in his pocket with his passport and heads to Kings Cross to catch the daily international service to Scotland.

ZARA

An iron bridge spans the platforms at Edinburgh station; you can look down from here and watch the trains arrive and leave. She's come here, often, just before four o'clock in the afternoon, in time to greet the international service from London. Leaning on the rail, she has watched the train pull in, slow and stop, and the passengers alight and shuffle and dodge along the crowded platform, dreaming of the day when she would look down, and see Ash among them.

She's not dreaming now, not today, not any more.

It's time.

She slips *Four Quartets* into her bag. The train eases to a halt, and she leans on the parapet, looking along the length of the platform, scanning faces in the crowd, remembering how she stood on a bridge and noticed him for the first time in London: a tall boy with fair hair and a faintly puzzled look. Her eyes search. . .

And see. Her breath catches, her heart beats and soars. For a moment, she watches him unseen and then she runs, to get to the barrier before him; to be there when he comes through.

ACKNOWLEDGEMENTS

So many people have supported, inspired and kept me company along the way while I've been writing this book. I'm grateful for the friendships I've made in the children's writing community, especially through SCBWI and the Book Bound retreat.

Ash and Zara's story began as a couple of scenes scribbled at high speed in a play writing class led by Tom Fry and Bernard Kops. My thanks to them for providing such a unique playground for ideas.

Much of this book was written in cafés around London alongside fellow writer Kimberly Pauley: thanks for all your optimism and advice, and for being there through thousands of words and countless cups of tea.

Writer K M Lockwood runs the best writerly B & B I know. Thank you for providing not only a place to work in peace, but also laughter, long walks and talks by the sea, and boundless friendship.

The members of my writers' group have known this novel since its first scrappy draft landed in their inboxes, and their collective thoughts have helped hugely to shape it through subsequent rewrites. A thousand thank yous, Carolyn Boyes, Sarah Dalkin, Julian Margaret Gibbs and Dale Mathers: I couldn't have hoped to find a wiser and more generous group of comrades.

I couldn't have hoped for a better agent either. Molly Ker Hawn: thank you for the passionate enthusiasm you've brought to this book and for guiding me so securely through everything with such wit and intelligence.

Thanks too, to everyone at Scholastic for giving this book a home particularly to Liam Drane for the cover design, and above all to my wonderful editor, Linas Alsenas: it's been a joy working with you.

Thank you Ioana Manoliu for sharing memories of Romania, and for reading two drafts of this book, and to Monica Blagescu, Alex Stranescu, Anna Pincus, Andrea Scherzer and the many others who took time to share their various experience and expertise. Special thanks to Ed Rayment for Ash's favourite equation and to Katie Bullard for the problem of the baby on the train track. Very special thanks to Liz McDonnell for friendship and long walks with the real Loulou.

And thanks, above all, to the people who are always there: my mother and father, and Jonathan, Katy, Bethan and Emily.